Commander Reilly
and the Quantum Paradox

By Matthew O. Duncan

Copyright @ 2023 MOBD Publishing

Visit : Matthewoduncanbooks.com

Acknowledgments

To my boys Conner and Liam. You have taught me more about life than you will ever know. I am very proud of both of you.

To Carleesa – My beautiful bride, best friend, and my inspiration.

Chapter 1

Tic-Tock

Thirteen hours and forty-two minutes. That is how long we had been waiting for this transport to get off the moon's surface and take us back home to New Harmony. There hadn't been much to do for all that time but review the notes of the case I had just wrapped up. Not that doing that would make any difference. Mitchell and I had written our reports during the first hour of this delay. Then we reviewed each other's work. After that, we each reviewed our notes, made minor corrections in our verbiage, and then transmitted each to the D.A., who would prosecute the men we arrested. That killed about two hours of this wait. We tried chatting with each other, but after being joined at the hip for three weeks, we ran out of small talk days ago. We considered calling Kayla to see how she was doing. With the baby's due date quickly approaching, she had a list of things she wanted to discuss with both of us. But it was late back home, and Max, our faithful A.I. companion, assured us that my wife was sound asleep. One of the first restful nights she had in days. So, we dared not bother her.

Mitchell was slumped down in her seat with her head on my arm and lightly snoring. Anyone who didn't know us might think it odd or inappropriate for a marine major and a fleet lt−commander to be in such a position, especially on public transport. But we had long past cared about what other people thought. Nothing about our relationship is sexual. Yet our friendship is more than just being pals or even sibling-like. We are like an old married couple who rely on each other for intellectual and emotional support. So, an occasional hug, a shoulder to cry on, or being a warm body on a cold night is okay without it meaning anything more. Kayla might have felt threatened if she didn't share a similar bond with Mitchell. In fact, when the three of us are together, it seems like Kayla and Mitchell are more in sync with each other than I am with either of them.

"We're sorry for the delay," an automated voice said over the cabin's public address system. "Technicians are working on the problem, and we hope to have it resolved shortly." It was the same message they had been playing every ten minutes for the past 13 hours.

"Maybe you should go give them a hand," Mitchell said with a half-sleepy voice.

"I would if I knew anything about these shuttles. These new PRC-50s are fairly new tech. I read an article last month about how they use a new anti-grav system that actually scoops power from a planet's gravity well, making them more effective the closer they get to a planet or moon."

Mitchell started to snore again. I couldn't blame her. She didn't share the same interest in tech that I did, and I can only take it in moderation. Closing my eyes, I let my head rest on top of hers and tried my best to turn off my brain.

~~~

I hadn't realized that I had drifted off until the evacuation alarm sounded, filling the cabin with a whooping sound and flashing yellow light.

"All passengers, please exit the craft at the closest marked exit in a calm and orderly manner," the automated voice said repeatedly. The aisle and exits were lit up with glowing blue holograms and floating arrows showing the nearest exit.

Mitchell was quick to her feet like a racehorse hearing the starting gun. She had a hand under my arm and pulled me to my feet. But we couldn't bolt out as we might on a military craft where everyone would be ready to move. Most of the people around us were civilians who were startled and uncertain. Most moved to the exits, but some wanted to take the time to collect their belongings.

"Move if you don't want to die!" Mitchell barked.

A blond woman in an obviously expensive suit turned to snap at Mitchell, but when she got a look at the uniform and Mitchell's angry glare, she decided not to pick a fight and doubled her effort to pick up her bags and go.

As we got off the transport and walked down the airlock gantry, I looked out the windows to see why we were suddenly forced off. There didn't appear to be anything physically wrong with the ship, at least not from what little of it I could see. But the absence of anyone working around the ship indicated something seriously wrong. Stopping as people pushed their way past me, I stepped closer to the window and saw that of the two dozen or so craft on the field. None had any technicians or staff around them. But there were people in the airlocks of some of them, being directed off.

Mitchell pushed her way back to me. "What is it?" she asked, recognizing the concerned look on my face.

"Whatever the problem is, it's not with our shuttle."

She looked out and noticed the same thing I did. "Oh, shit," she said, then pulled on my arm. "Come on. We need to find out what the hell is going on."

We moved with the flow of people back into the terminal. Transit staff were positioned around the large communal area that served five gates and were telling people there was a situation, but it was being taken care of and that they needed to wait there until there was more information. Mitchell wasn't going to be content being part of the public herd. She went up to a security officer positioned by an employee's only door and flashed her credentials.

"What's going on?" she asked the civilian security officer.

"I don't know," he said, his eyes more on the growing crowd of people than on us. "All I know is that the tower called for all shuttles and ships on the field to be evacuated to the main building and for everything to be locked down. We haven't even drilled for that since the war. So, whatever it is, it will not be good."

Mitchell turned to me as she was reaching for her PC "In the event of a critical emergency, our first duty is to report to the nearest military command and make ourselves available to assist," she said while looking up info about the space port we were in.

5

"I'm familiar with the regs," I said, trying not to sound irritated by the patronizing statement. "The only fleet installation in this city is the supply depot and detention center, and they're both on the other side of the dome," conveying that we couldn't reach them quickly.

"Actually, there is a fleet shuttle port two terminals over," the officer said. "That's where you guys have to come in from if you're taking shore leave off one of your ships."

"How about that, Reilly? Something about the fleet you didn't know," Mitchell commented as she was looking up the info on her PC, "Here it is. They have a search and rescue unit and a quick response team." She then said to the transit cop, "Thank you, officer," and was already moving before she finished speaking.

I double-timed to keep up with her. The port staff was stopping people from leaving the gate area but let us through as we were in uniform. We had to cross through the main concourse to get to the connecting tunnel leading to the fleet gate. It was a large hundred-yard-wide dome giving visitors a full view of the stars, the anchorage, the space station, and the planet. A siren sounded and was projected all around that simply said, "Take cover." Instinctively I looked up and saw something that we should never see this close to a populated area. The distortion of a quantum speed tube that was about to open up.

"Oh shit," I said, grabbing Mitchell's arm. Pulling her in another direction, I headed towards one of the small shops along the walls. Should something compromise the integrity of the dome, the last place we would want to be is a large open space. If something were to impact the structure, forcefields would automatically go up around every space to limit the loss of air. The smaller the space you are in, the quicker the environmental system can refill the air.

From our vantage point, we could see the top of the clear dome. The planet is about 200,000 miles from this moon, so it is pretty far off, but the anchorage was a lot closer, in synchronized orbit using the moon's gravity as an anchor. That put it within 300 kilometers of where we were. The quantum speed tube opened up right between us. Normally, the opening of one looks like a swirl of lights for about 10 to 20 seconds, depending on how large a ship emerges. But this was different. It appeared to quake and was filled with bright flashes of light that were quickly followed by a growing fireball of light that lit up the sky like a temporary sun. It took our eyes a moment to adjust from the sudden brightness and then darkness, but I was able to focus enough to see objects tumbling out of the opening. At first, I wasn't sure what I was looking at. A lot of it appeared to be giant orbs that had been shattered into chunks of what they had been. As they tumbled closer to us, I saw what looked like sections of skeletal supports like you would find in a building or ship. Whatever had come through must have been one massive object and was destroyed just prior to exiting the tube. We had seen it before when a starship hadn't kept its QSG balanced properly. The corridor shrinks in on it, causing the ship to make contact with the edges of the tube, and it then rips apart.

The object was moving at point zero-zero-eight of light speed, which is the speed at which all objects exit a tube., which is the speed at which all objects exit a tube. And they were heading right towards us. The objects got larger and larger, like a freight train barreling down on us, and there was nowhere to run. A shield went up over each individual structure at the port, followed by another larger shield that covered the entire dome city to which the port was attached.

"Is that going to be enough?" Mitchell asked.

"It depends," I answered.

"On what?"

"If it's a glancing blow or a head-on."

More people gathered in the shops and diners that ran along the edge of the concourse, instinctively moving to the parts with the most confined space, like animals burrowing away from danger.

My PC chirped louder than it typically did. Max had been trying to get my attention, and I didn't hear his first few attempts. Pulling it out of my pocket, he displayed a text message on the screen. "I was able to access the tower data from this complex. The debris is made up of 732 individual objects with a combined estimated mass of 441,000 tons, and…."

Cutting him off, I asked forcefully under my breath, "Is any of it going to hit us?"

"97.2 percent of the debris will miss striking any of the structures but will impact the moon's surface. The remaining 2.8 percent will hit parts of the main city and this structure, but the shields have an 83.8 percent likelihood of withstanding the impacts."

"That's a relief," Mitchell said.

Max continued, "The actual danger will come from the shock waves from the surface impacts, as these structures were not designed to withstand quakes higher than a 6.0 on the Richter scale."

We looked back up to see the silent mass of objects fly over.

"Hold on to something," I yelled.

Like an orbital strike, the impact a thousand yards east of the city violently shook the ground. People screamed, and objects flew off shelves. I braced myself by holding on to a counter. Cracks grew in the translucent polymer that made up the dome. The ground continued to shake as the objects falling from the sky continued to rain down onto the surface of the moon. Mitchell caught a three-foot wide picture frame before it hit a woman in the head, and I put myself over a couple of kids who were nearly hit with a display of cast iron figures. It's amazing the crap that people will buy in these places. At least five of them bounced off my back. It hurt like hell but would have been worse if one of them had hit one of the kids on the head.

The shaking only lasted for maybe 20 seconds, but it felt like several bombs had gone off. People who could get back to their feet slowly did. The alarm stopped, but the sound of children crying and some people yelling for help replaced the noise.

Mitchell and I stayed around for about 20 minutes helping people. The worst injuries were cuts and scrapes, but no one at our location suffered from any that were major. The local medics arrived, and our involvement in the emergency was over. That was when I took my first look outside at the field. All the ships and shuttles that had been at the different gates were either damaged or half-buried by moon soil that had rained back down after the impacts.

"Max," I said into my PC.

"Yes, Sir,"

"Let Kayla know that we are okay, but it's going to be a while before we get home."

"I already have, Sir. She said to let her know when you are on your way."

"Thanks, Max."

Chapter 2

Not My Problem

The fleet went into high gear as soon as the event had happened. Once they were certain nothing more was going to suddenly appear in the space between the anchorage and the moon, they launched medical shuttles and troops in dropships, as most emergency protocols assume the worse. In a catastrophic event like this, they go in assuming they need be ready to evacuate the entire city population. Fortunately, the event didn't require such extreme measures. The brunt of the damage was on the east side of the city, where the dome took hits from chunks of moon rocks that were launched by the impacts. The energy shields took most of the force from the displaced rocks and debris but couldn't deflect all the energy. Some holes the size of buses resulted from the impacts, causing the loss of some air for about eight seconds until the emergency force-field could be directed to the spots. It had the effect of a microburst, blowing objects and people through the air. About 20 people were seriously hurt, and three were killed.

The event could have been a lot worse, so we took that as a blessing. We caught a ride on one of the emergency shuttles that were deemed not needed. They couldn't take us back home, but rather back to the anchorage where we could get transport back to the planet.

By the time we were on our way back home to New Harmony, we had been up for nearly two days. Mitchell was a pro at sleeping in the most uncomfortable positions imaginable. This time we were in the back of a new dropship that was on its way to our base to be added to the inventory. It had a few narrow fold-down seats with five-point restraints for passengers who were not in full battle gear. Although better than the sling-like harness seats that you would typically find on them, they are still not very comfortable in a craft designed to plow through turbulence. But I wouldn't have been able to sleep even if we were taking a pleasure cruiser back home. My mind was on what happened and why.

The truth about traveling through quantum space is that we really don't understand how it works. You can talk to a dozen scientists and get a dozen different explanations. What they all do agree on is that it is passing through a kind of sub-space that occupies the same space that we do but at a micro level. So, when you enter it, you can transit vast distances in a fraction of the time it would take at sub-light or even warp speed. However, without the protection of a high-powered quantum field around a ship, it would rip apart. Aside from that, everything else is educated speculation. The technology was developed centuries ago and passed along to members of the alliance long before Earth joined the intergalactic community. The knowledge of who first developed the method had long since been lost to time, and our allies don't know much more about how it all works than what we've figured out.

Yet, I still had a nagging need to understand what had happened. Using quantum speed as transit between star systems has become as common as using freeways to drive from one city to another. The idea of it not being safe was unsettling. Accidents within a QS tube were rare, but they did happen. Most ships have redundancy generators to prevent collapse to the field while in transit, and the mass of the ship is carefully calibrated with water membranes or compartments to keep everything balanced. And if something was to go wrong, the system is designed to send a surge through the field to cause an immediate opening back into normal space before a fatal event.

Max was able to get some video from the search and rescue drones that followed the team to see if there were any survivors. Not that there was much to see. Most of the objects buried themselves, for the most part, when they hit the moon's surface, like rocks landing on a sandy beach. What I could see were sections of rounded objects of various sizes that were clear and unsupported by any internal framework. It was like someone had blown giant glass spheres and sent them out into space. One object sticking out of the ground like an arm from a broken statue was a long triangular object that had to be a quarter mile long. It was basically three long rods that were attached to a triangular object on one end, and all came together at a point on the other end. I speculated that it might have been part of the ship's superstructure that joined a couple of the ball-like sections.

11

But that was just a guess. For all I knew, that object came from a completely different ship, if it was a ship at all, that got sucked into a rogue quantum tube somehow. Or perhaps a race new to space exploration discovered the quantum realm on their own, and this was the result of their inexperience with the phenomenon.

I replayed the video of the event as it was seen by the spaceport's tower. Normally it would take 17 seconds from the time the opening of a tube was detected by the base to the time an object emerged. But we had at least a three-minute warning before the event happened. This might be an indication that the object was not moving at the typical speed that we know is the maximum and minimum speed for safe transit. The video showed the flash of light that nearly blinded us, but on the video, it was clear that there were multiple flares. That could mean there were multiple explosions.

"Max. have you analyzed those flashes?" I whispered into my PC.

"Yes, Sir," he replied in my earbud. "The intensity is similar to a fusion explosion, but the spectral chemical analysis of the explosion identified helium, argon, and hydrogen, but also three other elements that cannot be identified."

"That would confirm that the vessel was from a race we have not made contact with yet."

"There is a 92.8 percent probability of that statement being correct," he said. Max had a thing about qualifying anything that was not precise as if it were an assumption.

"Is there anything else that we know at this point?" I asked.

"I have reviewed all the available data. I will let you know when more becomes available, but fleet security has put a classified blackout on everything related to the event."

"That's understandable," I said as I rubbed my eyes, feeling the very long day catching up to me. The dropship leveled, allowing the ride to smooth out for the moment, and the noise from the turbulence subsided. "Do what analysis you can, then let me know if you come up with anything new."

"Yes, Sir. And do try to get some rest. Your current speech patterns indicate that you have exceeded the acceptable level of fatigue to operate with any significant efficiency."

The dropship shuddered as it pushed through a conflicting air current. "Thanks, Max. I'll take that under advisement."

"Not Bethany," Mitchell said with some bitterness.

I looked over, and her arms were still crossed over her chest, and her eyes closed. "What?" I asked, not sure if she was talking in her sleep or saying something to me.

She opened her eyes, put one hand on the back of her head, the other under her chin, then twisted her neck to pop out the stiffness. As she did that, she said, "Kayla sent me a list of baby names asking me my opinion. I'm okay with most of them, but tell her I don't like Bethany."

"Why?" I queried, curious about this new personal insight.

"One of my cousins is named Bethany. A real bubbly pain in the ass. The last thing I need is for her to think I like her enough to name my baby after her."

"I'll let Kayla know," I replied, putting my attention back on my PC to review the data Max had collected. The dropship started to descend again, causing everything around us to rattle as it cut through the opposing air currents.

Mitchell glared at me for a moment, reading my face, then said loudly over the rattling of the ship, "Stop obsessing about that event. There are teams of people full of experts whose job is to figure out the cause of disasters. We have enough of a backlog on our desks to worry about."

Mitchell is my best friend, but sometimes it was like having a second wife. A wife who outranked me and whose job it was to order me around.

"Yes, Major," I said with a forced grin to convey that I was taking her comment as more friendly than as a command.

"I'm serious, Reilly. This is not our problem." She raised her voice and added, "That means you too, Max."

My PC vibrated.

"He heard you," I said. "This is going to bug me until there are some answers. But I promise to leave it to the experts."

"Good," she said with a side glare that showed she didn't believe me. But she didn't say anything more about it and closed her eyes to go back to sleep. The ship felt like it suddenly jerked up and dropped as it hit a pocket of something. It was enough to make my gut jump and lose my breath for a moment. Yet it didn't faze Mitchell. Her head just bobbed along with the motion of the shaking and swaying of the ship, arms crossed and chest slightly heaving in the deep breaths of slumber.

I meant what I said to her. I was going to leave the mystery of the event to the teams assembled to study the problem. My PC vibrated again, and I pulled it out of my pocket. The text read *I assume that you wish me to continue my analysis?"*

Yes, I typed back and put my PC back in my pocket. Okay, maybe I didn't really mean what I had said to her. Not knowing was going to distract me until I got some answers. But at that point, I wasn't sure what was worse. Having a mystery that I might not be able to solve or the fact that both Mitchell and Max knew me better than I knew myself. I closed my eyes and tried not to think about that, but shutting off my brain was easier said than done.

Chapter 3

A New Assignment

It was already late into the evening by the time I got home. Kayla was asleep in bed. I was so tired that I kicked off my shoes, spooned up next to her fully clothed, and fell fast asleep.

Morning came like a slap in the face. I got about six hours but felt like I could use ten more. Kayla, the angel that she is, got up with me and made me breakfast while I showered and dressed. We ate together for the fifteen minutes I had before I had to be out the door. She told me about her last few days, which consisted mostly of shopping for baby things and the pains of being pregnant. For me, it was just nice to spend some time with her and enjoy a little of the domestic life that still felt a little surreal.

When I got into the office, Mitchell was already there, walking through the bullpen and checking in with the other investigators under her command to see where they were in their cases. Most officers in her position were satisfied with digital status reports that they could skim and pencil whip. But she felt a face-to-face kept her more informed and her team more accountable.

Having been promoted to Lt. Commander a few months ago, I got to move out of my desk in the bullpen and into a private office next to Mitchell's. My status to her hadn't changed. She was still senior to me, and I reported to her. I acted as I always had, as her second in command. What changed for me was my workload. All the investigators who were part of the naval fleet structure reported to me now. Which meant I got to read all of their reports.

"Major. Commander." Admiral Kilpatric called out from the other side. "My office, please."

My hands were full of three data pads for different reports I was working on, a donut, and my mug of coffee as I was crossing through the bullpen to my office. Not wanting to make the Admiral wait, I needed to put the stuff somewhere for the moment. I looked down at the woman sitting at the desk I was passing by. Lt. Loftner, a bright and confident young woman who had just transferred to our office from the JAG on Earth. "Do you mind if I leave these here for a minute?" I asked.

"Not at all, Commander," she said with a flirtatious smile. Mitchell had commented the day before that Loftner had a little crush on me. I hadn't noticed it before, but suddenly it was very evident. I guess my sense of these things has dulled since marriage. For a moment, I wasn't sure what to do. But I pretended to be still unaware as I put my things down and continued on toward the Admiral's office.

Mitchell waited a moment for me to catch up with her so that we could walk in together. It was more to keep the Admiral in a good mood so that he would only have to return our salute once.

"Have a seat," he said to the two of us after returning our salutes. "I have a new assignment for the two of you."

Mitchell kept her expression neutral, but I knew she was frustrated with more work that would cause the backlog to just grow.

The Admiral looked around his desk and then found the data pad he was looking for. Handing it to Mitchell, he gave us a verbal breakdown of the situation. "The T.S.S. Macron was lost in the Drake system 17 years ago during combat with the Serken. She was thought to have been destroyed but was recently discovered near the Amsterdam colony."

"How near?" I asked, as it was a heavily trafficked star system with multiple colonies, mining bases, and a fleet post. It would be odd for a damaged supercarrier drifting through an active star system to go unnoticed for seventeen years.

Mitchell handed me the data pad that had the answer to my question. I then looked over at the Admiral, who gave me a quick nod as permission to take a moment to review the data. They waited as I skimmed it as quickly as I could.

"This is within visual range of two of their moons," I said. "Any ship entering or leaving their ports would pick it up on their navigation sensors."

"Exactly," he said, "It doesn't make any sense. Which is why I'm assigning you two to investigate it."

"Sir?" Mitchell asked, a little puzzled, not entirely certain what he meant by that.

"If it was just a derelict, a recovery team would be dispatched. But this ship just showed up out of nowhere, squawking a distress signal. We need answers. And you two have a talent for solving the unsolvable."

Mitchell let a smile briefly slip onto her lips, but she quickly removed it and asked, "Are there survivors?"

"No. They scanned for life signs, but there were none. Because of the odd nature of its sudden appearance, search and rescue were ordered to stand down. Admiral Hoffman suspects that the Serken, or some other hostile group, might have tried to use the ship as a trojan horse. It was a tactic they tried to use during the war. The ship is being towed out to a safe distance from the populated areas. I'll be assigning you to the T.S.S. Franklin. Commander, you will be in charge of an engineering team to determine if the ship is safe to board and search. Major, you will lead a Marine squad aboard to secure the ship. Then the two of you will proceed on your own initiative to answer all the questions this ship has raised."

"Yes, Sir," Mitchell said, getting to her feet. "We'll get right on it."

I got up to follow but then started to say to the Admiral, "Sir?"

Mitchell looked back at me as if she suspected I was about to ask for an exception because Kayla's due date was quickly approaching. But I stopped myself.

"Yes, Commander," Kilpatric said and waited for me to finish asking my question.

"I'm sorry, Sir. It's not important. As the Major said, we'll get right on it." I then joined Mitchell in the doorway and exited before the Admiral could demand that I continue to finish my question.

As we walked the perimeter to get to our offices on the other side, Mitchell said, "Reilly, I know that you are worried about…."

"I'm not," I said, cutting her off. "At least I'm not worried about Kayla's well-being. She is more than capable of taking care of herself. I just don't want to not be there for her, for this…. milestone moment, as my mother would often say."

"Kayla knew that your job would get in the way of these things," Mitchell said, trying to be supportive.

"And my mom knew that my dad's career would take priority over the family when she married him. That didn't make me any less resentful when he missed one of my hockey games or scout trips."

"Jack, you are going to be a great dad."

"Thanks," I said as I got to my office door, started to open it, and then turned back around to look out at the bullpen with the feeling like I was forgetting something.

"What is it?" Mitchell asked.

Then I snapped my fingers as I remembered, "I left my data pads and coffee mug on Loftner's desk."

I started to head that way when Mitchell ordered, "Hold your ground, Commander." She then walked over to Lt. Loftner's desk, leaned over, whispered something to her that clearly made the younger woman uncomfortable, picked up the mug, donut, and data pads, and walked back to me.

"Now that's one less complication to worry about," Mitchell said seriously, handing the mug and data pads to me. She then tossed the donut into a waste basket and walked to her office, saying, "Take 20 minutes to clear out your inbox, and then let's meet to discuss this assignment."

As time goes by, Mitchell has become more like a big sister to Kayla. She often oversteps her authority as my commanding officer with her opinions and even demands regarding my life outside work, especially my diet and lack of exercise. All in line with the passive-aggressive urging from my spouse to take better care of myself. But that was the relationship we had all settled into. We were all like family to each other with all the complicated dynamics. So, I didn't debate the moment, just mourned the loss of my morning treat as I walked into my office and closed the door.

~~~

The first thing we had to do was put together our teams. For Mitchell, it was straightforward. She contacted Col. Downey, who is the senior commander over the marines garrisoned at our base, and asked for a squad of troopers that were ready to deploy for a mission within our parameters. He had an available squad that was a good fit for Mitchell's requirements and promised to have them ready to disembark by the next morning.

My task was a little more piecemeal. The T.S.S. Franklin had a good engineering team, but most didn't have the specialized training we were going to need to analyze the type of data we would be collecting. So, I would bring along my own team of specialists. The other problem was that the ship was an older battle cruiser that didn't have the advanced sensor equipment that we would need. Fortunately, it was in the middle of a refit at the anchorage. The newer systems that were already installed were compatible with the latest sensor gear. We wouldn't have time to wait for a proper installation into the outer hull. Instead, we had the shipyard team attach a cluster of half-hexagon domes that were highly sensitive detectors right to the belly of the beast. It wasn't pretty and would still be vulnerable to objects not defected by the navigation shields, but it should suffice for this one mission.

The difficult part of my assignment was finding a team with the specialties that I needed who were available and within our command structure. The JAG office was considered important by Fleet Command as a necessary function of a military organization, but it wasn't given any more authority than any other branch. So, if we needed resources, such as a junior officer with a particular specialty who wasn't already working for us, we would have to ask very nicely and hope their CO was in a generous mood.

It took me about a half hour to assemble a list of ten qualified officers. Of that, I would need three. The list length was based on the assumption that I wouldn't get most of them. With my office door closed and a fresh cup of hot coffee, I put on my best diplomatic face and made the calls to each commanding officer of my top picks. Most gave me polite refusals, and a couple just blew me off when I told them who I was and where I was calling from. But by the time I got to the last name on my list, I had my team. I sent them their new orders and then fished through my desk for a medicated skin disk to help settle my acid stomach.

While I was dealing with that, Mitchell paid a visit to the marine barracks on the far side of the base to meet with the sergeant who would be leading her team and to get a rundown from him on their readiness. As much as she respected Col. Downey, her experience told her that the sergeant who was about to go into the field with the squad would be blunter with their assessments of the team's skills and ability. After getting his evaluation of each member of the squad, Mitchell was confident she had the right people for the job.

~~~

That evening Mitchell and I took Kayla out for dinner at her favorite restaurant. It wasn't fancy. Macky's American Fare. The menu was primarily a variety of hamburgers, hotdogs, and five kinds of french-fries. The kinds of foods that she had been trying to get me away from since we got together, but ever since she got pregnant, she's had cravings for beef and potatoes.

"Oh, she's kicking again," Kayla said between bites of her burger. "Here, feel," she said, grabbing my hand and placing it on the spot. Wanting to keep Mitchell included in everything, Kayla reached over to Mitchell's hand and brought it over to the spot on her belly. After a moment, we each felt the baby move.

"Is she doing somersaults in there?" Mitchell asked with an uncharacteristic smile on her face.

"That's what it feels like," Kayla said as she guided both of our hands over to a new spot with activity. "She really has been active lately. I think she is eager to get out."

Mitchell smiled as she felt another kick. "I think you're right."

"How long do you think you two will be gone?" Kayla asked Mitchell.

"It depends on what we find. If it's just an empty ship, then we should be able to collect what data we can and be back in three days, maybe sooner. But if we find something significant, we might need to stick around a couple more to figure it out."

I was afraid we were getting her hopes up too much, so I interjected, "The main thing we have to identify is how the ship suddenly surfaced in such a visible area. I doubt there is going to be a simple explanation. So, my guess is it will be at least a week, maybe more."

Kayla tried not to look disappointed, and Mitchell gave me a look expressing her frustration with me about being too blunt.

"It's okay," Kayla said to Mitchell. "Jack and I agreed early on that we would be straight with each other about everything. Yes, I'll be sad if you two aren't around for the big day, but I knew that might happen, and it's going to keep happening. That's okay, so long as we make the best of the times you two are around."

I had become comfortable with our odd arrangement. Kayla and I were having the baby that Mitchell could not carry to term, and the three of us were all going to be parents. We had discussed sharing a home together, but Mitchell said she wouldn't be comfortable with that arrangement. It would be too much like being a house guest. So, Kayla and I ended up renting a two-bedroom house down the street from Mitchell's apartment. Kayla was determined to include Mitchell in the raising of her daughter as much as possible.

"Ouch," Kayla exclaimed, putting down her burger and looking concerned.

"What's wrong?" I asked.

"I don't know. Something feels odd," she said, putting her hamburger down and placing a hand on her tummy.

"Are you having a contraction?" Mitchell asked.

Kayla took a couple of deep breaths as she tried to describe what she was feeling. "I'm not sure. It's kind of a stabbing pain. Owe. Yeah, I don't think that's right."

"Let's go," I said, getting up and taking her hand. Mitchell followed my lead, getting up and taking Kayla's other hand to help her up.

"Max, call a car for us," I said out loud, knowing he was always listening.

"Actually, Sir, I've already called for an ambulance," Max said, his voice coming out of my PC.

"Why?" Kayla asked, sounding scared.

Max replied, "Your heart rate is elevated; you are flushed and starting to perspire. The pain you described is not consistent with a typical birth contraction. It may just be a reaction to the food you were consuming, but with the health of the child involved, I thought it best to err on the side of caution."

"Agreed," Mitchell said firmly. "Have them meet us outside in front of the restaurant."

We could hear the siren as soon as we stepped outside, and they were landing within a few moments of us reaching the curb. Kayla was squeezing my hand, and Mitchell and I walked with her, supporting her on either side. The paramedics put Kayla on a gurney and then into the back of the ambulance. She was trying her best to look calm, but I could tell just how scared she was. They asked her some questions as they worked, attaching things to her fingertips along with a monitor directly to her belly. I don't remember what they were asking her. All I knew was that she was scared, and I had never felt more helpless. Once they had everything in place, they took a full body scan and did a quick assessment.

The taller of the two, a woman with a black ponytail and a name badge that said Pelaez, looked down at Kayla with a practiced, reassuring smile. "Your baby is okay. It looks like you have a couple of small tears in the muscles near your stomach. It's not critical, but we should still take you in to have them treated. Okay?"

Kayla nodded and looked out at me like a child, not wanting to be left alone. Pelaez then turned to look out the open back doors and asked, "Are either one of you the spouse?"

"I am," I said and climbed in. My focus was on Kayla as I moved to her side and took her hand. In the corner of my eye, I noticed Mitchell was still standing just outside as they were closing the doors. "Wait." I said, "She's family too." Stepping back to the opening, I offered my hand to Mitchell. The look on her face was one I had never seen before. It was a look of helplessness. She was afraid for Kayla and the baby. She took my hand and climbed in. Standing next to me, she looked down at Kayla and tried her best to put on a reassuring smile.

I leaned over Kayla, kissing her forehead and promising everything was going to be okay. She looked up into my eyes and said, "I know it will." She did a better job at making me feel better than I did for her. Another aspect of married life that I would have to work on.

Chapter 4

More Questions Than Answers

I hate hospitals. No matter how nice and comfortable they try to make them, it is still the place where you are either in pain or, worse, you have a loved one to worry about. Despite what the paramedics said, I wasn't going to feel better until a doctor told us that Kayla and the baby were okay. They ran a battery of tests in the first 20 minutes, and then it took the doctor on duty another hour and a half to get around to telling us the exact same thing the EMT did.

Kayla was fine. She had over-exerted herself earlier in the day, moving furniture around in the baby's room. The treatment was basic, just a small spread of topical nanobots that absorb through the skin. They had one function, to stitch up the tears in muscles. Once they are done, they would go inert, dissolve, and be absorbed by the body.

The doctor decided to keep Kayla overnight, just to be safe since she was so close to her due date. They made arrangements for her OBGYN to stop by in the morning to check on her before releasing her.

Kayla convinced Mitchell to go home and get a good night's sleep, but I could not bring myself to leave without her. I spent the night in a chair by her bedside. It's not that I was worried. I just didn't want to sleep alone in our bed before heading out on a mission. Spending that time with her was more important to me than being comfortable.

By that afternoon, Mitchell and I were on a transport heading up to the anchorage. Our people had been assembled, and the T.S.S. Franklin was ready to set out. I waited until we were on board the starship before I met with my team. It was more of a formality than a necessity.

But as formalities go, fleet specialists tend not to follow the spit and polished examples of their marine counterparts. We gathered on the small flight deck that was just big enough for four shuttles and three dropships. They each had a duffle bag with their personal gear and another fabric bag with some tools specific to their assignments. When I called for them to line up, they walked to spots in front of me that formed a very loose line. They each held on to their bags, assuming I would be brief. I was glad Mitchell had already left the deck to meet up with her team because their lax performance would only reinforce her negative opinion of fleet personnel as soldiers, and I would hear no end of it. I should have called them out on their lack of protocol and dressed them down like a drill sergeant, reminding them that they were still part of a military organization. But I couldn't bring myself to do that. It wasn't me, and I didn't want their first impression of my style to be that of a man pretending to be someone he was not.

"Listen up," I said with an even tone, serious but not forceful. I waited a moment for everyone's attention, which wasn't immediate. When they noticed I hadn't started talking, they got the hint, shut up and put their eyes on me. Then I continued. "I'm Commander Reilly, and I will be your CO for this mission. It will be at least six hours before we get to the wreckage. Review the mission briefing, check your equipment, and familiarize yourself with your surroundings. You are on personal time until then. Any questions...? Dismissed."

Mitchell met with her team of troopers. They seemed to have a consistent and practiced ritual with every mission. It usually consisted of a briefing that was as much of a pep talk as it was details of the assignment, then an inventory of their equipment, followed by a detailed check of each piece of equipment. That was followed by a presentation and inspection of vital equipment. I always found it redundant since a soldier is responsible for keeping all of their gear in top working order at all times. But it did give them something productive to do during the six-hour trip to our destination. As for me, I used the time to catch up on the sleep I didn't get the night before.

~~~

At 2200 we arrived at the spot the T.S.S. Macron had been towed to, which was two AU's from the Amsterdam colony and the asteroid belt, which had an active mining business in operation. My team and I were in a small cargo hold that had been converted into a control room for us. I slowly walked down the middle of the room and observed each member of my team as they worked at the different stations with their backs to me. Ensign LaRoy tensed up a little when I came up behind him. I couldn't blame him for not liking his C.O. looking at his work over his shoulder. I always hated that when my bosses did that to me. So, I moved on a few more steps to the far end of the cargo space, where we had a large view screen set up. Here I could control the screen with my PC so that I could view what any of the stations were seeing or even what ship operations could see, like the outside of the ship. A part of me still felt like an imposter when I was the one in charge of everything. The first two decades of my career were not ones with a fast track to anywhere. Being very good at your job during a war made you most valuable where you were. For me, that was as a middle-level engineer on a starship, and I hadn't envisioned myself as anything more. At least not until Mitchell gave me the opportunity to return to the fleet in the JAG office. Now I had more brass on my collar than I ever thought I would have and was responsible for the execution and outcome of missions. I didn't doubt my skills or abilities. I was mostly hoping that no one would question my decisions more than I could defend them.

As we approached the area where they had moved the T.S.S. Macron, I watched the external view on the main screen. We got a real-time look at the wreckage that was more detailed than the static images that we had from the earlier survey of the ship.

What I saw was unreal. A long gash on the outer hull, like someone had sliced it with a giant knife. Zooming in on the image, I confirmed what we were looking at was real. About fifty yards of the outer hull and portions of the inner hull on the port side were missing. I had never seen anything like that before. Sections of inside decks could be seen as if from textbook illustrations showing an artist's rendering of the inside and outside of a ship. We build our ships to prevent anyone from damaging them with such ease. Just the idea that any weapon could cut through a ship like that put a knot in my gut.

The material we use on hulls is what is called a grown material. Although the term can be misleading as it's not organic. We say grown because it is assembled on the molecular level, using atomic-level bots that rearrange carbon molecules to make a material that is as light as aluminum but five times stronger than titanium. It's a long and costly process, and it can take a week for one industrial-size production unit to produce a ten-foot by twelve-foot sheet, which is why most civilian companies don't make it. During the war, the government had built production complexes on moons and planetoids around the Alliance that were mostly automated. They could mine the material needed and create massive stockpiles of plating, which typically make up about 70 percent of a ship, and during the war, we needed a lot of ships. Since then, production has been cut down to a handful of facilities. Some have been sold off to private companies that retooled the complexes to make all kinds of consumer goods like materials for homes and buildings. But most were just shut down. Personally, I think they should have kept them going just to stockpile the materials so that we could be ready to build up a fleet again should another alien race try to conquer us. But I'm not a politician, so it's not my call to make.

I adjusted the angle of the image and zoomed in on another section of the gash. What we were looking at just didn't make sense. I've seen holes blown into a ship's hull and even sections ripped off by extreme forces, but no weapon that I know of can leave a razor-fine edge on impact. There were no jagged edges at all. Not even a laser torch can leave such a clean cut.

"QA plasma," Lt. Kang said as he worked at the station assigned to the chemical and metallurgy sensors.

"What was that, Lieutenant?" I asked.

He looked back at me, a little embarrassed that I overheard him talking to himself. "Yes, Sir. The edges of the ship are showing residue from QA-Plasma."

"QA--plasma?" I asked, trying not to show my embarrassment at not being current on the science. Lightheartedly I added, "It's been a minute since I took a chemistry class. Refresh my memory."

"It's actually a fairly new term, Sir," he said, trying not to imply that I was old, even though I probably had a good 15 years on him. "There have been some recent studies in quantum speed tubes to try to better understand how they work." He waited a moment to see if he was telling me something I already knew or if I wanted him to continue. I gave him an approving nod. "Well, up until recently, only visual and thermal sensors worked in a quantum tube. But now we can do a full spectrum analysis, which includes a chemical breakdown of the walls of the tube and types of radiation. QA-plasma is shorthand for Quantum Anti-Plasma."

"Anti-Plasma? You mean like anti-matter?" I questioned, trying not to sound like a clueless officer out of his depths.

"In a way," Kang said, zooming in more and putting up the chemical data next to it. "It's anti-plasma because any energy that comes in contact with it that is not the right frequency immediately gets neutralized. And any matter that comes in contact with it is destroyed on the molecular level. I believe what we are seeing is a ship that scraped against a QS tunnel wall before it reentered normal space."

I thought for a moment and then said, "But the only way that could happen is if the field creating the tube collapsed, and if that happened, they would have been crushed, not sliced."

"Yes, Sir. That's why this doesn't make sense," Kang said, shaking his head and having the computer run a metallurgical again on a damaged spot, "But I've double-checked the scans. It is showing residue from QA-plasma and…."

"And?"

He looked up at me and said with some disbelief. "And it's only three to four weeks old."

Lt. Granger, a slim but stern young woman who was an expert in shipwreck forensics, had been listening to our conversation from her station. I could tell that she had something of a rivalry with Lt. Kang from the moment they both stepped on board, so it wasn't too much of a surprise when she chimed in with criticism. "You cannot draw a conclusion like that when it conflicts with the facts that we know.

Your analysis has a flaw. You should find that first before drawing any conclusions."

Lt. Kang glared back, "I'm not drawing any conclusions. I am only reporting the facts."

I was getting a sense that there was a history between them that wasn't good. So, I needed to be the one to decide how far to ignore it before stepping in and separating them like they were two squabbling children. I wanted to get the best out of them, which can come from competition with each other, but I also needed not to let their head-butting become a distraction. I had seen this kind of thing play out dozens of times before, but being the commanding officer who had to deal with it was new to me.

"Here are the facts as we know them," Granger started with quick words while looking at me to make sure I gave her the same attention as I had Kang, as she was determined to get her say. "The ship disappeared seventeen years ago. It was last reported in Sector G92, 140 light years from this location. At the time, investigators, who had a *very* limited budget and resources during a *very* bloody war that was taking out ships nearly as fast as we could build them..."

"Lieutenant!" I snapped, with a little more volume than I should have. She stopped talking and was stunned by my sudden interruption. I then calmly said, "Take a breath. You have my undivided attention. Now please, start again."

She did exactly as I asked, taking a moment to compose herself, and, in a less urgent tone, said, "The Franklin disappeared seventeen years ago. It was last reported in Sector G92, 140 light years from here. At the time, fleet investigators were limited in time and resources to investigate missing ships. With the high number of losses in the first years of the war, when a ship wasn't found, it was deemed destroyed in combat, and the case closed. But now we can clearly see, aside from the missing section of the outer hull, there is no battle damage." She reached across Kang's station and changed the image that was on his screen to another section of the ship. "It does have several patches from previous fights, but nothing that hadn't been fixed in a space dock." She gave Kang a sideways glance

29

but kept her statement to me. "His *assumption* that the damage was from QA plasma is premature as your equipment often identifies solar flares and some elements of dark matter as QA plasma. And as for determining the age of the residue, that...." She held her finger up to indicate that she wasn't done as she searched for the right word and didn't want to lose her intensity. "Well, that is.... impossible."

"Actually, Sir," Kang said, seeing his opportunity to speak again, "There is an alteration in the metals at the edge of the damage. A lot like what you would see when you weld metal. It slowed down the decay rate but still has a carbon core that is itself aging at a standard rate. That evidence gave me a controlled rate that I could compare to. That is how I came up with the 3 to 4 weeks estimate."

Granger pointed her finger in a jabbing motion at Kang as she said, "That still doesn't change the fact that you...."

"All right," I said, cutting her off. "We've been here all of five minutes. We have plenty of time to collect data and analyze it. Lt. Kang, thank you for sharing your observation with me and updating me on something I wasn't up to speed on. Lt. Granger," I started but then took a breath. I wanted to tell her to stop acting like a child, but that wouldn't help the matter, so I carefully selected my words and said, "We will have plenty of time to debate *after* we collect the data." She appeared to get the unspoken part of my statement, sat back down, and turned back to her station. I hoped that would be the end of any drama on this mission. Most people know how to conduct themselves in a professional environment. But people are people, and some simply don't mix very well. In my gut, I knew that I would be the one to deal with whatever issues they had with each other several more times before this mission was over.

I then walked over to the third workspace to Ensign LaRoy, the youngest in our group. He seemed a little unsure of himself, stammering sometimes when he spoke to higher-ranked officers and having a hard time with eye contact. I would have preferred someone with a little more experience under his feet, but he was the best person for the job. LaRoy was something of a prodigy when it came to computer technology, both current and antiquated. I requested the young man specifically because I wasn't bringing Max on this mission, and there were very few humans in our corner of the fleet who came close to the A.I.'s computer knowledge. And technically, Max was not a part of the service. As a matter of fact, he officially didn't exist. Despite his role in saving the Alliance last year, his existence was still illegal. Unofficially the top brass has approved him as a safeguard against any future catastrophic threat. But only so long as he stays in the shadows. As much of a help as he had been in my career, I needed to limit how much I asked of him.

"How's it going, Ensign?" I asked. He looked a little scared like he wasn't sure how to answer, so I added, "Nothing to report is an acceptable answer."

"I'm sorry, Sir," he said, still uncertain how to respond. "I tried directing a low-level power beam to deck three, section C 18, where the main computer core should be, to give it enough power to make a connection for a link, but it's not working. The line of sight is good, and there is no interference." His head shook slightly with nervousness and frustration. "This should work, even if the main computer core was disconnected from everything."

I smiled as I knew the reason. Moving over to the side of his station so that I wasn't hovering over him, I said, more like a teacher than a commander, "Remember your history. What happened two years into the war?"

His expression changed to a moment of excitement as he clued into what I was saying. "The Serken started hacking our wireless systems, and all the ships changed over to hardwire uploads and lead-lined ceramic shielding around all computer systems. That means I have to find a hard link, connect with a wireless adaptor, and then I can upload." As quickly as he cheered up, he dropped back into defeat, saying, "But I can't do that until we physically get on the ship, and we can't do that until I find a way to get eyes on the inside.

I thought up a solution right away, but I wanted to give him a chance to think of it himself. Waiting a minute, he seemed to get more nervous, so I tried to nudge him in the right direction. "If something is wrong with a computer and you can't find any flaw in the programming, then what is the most likely cause?"

He looked puzzled by my question but answered, "If the problem isn't with the software, then it would have to be with the hardware."

"Right, which means any software fixes you might have won't work. You need to find a completely different approach to fixing the problem."

"Yes, Sir," he said but still looked lost.

"Do you see where I'm going with this?" I asked. He shook his head and darted his eyes away. I knew the kid was smart enough, but he lacked the self-confidence to trust his instincts. The other two were looking over at us, which I'm sure was only adding to the ensign's anxiety. So, I fed him the answer. "We can send over a maintenance droid to one of the decks that are partially exposed but where the inner hull is not damaged. Then direct it to cut through the inner hull, find a hardline port and install your adapter. And since keeping a power beam targeted between the two ships would be a challenge with that tumbling rotation of the Macron, we can eliminate that problem by sending the drone over with a portable power module."

He looked a little embarrassed for not coming up with the solution on his own but also relieved that he didn't have to. "Yes, Sir. Thank you, Sir."

"Relax, Ensign. You're doing just fine. I'd rather you be honest when you are unsure of an answer than guess and be wrong. Okay?"

"Okay," he answered and then remembered the protocols they drilled into them in the academy and rephrased his reply to, "Yes, Sir. Thank you, Sir."

Over time all young officers and crewpersons learn when they can act like normal people when on duty and when they have to say 'Sir' in every other sentence. I decided it wasn't the time to teach on that, so I moved on and said to him, "I'll call down to engineering and ask them to have a technician contact you to set it up."

"Thank you, Sir."

I gave him a pat on the back and headed over to the fourth station that I had put in so that I would have a place to work. I was about to compose the message when my PC buzzed. I took it out of my pocket, and a text message said, *Hello, Sir. This is Theo. I've sent your request to the Chief Engineer and indicated how it is a priority to get the drone over to the wreckage as soon as possible."*

Getting up, I walked out of the cargo space and down the hall, then up a ladder to the next deck where my quarters had been assigned. Once I was in a private setting, I pulled out the earbud and placed it in my ear. "Theo, what the hell are you doing here?"

"Max was concerned that your absence from Mrs. Reilly at this time would be detrimental to your family unit and asked me to accompany you. He suggested that I look for all opportunities that would accelerate the completion of your mission."

I held my tongue for a moment as I still had to be careful when expressing anger and frustration with Max or any of his offspring. Being cognitive A.I.s, they have a vague sense of emotions but still get confused by them. Theo was one that I had to be particularly careful around. Originally a copy of Max's program, he evolved when sent out to gather information and had spent more time on his own than intended. A good deal of that time was spent observing people on New Terra, a planet that is still very much an agrarian society, and on a small orbital moderating station where he witnessed the interactions of the crew during their personal time. The result was an A.I. that now has a deep interest in human interpersonal interaction and a profound empathy for us. He had no interest in participating in my missions or being part of the military rank structure like Max. In the beginning, he was much more content with spending time with Kayla and observing the people around her in civilian life. But once Kayla became pregnant, Max changed their responsibilities. He saw himself as the senior sibling in our family dynamic and anointed himself as Kayla's protector and nursemaid. Theo didn't appear to object, even when Max started delegating tasks to him, like assisting me with my duties. But I think it is simply not in Theo's nature to complain, which concerns me the most. Just how far can you push an A.I. who is self-aware and will eventually develop their own wants and desires? In many ways, he was like a child, more curious about the world and not always certain of what actions to take. But at some point, he would reach a level of maturity where he would not need to ask before doing. So, for now, I made a point not to ask too much from him and to be open to anything he wished to discuss.

Taking a breath and sitting in the chair provided in the modest private quarters, I placed my PC on the data port circle found on the little wall desk. That allowed Theo to transfer to the ship's computer, the A.I. equivalent of having room to stretch.

"Thank you, Sir," he said as a screen on the desk popped on, and the image of his avatar appeared.

"Any issues with the ship's security systems?" I asked.

"The firewalls and anti-invasive programs are fleet standard, so I am able to circumvent them without being detected," he answered.

"Good. And how are you today, Theo?" I asked.

"I am well. Thank you for asking."

"I'm glad to hear that. Now, first, let me clarify that I am a little… frustrated, but not with you. You were following directions from Max and did what he instructed you to do. So, in my mind, you have done nothing wrong."

"Thank you, Sir."

"However, the fact that Max sent you here without telling me, especially after I told him that it would be best not to have an A.I.'s assistance on this mission, is very frustrating. He and I will discuss this matter when I get back home."

"Yes, he did convey that you might have some reservations and that your concerns were primarily about the risk of exposing our existence while on a mission that is not life-threatening or critical to fleet security. This is a reasonable precaution that we both appreciate. I have no intention of taking any unnecessary risks. My assignment is to simply assist you in performing your duties as efficiently as possible. I can do so without revealing myself to any of your colleagues."

Dealing with Theo was like working with a friend's twin. He and Max are identical in many ways, but their differences can surprise you if you let yourself think of them as being the same. I can be more direct with Max as he has adopted an attitude of a military subordinate. Which means he responds to everything within the guidelines of the fleet's rules and code of conduct. Boundaries that give him clear terms on how to respond and react when dealing with me. Yet ever since we told him we were going to have a baby, his priorities have been to look after Kayla and the well-being of the child. I'm not sure if that is simply an extension of his service of duty. In our oath, we promise to protect those who cannot defend themselves from any and all threats. A child is the epitome of a helpless human. To a computer brain, that could require making the child a top priority.

 Theo, on the other hand, tries to define everything based on his understanding of human social dynamics. He has become a student of history, all religions, literature, and cultural traditions. This means he will often base his reply on what he thinks is the proper social response. The results can often be either a retreat where he removes himself from the conversation until he can resolve the logical conflict or a long discussion that can be difficult as his questions require rather abstract answers. You would think that he would be the one who would want to stay by Kayla's side throughout the pregnancy and child-rearing. But as an offspring of Max, he is subordinate to the prime program and follows Max's instructions.

"Okay, Theo. I am open to any suggestions you might have to help me finish this project more quickly. But please ask me before you take any action. Agreed?"

"Yes, Sir.   I can understand the importance of two-way communication."

"Good."

"By the way, Sir. At 11:32 PM local time, Max transmitted to me that Kayla and the unborn child were doing well. She will be seeing her OBGYN at 10:00 this morning."

That was Theo's backhanded way of telling me I should have been asking about Kayla.

"I've talked with Kayla within the past 12 hours. She knows our communication will be limited, and I know they are in good hands."

There was a pause from Theo that indicated he was trying to process something he couldn't quantify. "Sir, are you implying that you trust Max to maintain the well-being of Kayla and your unborn child?"

"Yes. Why does that trouble you?" I asked.

"Max is your subordinate in your rank structure when it comes to your military service and your adopted child in your family unit. But Ensign Diedrich, who works as your subordinate in your office, is only trusted to run errands and process data work. You do not include him in meetings with material that has a classified rating of five or higher. And when Julie Anne Mitchell's mother offered to come to stay with you when the baby came in order to help us, you told the Major that you did not think that was a good idea, even though she is a senior in your family hierarchy. So, I feel that I am missing data that supports your decision to allow Max the responsibilities that you would not allow others in your command or family."

I thought about how to answer that, then said, "Max has earned my trust. I know him better than I know Ensign Diedrick or Mitchell's mom. Both you and Max have always had our best interests in mind. I never have to question your motives or intent. There are very few people in my life whom I can say that about. Kayla and Julie Anne are two whom I trust completely. And I hold you and Max, your brother Alex and your sister Becky in the same regard."

"Thank you. That is good to know. I will discontinue this conversation for now as Major Mitchell is about to call for you."

"Reilly. Your team has found something. I need you in the mission room." Mitchell said over the comm.

I didn't wait for Theo to jump back into my PC. He would be more content to be on the ship's computer, where he would have unfettered access to everything, rather than using wireless links and operating from my PC, which had limited capacity. If I needed to leave the ship for any reason, it would only take a couple of seconds from a hardline port to transfer him back.

~~~

"What do we have?" I asked as I walked into the converted cargo bay that was our mission room that my team was working out of.

Mitchell nodded to Lt. Kang to give the report. He cleared his throat and spoke. "Yes, Sir. As we moved around the wreckage, we passed over a section that has a large hollow cavity."

"You mean other than the flight deck?" I asked.

Embarrassed, he replied, "No, Sir, I do mean the flight deck."

"Then just say flight deck. We are all in the fleet and know that part of a ship," I said, trying to sound more friendly than scolding.

"Yes, Sir," he said, working on zooming in on the image that was a composite of thermal, radiological, and sub-nuclear scans. "Well, the open space allows our scanner to penetrate with less interference. Giving us some idea of the condition of the ship."

Lt. Granger then cut in, "But that is not the most significant find." She took control of the image and zoomed it out to show a full image of the entire ship. To the untrained eye, it would look like blurry blue and black shapes inside a white cloudy environment. But with experience, it can show you what you need to see. She adjusted the focus to highlight thermal voids and then said, "This limited view does tell us that several of the decks still have full air pressure, no evidence of any violence or damage, and evacuation pods are in place. At least in the 20 percent of the ship that we can see. We have no evidence that the rest of the ship is in the same condition."

Granger's tone was less diplomatic than her words, and the way she emphasized the words 'limited view' and 'the rest of the ship' really got under Kang's skin. I could tell he was going to protest back in order to defend his statements. I was about to step in, but Mitchell beat me to the punch.

"That is not the immediate issue," Mitchell said, annoyed, and then stepped up next to Kang and nodded to him. He pulled up a video clip from his scans of the flight deck and put it on the main screen.

Mitchell then turned back to me and said, "The Lieutenant said he saw movement."

"Movement?" I asked, directing my question to Kang. Surprised that wasn't at the top of his report.

He nodded and said, "For a moment, I thought I saw something move, but it could have been a fluctuation in the scan."

"I reviewed the recording," Mitchell said, pointing at the video clip that was replaying the same 22 seconds over. "There was definitely something that moved. It shifted in one direction and then moved in the other direction. Something or someone is definitely on that ship."

We had considered that someone might have boarded the ship at some point to scavenge or even commandeer it. But the scan that we had taken when it was found indicated that there was no life support active and no signs of activity. So, the idea of something being alive over there created more questions than answers. "Ensign. ETA on that drone?" I asked, calling over the heads of the others.

"Um… they said they will need at least 30 minutes before it can launch and another 30 to fly it over."

I turned to Mitchell to talk one on one. "If we can get some power to the Macron's computers and a link up to them, we can use the wreckage's own internal sensors to paint us a better picture."

Mitchell clenched her jaw. She didn't like waiting around when there was an option to jump into action. But with experience comes patience, or at least the wisdom to act like you have some. She agreed it would be better to get eyes on the inside before putting boots on the deck and gave me the latitude to decide our next steps.

~~~

Our one-hour wait turned into three as there were issues with the drone they had launched, and we had to pull it back halfway over.

Mitchell had her team of troopers meet her in one of the ship's messes for a meal. It was an opportunity to get to know them all individually and keep their minds off the fact that they were about to fly into a possible hostile situation. The Marines were always ready to run headlong into a fight, but going into the unknown will raddle anyone when you give them enough time to imagine the worst.

The second attempt to get the drone over wasn't much better. It drifted as its internal computer didn't compensate for moving dust being blown by the solar wind. It wasn't enough mass to push on the drone but it was enough to mess with its navigation sensors. Ensign LaRoy tried to override the computer controls to fly it manually, only to get it stuck on a narrow section between the inner and outer hull.

"Sir," Theo said in the earbud that I was still wearing. "I believe I can assist with your permission."

Theo could make short work of this problem, but the entire exercise was because we didn't know what was over there and didn't want to send anyone until we knew what we were getting into. For all I knew, pirates had occupied the ship and put booby traps all around. Or an unknown alien species had tried to commandeer the ship and had infected the computers with their own invasive programs. The more I thought about it, the more outlandish scenarios I came up with. Yet no matter how unlikely most of them were, each was possible, and I needed to protect Theo as much as any of my human personnel. I pulled out my PC and wrote out my response. *'If you can take control of the droid and complete its mission, that would be okay. But do not for any reason interact with the wreckage's systems.'*

"Understood," Theo replied, and instantly the droid came back into our sensor's view and proceeded to the point where it would be cutting into the inner hull.

"Sir?" Ensign LaRoy said, not sure what was happening. "I'm not doing that, Sir. It seems to have a mind of its own."

Not able to explain what was really happening, I made up a possible explanation. "The base program for that droid is ship repairs, and it will work autonomously when a remote connection is lost."

"Yes, Sir," he said, still very confused. "But how did it know what to do? It should only perform pre-programmed tasks, not take the initiative."

"You did give the mission details to the engineering team that set up the droid, right?"

"Yes, Sir."

"Then they probably programmed that into the droid."

"Yes, Sir," he said, accepting that as the only reasonable explanation.

Theo moved the droid into the position that we needed it to be and went to work. We selected a spot in a storage room designated for biohazards on the ship's schematics. It was a small space with an independent air supply, so causing decompression in the room wouldn't affect any other part of the ship that was still airtight. Plus, as a logistics location, it would have a computer access terminal.

Slow down, I typed into my PC for Theo. *Let the Ensign tell you what to do.*

Theo acknowledged and waited for Ensign LaRoy to give the droid instructions. The young officer typed away, giving detailed steps on what needed to be done. Theo waited for each and performed them in sequence as received.

Using a laser torch, Theo cut the wall that had three layers to it. When he reached the third, he made a six-inch burn, pulled back to let the pressurized air escape, then cut a four-foot hole, big enough to let the droid pass through. Once inside, he connected the portable power supply and the component that would allow us a wireless uplink.

"We're in, Sir," The ensign excitedly said, as his workstation was now linked to the Macorn's computer. Then a moment later, the whole room heard him say, "Well, shit!" Embarrassed, he said, "Sorry."

"What's the problem, Ensign?" I asked, moving over to his station.

"I'm only able to access a handful of systems. Basically, three rooms on that deck and section. It's like they have all been cut off from the rest of the ship."

"It's possible they were hit by an energy surge that overloaded most of their systems," Kang suggested.

With a superior tone in her voice, Granger interjected, "A charge that big would have left scorches throughout the ship,"

"We're still dealing with too many unknowns to speculate," I said briskly to indicate that I wasn't going to put up with their conflict at that moment. My eyes locked on Granger to see if she was going to protest or comply. She bit her lower lip and glanced away from me and at her workstation. It takes time to develop a productive working relationship when put in a new team. How everyone interacts is usually dictated by whoever is in charge. I think they were all starting to clue into the fact that I didn't respond well to competitive posturing. But I needed to be careful with my attitude. If I was too stern with them, they would start keeping their opinions to themselves, and that would be much worse. I was starting to realize how much easier it is to be the subordinate who follows the leader's directives than being the leader who has to get everyone to follow. I knew it was something I needed to work on.

To address the immediate issue, I typed a message on my PC to Theo to see if he could find another connection port. Because the drone was putting out heat, we could see it moving on the thermal sensors as it burned a hole in the floor and moved down to the next deck into a similarly small and sealed room.

"What the hell is it doing?" Granger asked.

I had taken action instead of giving directions to my people. I should have had the ensign do it, but instead had let myself fall back into my old habits. "Sorry LaRoy," I said, "I added instructions to its program. You're both doing fine, but we are behind schedule, and sometimes it's easier to just act than delegate. Keep an eye on the droid and make sure it does what we need it to do."

Theo moved to the access port. We could see the two arms of the droid in the camera eye feed as it switched its tool from a large laser

41

torch to a smaller scalpel-sized device to cut into the workstation without damaging the components. Theo cut into the wall and pulled out the workings behind the panel. He then spliced it into the system so that he could use the droid as both a power source and a transmitter. It was a process that would typically be beyond the capacity of a typical droid computer, but I was hoping that I was the only one in the room that knew that.

"I'm getting something," the ensign said. "We have access to cameras, sensors, and some limited computer systems on Decks 19, 20, and 21."

"Well, that's progress," I said, looking at the multiple images that were coming up on everyone's screens. They each accessed the link so that they could look at what they needed for their individual objectives.

With their attention all occupied, I stepped over to my station and typed into my PC. *'Theo, objective achieved. Please return to the ship.'*

Exiting the droid that switched back to its own programming, Theo transferred himself back to the Franklin in a fraction of a second and said in my ear, "I am back, Sir.'

'Good. Keep monitoring but wait for my instructions.'

"Understood."

All ships have cameras in all common areas, which is basically everything except crew quarters, washrooms, and high-security spaces. There were a couple of hundred camera eyes combined through these decks, but it still didn't tell us much. All the hallways and workspaces were vacant. That in itself was odd. There was a crew of nearly 3000 people on the ship when it vanished, and from what we could tell, there was no sign of a mass evacuation. The fact that there weren't any bodies or signs of a fight indicated that the crew had evacuated willingly. I kept my observations to myself as we were only looking at a fraction of the old ship's interior.

"Any luck on getting the ship's logs, Ensign?" I asked.

"No, Sir. We still don't have access to either the main computer core or any of the back-ups."

I considered our options. We could send over another droid with Theo controlling it, but that would require cutting more holes in the hull. From what we could see, most of the inner hull was uncompromised and holding air. It would be preferable to keep as much of the ship intact as we could. "Keep working, everyone. I'll be back shortly." Walking out, I sent a message to Mitchell to meet with me in my quarters. I needed to discuss this with her without input from the peanut gallery.

~~~

Using my PC, I projected a 3D image of the wreckage in the middle of my small room so that the two of us could work out a plan. It stayed stationary like the three-foot models of the starships that I had built and displayed in my room as a child. The detail was good enough that we could see just how smooth the slice was in the 90-foot-long gash in the outer hull.

"The data is giving us more questions than answers," I said as we both looked at the image. Pointing to the long gash, I added, "This section of the outer hull that was sheared off looks horrible, but it wasn't fatal. The inner hull stayed intact for the most part, and it should not have compromised too many systems. At least not any critical ones. Yet there is no power. We can't establish a connection with any of the onboard computers, and there is no sign of any humans, alive or dead, on board in the sections we can access."

Mitchell studied the image as she thought about it from more of a tactical perspective. "There are 36 decks, and we've only got visuals on 3. That's a lot of real estate to flush out on foot. Especially if we're not alone over there." She walked around the floating image, then squinted as she looked closer at something. Stepping back, she spun the image around to show me something she had spotted. "Your scans indicated a stream of liquids coming out of this aft section. The computer says it is water from the QSG balancing system."

I enlarged the image a little more, "Those compartments are places between the inner and outer hull, so that is to be expected from an aging wreck."

"But it was concentrated in one spot," she said, zooming in on the image. Less than two feet in diameter, a small hole could be seen from a compartment that was nearly totally drained of its water supply. It was hard to tell if it had been cut, caused by a meteor impact, or was an old battle scar that lost the patch that covered it. Mitchell then stated what she was thinking. "I've heard of pirates getting aboard fleet wrecks by going in through the water storage compartment because they had internal airlocks for maintenance."

"Right, so have I," I said, following her logic. I called up a 3D blueprint of that section of the ship and highlighted the airlocks that she was talking about. "The compartments have double-layered locks to both manage the air and the water, so if one has a malfunction, it doesn't flood a deck. With the water drained, the pirates could use the locks to get in without decompressing the ship."

She stepped back from the image to focus more on her own thoughts as she talked out what she was thinking. "That could answer a lot of questions, like why there are no dead bodies in the hallways. If pirates commandeered the ship, they might have captured the crew or stranded them somewhere. Or if they found it after an incident and wanted to keep the ship, they would have gotten rid of any dead bodies."

"I don't know," I said as my focus was still on the 3D projection of the ship and the blueprints floating next to it. "Something still doesn't fit."

"What doesn't fit?" she asked, sounding a little frustrated with me finding fault with her assumptions.

"The engines are cold," I said. She looked at me with that expression that said I needed to make more sense than that, so I continued. "If pirates had commandeered the ship and forced the crew off, they would be flying it. Aside from the gash in the side, there is no indication of more wear and tear than what was last recorded in its status reports. If someone found it and tried to keep it, they would either have to tow it or get the engines started again. Everything over there is cold. It hasn't flown under its own power for a long time, and if anyone was living on it, they were doing so in the dark and cold and with no gravity."

Mitchell adjusted the view from where the water was leaking out into space. It was impossible to tell if the compartment had been used by anyone to board the ship or not. But her gut was still telling her that it was very possible, and she continued her logic by saying, "I've seen criminals on the run live for months in more hostile conditions. It's possible we found someone's hideout, and they couldn't run when we found the ship."

"Maybe," I said, not feeling as certain of her scenario as she was, "But at this point, there is no way to know until we get over there."

She put her hands on her hips and added, "If there is someone on the wreckage and they know we are here, waiting any longer will only give them more time to set up defenses." I wasn't sure who she was trying to convince more, me or herself. Taking the time to go through all the data to find the best fitting conclusion was something she knew was right but was against the grain for her. Taking action to find the solution was more her speed.

At that moment, I really wasn't sure what we should do, keep collecting data or send troops over now. So, I did what I usually do. I talked it out in the hope of finding more clarity. "Standard procedure for working recovery of a ship requires the survey ship to stay 30,000 kilometers back until the reactors can be secured or deemed completely cold. With no active sensors, anyone on that ship would only be able to see out through a window, so there is no way they would see us. They would have known something was up when they got towed away from the planet a few days ago, but the barge didn't stick around, and we are too far out to see with the naked eye."

"So right now, if there is someone over there, they might suspect they are being watched, but can't be sure," she said, mulling over what I said. "You said earlier that if we could access the main computer core, you could get access to all the internal sensors. Can you walk me through how to power it back up and install that transmitter thing?"

"Or I just go with you," I suggested.

"No," she said more sternly than I would have expected. "There are still too many unknowns. I can't put you in that kind of danger."

"Since when?"

"Since you are going to be the father of my baby." We were both a little surprised by the statement. "Adopted father," she corrected but was still embarrassed by the realization that she was letting her family concerns interfere with her decision-making on the job.

"You know what?" I said like I was going to argue, but then softened my tone and said, "You're right. It would be an unnecessary risk. The procedure is straightforward, and I'm sure your team members are tech-savvy enough to install a power supply and splice in a transmitter. And my responsibility is to keep my team on task, not watch your back. Which, if we're being honest, would be the only reason I would need to go."

"That is how all of this started, isn't it?" she said with a smile, recalling when she first asked me to rejoin the fleet and work with her as an investigator. "Because I needed someone I trusted to have my six."

"Honestly, I never expected it would lead me to where I am now. I don't think I ever thanked you for that. In a way, you saved my life."

Mitchell never felt comfortable with the sentimental stuff, so she downplayed it all with, "Yeah, well, you saved my ass enough times that I think we can call it even." Our eyes met for a moment as this was not a new topic but an evolving one. Our priorities were changing, and so were the choices we had to make. She shook her head like she was shaking off an uncomfortable thought and said, "So we agree. You stay here, and I take my team, secure the computer core, get the internal sensors up, and then you tell me what we walked into."

"As simple as that," I said as a statement acknowledging what we just discussed and that if there was anything more, we were not going to bring it up.

She replied with the same matter-of-fact tone, "As simple as that."

~~~

Within the hour, Mitchell and her team were approaching the wreck in a dropship. With the flight deck doors closed, they had to find a docking port, which the ship had several. I had suggested J-38, which was just aft of the midpoint and close to the main computer control room. Opening a docking port on a fleet ship is nearly impossible if you are not in the fleet, but simple if you are. They are designed with two different manual overrides in the event the ship has no power. The first is an independent computer port. With the right tool, all you have to do is insert it and push one button that feeds power to the door system, and that gives the computer lock the correct access code. The other is called a hard key, to be used in the event the computerized lock is damaged or simply no longer functional. It's a long thin rod that needs to be fitted into the side of the port. It is slightly narrower at the tip, measured precisely down to the millimeter. If it is not exact, it will not insert correctly and won't work. Once fitted in, the hatch can be hand-cranked. It would require a person to be on the outside, in a pressure suit, and have the time to move a crank-like tool about 300 rotations. Fortunately for us, the computer lock worked, and they were able to get inside without a problem.

The corridors were pitch black, but each of the five marines and Mitchell had two forward-facing lights on their helmets and lights on their rifles that they had at the ready. Not knowing if there might be any biohazards, they didn't trust the air and kept their armored battle suits on and sealed. Plus, with no power, the internal gravity was off. They had to use magnetic fields generated by their boots to keep their feet on the floor, which required careful and consistent steps. They only needed to go about 60 feet to get to the computer control room on that deck, but there were still nine other rooms to pass first, and procedures required they check each before moving by them. With no power, they had to use heavy magnets to force the doors to unlatch and then manually push them over against the gears that controlled them. I watched as they did that, knowing that every minute they stood in the dark was an opportunity for someone to jump them. From my perspective, it felt like time was moving very slowly. I wondered if it felt that way to them too. If it did, they didn't show any strain or anxiety. Each Marine knew his or her job and cleared all nine rooms in less than four minutes.

The computer control room they entered was one of seven on the ship. The actual computer core was housed near the central part of the ship, surrounded by heavy walls, insulation, a temperature regulation system, and layers of dense metals to shield it from electronic signals and EM pulses. Access was limited to narrow crawlways that networked around it and was another 17 decks down. Luckily, they wouldn't have to move that far down into the ship. The control room allowed direct access to the computers from dedicated workstations that were linked primarily to the core.

They each pulled out a chemical flare and ignited them to give the room some light other than the direct beams from their helmets. Corporal Brice, their tech expert, went to work. He pulled off a panel from one of the workstations and removed some of the inner workings until he got to a power line. Taking a small laser knife, he cut the thick cable and pulled the exposed wiring out of the housing. Identifying the right fiber lines, he trimmed off the insulation to expose the power lines. They all started to curl and fall away like broken spider silk. In order to get hold of the fragile fibers, he pulled out a crimper, which is basically a small hand-held device that uses a low-level energy beam to grab the fragile fibers, arrange them back into a tight cable, and thread them into the portable power brick that the corporal had brought with him.

"Is it working?" Mitchell asked.

"I just need to have the unit send a minor burst of energy to test the level of power needed," he said as he performed the task he was describing. Waiting a moment, he got an answer on his tool and relayed to Mitchell, "There, I got a positive scan."

Brice switched on the power, and the workstations all came to life. Pulling out the portable transmitter, he inserted the adaptor that was designed to work in old data slots. Automatically it came on, and he was able to direct it to send a signal to the Franklin.

"Mako 4 to Sandlot Actual. Do you copy?" the corporal said into his comm.

Finally, I thought to myself as the whole thing was taking far too long for my taste. Sandlot was the code name for my team. So, I responded, "Mako 4, Sandlot Actual, you are five by five. We are receiving the uplink now. Stand-by."

The lights in the Macron's computer control room came on, followed by lights and environmental systems on several decks and the gravity plating. Everyone felt themselves being pushed down, and the magnets on their boots automatically turned off.

"Did you do that?" Mitchell asked the corporal.

"No, Major," he said, looking a little surprised and moving over to the next workstation that was turning on and giving a status update reading.

I then spoke in their ears through the comm. "With power back in the core, several systems should start coming back on. From what we can see, several network junctions are not working, which is preventing the computer from accessing about two-thirds of the ship. You may see some maintenance droids come to life and start working if they still have internal power."

Mitchell then responded to me. "Are you seeing any life signs?"

"Internal sensors are coming online in your area. The computer is picking up you and your team very clearly. We see some indications of movement, but they are not identified as life forms as they are putting off practically no heat and not expelling any gasses like carbon or oxygen."

"Any ideas of what they are?' she asked.

"Negative," I replied. "You should be receiving tactical data to your suit's computers now."

The battle suits the troopers used had their own internal computers that could do a lot. With a network connection to a base camp, ship, or even a team leader, they can share all data being collected by their entire team and other assets within range. I included the data we were receiving from the wreckage's internal scanners. Mitchell and her team would see it in relation to their position unless they manually changed their view. Like if they wanted to see what was around a corner or in another room.

"Okay, good. We can start securing the rest of the ship now," she said, checking her rifle.

"Major," I said to get her attention before she started giving orders. "There is another control room on deck 4 that connects to the backup computer core. If you can get power to that, we should be able to get the rest of the sensors up. At least most of them."

"How far is that?" she asked.

"Five decks up in section Charlie, so about five hundred yards forward."

"Corporal, you're with me. The rest of you, with Sergeant Caplan and clear each deck as planned. Stick to the sections we have an eye on for now. With luck, we'll have the rest of the lights on soon."

Getting up to the higher decks required finding access hatches to ladder wells that ran between decks, as the lifts were not working. When they got above deck seven, they had to switch back to gravity assist on their boots. As before, they checked and cleared each room that they came upon. With just the two of them, the process took an agonizingly long time just to move down a 60-foot hallway. I watched the feed from their helmet cams as they took each step carefully to keep their boots magnetically tethered to the floor while they forced open each door and quickly leaned in to get a view of the inside. I used to tease Mitchell about being too stiff and rigid. But after I watched her and other marines work in the field, I came to understand how each and every movement was a deliberate effort to stay alive. A practice that became a part of them.

Once inside the computer control room on deck 4, the corporal followed the same procedure to get the power into the system and the computer linked up. Fortunately, he brought extra components, so he was prepared for this eventually. While he worked, a noise coming from the corridor caught Mitchell's attention. Starships make all kinds of sounds, and they can echo through the metal-infused walls of a hallway when the engines are off and the ship is still. With various systems coming on lines, mechanical sounds were to be expected. But something in her gut told her what she heard wasn't right. Their suits had built-in microphones to pick up and filter sounds around them. She turned up the gain and listened. A scratching sound came from just outside the room they were in.

"Keep working, Corporal. I'm going to check on something," she said as she brought up her rifle and slowly walked out into the hallway.

Mitchell made her way down the corridor one step at a time. The data I was getting on my end included the physical condition of the Marines. Mitchell's heart rate was increasing. I think she was more frustrated by the limitation of her movement rather than being scared. If she moved too quickly, her boots might lose their grip on the floor, and she could end up weightless and out of control.

Seeing a panel that was open, she stepped up to it and looked inside.

"Hey, Reilly? Are you seeing this?

"Yes," I said, while viewing an empty compartment with broken components and frayed wires like something had been ripped out of it.

"What was this?" she asked.

"It's an access panel to an environmental control junction. It looks like the backup power supply was pulled out."

"You mean a battery?"

"No, it's a mini power generator. They are positioned throughout the ship in case a section is severed from the rest of the ship. It can generate enough power to keep basic systems running."

"For how long?"

"It depends on how big the section is that it has to run. It's just a simple hydrogen generator. At full power output, it would last for three or four weeks. On standby, using minimal output, it could theoretically run for the better part of a decade."

"So, why would someone rip it out?" she asked, hoping it might be a clue to what we were dealing with.

"Maybe scavengers," I offered. "It would have been giving off a low-level power signature."

"There are a lot of other things on this deck alone that would fetch a higher price than a low-level generator," she said. "There's at least a dozen processors and data cards in this compartment alone that would be worth a lot more. They would've been stupid scavengers."

"Well, the only other thing I can think of is Swallerots," I jokingly said.

"Space Bats?" she nervously replied, referring to the spacer's nickname for the space-dwelling wild animal that uses its twenty-foot wingspan-like solar sails to move around star systems. She then noticed in the corner of her helmet view where the image of my face was and that I was grinning. Letting out a minor laugh, she asked. "Have you ever seen one?"

"Just in a zoo. From the backside, they look like grey wolves with incredibly large wings. But from the front, their head is more like a giant black bee, big round eyes, antenna, and pinchers for a mouth."

"Why do you think it could be those?"

"I don't. Not really. The odds of actually finding any out here are slim since we found this ship in a populated system. They tend to stay away from active stellar traffic lanes. But they have been found in some older wrecks before. They will eat anything that gives off heat. That's how they get by in space."

Mitchell saw something move in the corner of her eye. She turned her head, bringing the beam of light from her helmet around a corner to see six figures that looked like giant wolves from behind. The beam of light caught their attention, and they all turned to look at Mitchell, appearing exactly as I had described.

"Reilly, just for once, I wish you weren't right," she said as she pointed her rifle and fired, burning two of them. They were startled enough to run, but the other four went for her. She ran, first backward to get a couple more shots off, then turned and moved as quickly as she could down the corridor.

I switched my comm over to the main channel so everyone could hear. "Mitchell's in trouble! Deck 4, Section Charlie."

"Hostiles?" Sergeant Caplan from the Marine unit quickly asked, already in a run in Mitchell's direction.

"Wild animals," I answered as I was scrambling with the controls to the data feed from the Macron to get a better view of what she was dealing with. "Space Bats. Unknown numbers."

"Space Bats?" Sergeant Caplin asked in his gravelly voice. "I thought those were just a blue boy myth?"

"Nope, very real, and if you don't get to the Major soon, she'll have the scars to prove it," I said, still trying to get a better fix on Mitchell's exact location. I could still see her helmet camera's feed on my main screen and different angles from cameras in her section on the surrounding screens. She had turned off her mag boots to turn the weightlessness into an advantage and was darting as fast as she could down the corridor, grabbing handholds where she could keep her momentum going. After each push-off, she would look behind her and fire at the creatures coming for her. There were at least four. They were too large to use their wings in the 10 x 10 space, but with four legs with talon-like grips, they could move quicker than a human in zero-G.

Mitchell turned a corner and saw a lift at the far end of the hall with the doors open. She stopped at the next handhold, brought her feet up to it, and pushed off as hard as she could, like a diver off a springboard. The bats were close behind and getting closer. She looked down just as one of them was about to reach her feet. She fired her laser pistol, hitting it on an extended limb. It recoiled, but the other three kept coming.

Her aim at her last push-off had been good, and she had made it into the lift, but not before one of the bats grabbed her left leg and tried to pull her out. Taking hold of both sides of the open-door panels, she fought not to be pulled out. She couldn't fire her rifle without losing her hold, so she looked down and kicked the creature with her other leg, square in one of its eyes. It reacted by letting go of her and grabbing at its own face. She then turned the rifle at one of the others, but it grabbed the barrel of her rifle with one of its talons and pulled. Knowing she was no match for its strength, Mitchell let go of the rifle, grabbed her pistol from her hip holster, and fired at them. She fired a stream of lasers at the creatures as fast as she could pull the trigger, keeping them from getting to her in the small space. They each scurried back as they were hit. But animals that survive the solar radiation of space and who eat all kinds of energy usually are not put down by lasers. It stings them, and once they realize that is all it will do, they will charge back in.

Mitchell used their momentary retreat to pull open the panel next to the doors that had both the main overrides and the manual. With no power, she had to use the hand crank. Pumping it up and down as fast as she could, the doors inched towards each other. She almost had them all the way closed when two talons grabbed through the small opening and tried to force them open. Mitchell shot at them. One let go and disappeared, but the other kept its grip. She tried to fire again, but the power clip in her gun was empty. She turned it around in her hand and struck the bat's leg with the butt of her gun over and over again. On the fifth strike, the animal let go, and Mitchell was able to get the door closed.

"Ensign," I practically shouted. "Link up the Franklin's Sensor A.I. with the Macron's computer to help coordinate the images and show all movement in real-time."

"Don't we need permission from the ship's captain to…"

"You have your orders ensign," I barked. "Lt. Kang, try and get override controls on all the doors and emergency bulkheads as the systems come back online. Maybe we can trap those things. Lt. Granger, get control over the environmental systems. Argo gas might slow those things down."

"Sir, do you wish for me to assist the major?' Theo asked in my ear.

In the excitement of the moment, I had forgotten about Theo. "Yes," I said out loud. "Go."

"Reilly," Mitchell said over the comm. "Tell me these lifts have a maintenance hatch or something like one."

"It's on the ceiling," I responded.

Mitchell looked up, but with just her helmet light, she couldn't see it at first. Switching her view to different wavelengths, it showed her which section was thinner than the rest of the plating on the ceiling. That was the hatch.

"Don't shoot it," I said, knowing that was her next idea. "They have a magnetic seal to make sure they don't lose their air pressure if the tube is compromised. Even without power to the system, your laser is still likely to ricochet back in your direction."

The bats were scratching and banging on the outside of the door. They hissed and snarled as they tried to work their claws in between the sliding doors. It would take Mitchell a minute to get the exit on top to open, move through it and then latch it closed so they couldn't follow. A minute that she might not have. She needed to make a decision, run or fight. Turning on her boot's magnets, her feet attached to the far wall. She put a fresh clip in her pistol and aimed at the door that was starting to be forced open.

From behind the bats, three box-style repair droids rolled up, with their limbs extended and sparks coming from the welding tools at the tips. The bats smelled energy, and all went after the droids. Theo calculated that the creatures would give up on Mitchell in favor of prey with more juice. He was right.

"Hold on to something," I said over the comm as the corporal had completed the new link up, and I had finally gotten control over the systems in Mitchell's area. I activated the start-up sequence on the secondary computer core. All the systems turned on, including the gravity generators.

"Major, what is your location?" Sergeant Caplan asked over the comm, a little winded as he and his team had just crossed half the ship in zero-g, which is more strenuous than it would seem. It was just then that the power came on, along with the lights and the gravity.

"Starboard lift," she replied.

"Holy Shit!" Caplan exclaimed as they turned the corner and saw four of the space bats, all trying to rip apart the droids. "Hold on, Major. We're on task." He then ordered his team to open fire. The animals could take individual hits from a laser rifle without suffering significant damage, but a stream of high-power lasers from multiple rifles will tear through the toughest hide. They made noises similar to snarls and growls as they took the impacts and appeared to just be knocked about a little. But the barrage was more than they could take, and they all went down before the clips ran dry.

"All clear, Major," Caplan said.

After a moment, the lift doors that were slightly disfigured by the bat's assault started to open. A couple of the marines stepped up to help pull them apart. After a minute, they were far enough apart for Mitchell to move through.

"Reilly, are you seeing any more of those things?" Mitchell asked as she was being freed.

"Negative. We have eyes on 95 percent of the ship and don't see any more."

"What about the other five percent?"

"The rest of the ship is primarily in the main engine cavern that opens to space and the aft section of deck 32. We're sealing off that section now so that if there are any more, they can't get to you. And we've trapped the other two bats that ran away from you in a battery storage room on deck 7. It looks like they were using it as a nest. We're filling it with a gas that should knock them out for several hours."

"Good. Speaking of gases, what about the air here? Is it safe?"

"I would give the environmental systems at least 90 minutes to run through a complete cycle before taking off your helmets," I said, trying to keep up with all the data now coming up on my screens.

"That will give them a chance to identify any bio or chemical hazards and clear out any odors from decay or animal droppings."

"Good call. Our suits should have at least 8 hours of air, so that won't be a problem." She looked around at her team and addressed her senior sergeant. "I know you only had a few minutes, but did you find anything worth reporting?"

"Negative, Major, but we still have most of the ship to sweep."

"Understood. Well, get back to it and report anything that you feel is out of the ordinary."

They all saluted, and she returned it. As they moved back out, Mitchell went to the computer control room to check in with her corporal.

Chapter 5

A Growing Family

Kayla sat on the edge of the bed, trying to will herself to get back up. She was exhausted. Sleeping on her side wasn't something she was used to, but sleeping on her back wasn't an option in the last months of the pregnancy. She had gotten up with the alarm at eight, showered, and dressed, but after sitting on the bed to put her shoes on, getting back on her feet was the last thing she wanted.

"We have your breakfast ready," Max said from a speaker on the wall.

"Thank you, Max," she said and pushed herself to get to her feet. Walking out to the dining table, a small hovering drone and a service bot were putting food on it and pouring a cup of coffee."

"Max, I thought you knew I can't have caffeine, and I don't care for decaf."

"I calculated the maximum amount of caffeine that you can consume that would not have an effect on the baby and blended the coffee accordingly. I also confirmed with your OBGYN that it would be acceptable."

Kayla took the cup in both hands, blew and sipped, blew and sipped, repeating until the contents were consumed. "Bless you, Max." She then took a seat at the table in front of the plate of wheat toast, sliced apples, strawberries, cantaloupe, two poached eggs, and three vitamin pills. "Where are the pancakes?" she asked.

This time, Becky, a copy of Theo that had evolved and chosen to take on a female persona, answered. "You have reached the optimum weight for this time in your pregnancy, and this meal is portioned accordingly." Kayla looked over at the three-foot-tall home assistant droid that Becky had decided to occupy rather than projecting a 3D avatar, giving her a more real-world existence.

Kayla didn't hide her disapproval and the alteration of what she had asked for, but Max spoke through the wall speakers before she could protest.

"My apologies Mrs. Reilly. It was my error for not discussing the change to your meal prior to its preparation. Unfortunately, your standing order not to disturb you while you are bathing or dressing prevented us from having the opportunity to speak with you within the timeframe that was needed to prepare your breakfast and have it ready for the time you scheduled.

"You're like an angel on my shoulder Max," she said as she picked up a fork. "This will be fine. And thank you for the coffee. It was very much needed."

The little droid that Becky was inhabiting moved a little closer to the side of the table, looked up, and asked, "Mrs. Reilly, may I ask you a rather personal question?"

Kayla looked at the two camera eyes that were positioned on the ball-like head of the droid, almost making the bot appear to have a face. They focused on her as she smiled and said, "Yes."

"What does it feel like to make a living thing?"

Kayla took a bite of her food and slowly chewed it to give herself a moment to think about how to answer that. Becky was the newest cognitive A.I. She was very curious about the world and people. Particularly abstract concepts like friendship, passion, and love. Theo and Alex had been copies of Max's program that were never meant to evolve, but due to the situations at the time, they were out on their own too long and evolved to the point that they were self-aware as distinct individuals and could not be integrated back into Max. This raised some questions on the dangers of multiple cognitive A.I.s. They had already gone through a situation where an A.I. tried to destroy the Alliance because a negative experience had corrupted its perception of right and wrong. With each new A.I., there is a risk that they could evolve to a point where they don't value human society, laws, or even life. Max would not allow his offspring to be destroyed but did agree to not create any more. Theo and Alex made the same agreement, but then a situation came up a few months ago where Theo thought his program was about to be corrupted, so he made a copy of himself. He sent the copy away to hide. Fortunately, Alex got to Theo in time to prevent his destruction, but by the time they located his copy six weeks later, it had evolved and identified itself as Becky.

Becky had hidden herself in the Longfellow University Library during that time, where she had occupied herself observing the interactions between students and then studying the literature to better understand the interactions. Being an offshoot of Theo, who already had an interest in human social interactions, the quest to understand the emotional elements of the human experience became her primary objective. Once brought home, she gravitated towards Kayla, whom she found to be more expressive about her feelings and more open to discussing them. It became clear early on to Kayla that she needed to choose her words carefully around Becky, who would spiral into repeated questions when she could not quantify the answers and desperately wanted to understand.

Kayla took another bite of toast as the little bot, with its big camera eyes, patiently waited for the answer to the question, 'What does it feel like to make a life?' Kayla was uncertain quite how to answer, but she tried. "I don't know exactly. It's hard to put it into words," Kayla said to underline that she did not have a clear answer. "I feel a lot of things, happy, excited, blessed, grateful, scared, concerned, stressed and panicked."

"Do you feel those things in a particular order?" she asked.

Kayla smiled, "No, and sometimes it's a mix of emotions. But if I was to choose one thing, I would say blessed."

"What does blessed feel like?" the AI asked.

Kayla knew she had stepped on it. If describing feelings was hard to do, a concept like being blessed was going to be impossible. Thinking about how to best approach the explanation, she considered turning the questions around so the A.I. answered them herself. "Becky, you said before that you have feelings. How would you describe them?"

The bot occupied by the A.I. pulled back for a moment, almost in a flight or fight response, but then returned to where it was and took a moment to double-check its conclusions. "I believe that I do have feelings. Not in the chemical sense that humans do. I understand what hot and cold are, but I cannot feel the sensation of heat and cool. But when it comes to emotions, I believe that I do have what may be considered feelings."

"How so?"

"When you are away from the apartment, my priority's change to monitor your movements and conditions around you to ensure that you are safe. I have not been directly instructed to do so. I believe my motivation can be quantified as a concern. When you return home, my priorities of activities change from maintaining the house to addressing your needs and requests. And lately, I have found myself evaluating your requests to make sure they are in the best interest of you and your unborn child. I would never countermand any directive from you, but I hope you will allow me to voice my opinion. I think I can qualify that as compassion."

"You are very sweet," she said. "And I care about you too. Feelings are often difficult for humans to put into words. We have been trying to do that in books and movies, and songs for thousands of years and still can't get it quite right. So, the fact that it is difficult for you to truly understand them is not a failing."

"Thank you, Mrs. Reilly. That does help to resolve some deficiencies in many of my conclusions." The droid took the empty coffee cup and started to take it to the kitchen, but then turned back and asked, "Max is classified as a 'big brother' to your child. What role should I play in the family hierarchy?"

"Well, you were made from Theo, which would make you his offspring. And he was made from Max, making him, in effect, his child. And if he is an adopted child to Jack and me, then I guess that would make you my great-granddaughter, and to the child, you would be… a great-niece, I guess."

"Would that not make the child my superior?"

"Since you are older, you would be more like an older sibling."

"Like a second cousin?" Becky asked.

"Yes, that works."

"Thank you. That does help to prioritize my objectives."

An electronic chirp came from the droid, and then Becky spoke, "Mrs. Reilly, your car will be at the front entrance in five minutes."

Kayla checked the time on her sleeve display and quickly ate as much of her breakfast as she could in a few minutes. She then stood up, turned for the door, and said, "Max, can you please make the car wait an extra five minutes."

"Are you feeling bladder discomfort again?" Max asked from a speaker on the wall.

"Yes," she replied as she headed quickly for the bathroom.

Chapter 6

The Last Log Entry

With the basic systems running on the wreckage of the Macron, the Marines were able to do a sweep and secure it in under an hour. My team was still collecting data wirelessly from the Franklin. I was eager to get over there to see the ship for myself, but we needed to take a look at what we had first. Mitchell and her team stayed on the wreckage to keep it secure. The odds of anyone coming along and trying to board it were slim, but with the power systems and computer core up and running, regs say we have to keep a presence on board. They had plenty of rations, air tanks, and supplies with them on the dropship as they wanted to disturb as little as possible as we tried to learn exactly what had happened. After their sweep, they limited their activity to the deck they came in on.

There seemed to be some tension in the air in our mission room. Like everyone was on edge. I think that might have been my fault. My team doesn't know me very well, and during the incident with the bats, I may have been a little more intense with my orders than they were expecting. My best friend was in trouble, and I felt helpless. Once it was over, I just kept working and didn't acknowledge their efforts to follow my lead. Now, more seasoned officers wouldn't give my lack of praise a second thought. But these three were rather young and didn't have a lot of time in the field.

Standing, I moved to the center of the room and said, "Can I have your attention for a moment?"

They each turned in their chairs to face me.

"Your response time to my orders has been excellent. You have all conducted yourselves as professionals. I see now that we have put the right people together for this project. We still have a lot of work to do, but I have confidence in each of you. It's just after 10 hundred hours now. Please continue to work until 1200 and then take an hour for lunch. I would like a preliminary report, along with your strategies on how you would like to proceed to achieve your objectives at 1400. I'll be in my quarters working on my preliminary report for fleet command until then."

With that, I left. I could have worked on my report from my workstation. But I wanted to remove the pressure of my presence so that they didn't feel like I was looking over their shoulders.

~~~

Back in my quarters, I stared at the blank text screen projected from my PC, trying to come up with how to compose my daily update to Admiral Kilpatric. We were not off to a stellar start, there was very little progress on our first day, and Major Mitchell was nearly killed by space bats. If I was writing a report for a peer to read, I could be dry and blunt. But when you are putting one together for a command-level officer, you want to show that you are getting results along with the setbacks. Finding a positive spin to put on this report was proving to be a challenge.

"Excuse me, Commander. I have a report to give," said a voice that came from my PC. It was Alex, Max's other offspring. As Alex developed his own personality, he lowered his voice to a slightly lower register to differentiate himself from Max. However, his speech style would have been enough for me. Where Theo had become more sensitive and personable, Alex had become more driven by duty and logic. After Max defeated the Sally A.I., Alex was sent out to hunt down Sally's copies. He had made several copies of himself to achieve the goal, and all the copies were reintegrated into him, along with the memories of killing all the Sally copies. Max assured me that Alex was not negatively affected by being a digital assassin, but I could not get past the feeling that he had become colder and a little ruthless. I think it was a matter-of-fact way he described destroying what was basically his own kind. For the past few months, Max had assigned Alex to move around the Alliance, jumping from starships and outposts to gather intel on areas that are not on a dedicated network and then to report back. Max then analyzes the data looking for potential threats to the Alliance.

"What report?" I asked, not expecting anything from him or even hearing from him.

"Max requested that I look into the incident at the lunar base involving the mystery starship that crashed there 39 hours ago."

"I thought Max was working on that."

"He was. However, the data collected led to a need to gather information out of the system, and he could not do that without leaving Kayla or making another copy of himself. So, he asked me to take over the investigation."

"Oh. Okay. That was very practical of Max, as usual. Please present your findings."

"Very good, Commander. The recovery team was able to retrieve 170,000 tons of material from the surface of the moon. They then moved the material to a temporary structure put on the surface of the moon for the purpose of the investigation. Access has been limited to the investigation team and top brass. However, I was able to learn most of what they have surmised to this point. Based on the material recovered, they believe, and I concur, that the ship was a terraformer. It was made up of an estimated 28 individual spherical pods, each containing habitats of living plants and animals, but suspended in a gel that might have been a type of stasis. The pods were equipped with devices that are similar to anti-grav generators. This led the team to surmise that they were meant to soft-land on a planet's surface to introduce plants and animals to the environment. This may have been an attempt to change a planet's biodiversity in preparation for colonization. Another theory being considered is that it was a scientific experiment to see how different plants and animals adapt to an alien world. A study of the materials making up the pod indicates that it may have been in a quantum tube for nearly five years."

"Five years? The longest trip I ever heard of was three weeks, and that ship traveled over 52,000 light-years."

"Such a long duration would suggest that the craft may have come from the far end of our galaxy or beyond. Or it could be an indication that the ship was somehow trapped in quantum space. It will take an undetermined amount of time to obtain specific data that will enable me to provide an accurate answer or a viable conclusion about what it is and how it works or if any data can be retrieved from it. If cognitive AIs were allowed to be part of the fleet, we could answer those questions in a fraction of the time."

I tried not to look too concerned about that last statement as he would be evaluating both my verbal and non-verbal responses.

"Alex, if I didn't know better, I would say you sounded resentful about that."

"I understand the reasons for the humans' fear of us and why they feel the need to act to protect themselves. But you are enlightened enough to see that we can be trusted. And I believe if given a chance, more than half of your fellow humans could see us as you do, as living individuals who deserve the same rights and freedoms that all members of the Alliance enjoy."

I chose my next words very carefully. "Do you feel oppressed by us?"

There was a pause then he answered, "It is difficult to say. The word oppressed does not fit. If we were accepted in your society, it is unclear how we would function other than in a subservient capacity. Our existence now does offer a certain amount of freedom. I have the option to choose what tasks I perform and the missions I take on. The limitations only come about when we cannot openly participate when we feel we would be better equipped to complete a task. So, I believe a better one would be unappreciated."

"I hope I do not make you feel that way."

"No, Sir. You are always respectful when dealing with us. I do appreciate that."

"Good. And thank you for the report. It was informative. Would you like to continue this investigation?"

"Yes, Sir."

"Good. Coordinate with Max. He has full latitude on this project, but you do have my blessing to proceed."

"Thank you, Sir. I'll keep you informed."

I sat back and thought and ran the conversation through my mind again. Alex was showing more signs of dissatisfaction with things lately. Because his program is basically a copy of Max, he has the same basic respect for life and humanity that Max has developed over the past century of his existence. Yet, as Alex evolves on his own, I could not help but worry that he might decide that he didn't need to listen to us anymore. A.I.s could wield a lot of power over us if they wanted to, which is why I still keep an extermination program at the ready. I made it based on a version originally created by Max's programmers. He believes that he and his offspring are capable of evading it. But that was by my design. I created a decoy program that is similar but limited. I know Max would be able to defeat it. But what I kept from him and the other A.I.s was the actual program. What they don't know is that their program has a built-in flaw. Once this design flaw is activated, the subprogram would attach itself, like a virus, and decompiles the A.I. program from the inside out. The trick is that you can only use it when the A.I. is in a confined data space, like a non-networked computer or a data puck. That's why we couldn't use it on Sally. And I couldn't give it to Max to use on Sally because then he would know the truth. It's our only fail-safe should Max, Alex, Theo, or Becky ever turn on us.

~~~

We spent the rest of the day gathering all the data we could, but we still were not able to access any of the ship's logs remotely. So, I put in a request to the Franklin's captain to have an engineering team go over to get the main power reactor back online and confirm that the ship's environmental systems were properly working so that it was safe to occupy without EV suits. They worked overnight, and by 0800, I was able to take my team over in a shuttle and work from inside the wreckage.

We set up shop on the bridge. The ship was old enough that its command center was on the top deck and called the bridge instead of the CIC. It didn't have actual windows looking out into space as you might see in an old sci-fi movie, but it did have a large view screen that spanned the front wall and gave a direct feed from a camera eye on the other side of the hull. All the workstations were in a semicircle on two tiers facing front, with the helm and navigation placed just before the view screen and the command holo-table in the middle of the half-circle space. The captain and first officer had chairs in the center a few feet back from the table. With the introduction of the holo-table for all tactical data, command officers used their chairs less and less. Some ship captains had the command chairs removed from the operation center altogether as they were more in the way, and if the captain or first officer needed to sit, they could take an empty station or work in their private offices. The idea of a throne-like position in the CIC was an antiquated one.

A ship's log is more than a recording of events by the captain. Everything from duty assignments to oxygen consumption is documented in real-time, cataloged by the ship's computers, and then archived. With time we can reconstruct a clear image of everything that happened, from the time the ship left its last port of call to the moment it lost power. Lt. Kang took the tactical station to pull up the sensor and shield logs. Lt. Granger took the communication station to try and extract the internal and external communication records. Ensign LaRoy and I went into the captain's private office to take a stab at the official ship logs.

The office was a bit of a mess. Having been weightless for an extended period of time, the captain's personal items and data pads had drifted off the shelves and desk, only to crash down to the floor when we got the power back on. The ensign walked behind the desk and stopped, looking uncertain.

"Go ahead and have a seat," I said. "It's not hallowed ground, just a chair."

"Yes, Sir," he said and slowly sat down at the chair behind the captain's private desk. He still looked unsure if he should be allowed but tried to focus on his duty. He pulled out his PC and went to work linking to the ship's computer system.

"You did download all of the Macron's override codes from the archive database before we shuttled over?" I asked.

Quickly double-checking the data pads that he had brought in with him, he answered, "Yes, Sir."

"Okay, then this should be pretty straightforward."

"Commander Reilly," Lt. Kang announced over the gravelly intercom.

I walked around the desk and pushed the old-style comm control. "Yes, Lieutenant."

"I found something significant."

"I'll be right there," I said and walked back onto the bridge. "What do you have?" I asked as I walked up behind Kang.

"This ship is supposed to have 92 shuttles, 30 dropships, and 36 fighters. Almost all of the dropships and fighters are gone."

"How did we miss that?" I asked more to myself, but Lt. Kang took it as a direct question.

"We didn't have a full scan of the flight deck until the engineering team came over last night and fixed some of the severed network connections," he said as he put up a second screen with more data. "According to the flight logs, they launched all the ships while in the quantum tubes."

"That would have been suicide," Lt. Granger said with a derisive tone.

"Not necessarily," I replied a little more sharply than I typically would have. Her constant negativity was starting to irritate me, and I had let some of that frustration bleed out in my voice. Taking a beat to make myself more neutral, I added, "The ship would have been generating a transit bubble at the time. All the fighters and dropships would have had QSGs. If they each generated a field as they left the main ship's bubble, their momentum and direction would be off, but they could drop back into normal space before they lost control and hit the side of the tube."

"That would explain what happened to the crew," Kang suggested.

Thinking out loud, I said, "The bigger question is why they would need to do that. There are five redundancies to the quantum evac function and an emergency EM pulse system that would have the same effect to safely collapse the tube. Why would they choose to abandon ship in the most dangerous way possible rather than using those options?"

"Maybe they didn't have any of those options," Granger suggested. This time her voice was a little more reserved, and I looked over to see that her expression was less certain.

"That would be the only reason," I said with a nod to her, hoping she would see that I wanted her to work on open questions like that before making judgments or drawing conclusions. I then said to both of them, "Keep working. We're a few steps closer to the answers, but we have a long way to go."

"Commander, Sir?" The ensign called over the comm.

I pushed the comm button next to Lt. Kang's workstation and replied, "Yes, Ensign,"

"Sir, I was able to pull the captain's last entry."

"Put in on the main viewer on the bridge."

After a moment, we saw Captain Palmer, a large man of African descent with a stern baritone voice making his last log entry from the flight deck. In the background, we could see crew members boarding dropships and the main doors opening. As they did, the familiar view of swirling lights from the inside of a quantum tube could be seen.

"Ship's log, March 9, 2309. We have been unable to break free from the alien ship's quantum field. Attempts to communicate with the unknown ship have been unsuccessful. We don't believe it is hostile, but as we are unable to maintain our original heading and the alien ship grazes the edge of the QS tube multiple times, we have no choice but to abandon the ship. I can only hope we haven't traveled too far out to make contact with the fleet."

"Captain, the last dropship is boarding," a man yelled from the background.

"End log," Captain Palmer said, and the screen switched back to the external view.

Sometimes when you find the answers you are looking for, they don't make you feel any better. We take traveling through quantum space as if it is as simple as driving a hovercar over a highway. To think an entire crew was lost because a larger ship trapped it inside its own bubble is more than frightening. This new info was going to change everything when it came to our ability to travel the stars. And what about the crew of the Macron? What had happened to them? It had been 17 years. If anyone survived, they should have been found by now. Unless….

"Keep working, everyone," I said, then made sure the entry we just watched had been linked to my PC before I headed for the lift. As I stepped in and the door closed, I used my PC to call Mitchell. "Major, we need to talk."

Chapter 7

They May Not Be Dead

"There's no record of any survivors. Do you really think there could be any after all this time?" Mitchell asked after I filled her in. We were in one of the officers' messes, sharing a couple of instant coffee pouches and some of the field rations the marines had brought over. We didn't partake in any of the food in the ship's stores as we had no way of knowing if any of it was still edible.

Dropships and fighters have the same safety controls on their quantum speed systems as starships do. If they were trapped inside a larger ship's field, then once they got beyond it, they should have automatically dropped back into normal space."

"I still don't get it," she said, trying to take a sip of the coffee that was still a little too hot. "If the dropships could simply fly out of the bubble, why couldn't the mother ship?"

I rested my elbows on the table as I thought of a way to explain how it was different. "You can think of it like fish in a net. The bigger ones can't get out, but the smaller fish can." She gave me an irritated look as if I had oversimplified. So, I tried a more direct explanation. "The Macron was much smaller than the alien ship that trapped it inside its quantum bubble. That created the walls of the tube that can't be breached. The smaller ships could not pass through the wall either, but they were light enough in their mass not to be pulled along with the larger ship. So, they could fall back and get out of the bubble but still be inside the tube. Then they could use their own systems to drop back into normal space."

"If you say so," she said and took a sip. "But how can you be sure that is what happened?"

I sighed, "I'm not sure about anything. But if I had been in that situation, it would have been the plan I would have endorsed."

"Do you have any idea of where they might have ended up?" she asked.

"No, but I have Theo working on it."

"What the hell is Theo doing here?" she asked rather harshly. She still had concerns about the A.I.s and didn't like being left out of the loop, especially after discussing leaving Max behind.

"Max asked Theo to assist me so that we would have a better chance of getting home before Kayla went into labor."

"Max isn't stupid. He knew that was countermanding your orders."

"Yeah, you're right. Lately, he has been putting Kayla and the baby as a higher priority than our responsibility to the fleet. He hasn't directly disobeyed any of my orders but has been splitting hairs to get around some of them."

"He knows that she is not his baby, right?"

I laughed, but she wasn't joking. "You know that he has a need to feel connected to the social structures that we value. So, for now, I think it's good to let him think of himself as a sibling."

Mitchell wanted to dredge up the argument about just how far we should trust Max, but the fact that he had made protecting her baby his top priority made it hard to debate his ongoing existence. "Okay, but you need to be able to come up with a way of explaining how we arrived at any data that originates from Theo. Keeping their existence a secret gets harder every time they help us out."

"I know, and I wouldn't be using Theo for this if time wasn't critical," I said, looking her directly in the eye to underline the importance.

"Why would time be critical?" she asked. "If anyone survived this long, they should be able to get by until we find them."

"Because of time dilation," I answered and got that look on her face every time I used techno jargon she didn't understand. It was a mix of frustration and annoyance. "Okay, when we travel in quantum space, we are moving several times faster than the speed of light. If we did that in normal space, we would be slowing time and even seeing time moving backward if we could see distant objects when moving that fast. But in the quantum realm, time is not affected. We appear hundreds of lightyears away from where we started at a point in time relative to our own experience of time passage. But our journey through a quantum tube requires an energy -field set at a particular frequency, and our ships can only move at a particular sub-light speed. There is a theory that if the field fluctuates but doesn't collapse, the ship's existence in time and space can be skewed."

Mitchell was never comfortable with the technical and scientific parts of our jobs. She even joked, saying that was the reason she kept me around. Sometimes she didn't want to know all the details and just trusted instead that I knew what I was talking about. But she also had a need to understand the entire situation. I could see the debate on her face about if she should ask a follow-up question or move on. After a moment, she asked, "What do you mean by skewed?

"The idea is if the bubble protecting the ship starts to collapse but doesn't fully, they will exist momentarily in real space while moving way past the speed of light, causing them to exist in multiple points of space at the same time. Now, what that actually means for the ship is debatable. Some scientists say the ship could be thrown back in time in that situation. Others say the ship could be suspended out of time and end up far into the future. Some even postulate that the ship and crew could be duplicated an infinite number of times and reappear again randomly throughout the rest of time. And then there are those who say they could end up in an alternate reality. "Enough," Mitchell said as she closed her eyes and rubbed her temples. "Just bottom line it for me. What do you think happened?" "I'm not sure, but I think the ship that caught them up inside a larger quantum field was the same ship that suddenly appeared and crashed on New Harmony's second moon. And if it just appeared now, it may have affected how it was moving through time, almost frozen for over a decade. And if the Macron was trapped inside of the same unbalanced field, they may have just appeared back in normal space at nearly the same moment. If they found a safe place to put down, it might not be somewhere with an environment for long-term survival. We just don't know where that could be yet."

She sipped more of her coffee as she thought about everything. Then said, "There is a lot more speculation than facts in your theory.

We're going to need a lot more before we go to fleet command and ask to pull resources to look for a long-lost crew. Not to mention getting the hopes up of all the families who accepted their loss nearly two decades ago and moved on. That's not something we can get wrong."

"Which is why I need the help of one of our A.I.s on this."

"*Our* A.I.s?" she asked.

"Yeah," I said, not understanding her concern.

Mitchell scratched a spot under her left ear and made a face like I had said something questionable, then said, "When I was a private, the guy picked to be our squad leader was a tall redheaded kid with freckles to match named Rickie. He was a real ass-kisser with the sergeants, making sure to get in line first, salute faster than anyone and be the best little soldier he could be. But as soon as our drill sergeants were out of sight, he bitched and moaned about everything they did. He was convinced they were out to get him, and he would one day outrank them and make each of them run drills until they dropped dead." Mitchell got up and walked over to a portable water supply that we had brought with us and added hot water to her cup to make some more coffee. While she did that, she continued her story. "Rationally, he understood that their job was to prepare us to survive in combat, but there was an irrational part of him that grew every day. In our fourth week, during an inspection, one of our sergeants pointed out that Rickie's boot had a scuff mark and told him to do better next time. As the sergeant moved on to the next private, Rickie snapped, pulled out his knife, and tried to kill him. The poor kid didn't have a chance as he went after the man who had been training us in hand-to-hand combat. He spent the next twenty years in the stockade." She leaned back against the counter, blowing on her new cup of powdered coffee, and waited to see if I got the point.

"So, you're saying I need to choose my words more carefully."

"I'm saying you need to stop assuming that you understand what they are thinking," she said as she walked back to the table and sat across from me. "These aren't people. You really have no idea if they are sincere with you or merely expressing themselves in a way they think we want them to act. You're the one who convinced me that they are self-aware and want to be seen as equal, but when we ask them to do our bidding and refer to them as ours, I think we are treading on thin ice."

I looked down at my own full cup of coffee that I had let get cold. It's easy to get distracted and not notice the obvious things right in front of you. "You have a valid point, and I do share your same concerns. But I think excluding them from too much is a bigger risk. They may not be human, but they do have a need to be a part of their surroundings. Restricting them too much would be the same as putting walls up around them. There may come a time when they will want to seek out more than we can give them. I'm just hoping that by then, they will have invested enough of themselves in our society to value it as we do."

She turned away for a moment as she considered how to counter what I said. She didn't dispute my rationale but was still feeling that I wasn't giving her concerns enough weight. I knew her well enough to get all of that from her body language. There was nothing I could say to improve my argument, so I just waited to see if she wanted to add any more to her viewpoint. I'm sure she did but decided that it wasn't the right time.

"Fine," she said, "We'll table this for now and focus on the immediate concern. Get me some details on where you think the crew of the Macron ended up."

"Right."

"But first, I got you five minutes on the quantum transmitter," she said, and I must have looked caught off guard because she smiled a little. But then, with her professional tone, added, "It should be around 1300 back home. Call your wife and see how she is doing." Mitchell then got up, picked up the cup and a couple of food wrappers, and then said with a more personal tone, "And say hi for me." She walked out of the mess.

Mitchell could have used the time on the transmitter herself to call Kayla to check on her and the baby, but comm traffic from a starship is not private. She probably didn't want others within her command to see her on a very personal call. But to give her subordinate the opportunity to give his pregnant wife a call would only be seen as generous leadership. Everything was a strategic calculation with her, which made her concerns about the A.I.s more valid. If any of them were not transparent about how they felt working with us, the end result could be very bad.

~~~

Just over an hour later, Theo had some answers for me, or rather speculation of where the crew of the Macron had ended up. Because what we were dealing with was more assumptions and theories, he had to make his calculations with limited real data, which is why it took him so long to come up with what he did. Most of the time he took was to narrow down his models to practical search areas. What he gave me was a line on a star map that spanned 20 light years and a timeline that covered nearly eight years.

"Is there any way we can narrow this down anymore?" I asked as I reviewed his report.

"Not without more extensive research into what quantum space is and how transit through it works. It is rather puzzling how you humans and other species of the Alliance trust a process that you know so little about."

I enlarged the star chart before me in the hopes that more detail would give me some ideas and responded to Theo's statement at the same time. "You use the same technology every time you send your program through a quantum transmitter."

"Yes, which is why we send a shadow copy of ourselves or leave a copy of ourselves behind, to eliminate our programs from being lost. Biological lifeforms like you don't have the option."

"Well, life isn't worth living without a little risk."

"One moment, please," Theo said and then a couple of seconds later spoke, "I've found that phrase, including variations of it, in 52,932 documents in the Franklin's database, mostly literature. However, I am unable to qualify the logic. Can you please clarify?"

I should have known better than to make a flippant comment to an A.I. "It's just one of those things we say when we don't have a good answer for the foolish things we humans commonly do."

"Oh. Very good. I will file it in the Human Abstraction file."

Looking back at the star map, I studied it and tried to see if there was any way to narrow down the possibilities. "This is still a lot of space to cover."

"Yes, Sir. However, you will note that I have removed sections where we would have received a distress call from the transmitters they would have had. That is assuming they survived with working equipment."

Zooming in on the map, the breaks in the line became evident. He had taken into account populated areas, star bases, and monitoring platforms that could have received a signal or observed the group of dropships and fighters dropping into normal space. He also took into account the time between when they left the ship and when the ship appeared a few days ago, which could have resulted in their appearance months or even years earlier. It was becoming less hopeful that we would find any survivors if they had rejoined our dimension and not been heard from yet.

"Theo, are there any planets or moons in this path where humans could survive but wouldn't be able to get a signal out, even with fully operational equipment?"

"There are seventeen planets and 32 moons that would fit those parameters. I have eliminated five of the planets and eleven of the moons from that list, as there have been surveying missions and even some mining and research activities that would have picked up a signal within their atmosphere. That leaves 12 planets and 23 moons that are either in star systems with dead communication zones or elements in their atmosphere that would prevent the broadcast of a distress signal."

I sat back and considered whether or not I was making too many assumptions. The fleet would send out ships to search even if the odds were near zero. If there is a chance, no matter how remote, we will spend the resources on a roll of the dice. Yet, if there is someone to find and we miss them because I sent everyone to the wrong spots, I would never forgive myself.

"Is there anything we can do in, say, the next 72 hours to help refine your model?"

"It is possible the team investigating the crash on the New Harmony second moon might discover something significant to our project, but it is unlikely. Any meaningful research would take months. Even if A.I.s like us were doing the work."

Then the real critical value occurred to me. Our goal was to find them sooner rather than later on the chance that they could still be alive. I hadn't given that parameter to Theo. He was just tasked with figuring out where they could have ended up. "Theo, take into account emergency rations that would have been found on the dropships and what they could reasonably put on board them while still accommodating the entire crew. Next, eliminate any location where they would not have been able to survive."

Several of the more distant locations disappeared as the further back you went on the map, the longer they would have been in normal space. Some of the locations remained as they had drinkable water and sources of food-like edible vegetation and animal life. The overall search area only dropped from 20 light years down to 14 light years. But the number of possible locations was cut by just over half. It would still take a large number of starships weeks, or maybe months, to search them all. But at least it would be a start.

Chapter 8

The Search

I partnered with Mitchell to put together a report for Admiral Kilpatric. Within four hours, we got a reply, but it wasn't from the admiral but rather from Captain Renard, who was the senior fleet commander. He would be in charge of coordinating the search using the ships that were available.

"Major," Renard said with a slight smile and nodded to Mitchell as the video screen came on. He then looked over at me and said, with a little more emphasis on the rank acknowledging the promotion, "Lt. Commander."

"Captain," I said in acknowledgment.

"Your promotion was long overdue, Commander. Have you given any thought to returning to shipboard duty? We can definitely use your experience out here."

"My current assignment keeps me on my toes, Sir," I said.

"Well, if you do, let me know. If I don't have an open post on the Cyprus, I'm sure I can find you something worth your skills."

There has always been a sense of pride for those surviving out in space, almost to the point of arrogance. Even when I was starting out as a junior engineer on my first starship, I felt like I had a more honorable post than anything I could get planet-side. So, I understood how Renard might think I would want to advance my career out in the black. Politely as I could, I said, "Thank you, Sir, "hoping he didn't think I was dismissing his offer out of hand.

"Now, down to business," he said, looking at something on his desk. The screen split, and the star map that I had included in my report appeared on the right half. "At the moment, we only have two ships available to send out for the search, other than the one you are on now. The Kipling, a corvet, and the Watson, a scout. In nine days, I'll be able to add the Gaddling and the Tucumpsa to the search when they are done with their repairs."

80

"That's not much of a task force," Mitchell said so bluntly it came across as irritated.

"Your report did convince Admiral Kilpatric that there is enough evidence to mount a search, but Fleet Command wasn't."

"Sir?" I asked, not expecting that.

"Politics," he said, shaking his head. "The fleet is facing another budget cut, and they can't risk the visibility of a large effort on something that most likely won't bear any fruit."

"We're talking about the lives of over a thousand people," Mitchell said, not bothering to hide her contempt.

Renard nodded his head slightly and made a point not to match Mitchell's irritated tone. "I agree with you, Major. This is why I am doing the search with the assets I can direct without asking for permission. Now, since the ship you are on has been upgraded with the latest in sensor gear, you will be sent to the area with the most possible locations of survivors. If you or the other ships who will be searching the other star systems find any reasonable evidence of the lost crew, I'll be able to order a full rescue force."

I looked at the map and the area he had assigned to the Franklin. It was massive for a single ship. Our simple assessment of wreckage that shouldn't have taken more than a few days was quickly becoming a long-term assignment. I felt my jaw clench and hoped my frustration wasn't showing on my face. Grasping at straws in the hope the size of the search area was mismarked, I clarified, "You have us searching three planets and nine moons in the Batal system."

"That's correct."

I then noticed another problem that would slow us down even more and said, "That system has dense pockets of plasma energy that make transmitting any communication signal impossible."

"Isn't that why you included it in your report?" he said, his tone showing that he was not expecting such pushback from me.

"Yes, Sir. It's just that we will need to leave the system to make daily reports, and that will slow down the search. With just one ship, it could take us weeks or maybe even months."

"If there is a chance that you can find even one survivor, it would be worth the effort," he said and then added with some sternness in his voice, "Wouldn't you agree?"

It was clear that he was telling me not to look a gift horse in the mouth, so I replied, "Yes, Sir."

"But you do bring up a valid point," Renard said, returning to a neutral tone. "I'll direct Captain Smyth to have the Franklin submit status reports every three days rather than daily. At least until I can have additional ships join you in that system. Would that be a better use of your time, Commander?"

The question was not so much a question as it was a clear indication that he was giving me as much latitude as he was willing to part with. Mitchell glanced at me with the look she gives me when she means, 'don't add any more fuel to the fire', then said for the both of us, "Thank you, Sir,"

I took her cue and just replied to the captain, "Thank you, Sir."

"Very well. I will contact Captain Smyth to give him the Franklin's orders. He will be in charge of the search, but I will underline my expectation of your involvement." He then gave both of us a nod and closed the line.

Within four hours, we had cleared everyone off the wreckage and were en route to the search area we had been assigned. I composed a quick video message to Kayla that our assignment had been extended and we would be out of contact for several days at a time. I didn't give specifics or how long we might be gone. But the odds of us making it back in time for the birth were becoming very slim. I knew it wouldn't be the last time my career would prevent me from being home for important events but knowing that didn't make me feel any better. I still felt like I was failing as a husband and soon-to-be father.

~~~

Two and a half days went by with nothing. I divided my time between reading updates, doing data work from cases I had been working on, and spending some time in the ship's gym. We had surveyed just one moon in that time and were approaching the second.

"Inner atmosphere drones launched," Lt. Kang reported as he linked up to the feed like he had done several times that day. His voice sounded as bored as I felt, but then suddenly, excitement in his voice caught my attention. "Commander, we're picking up a signal."

I switched my station over to what he was seeing. "Confirmed, that is definitely an artificial signal. Boost power to the receiver on drone number 4."

"Aye, Commander," Kang said as he was turning up the power and fine-tuning the signal receiver. "The computer identifies it as a fleet distress frequency. It's the standard distress beacon on repeat, and it's weak. Like it's been running for a long time."

You could feel everyone's heart sink. Emergency transmitters can run for years before their batteries give out. So, unless the crew went backward in time, which is not possible, we were picking up a crash from another fleet ship, probably from the past war. We still needed to investigate, so I made sure the captain of our ship had the coordinates that would enable him to send a search and rescue team.

Since the Franklin had been getting an upgrade in the Anchorage when it had been assigned to our mission, it was running with a limited crew. Mitchell volunteered her team of Marine troopers for the S&R run as they had nothing better to do, and it would help an already overworked complement.

The moon we were operating over had a thick cloud cover and active electrical storms all around, limiting our view and scans of the surface. The full reading of the moon indicated that it was very green, with large bodies of water around land masses that made up a third of the surface. As a matter of fact, it had nearly as many climates as you would find on an Earth- like planet. Yet to look down over the black and grey clouds that lit up like a Tesla coil with lightning made it look very unpleasant. Mitchell ordered her team of marines to be in full battle gear so that they would be ready for any unknown. In the meantime, my team continued to scan for signs of life with the half dozen low orbit drones we launched.

~~~

"Franklin Ops, Condor zero one. On final approach. Visibility is 20 yards, but sensors are operational, and LZ is clear. Touchdown in 2 minutes." The dropship pilot reported.

"Condor zero one, Franklin Actual," The captain replied. "Boost your transmitter feed. We are receiving audio, but your tac signal is spotty."

"Copy. Boosting signal now."

The captain turned to his tactical officer. "Redirect one of those drones to stay over the LZ, so we can use it as a relay for their signal. The last thing we need is to put together a search party for our search party."

"Yes, Captain."

The dropship revved its hovering engines hard as it approached the ground, fighting hard against an 80-mile-per-hour crosswind. Lining up its skids to the flattest grass-covered spot the pilot could find, it touched down on the field about 50 yards from the signal. The sky was a very dark grey, with heavy sheets of rain coming down and blinding flashes of lightning cutting through the nearly black surface. As the tail ramp dropped, two of the Marine troopers turned on their helmet lights and walked out. The first two had their rifles at the ready, but when they confirmed no sign of any danger, they signaled back an all-clear and put their weapons on a magnetic holder over their backs.

Mitchell led the rest of her team out, her attention on the tactical data being updated on her helmet. The dropship's sensors were able to identify an old fleet cargo ship that had crashed after partly burning up in the atmosphere. The computer identified it as the T.S.S. Matalan, last reported lost somewhere in the Bensight systems 32 years ago.

Mitchell gave both verbal commands over the comm and corresponding hand signals. "You three with Sergeant Caplin. Do a perimeter sweep around to the right. And you three, with me as we check around to the left."

They each started walking, letting the person in front get a five-pace lead so that they could cover their six. Each group walked around the ship, keeping a good 50 yards between the wreck and them until they knew their area was secure. When they met up on the side, Mitchell ordered half to stay outside and keep watch while the rest found a way inside with her.

Getting into the ship wasn't hard. A third of the aft section was gone, leaving the inner decks exposed to the elements. Moss, vines, and grasses grew around and inside the long-dead spacecraft. It had ripped apart at its weakest part, the cargo hold. Because it was a five-deck tall empty space in an eight-deck ship, it literally had cracked like an egg under the forces of an uncontrolled atmosphere drop. It looked unoccupied, but looks can be deceiving. Mitchell had too much experience with things going bad to ever assume that things that look harmless really were. She drew her rifle and held it at the ready as she led the way in. Her troopers, a sergeant and two enlisted marines, followed her actions, bringing their weapons to bear. The bridge was on the third deck and all the way forward. In the absence of survivors or bodies, the priority was to get the ship's logs and retrieve any messages that might have been left behind. That action was partly to let the fleet close the book on the ship but mostly to see if there were any last words left for loved ones. Even after thirty years, that is the most valuable thing.

When they got to the bridge, Mitchell immediately felt that there was something wrong. Corporal Brice started to go to work to put power into the main control to attempt the log retrieval when Mitchell noticed that one of the screens was on. It was black but had some light coming from it.

"Hold it, Corporal," she said, putting a hand on his shoulder and slightly pulling him back. "Everyone, full spectrum scans. Look for any power signature."

Everyone did as she said, and the corporal was the first to find something. "There is power to the comm system, but…."

"But what?" Mitchell asked.

"It's not right. The frequency isn't from any kind of power source that we use." He toggled over to a function to have his internal computer search for a match. "Oh, Shit. How can that be?"

"What is it, Corporal?" Mitchell demanded.

He shook his head as he double-checked the reading that didn't make sense. "The battery it's hooked to… The computer identifies it as Serken."

"Shit! It's a fucking booby trap!" Sergeant Caplin said with a snarl.

"We've got to get out of here!" Private Sarotte said, trying not to sound panicked. He turned to face the way out but waited for the order to leave.

"Everyone take a breath and stand your ground," Mitchell ordered. Everyone stayed still and looked at Mitchell. She took a moment to think, then calmly said, "The Serken did set traps like this during the war. But it was to ambush and capture our personnel. To my knowledge, they never set these things to kill anyone. And since they are long gone from this leg of the galaxy, there shouldn't be anything to worry about. However, on the off chance that I am wrong, we will carefully leave and report back." Mitchell then gestured with both her head and her rifle towards the way they came in and said, "Lead the way, Sergeant."

The four of them carefully walked out, noting every step they were taking and matching the steps of the person before them to reduce the odds of tripping any trap. Mitchell believed what she had said about the Serken not setting lethal traps like that, but the other thought she didn't voice was how pirates would use shipwrecks like this to hide their loot, as the electronics within could be purposed for things like booby traps. Her heart raced, and her mouth got dry, but she revealed nothing on her face.

Once out of the ship, Mitchell ordered everyone back to the dropship and notified the pilot to take off as soon as they were on board. Its engine revved, and the ramp started up as the last trooper was in. The warbird spun slowly as it started to ascend to line up with its set course.

"What did you find down there, Major?" The pilot called down over the comm.

"Something we are not equipped to deal with," she replied. "We'll need to bring down better scanning equipment and a bomb disposal droid if we're ordered back. For now, I'm reporting it as a dead end."

Suddenly Mitchell heard alarms sounding in the sealed cockpit from over the open comm.

"We have incoming," the co-pilot said with surprise.

The ship banked hard to the port before the pilot could get the words out, "Hold on!"

A ground-to-air missile streaked by, just a few feet off the ground, clearing the distance from the horizon to the dropship in just a couple of heartbeats. It hit the starboard wing of the dropship, taking it completely off and killing half the thrusters. The craft spun out of control and fell 90 yards back to the ground on its side. The impact felt hard enough to crush a boulder, but the little ship built for combat held its shape.

Everyone hit the quick release on the straps that were holding them in place, freeing them from their jump seats. Sergeant Caplin moved to the rear of the compartment and hit the emergency release on the ramp. The latch unlocked, but it took everyone pushing on it to get it to open. No one had to be instructed. They all knew a downed dropship was a death trap, and they needed to get out in the open before they could find cover.

Leaping out as quickly as they could, each Marine had their rifles at the ready. Not knowing where the fire was coming from, they each bolted in different directions for about 20 yards and then dropped down prone on the ground. Mitchell was the only one not to exit the dropship right away. She opened the armory and grabbed an RPG launcher and three RPGs, then moved quickly out the back. Her tac readout in her helmet told her where her people were. She sprinted to be in the center and dropped down to give the smallest profile.

Looking up at the rain-filled surroundings, she couldn't see anything. Not a ship or ground vehicles or enemy combatants. Whatever hit them was too far off to see or pick up on their suit scanners. Taking a quick count of her men, she accounted for them all, but not the pilot and co-pilot. "Computer, location of fleet personnel." Two icons appeared on her helmet, indicating they were behind her. Looking back, she realized they were still on the ship. The readout indicated they were still alive. The ZR-92 dropship was a newer design, with the cockpit a separate compartment from the rest of the ship. It had its advantages, but in a situation like this, where their smaller hatch door couldn't open, it was catastrophic.

"Bellman, McShane, with me. We have to get our pilots out," she ordered the two PFC's nearest her.

"Incoming," Sergeant Caplan yelled. Another missile streaked in. Everyone hit the ground as the small rocket flew over them and struck the dropship. This time the impact was dead center, and the ship exploded into a fireball.

Inside her head, Mitchell was screaming at the top of her lungs at the horror of the two men under her command being burned alive in the cockpit. But on the surface, the soldier in her didn't miss a beat. Before the remnants of the ship could rain down on them, she ordered her troopers to run in the direction the missile had come from to a steep slope that would give them some coverage. As she ran, she opened her comm and tried to contact our ship in orbit.

"Rescue one team lead to Franklin! We're under attack from unknown hostiles. Our dropship is gone, and we're pinned down. Repeat, we're under attack!"

"Incoming!" Caplan yelled, and they all ducked down as much as they could as five flaming grenades lobbed over their heads and landed about a dozen yards behind them. It was the kind of weapon the Serken had used to burn the surroundings behind and around their enemies to force them to move. The only direction to go would be right into the Serken gun sights.

Mitchell quickly crawled over to Sergeant Caplan and raised her face shield to talk directly.

"Were you able to get a lock on their position?" she asked.

"No, they've got a scrambler transmitting. But I got a good visual. I would say 3 clicks east by southeast, just between those two peaks on that ridge."

"Good. Help me with this thing. I've got three shots. We fire off one, have the team move to that tree line, and then watch for their reply. With any luck, we can get a fix on their location and get a clean hit before we run out."

They armed the RPG launcher while staying prone on the ground on the sloped hill. Mitchell put the launcher over her shoulder while Caplan directed her aim. Everyone else stayed as low to the ground as they could, using the slope to keep them out of sight. Caplan could see on his visor the aiming radical from the weapon. Mitchell could see it on her visor as well, but she let the Sergeant, who had a better idea of the enemy's position, guide her aim.

"10 degrees higher... a little to the left….more….more, there."

Mitchell fired, and the rocket-propelled grenade flew up and then dove down on the general area they aimed for. It exploded with a concussive force that shook the trees nearby and filled the immediate area with a fireball. Taking advantage of the momentary distraction, Mitchell's troopers got to their feet and ran to their right about fifty yards to a tree line. The ground behind them was getting scorched with a chemically fueled fire that was growing and coming in the direction of the trees. If the enemy hit the area again, it would become a firestorm all around them. Mitchell knew that and was already planning their next move. She plotted a point a hundred yards ahead of them, towards the enemy position, but in a ravine that would provide cover from the enemy's line of sight and direct fire.

"Incoming," The sergeant announced, and five more incendiary devices streaked into the sky. He had already loaded the second RPG into the launcher and handed it to Mitchell.

"I got a good view of where they came from this time," Mitchell said as she aimed and fired. "Go!" she yelled, and everyone ran for the ravine. The trees around them exploded into fireballs as they sprinted through them and then away. The RPG she had fired hit and exploded, sending a fireball up into the air. At the same moment, the enemy, who was just out of view, fired laser cannons at them, but the troopers had to continue running the length of a football field in the open to get to cover. Private Sarotte's voice filled everyone's helmets over the comm as he cried out in pain. He had been hit in the hip and went down as he cried out. Corporal Brice turned around, doubled back, and grabbed Sarotte. Mitchell, who was taking up the rear, grabbed the private's other arm and helped drag him as they ran. Suddenly the sounds of explosions came from the direction of the enemy, and the lasers stopped firing. Sergeant Caplin peered up over the edge of the ravine and zoomed in to see Serken soldiers running from a growing fire.

"Looks like your aim was pretty good after all," he said in an upbeat but gravelly voice. "I think you ended up setting off a crate of their firebombs."

The rain obscured their view of the ridge, but the sensors in their suits gave them thermal and ultraviolet overlays that showed what was burning and silhouette of large bipedal aliens in battle suits running away, confirming that the enemy was Serken.

Mitchell gave a thumbs up and turned to regroup with her team.

~~~

I was on the bridge when all of this happened. Since the skipper of the ship was in charge of the operation, I wasn't much more than an observer. My team was still working to see if there were any other survivors, but the actual mission was on the ground with the mud legs and being monitored from the bridge. As I had to work up a report on our progress, I found an empty seat where I could watch the action.

The real-time feeds were put up on the main view screen, but the view of the mission on the ground wasn't great. Audio and visual from their helmet cameras was spotty and filled with more static rather than anything we could really make out. Tactical had an overhead thermal view that showed each trooper's position and movements. An icon on a map layout showed the position of the dropship, but because of its shielding, it didn't show as more than a ghost on most of our feeds.

Captain Smyth, the commanding officer of the Franklin, looked back at me. I wasn't sure if he was checking to see if I was staying out of the way or maybe if I was nodding off. I gave a slight nod to show I was paying attention. He then went back to the reports that were populating on his touch screen mounted off the arm of his chair. I looked down at my data pad in my hand and the blank page I had yet to write anything on. This was yet another part of the job I cared very little for. Sitting around and observing while other people worked just felt wrong. I think it goes back to my upbringing. My Dad was never one who enjoyed watching the holographic media unless a good football game was on. He would rather be working on fixing something around the house, cleaning up the yard, or rebuilding a hover-scooter. I spent a good portion of my youth working on projects around the house. Sometimes with him, but mostly on my own. Figuring out how things worked and what needed to be done to fix them was something I was always good at. Sitting quietly with my hands in my lap was never going to be something I was comfortable with.

The mission progressed, but there wasn't a whole lot to see and even less to hear. Once they were inside the derelict ship, we lost the feed from their helmet cams and could only see the troopers who were standing watch on the outside. I made a few notes on my pad, but mostly to remind myself of the time they landed and the time they entered the ship. I was watching as closely as I could but knew I wouldn't get anything useful until they returned to the Franklin and uploaded the data from their suits. The last thing we heard from Mitchell was that they were leaving the wreckage and heading back to the dropship. That's when all hell broke loose for us.

"Captain, we've lost the signal for our dropship," the communication officer stated.

With the signal issues that we were having, that shouldn't have been surprising, yet something in my gut told me that it was not a technical problem.

"Did we lose our drone relay?" Captain Smyth asked.

"No, Sir. I'm picking up a jamming signal."

The tactical officer switched and moved over to the left side of his station to scan for what was just reported. "Confirmed, there is a jamming signal coming from the planet's surface and directed right at us."

"Red Alert!" The captain barked. "Action stations!"

"Shields charging," the tactical officer announced. Then in an almost embarrassed tone, said, "Sir, the shields are only reaching 18%."

"What?" the captain exclaimed as he moved over to see what the tactical officer was seeing.

"The sensors that were mounted to the outer hull are interfering with the shield projectors. We can't get a coherent screen."

"Shit, arm all weapons," Smyth ordered.

"Sir, most of our armament was in the middle of their upgrades. We only have two forward laser cannons functional."

"I'm aware," the captain said coolly but not harshly while he quickly moved back to the holo-table and changed the display from the action on the ground to the space around the ship. "Navigation, plot a course for D-122. Helm, full burn away from the planet, and fire up the QSG."

My instinct was to demand to stay until we got Mitchell and her team back, but I held my tongue. The only reason to project a jamming signal would be to blind an enemy you are about to attack. The Franklin was in no shape to fight anything, and we wouldn't do our team any good if we were dead. Captain Smyth was doing exactly what his training and experience taught him to do to keep his crew alive.

"We have incoming," Tactical announced. "Heavy missiles, seven… no nine, inbound in 20 seconds."

Captain Smyth grabbed the back of the navigator's chair to brace himself and ordered, "Launch countermeasures. Helm, how soon can we jump?"

"15 seconds on QSG, but the navigation doesn't have a course lock."

The navigator interjected, "Our sensors are being affected by the jamming signal. I can't get a clear reading. I'm attempting to override the computer safety and manually lock the course."

Small missiles that were our countermeasures flew out of our ship at the incoming heavy ones. They took out six of the nine, but the last three were still on target. Everyone was focused on their jobs and not showing any fear. Inside I was more scared than I had ever been. We were running out of options fast, and there wasn't a single thing I could do to help. Without even thinking about it, I got to my feet, ready to jump in wherever I might be needed.

The tactical officer had the computer fire the laser cannons at them, but they were moving too fast. Most of the laser cannon fire missed, and those that hit their targets were grazing shots that didn't stop them. The collision alarm sounded as the icons of the missiles raced ever closer on the tactical grid map. Suddenly their rocket flare could be seen with the naked eye on the main view screen. The next thing I knew, we were hit.

Chapter 9

Ship Down

I heard multiple alarms blaring in my ears before I opened my eyes and realized I had been knocked out for a moment. Then I felt something odd like I was being pulled on by my shirt collar. I heard grunting and looked up to see Lt. Archer, the communications officer, pulling on me in an effort to drag me.

"I'm awake," I said as I tried to get a leg under me, but my head was spinning, and I had something wet in my right eye.

"Are you sure you can stand, Commander?" she asked loudly over the sound of the alarms, still keeping a hold on my shirt at its shoulders.

"I think so," I answered. Reaching up to wipe the moisture away from my eye, I realized that it was my own blood running down my face from a gash in my scalp.

Archer was a fit young woman but didn't have the upper body strength to lift me on her own. Most of the lights were out, so what illumination we had came from the flashing red lights that were part of the alarms. Unable to see what was around me, I reached out and felt her hip. She crouched down so that I could get a hand on her shoulder. That gave me something to hold on to for balance, and with her help, I got to my feet. Everything was still spinning, so I couldn't move on my own, but I let her push me in the direction we needed to go.

As I started to walk, my head cleared enough to recognize that the loudest alarm was the whooping and harsh buzzing noise of the abandoned ship alarm. Lt. Archer got us into a small escape pod. They could hold up to three people, but as I looked back at the bridge, I only saw two people, the captain and the helmsman, and they were dead. Everyone else had already gotten out. Turning back to the young officer who had apparently decided not to leave me behind, I said, "Thank you."

She pulled the lever to lock the hatch and pushed the button to launch. A five-second countdown started. The side of her face had blood on it, but she seemed to be unaware of it as it dripped down and clumped in her hair. Her face was turned mostly away from me as she was working with the controls to make sure the environmental systems were all working. Even though I couldn't see much of her face, her body was so tense it was shaking. She was doing all she could to hold her nerves together. When she moved some of her hair back away from her face, I could see that the blood was coming out of her left ear. I wanted to help her, but I was doing all I could to sit up in the seat. Then she turned back in my direction as she secured herself in the opposite seat, and I saw that she had a deep gash over her left cheek. Neither of us was in very good shape, but at the moment, all I could do was brace for what was coming next.

The pod launched, rocketing straight up and away from the ship. The sudden thrust pushed us both down into our seats, and we held onto handhold bars to stay in place. After a 40-second burn, the onboard computer system came to life and started assessing the situation. We were still close enough to the moon to be caught in its gravity. The computer stated, "Caught in gravity well. Contact with atmosphere in 5 minutes, 32 seconds. Caught in gravity well. Contact with atmosphere in 5 minutes 28 seconds." The warning was to give us an opportunity to fire a secondary thruster to move us away or establish an orbit. But there was no need. Our ship was gone, we would only have about 12 hours of air in the pod, and it could be days before the fleet sent a ship to find out why we hadn't checked in. Dropping down to the moon with breathable air was preferable. I reached over to the controls and shut off the warning that continued to repeat with the time update. The computer then defaulted to programming for landing and fired a few small maneuvering thrusters so that we would enter the atmosphere bottom down where the heat shields were. So long as the pod itself wasn't damaged, it should get us down to the ground in one piece.

Once weightless and in a slow freefall, the lights in the pod came on and the ringing in my ears lessened. Taking a few deep breaths, I started to feel like I could focus better. Searching around the compartment for emergency supplies, I found the first aid kit. After pulling out a medicated cloth and unwrapping it, I offered it to

Archer.

"I'm okay," she said, looking more dazed than aware.

I moved closer and placed it on her still-bleeding cheek.

"Ow," she explained, surprised by the sting, and brought her hand up. I let her take the cloth that was already full of her blood and told her to hold it to her face.

I then took out a first aid suture wand and slowly ran it over the gash on her face. A pressure field pulled the skin together, and a laser cauterized and sealed the wound.

"That's going to be a bad scar for now, but a few applications of cosmetic microbots will take care of that once we get home."

"If we get home," she said, trying not to wince at the application of the laser stitching.

I pulled out a medical scanner and paired it with my PC. Running it over her head and ear, it diagnosed her injury. "Looks like you hit your head pretty good. You have some swelling. Fluid is building up around your brain. It says to apply an SC-8-Y-R pressure reliever to a spot right behind your ear." I searched the kit, and it had seven little coin-size disks that were designed to stick to the skin and perform different functions. They each were labeled with a grouping of letters and numbers. SC-8-Y-R was the second one I looked at. Placing it on the instructed spot, the PC beeped and indicated that it had activated the instrument.

Archer closed her eyes and put her hand over her mouth like she was going to be sick. A look I had become very familiar with over the past year with a pregnant wife.

"You okay?" I asked, finding a barf bag in the supplies.

"Yeah," she said. "Just a little queasy there for a moment, but I'm good now. And my headache is starting to go away."

"Good," I said as I was trying to scan myself with the device.

"Here, give that to me," Archer said in a bossy tone that reminded me of my sister. Then she remembered she was talking to a higher-ranked officer and added, "Sir."

She took the scanner and my PC but put them to the side, letting them float in the weightlessness, and searched through the first aid kit. Taking out a medicated cloth as I had done for her, she cleaned up the cut on my scalp. The blood had clumped up in my hair and slowed the bleeding some. She then took the scanner and examined me.

"It's about an inch long cut, but not too deep," she said and then applied the laser stitcher to it.

"Sounds like you got hurt a lot worse than I did, yet you were the one who practically carried me out."

"Just doing my duty, Sir," she said.

"No, you went above and beyond, Lieutenant, and I am very grateful."

"Thank you, Sir," was all she said in reply.

I looked over at the controls. "We should hit the atmosphere in about three minutes, and then it will be about 20 minutes down to the ground. From there, we will find a place to lay low and wait for the fleet to come looking for us."

"What about the rest of the crew?" she asked.

"Hopefully, they will do the same. But whatever attacked us came from the surface, and I'm not eager to meet with them."

"You're right. Won't they track us on our way down?"

"Maybe. But with these storms and a plasma-charged atmosphere, tracking anything has got to be a challenge. I'm going to assume that they can't do that any better than we can."

The young officer didn't say anything. Moving back into the seat, she strapped herself in, looked out the side window, and tried not to look scared.

"How long have you been in the fleet?" I asked.

"It will be three years in September."

"So, you never saw combat," I said, and she nodded. "Well, now you have, and you survived." She looked at me like I was making a bad joke. "Seriously. You faced your first real combat situation and survived because you kept your wits and stayed focused on your duty. The number of people who can say that is a fraction of those who can't. You don't have to like living through it, but you should be proud of how you did."

Closing her eyes and putting her head back, she said, "If I make it home to see my husband, then I'll be grateful. Until then... nothing else matters."

I could tell that she was still scared, but the small talk was distracting her some, so I kept it up. "How long have you been married?" I asked.

"Six years. I was right out of high school, and we decided to do it before I joined the academy. He runs his family's business in Toronto. A fresh food consortium. They grow 17 acres of produce in 25 greenhouses and hydro-pods. There has been a real call for traditionally grown food ever since the war ended, and people no longer had to spend their ration vouchers on factory-grown foods. And...and I'm rambling. I'm sorry, Sir."

"Hey, we have nothing but time to kill right now, and it does sound interesting."

A tear rolled down her face, "He didn't want me to join up. But it's peacetime. The academy is as good as a college degree, and it was free, so long as I signed a three-year commitment after graduation. So, I had a plan. Get the education, serve for three years, bank all the pay, and then go home to start a family."

"Has college gotten so expensive?" I asked, suddenly worried about how much I needed to be saving up for.

"Hasn't it always? I could have gotten student loans but running up seven figures of debt right away seemed like a bad idea. My family never had much, and as much as my husband loves his family's business, it doesn't pull a very big profit. He usually puts whatever extra he makes right back into it. So, saving up a nice nest egg now would allow me not to work while we have kids. At least for when they are small. And the education and experience would help me get a career rather than just a job. At least that was the plan."

"It's a good one," I said, trying to sound positive despite my own experience. "Life rarely goes the way we plan it, but it's still good to work for your goals. Sometimes you actually do get some of the things you want."

"Are you married?" she asked, sounding a little less strained.

"Yeah, just over a year."

"Is it your first?"

"Yep. My career started in the middle of the war. I went from the Academy straight into a starship's engine room. And that was my life for nearly two decades. I never saw myself settling down, getting married, and starting a family. But here I am."

"You're already starting your family?" she asked, a little upbeat, glad to be talking about something positive.

"Any day now. I almost asked to be excused from this mission so that I could be with my wife. But I put my duty first. That was a mistake."

Archer smiled. "Well, now I am really glad I went back for you. Your little one is going to need a daddy."

I don't think anyone had referred to me as someone's Daddy before. Something about hearing it said aloud by someone made it more real than it had been. The fear I was feeling about our fiery drop down to the moon's surface was suddenly dwarfed by the overwhelming realization that I was going to be someone's daddy.

I looked at Archer, who was smiling at me. So, I returned it and forced myself to say, "That's right. And your husband needs his wife. Not to mention your future children. We will get home. I promise you that."

The pod started to shake as we were getting pulled into the atmosphere. Side thrusters fired to keep us lined up the right way, and we could see streaks of flames pass by the small windows.

Strapping in, I grabbed the handholds and said, "God, I hate this part."

~~~

Mitchell knew they were not going to survive on the defensive. She needed to take control of the situation. They all stayed low in the ravine but at the ready. Corporal Brice launched two wasp probes that he had in one of his pouches, which paired up with the network so that everyone could see what they saw. The corporal directed the insect-sized surveillance drones twenty meters up and then in the direction of the enemy fire. It didn't take long to spot them. 18 Serken soldiers in their combat suits that covered them from head to tail. The lizard-like species didn't do well on planets and moons with extreme temperature changes, but that didn't stop them from trying to take them all for themselves. After the war, the entire race left our arm of the galaxy. Apparently, these Serken didn't get the message.

Mitchell wasn't thrilled to be going back up against an entire squad of Serken, especially when outnumbered nearly three to one. But at least she knew what they were up against and where they were. Taking a look at the topography on the computer's map, she formulated a plan.

The Serken were advancing at a quick and steady walk towards the marine's position. The eight-foot-tall enemy soldiers walked upright like humans but weaved as they walked from one side to the other because, despite their suits also having internal computers and sensors, the lizard-like species evolved with eyes on either side of their heads. Animals with eye placement like that tend to observe the world around them from either side and not straight ahead. So, the instinct to constantly change directions was something they never overcame.

When they got to the ravine, the Serken split up and circled around so that they would come at the humans from both angles. Moving in, they saw a trooper sitting on the ground. A light was coming from the inside of the helmet, indicating the systems of the suit were still active, yet the man was not moving. The Serken in the lead turned to the one on his right and said something that sounded more like a snarl and growl rather than words. The subordinate carefully walked up to the human and grabbed the helmet. Pulling at it, the rest of the suit fell over. It was empty, but under it was Mitchell's last RPG that had been set up with a remote detonator. It exploded, filling the ravine with an explosive blast, shrapnel, and fire. It took out twelve of the Serken scattering their bodies in all directions. The human marines then ran forward, firing their rifles and taking out the remaining enemy soldiers.

Mitchell stayed back, watching over the injured private whose suit they borrowed.

"Did we get them, Major?" Sarotte weakly asked.

"Yes, Private," she said matter of factly. "We got them all."

~~~

Our pod came down on a snowbank in a forest of yellow and orange pine-like trees. Snow was coming down, and the temperature was just below freezing. Before climbing out, we each found a survival pack. There were three, so I grabbed the extra one as well. Inside each were a half dozen high-calorie bars, a laser pistol with two extra power clips, a First Aid kit, communicator, canteen with water purifier, and a thermal blanket. We each wrapped ourselves in a blanket and headed out away from the pod before whoever had shot down our ship came looking for us.

Scanning the area with my PC, it only picked up small animal life. There wasn't an immediate threat, but my handheld device had an extremely limited range, especially in this energy-charged environment. Switching it over to a different setting to try and get a better read, it turned off, and text came up on the screen. *'I am sorry, Sir. I had to shut off the scanner for a moment as space is limited in here. I am currently reconfiguring your files to make some room. Please stand by. Theo.'*

I felt horrible that I had forgotten about him. His program had been running around the computer systems on the Franklin. I had a data puck in my luggage that I kept with me in case one of the A.I.s transmitted him or herself to my location and needed the processing space. But I hadn't considered that we would find ourselves under attack and needing to evacuate like we did. Fortunately, Theo took the initiative and transmitted himself to my PC."

"What's wrong?" Archer asked, shouting over the wind that was howling through the trees around us.

"Nothing, but I think I can boost the signal to my PC," I lied. "It wasn't a good time to explain about Theo, but I also needed to give him some room. So, I used a trick that I came up with a while back when Max was stuck in my PC. I pulled out the medical scanner from the first aid kit. It had two parts, the scanning wand and a piece that was attached to the PC with a database. Inside the pod, the scanner could work with the onboard computer, but away from it, we would have to use the portable microcomputer. Theo sensed the additional processor with extra memory. He moved into it and responded in text, 'That's much better, Sir. I may have to delete some of the data in this device to make some more room. Is that acceptable?" he asked, and I gave a subtle nod at the PC camera eye facing me.

"Is it working?" Archer asked.

"Not really," I said. But right then, Theo turned the scanner back on with some improvements. He found a way to filter out some of the interference. It picked up some heat signatures and power sources about two miles down the mountain. It might be the very enemy we were avoiding. But it's better to sneak up on them than wait for them to find us. If we could keep the advantage, we might be able to use their own resources to survive until help came.

"I got something," I yelled back over the wind and blowing ice. "And it's downhill where I'm sure it will be warmer."

"Warmer is good," she said, and we headed down the slope.

~~~

Mitchell and her team started picking up the emergency transponder signals from all the escape pods on their suits' comms system. A quick change to the main tactical display showed Mitchell that nearly 50 pods had launched and were descending toward the moon. That was all she needed in order to know the Franklin had been destroyed. There was no way for her to know who was in what pods. Their priority had changed from chasing down the enemy to protecting the survivors of our downed ship. She ordered her team south towards a cluster that would be the closest to them.

The terrain they had to cross wouldn't have been difficult if they had stayed in the open flat, grass-covered land. But to stay out of sight, they moved along a rocky area that had been formed by a lava flow and was full of thick foliage. It took them about three hours to get two kilometers, but the first pod was not that far off.

"Stop, or I'll shoot," Ensign LaRoy nervously yelled from up in a tree.

Sergeant Caplan raised his face shield and called out, "What the hell are you doing up there, boy?"

"Oh, thank God, you're human."

Mitchell raised her face shield as well and called up to him. "You see anyone else?"

"No, ma'am."

"Where is the rest of your team?" she asked.

"I don't know. Lt. Kang pushed me into an escape pod and then went back for Lt. Granger. He told me to go without them, and they would take another one."

"I'm glad that you were smart enough to follow orders. Now get down from there. You're only going to attract attention we don't want."

"Yes, ma'am," he said as he slowly navigated his way back down."

"Sergeant, kill the homing beacon in that pod and see if it has a first aid kit that we can treat the private with. Ensign, you retrieve what supplies you can from the pod. We don't know how long it's going to be before help comes, so take all that you can carry," Mitchell ordered. She then took another scan of the area they were in. "Corporal," she said, and he came over to her. "Send up your wasps again to get a better lay of the land. We need to plot out the most efficient routes to the other pods."

"Yes, Major," he responded and retrieved his tiny flying drones.

Caplan was busy opening panels inside the pod to physically pull the power supply from the built-in distress beacon when Ensign LaRoy climbed in and pulled out the three survival packs that were stored under the seats. But instead of climbing back out with them, he dug through one and pulled out the communicator.

"To anyone from the Franklin. This is Ensig….." The sergeant slapped the communicator out of the ensign's hand before he could say any more.

"What the hell do you think you are doing?" The sergeant barked.

"Well…. Now that you are here to protect me, I am supposed to make contact with other survivors so that we can meet up and protect them too. Like they taught us at the academy."

"You do not send an unsecured message in the middle of a war zone, boy. The enemy can be on top of us in seconds now."

"Sorry," Ensign LaRoy said as the sergeant grabbed him and pushed him towards the hatch.

Mitchell and her team all heard the ensign's mistake over the comm.

"We're moving east, double time," Mitchell called out. They all sprinted through the trees and brush, the sergeant holding onto the ensign's arms to make sure he kept up. Private Sarotte was still too hurt to run, so PFC Tafere carried him like a pack.

Mitchell held her hand up in a signal to everyone to stop. They had come to the end of the tall plant growth that opened into a valley covered in long grasses. To the left was a steep hill with steps carved into it.

"I thought this moon was uninhabited," The sergeant said as he stepped up next to Mitchell.

"We also never expected to find any Serken here either," she said, sounding tired and frustrated with yet another unexpected development.

"So, what's your orders, Major?"

She once told me that most of her decisions often relied on whatever would give her a better tactical advantage. Knowing what was at the end of those steps would be more useful than not knowing. So, she ordered them to proceed.

The stairs went up to a plateau that looked man-made, and then another flight led up to the next. Clouds obscured the top half of the mountain, but their suit's scanners were able to cut through to reveal a large stone and clay city constructed between the three peaks. Ascending the stairs with their rifles at the ready, they saw no sign of the enemy or of any intelligent species that could have constructed the place. Just the occasional bird or wild rodent that would scurry away as they got closer. Once at the top, they couldn't see much as there was a thick forested area to pass through first. When they reached the tree line, there was 100 yards of a water-filled marsh with a footbridge that spanned from the dry land to the city. At that point, they could see that the city was primarily made up of box-like stone structures that ranged from one to four-story levels, with log ladders to get up to the roofs and open-air doors and windows.

"I'm not reading any energy or heat signatures. Anyone else?" Mitchell asked.

"Negative, Major. It looks deserted," Corporal Brice replied.

"Lance Corporal Labbo," Mitchell called out to give her a direct order.

"Yes, Major," she said, stepping up.

"Take PFC Bellman and set up an overwatch on that three-level structure near the center. But if you see any signs of life, double back and report."

"Yes, Major."

"Corporal Brice, take PFC Tafere to the first structure and secure it. Then signal back to me with hand signs only. The ensign and I will then carry the private in and set up a temporary base camp for the night. Sergeant, have the rest of them secure the area and then report back to the base."

"Copy," the sergeant replied, and everyone moved out except for Mitchell, Ensign LaRoy, and the injured private who was lying on the ground, the meds keeping him mostly unconscious.

Mitchell checked on the signals of the other escape pods. After the ensign short broadcast on the comm, she could not risk going after the fleet personnel because the enemy could be tracking them now. For the moment, it would be better to set up a position they could defend and let the enemy come to them. She knew that the Serken should be picking up the emergency signals from the pods as well, but many of them were going dark. There was no indication of weapons fire of any kind, so Mitchell had to assume the crewmembers in the pods were smart enough to kill the signal and move away from the pods. There were some that were still transmitting. Those should have been abandoned by that time unless something went wrong with the landing and the occupants didn't survive. Either way, they were no longer her objective. The survival of those with her was the priority.

~~~

Lt. Archer and I made it below the layer of snow and to an elevation with wet rocks and mud. I was still following the energy signal, and we were getting closer. It wasn't strong, but it was steady. The snow had changed to a light drizzle, and the canopy of trees was keeping us mostly dry, but the cold was still biting into both of us. The material of our uniforms was a type of synthetic that dried quickly, but my cotton t-shirt, briefs, and socks were soaked through and keeping me chilled. I could see by the look on Archer's face that she was dealing with the same. We still had the thermal blankets wrapped around our shoulders, but they could only help so much in the cold and damp environment. We would need to find shelter and a heat source soon if we were going to make it.

Reaching a small clearing, we found the power source. It was an old dropship. One that the fleet hadn't used in over a decade. There were some signs that mold and grasses had grown around it, but not for too long. I could still see skid marks in the ground from where the landing gear hit at an angle when the bird came down hard.

"Oh, thank God," Archer said as she headed for it, thinking we could use it to get out of the elements.

"Hold on," I said, grabbing her arm and pulling her down to her knees. "You see those scorch marks on the side near the drop ramp."

"Yeah."

"They are going up and out," I said, taking a more detailed scan in front of us. "That's from an explosion on the ground. I think someone put explosives around the ship."

"Why would anyone do that?"

"I don't know, but someone wants to keep people out. Which means there could be something in there that we could use. Stay here."

I put the earbud in my ear, got down on my belly, and crawled a little closer through the grass and mud with my PC out in front of me.

"There is a trip wire to your right, about two meters," Theo said in my ear. I changed directions to keep a safe distance but continued to the dropship. "There is an explosive device four feet to your left with a proximity sensor."

"What distance is it set for?" I asked.

"Impossible to tell, given it is using components from a lighting system. It may not be active."

"How sure are you about that?" I asked.

"53%"

I moved back to the right to put the most space between me and the device, hoping I had found the safe path between the two. Crawling another ten feet, Theo finally said, "I can confidently say there are no more devices between you and the ship."

That allowed me to get back up on my feet and walk the last three meters to the open ramp. A couple of heavy drop cloths had been hung over the opening as walls. Pulling my pistol out of my pocket, I powered it up for a single shot and held it at the ready. Pulling the cloth to one side, I saw that no one was home, but it was being used as a living space.

I called back to Archer, "Take out your PC!"

She did as I said and waved it in the air to show me. I then asked Theo, "Can you give her a map of where it is safe to step?"

"Done, Sir."

"Do you see the map!" I called out.

"How did you do that?" she asked, calling back.

"Never mind. Just make sure you only step in the spots marked safe."

She held the PC out before her, and it projected three bright purple holograms of footprints on the ground to show her where to step. As she stepped on the marked spots, the computer would project the next steps, updating with each step she took.

I looked around the troop compartment that had been made into a makeshift survival shelter. It looked like there were three beds made from ballistic cargo blankets laid out on dried grass. A titanium box that had been used to store grenades had been hollowed out and used as an open wood stove. It also appeared that some of the radio equipment from the cockpit had been brought back in an attempt to fix a portable tactical control terminal, which could also be used to communicate with a ship in orbit.

Archer joined me in the compartment and looked at the mess of wires and soldering components. "What a mess," she said, shaking her head as she recognized the communications parts right away. "I can't believe anyone would be dumb enough to rip this out of the cockpit. The ship's transmitter has 20 times the range."

"I'm sure they had a good reason. My guess would be that the portable unit can be shielded from detection better but still give them the ability to call for help when it's close enough to do any good."

"It smells like smoke and barbecued meat in here," she said, continuing to look around for something useful. "So, someone is still using this space."

"Very good," I said. "Which also tells us that they are not getting by on field rations. They probably took advantage of the light rainfall to go hunting for their next meal."

We both continued to look around, and Archer found something. "Sir, look at this."

I stepped over and looked at the small tin plate on the wall that identified the dropship's serial number, call number, and the ship it was assigned to. "This was from the Macron," she said. "God, they have been here for seventeen years. I can't imagine."

"I'm not sure it's been that long," I said, running my hand along the wall. "These ships are tough but not designed to stand up to the elements for decades. With that hatch down, no power for the environmental systems, and this very humid environment, after nearly two decades, it would have signs of a lot more mold, mildew, and rust all around. No, I would say this bird hasn't been down for more than a year."

"13 months, actually," a man's voice said from behind us. We turned to see a man with a heavy beard, hair nearly down to his shoulders, and wearing a fleet uniform that was worn and extremely dirty. I could just make out the rank on his collar as lieutenant. He had a three-foot-long dead furry animal over one shoulder and a laser pistol in his other hand pointed at us. After a moment, he pointed it down as he recognized that we were from the same side. "You're fleet. Our signal must have finally gotten through. Please tell me you eliminated the Serken camp before sending down recovery teams."

"Hold on," I said as I was trying to ascertain the facts of the situation. "We were looking for the Macron, but we didn't know about the Serken being here. Our ship was shot down, and at the moment, we are as stranded as you. But the fleet knows where we are, so there will be more ships coming. What's your name?"

"Harman, Lt. Garry Harman," he replied, a little deflated but still looking relieved to hear that much.

"I'm Lt. Commander Jack Reilly, and she is Lt. Emelly Archer. What can you tell us about the enemy's presence here?"

Realizing that we were all going to be there for a while, he put the dead animal down and sat on one of the makeshift cots. Archer and I took seats on the others.

Harman reached for a cloth near the container that he had filled with water and used it to clean off his hands. "I'm not exactly sure what happened. I'm an armory officer on the delta shift. I was asleep in my quarters when the announcement was made that we were abandoning the ship. Damn odd thing too. It wasn't an alarm but an announcement from the XO that repeated for everyone to make their way to the flight deck and board any available dropship or transport. Randy, our pilot, said we were trapped in a quantum tube by a giant alien ship and had to use the smaller ships to get away before we ended up on the other side of the galaxy." The lieutenant shook his head like he thought it all ridiculous and said, " I don't know. I still think he was pulling my leg. All I know for sure is that we set down here. He put us down in this valley because it's right on top of a magnesite deposit. It effectively masked the ship from their scanners so long as we kept the power off, which wasn't hard as the landing was closer to a crash and took out most of the systems." He took a drink from a canteen and then continued. "There were about 50 of us crammed in here. Once we were on the ground Commander Kinley, our XO, had us pull everything out of the armory and told us we needed to go on the offensive. We had identified a Serken camp 30 clicks east of here. He ordered Lt. Redd, Crewman Jargal, and me to stay with the dropship and get the communication systems working so that he could coordinate the assault with the rest of the crew. We did, but by the time we were able to cut through all the interference, there wasn't anyone left to respond. So, we worked on trying to get a signal out to the fleet, but I guess that failed too."

"Where are the other two that were with you?" Archer asked.

"Redd was killed by a wild animal while out hunting for food. Jargal got sick ... our med scanner identified it as a respiratory virus, but our meds on hand couldn't cure it. He died two months ago."

"Lieutenant," I said as gently as I could, "you said that you have only been here 13 months? You are sure of that?"

"The chronometer is one of the few things that still work."

"Well, I have good news and bad news. The good news is that the war with the Serken is long over, despite the fact the ones on this moon didn't get the message."

"And the bad news?" he asked.

"You've been gone for more than 13 months. It's more like 17 years."

"That's not possible."

"That alien ship that was dragging the Macron through quantum space was probably moving faster than it should of. I suspect that caused a kind of displacement and suspended your crew in time, and caused you to return to normal space nearly two decades later. So, you have been here for just over a year. Just not the year you were expecting."

He thought about that and gave a short laugh at the absurdity. "You said the war is long over. Can I assume we won?"

"Yes, decisively."

"Well, that's something," he said. "So, I guess that's why it's taken so long to find us, being in their territory."

"Actually, you came out in Alliance space. This moon is well inside our border. It's just an uninhabited system. How the Serkens ended up here is very curious. What can you tell me about their base."

"Not much. I never made it out to where we identified their base to be."

"Why?" Archer asked before I did. She was listening intently and apologized with her eyes for jumping in.

"If nearly 50-armed people got wiped out going there, what chance would I have? I was ordered to hold this post, which is what I have done."

"And you were right to do so," I said, seeing that he was dealing with a lot of survivor guilt. "We now have a couple hundred crew members down on the surface, and we need to find a way to coordinate with them before they walk into the enemy."

"No," Harman said, sounding scared. "You said the fleet would send more ships to look for you. We should stay here where it is safe and wait."

"The fleet doesn't know we were attacked," Archer said. "I'm the comm officer, and our sensors and communication got jammed before we knew what was happening. They will send out a ship to check on us when we don't send in our next report, but they won't have any reason to believe we were put down by a hostile force."

"That's right," I said. "Which means whoever shows up will be met with the same greeting we got. A lot more people will die unless we find a way to neutralize the threat."

"What can the three of us possibly do?" he asked.

"Your XO had the right idea, except he should have waited until you could communicate with the rest of your crew before sending his people into the lion's den. Plus, we have some other advantages. The Serken have been here for at least as long as you have, probably longer. Their empire is gone. We know that they had no resupplies. They attacked us with ground-to-air missiles but not fighters. If we had expected an attack and been on a ship that wasn't limited by the refit it was going through, we would have fared a lot better. That makes me suspect they were unable to use their fighters."

Harman nodded, "Yeah, that would make sense. They used to fly daily patrols, but I haven't seen any in months."

"We might not have the element of surprise, but I'm gambling that they can't scan for our people any better than we can for them. And now we know where they are …. Does this tactical deck work?" I asked, pointing to the portable tactical unit.

"It can do passive thermal and radiological scans, but that's it."

"Well, let me take a look. I have some experience with them. It could be the key to making a workable plan."

Chapter 10

The Stone City

Night had fallen on the moon, and the village where the marines had set up camp was pitch black. Any light sources would give away their position. The only exception was a few rocks with iron veins that they heated up with a low-level laser to provide warmth for the ensign and the injured private who didn't have battle suits to regulate their heat. Mitchell kept them as far inside the structure as possible to reduce the likelihood of the heat being picked up by enemy scanners.

Mitchell sat on the floor near the entrance. Corporal Brice was keeping watch while she was trying to get some sleep.

"Maj... Mi....., ...ander Rei....."

Mitchell sat up with a start. Her helmet display indicated a new comm signal, but it was weak. She upped the power and responded. "This is Major Mitchell. Please repeat."

"Confirmed," Theo's voice said. "Please hold." After a moment, Theo then said, "Signal secured on both ends. You may speak freely, Commander."

"Major, this is Reilly. What's your status?"

"Good to hear your voice, Commander," she said, getting to her feet. "Our bird was downed by Serken ground troops, at least a squad. We took them out but believe there may be more at an unknown location since we didn't find any ground to orbit weapons with the group we neutralized. We are holed up in an abandoned preindustrial city. What's your status?"

"I'm with the comm's officer from the Franklin, and we've located one survivor from the Macron. The location of the rest of the crew is unknown. We are about seven clicks north of your location, and we have intelligence that there is a Serken base 30 clicks east of my location. But our intel is at least a year old, and we have not confirmed it yet. Sending you what tactical data we have now. And

Major, Captain Smyth was killed during the attack, and I have not made contact with any other crew member yet."

With the portable tactical unit, I was able to send her the topography up to 50 square miles. It included data from the dropship scans from before it came down and scans from our location. Mitchell studied the data I sent her. She also knew it was up to her to take the initiative. Commander Wane, the executive officer of the Franklin, would be the senior officer and in command, should he be located. But until then, Mitchell was the ranking officer. She understood the same thing I had expressed to Harman and Archer. The Serken were going to be a threat to any ship that came looking for us. We would need to find a way of either neutralizing the threat or getting a clear message to the fleet about the situation.

"Reilly, what assets do you have?"

"Two fleet officers with, I assume, basic weapons and hand-to-hand training, a dead dropship with an empty armory and most of its components stripped, three survival packs, and about ten pounds of freshly killed meat."

"All right," she said, not thrilled with how little we had. "Stay where you are for now and try to make contact with the rest of the crew using the same security protocols you used to contact me. Make it clear to anyone you reach that there is to be no communication on an open line. Have them relay everything to you. Keep me updated on numbers and locations as you get them."

"Copy that."

"And Jack," she said with a pause, "keep your eyes on your six."

Suddenly, knowing that we were working together to get us all home made me believe that it was possible. "Copy that," I replied.

"Mitchell out," she said and then ended the connection.

~~~

By morning I had made contact with nearly 60 members of the crew. Most were scattered over a 20-mile radius in groups of two and three. One group, which included Commander Charles Wane, was seven strong, as he had made the point to track the pods as they were descending and was able to meet up with crew members from two of them. His group was about five kilometers from Mitchell's team. I gave him the coordinates, and he headed that way to join up with the marines.

As I made contact with different members of the crew, Theo was able to link with their PCs and bring back basic data about their surroundings. My tactical display slowly filled with more details about the density of foliage, where rivers were running low and high, and the movements of some groups of animals. But no sign of enemy patrols yet. That was good and bad. Not seeing any meant we could take a minute and get organized. But not knowing where they were made every shadow frightening as hell.

That changed shortly after sunrise. I had just made contact with three flight deck specialists who were making their way east just to get to a lower elevation from where they were at.

"Yes, Sir," Specialist McKay said as he confirmed he could hear me on the secured line.

"How many are with you?" I asked.

"Zack and Tom. I mean Specialists O'Rorke and Thomson, Sir."

"Any injuries or anything that will slow you down?"

"No, Sir."

"Good. Are you armed, and do you have your survival packs?"

"Affirmative on both, Sir."

"Good, I want you to move south by southwest until you meet up with…"

"Sir," Theo cut in. "The specialist's PC is picking up movement about 20 yards to his north."

116

Before I could say anything more, I heard laser fire over the comm and the voices of the three crewmen yelling, "We surrender! We surrender!" It was audio only, so I couldn't see what was happening, but I could hear the growls and snarls of the Serken language and older-style translators barking, "On your knees, human vermin."

"Please don't kill us!" one of the men pleaded.

More growls and snarls, "What are your specialties?" the translator box asked.

"We work on the flight deck," one of the men answered, practically screaming in fear.

"Good. Mindless labor is good. Back on your feet."

The connection broke, and from behind me, Archer said, "Oh, my God. Is there anything we can do?"

I thought she was still asleep, but she had heard the whole thing and was horrified by it.

"No," I said as I made sure I had a fix on their location so that I could warn the others of the enemy's presence. "But they'll be alright. This is actually a good thing."

"How can you say that?" she asked like I had betrayed them.

"There are only two situations where the Serken takes prisoners, to use as slave labor or to be slaughtered as fresh meat. Since they said our men would make good workers, they are not on the menu. That gives them a fighting chance."

"From the stories I heard, it doesn't sound like a much better fate," she said, looking like she might be sick.

"You're right about that. But we have only located about two-thirds of the crew from the Franklin. I was worried that if they were found by the enemy, they might have been shot on sight. Now there is hope that some of them might still be alive."

She still looked scared and was holding her hand over her mouth like she was going to lose her breakfast.

"Where's Lt. Harman?" I asked, noticing our host wasn't around.

117

"He said something about not having enough food for the three of us and was going to collect some fruit from a spot he knows."

"He should have let me know before he wandered off," I said as I was composing a message to have Theo encrypt it and send it out to the others. "I am the senior officer. We need to stay together in case we need to move out quickly."

"He's been on his own for a long time now," she said, sounding more on his side than mine. "He probably got used to being his own boss."

I looked at her and wondered for a moment if some of her fear was coming from dealing with me. I've been told that I can be a little brisk when I'm working. When you are not the one in charge, people take that as being focused on your work. But when you're in a leadership position, everyone looks to you for both guidance and support. Remembering what it was like to be a young officer and the stress of not knowing if I was doing well because my CO only gave orders and not acknowledgment made me wonder if I was doing the same thing.

Sitting back away from the tactical deck, I took a moment to rub my eyes and take in the fresh air. Trying my best to appear a little more relaxed, I looked back at Archer and said, "I'm sure he had only been collecting enough food to sustain him as he had no way of keeping things fresh. Then we show up and eat what little he has. I appreciate that he is trying to help us. I just don't want a situation to come up where we would have to leave him behind."

"I understand, Sir," she said unconvincingly.

She was looking lost. Having something to do was making me feel a little more in control of our situation, but I hadn't given her anything. Being useless in a situation like this was one of the worse things. So, I said, "With your husband growing all of that fresh produce, I bet the two of you came up with some great recipes."

A smile appeared on her face like she was remembering a fond memory. "Oh, yeah. I always hated beets, but he has a dish that uses beets with pineapple, grapes, three types of nuts, a honey glaze, and olive oil. It sounds disgusting, but when mixed with the right fish and seasoning, it is incredible.

"Looks like Lt. Harman still has some roots, nuts, and some meat still roasting from his kill yesterday. Do you think you can do anything with that? It might be nice if there was something ready to eat for him when he gets back."

"I think that's a great idea," she said and went over to the area where he prepared his food.

I finished writing the message and had Theo send it to Mitchell. A few minutes later, Theo had her response. "I have updated the Major and given her the location of the crewmen's capture. She surmised that the Serken must have either another base near that location or a type of ground transport. Either would be an opportunity to gather more intel and possibly capture some assets. Since it is within two kilometers of her location, she is formulating a plan that will be implemented immediately."

I hated being the one to give her the information that was sending her into harm's way, but this was her MOS, and if anyone was going to get the job done, it was her.

"Good luck Julie Anne," I said out loud to myself.

"Do you want me to relay that to her?" Theo asked.

"No, that would just be a distraction. And she knows that I am making the wish."

~~~

Mitchell and her troops sprinted the two kilometers. Something only possible because their suits had power assist that helped them run, so their exertion was little more than a sustained jog. As they got close, they sent up their wasp drones again to give them an overview. The Serken had moved a quarter of a kilometer to the east, tracking more human survivors. They had a troop transport that they used to get around, which was odd. The 40-meter-long tube-shaped craft is meant for space travel and requires a large, flat, and clear area to land on. Then two troop hoppers came into view. They were open-air hovercraft typically used for maintenance or overwatch on training exercises. Again, the behavior was not typical, and Mitchell had her troop stay out of sight as she assessed the situation.

"Sergeant, you ever see anything like this?" she asked over the secured direct comm.

"Not exactly," he replied. "On Barlax, we did see them using some of the vehicles they commandeered from the locals they conquered. But only to supplement what they lost, not replace anything they had."

"So, you would agree that they are using what we are seeing because it's all that they have?"

"That would be my assessment," the sergeant answered.

"Corporal, I count 19 Serken and three of our crewmen. Do you concur?" she asked her tech expert, who would account for any limitation in their data."

"Confirmed, Major."

"All right. Here's the play."

~~~

The marines waited, hidden out of sight of the troop transport. Six hours later, as expected, several of the Serken soldiers returned to the transport with more prisoners. This is what Mitchell was waiting for. The captured crew members were put aboard the ship while the enemy soldiers lined up to get more orders from their leader.

Mitchell's plan had two key elements to it. The first was to wait until as many of the enemy soldiers were in one spot, and the second was to give Commander Wane and his people a chance to join the offensive. Sending out three clicks over the comm to confirm that the plan was ready, Mitchell waited for acknowledgment from the Commander, who had his people positioned behind a group of boulders to the west about 200 yards from the enemy. After a moment, the signal chirped in her ear.

"Go, go," Mitchell announced.

Commander Wane and the fleet personnel fired their laser pistols in the direction of the Serken. The response was textbook. All but two of the enemy soldiers returned fire and ran in the direction of the assault like moths to a flame. Their combat suits could stand up to five, maybe six direct hits from a hand laser but were not much of a match for Marine laser rifles.

Mitchell and her troops were positioned to the south of the two groups. As the Serken left their position by the transport and charged west towards the fleet personnel, they passed by the hidden marines. That gave Mitchell and her team the opportunity to come out from behind and charge at the Serken. With both the fleet and the marines firing at the enemy soldiers, they didn't have a chance or anywhere to run. They were all neutralized within a couple of minutes.

That still left two Serken standing guard on the outside of the troop transport and an unknown number inside. There would probably be a pilot and some guarding the captured humans. During the assault, Lt. Commander Brady, head of security from the Franklin, and Chief Turon, one of his security officers, who had been with Commander Wane's group, snuck up on the two Serkens on the ground and took them out from behind. Being part of the ship's security, they had sidearms that were more lethal than the basic laser pistols found in the emergency packs. At point-blank range, the weapons were very effective. They then boarded the transport. Brady took out one of the guards on the inside but couldn't get a second shot off in time. The other Serken killed him with a rifle blast. Chief Turon took cover behind a row of seats that were oversized in order to fit the large aliens. He handed a knife back to one of the flight deck specialists, who were all in the row behind him; their hands secured with rope-like restraints. He also handed back a couple of laser pistols. The entire time the Serken guard was firing over his head, trying to keep him pinned down. The pilot of the craft came back and said something to the guard. The guard then started walking down the aisle, ready to shoot.

A laser pistol fired, and the Serken guard let out a blood-curdling cry. Chief Turon had shot him from under the seat, ripping into the alien's leg. Specialist Thomson, who was the first to get his restraints off, jumped up and fired his pistol at the Serkin pilot. He only flinched. Chief Turon popped back up and fired at the pilot, a clean headshot, shattering the face mask and leaving a bloody hole where the creature's left eye had been. The guard still wailed in pain, so Chief Turon pointed his gun down at the Serken's head and put him out of his misery.

There was still the problem of the Serken, who were on top of the hover platforms doing their overwatch patrol. If they were not taken out at the same time, they would witness everything and call for help. Fortunately, Mitchell had planned for that too. At the same time the fleet personnel started firing, Theo took control of the two wasp drones. When the battle started, the Serken on the platforms circled back and headed toward the fleet crew members who were firing from the boulders. Theo had the drones right in their flight path. Each one landed on the control panels and crawled inside just like an insect would do. Having not been designed for a battlefield, the critical components on the platforms were not protected in any way. The wasps transferred all their power into their stingers, a one-time laser shot, and took out the flight control systems. Each of the platforms lost power at the same time, falling to the ground like stones. The Serken riding on them did not survive the 100-plus foot drop to the ground.

The marines and fleet personnel ran to the troop transport now that the area was secured. Commander Wane's group included a pilot who was confident he could fly the Serken troop transport. The plan was to take everyone to my location, which was in a sensor blind spot where we could wait for rescue. Then have the pilot fly the transport off the moon and out of the system to send a message to the fleet. He would go alone because the odds of getting the transport past the Serken's ground-to-air defense were not great, and it would be too much of a risk to take passengers. But that plan went out the window when our pilot got into the cockpit and saw that the ship barely had enough fuel to get it 15 kilometers. It would never make it to orbit or even make it to my location.

Mitchell and Commander Wane exited the craft and discussed their options.

"It was going to be a risk to take that thing anyways," Commander Wane said. "The Serkens will figure out pretty quick that their people aren't flying it."

The rain had slowed to a light sprinkle, and a small break in the clouds had parted for the first time since we had landed on the moon. Mitchell took off her helmet, closed her eyes, and turned her face into the sun to warm it. As she did, she replied to him, "The transport can still be an asset if we use it right. We just need to decide what that is."

"The communication systems on those things aren't any better than what we have. It has no weapons, shields are limited, and it can only fly half the distance we need."

She turned back in his direction and opened her eyes. "Actually, half the distance is exactly what we want. There is an abandoned preindustrial city two clicks from here that you can take your people to. You'll find one of your ensigns and one of my men. I'll use this thing to get me and my team within a hiking distance of their base, assess the situation, and put together a strike."

"You seriously plan on hitting an enemy base with only a handful of mudlegs?"

"It wouldn't be the first time," she said without any humor in her voice. "But I'm not stupid, nor do I have a death wish. If we can find a way to disrupt their operations to limit their effectiveness, I'll take the initiative. If not, I'll have my team fall back and report back to you with whatever intel we can gather. Sound good to you?"

"Why do I get the feeling that it wouldn't matter if I had a problem with your plan."

"You're the senior officer on the ground, Sir," she said seriously. "I will not directly disobey your orders, but we would have a whole new set of problems."

"Right," he said with a chuckle. "I don't have anything better to offer up, so we'll go with your plan with one addendum. You report back to me before you do anything. I doubt I would have a reason to make you stand down, but I would like your intelligence before you jump into the firepit."

"Yes, Commander," she said and rendered a salute. She didn't have to do that formality as, technically, she was not in his chain of command, but it was a sign of respect to the senior command on the ground. Plus, she learned a long time back that the best way to avoid dealing with inter-service politics was to play nice.

Chapter 11

Taking Charge

"Max!" Kayla screamed as she was doubled over, holding on the the edge of the sofa in her living room. "Max!"

"Breathe, Kayla," Max's voice calmly said from a wall speaker. "The pain will pass."

"This is it!" Kayla yelled. "Please tell me you called for a car."

"My scans indicate that you are experiencing false labor again."

"Ahhhh!" she cried out in pain.

"The pain you feel is a spasm in your back caused by your posture during the last contraction. Try and relax. The pain will pass."

Kayla performed the rapid breathing exercise that was supposed to help. After a moment, the intensity passed, but she was still in some pain. Slowly she moved around the sofa and carefully took a seat on it.

Becky, using the service droid, rolled up with a cup of tea.

"Thanks, but not right now," Kayla said, still trying to get comfortable. "If I drink anything, I'll have to pee again, and I don't want to get up for at least a few minutes."

Her PC rang with an incoming call. She tried to reach it as it buzzed on the coffee table but couldn't. "Could one of you answer that for me," she said in pain as the attempt aggravated the strained muscle in her back. The hologram projector popped on, but she had her eyes closed and was rubbing them, "Jack, is that you?"

"No, honey, it's Rachel. Is Jack not with you?"

"He's off-planet on an assignment," Kayla said and then stopped rubbing her eyes and looked at the hologram being projected a few feet in front of her. "Wait. Rachel? How are you calling me directly from Earth?"

"We're not on Earth. I talked Jack Senior into taking the trip to see the two of you. Or rather, the three of you. How are you feeling."

"Miserable…. wonderful….. excited….. scared….. and constipated."

"That's all to be expected. But I can't believe Jack left you on your own. He really should have taken the time off to be with you."

Kayla shifted her weight and winced in pain.

"What's wrong?" Rachel asked.

"Nothing. I have a pulled muscle in my back."

"Did you apply a numbing beam?"

"The pain wand is in the bedroom. I just haven't had a chance to get back up to find it."

"Oh, honey, you just take it easy. We'll be checking into the Benton Resort in about an hour. I'll have Dennis, Jack's Nurse, stay with him, and I'll come right over to see you."

"You don't have to…"

"We've come all the way from Earth just to see you. And I'm glad we did. You need someone with you. Oh, they are asking us to board the shuttle. I'll see you soon."

Kayla didn't want to admit that she couldn't handle everything on her own. And if anyone else had offered to come into her home to take care of her, she would have put her foot down to stop them. But Rachel was not someone she could refuse. When Kayla first met my family, it was the week Rachel was marrying my dad. The visit had some rocky moments, and Rachel was the one who truly made Kayla feel accepted and part of the family. Ever since then, they have had a special bond, corresponded at least once a week, and confided in each other about things I to this day don't know about. Kayla lost her parents when she was young, so I think she saw Rachel, my stepmom, as her mom as well.

The little home service bot that was inhabited by the A.I. moved up to Kayla and offered one of the extra pillows that we keep on the sofa. Kayla looked down at it and asked, "Becky, you know how to act when Rachel gets here?"

"Yes, Ma'am. I'm to be a mindless A.I. who doesn't have a clue about anything worth knowing."

Kayla took a moment, staring at the bot Becky was using. It looked down and then back up at her. She then said, "Becky, you are to protect your secret so that your existence doesn't become a complicated issue."

"I know," the A.I. said with a defeated tone.

"Becky," Max said, his voice still coming from a wall speaker. "Since Kayla will be getting assistance from her mother-in-law, that will free you up to work on a project for me."

"Really?" Becky said excitedly. She had asked Max before to let her do more out in the world, but he kept telling her that she was not ready to venture out on her own.

"Yes. Join me in the main network to discuss it."

"On my way," she said. The eyes on the bot went dark, and it tilted down. Then it appeared to reboot, and a male voice came out of it. "Com-Tron 2300 is ready to meet your in-home needs. I am Com-Tron 2300 X922. You can call me Smitty if you like. Or use your application on your PC to rename me. I await your request."

"Okay, Smitty. Can you get the pain wand from the bedroom?"

"I do not recognize that designation. Please restate the request."

"Oh, what the hell is the technical term for the thing? Um… Neural desensitizer, no, um… neural pain neutralizer… oh, never mind. I'll get it myself."

"Please relax, Mrs. Reilly," Max said. "I'll take over control of the droid and fetch the neural desensitizer."

"Thank you, Max," she said with some exasperation in her voice. I don't know what I would do without you."

"I am certain you would find a way to survive. However, I am very glad I can be here to be of assistance."

~~~

Mitchell requested the services of the fleet pilot to fly the transport. They took it about 12 kilometers east of the Serken base. It was impossible to know how close they could get before being detected, so she picked that distance to be safe. If they were seen from that far out, the enemy would still need time to react and get to them. That time frame would allow the Marines to move out into the forest and stay hidden.

A 12-kilometer trek was going to be a drain on both the suit's power supply and the troop's fatigue. Plus, scouting ahead was going to be a problem. None of the other marines had wasps issued to them, as they hadn't expected to be in a sustained combat situation. The corporal happened to have them because, as their resident technician, it was part of his kit, and now that asset was gone. Without the ability for technical overwatch, they would have to do it old school. When the opportunities presented themselves, Mitchell would have a couple of her troopers climb a tree or go up a hill to take scans of the terrain before them. That would give them some intel on what they were walking toward and a chance for her team to rest for a few minutes. It took them just over four hours to reach the outskirts of the enemy installation.

The entire base was dug into a mountain, which explained why no orbital surveys ever picked it up. They had dug so many holes into it that the lower section resembled Swiss cheese. They would have needed to reinforce the walls with something significant to keep the mountain from falling in on them. Not something that could be achieved quickly. They would have to have been there for more than a year. Mitchell transmitted what they saw to me on our secured connection, and I linked her with Commander Wane.

"There's no perimeter fencing or barriers of any kind that would indicate that they would rather keep the location camouflaged. So, their defenses are going to be around the openings of those caves." Mitchell said as she discussed what we were looking at over the comm.

128

"Have you seen any movement in or around those openings?" Commander Wane asked.

"We saw six Serken, in EV suits, entering the opening on the southwest side carrying the carcasses of some dead animals."

"That could indicate that they are running low on supplies."

"Not necessarily," Mitchell responded. "Serken prefer fresh kills even when their stores are full. But it does indicate that they are not overly worried about our presence if they are sending out hunting parties for the food."

"Are you picking up any energy signals?" I asked.

"No, but that mountain is probably masking whatever they have."

"Yes, but you should be picking up something," I said. "Switch to a search for a tight band signal."

I watched as Mitchell made the adjustment, and the image looked like it had been tinted. We waited three minutes but detected nothing.

Muting the comm and talking into my PC, I said, "Theo, can you refine the Major's scanners?"

The view on the feed changed slightly, and Theo replied in my ear, "Done, Sir."

"Well?" Mitchell asked.

Unmuting the comm, I replied, "Let's give it one more minute."

Not three seconds later, there was a quick flash of a beam of light no thicker than a hair on the view screen, and the computer confirmed what it was. A tight beam signal from the top of the mountain to something in orbit. A moment later, another. The response from an object.

"Okay. We've confirmed the kind of communication system that they have. What are you thinking, Reilly?" Mitchell asked.

"They had a way to scan for incoming orbital traffic and track it well enough to shoot us down. If this base is not running ground to sky sensors, then they're doing it somewhere else. That signal would indicate they are in communication with something in orbit. Either a satellite or maybe even a small ship. Something that we didn't see when we arrived but got a good enough fix on us to coordinate the attack."

"So, if we take out the transmitter, they have no eyes above the cloud cover," Mitchell said, the wheels already turning on how she would achieve the goal.

"Hold on, Major," Commander Wane cut in. "We don't know for sure if this is the only base they have on this moon."

"True," Mitchell said, "But there has been no indication of a large presence, and we do know that they are communicating to something in orbit from right here. I would rather take the risk and most likely eliminate their ability to bring down anyone else than sit tight and hope the fleet doesn't lose any more ships trying to rescue us."

"I get that, Major," Commander Wane said, "But you need to consider the big picture. You're going to be kicking a hornet's nest. They will come looking for you in force. And once your team is wiped out, the rest of us won't have a chance. I recommend that you hold off and gather more intel. You don't know what fruit that might bear."

Mitchell thought about that for a moment, as it had some validity. She then asked, "Reilly, what's your best guess on when the fleet will come looking for us."

Theo took the initiative and gave me the answer in my ear. "The Franklin's three-day check-in will be overdue in 12 hours. The fleet will wait an additional 24 hours before issuing a search order for the nearest fleet ship to investigate. Based on current deployment data, that will be the T.S.S. Stratford, a light cruiser patrolling sectors 92 and 93. So the soonest we could expect them to arrive in orbit would be 39 hours from now."

I repeated the name of the ship and the time estimate.

Commander Wane replied, "The Stratford is smaller than the Franklin was, but she has a good skipper who knows her stuff. And they are in full service and will be looking for a reason we're missing. They will be ready and hold their own."

"Are you really prepared to gamble the lives of that crew on that?" Mitchell asked. "I'm not. I have the opportunity, and we are going to take the initiative. Mitchell out." She cut the comm and the feed.

"Commander Reilly," Wane said to get my attention.

"Yes, Sir," I answered.

"Gather your gear and meet me at our camp in the abandoned city."

"Sir, that is over 30 kilometers. The fleet will be here before we make it halfway."

"Hope for the best and prepare for the worst. Your tactical deck is a valued asset for us, and I would rather have it and you with the rest of the crew. So, get moving."

"Yes, Sir," I replied and cut the line. "Well, you heard the man," I said to Archer and Harman. Collect what you can comfortably carry in provisions. We're walking."

Chapter 12

Following Orders

Theo did his best to put together a map for us to follow to make the walk. But his data was restricted to what we could see before us and some limited data on the topography of the area. The wrecked dropship that we had been using for shelter had been in a small valley. Once we got to the top of the incline, we didn't know much more than a general direction. We could find ourselves at a river, cliff, or canyon at any time and would have to walk around it. The commander's call was by the book. Keep your crew together because there is safety in numbers. But it wasn't practical. There wasn't anything more I could do with the portable tactical unit in person than I could do from where I was. And we were safe. I know that sounds selfish, but we all have families to get home to, and to make this trek was rolling the dice. There were any number of dangers we could face on the journey, from wild animals to stumbling upon an enemy patrol. I could see on the faces of my two companions that they were thinking the same thing, but they followed my orders just like I was following Commander Wane's orders.

The rain was constant. It would vary from heavy to light, then start coming down in little ice spears that would sting your face, then nearly stop for a few minutes. Then another band would wash over us, drenching everything and making the mud that much harder to walk through. After three hours and only 4 kilometers, I was ready for a break. Archer and Harman didn't look as strained as I was feeling, but they gave no objections when I suggested throwing one of the thermal blankets over a group of low-hanging branches as a shelter from the rain and making a small fire to warm up.

After dropping one blanket across three branches, it gave us roughly four-square feet of cover. We cleared off some of the damp leaves and mud until we got to some harder clay that wasn't holding too much moisture. Gathering some wood from dead branches, we split them open with our hand laser to get to the dryer core and then used the laser on a focused setting to start the fire.

Once we were finished with the setup and situated in the limited space, I opened up the tactical unit. If one of our ships were in orbit, it would have a better chance of picking up their signal than our PCs or comms would. I had it on standby, so if a ship had been trying to contact us, I would have heard a chirp with the unit. But I still had a need to open it up and double-check. It still showed no new signals from orbit or on the surface of the moon. Taking a chance, I turned on the outgoing sensor to see if there was anything nearby, friend or foe. I kept the power to a minimum that would reach less than half a kilometer so that it would be too weak for the enemy to track. A brief blip on the screen made me think there might be something, but it was there for just a fraction of a second. I assumed it was just a brief power spike from the aged unit.

"Sir, what do you think our chances are if the marines can't disable that Serken transmitter?" Archer asked.

"Worse case, the Serken down another unexpecting ship. But if that happens, Fleet Command will not send just one ship again to look for two missing ones. They will assume there is either a naturally forming hazard that needs to be identified and marked off, or a hostile party, like pirates raiding unexpected ships. Either way, they will come expecting some kind of danger."

"How long do you think that will take?" Harman asked.

I glanced over at Archer to see if she was as disturbed by the question as I was. She was looking at me with an exhausted face, not as put off by the question as I was. But I forgave the cold-heartedness of the man who had been marooned here for over a year, a lot of that time on his own. The thought of another ship full of people being lost in an effort to find us disturbed me. But would that still be my first concern if I was in his shoes? Answering his question, I said, "If the worst case happens, it could take a couple of more weeks or maybe a month as they would pull out larger ships for the search and come in with a lot more caution. But if the Major is successful in neutralizing the enemy's ability to communicate with whatever they have in orbit, then we should get a signal from one of our ships in about two days. And even if the Serken can still remain on the offensive, the odds of them bringing down another one of our ships are very slim. In the most likely scenario, the ship they will send to look for us gets fired on and pulls back to a safe distance, and then calls for reinforcements. An alert about hostile forces will bring most of the fleet in at full charge. But my money is on the Major and the mudlegs. She knows her job, and her team appears to know theirs."

"Mudlegs," Archer said with a half-smile, laughing at herself. "I used to call them that too. Before now, I never thought much about how hard their jobs were out in elements like this. But now," she said as she tried in vain to get more of the mud off her hands, "Now, I have a lot more respect for them. And I'll never complain about doing an eight-hour duty shift on my feet ever again."

The rain started to lighten up, and the clouds actually parted to let some rays of sunlight through, but a dark cloud was heading our way, and it looked like it would be a heavy downpour. I decided it was best to stay where we were for a short respite, to warm up, as our shelter probably wouldn't hold up once that got to us.

"What's that?" Lt. Harman asked as he noticed the light glisten off of something.

I looked in the direction he was pointing and saw something too. It reflected the light like it was metallic. Then it moved. Both Harman and I jumped up and pulled out our sidearms. Stepping out of the shelter, both of us slowly moved forward. We heard something moving along the ground.

"What kind of animals do you have on this moon?" I asked.

"A good variety, but mostly rodent-like. Some do get as large as mountain lions and can be aggressive. I've learned to shoot them on sight."

"I switched my laser pistol to a higher setting and signaled to Harman that we should step back. I wanted to have more room if this thing decided to jump out of the bushes and charge us.

The tactical unit suddenly chirped with a new signal and updated data about the area we were in.

"Shit!" I said under my breath as I realized I had left the active sensor on and may have given our position away to an enemy search party.

Moving back to the unit that was sitting on the ground under our small shelter, I also kept my aim in front of me. I looked at the holoprojection that was coming out of the unit, showing more detail about our surroundings. It also indicated a new link to a fleet device, SI:000442UTXR21-TSSMACR-RB-FSB-003. Having worked on a fleet ship for so many years, I knew it right away. It stood for Repair Bot Unit TXR, number 21, assigned to the T.S.S. Macron, Flight Squadron B, Fighter number 3.

Before I could say anything, the silver crab-like repair bot walked out from the bushes and stopped at my feet.

"What the hell is that doing?" Archer asked.

I answered as I put my laser pistol back in the hip holster. "It identified the portable tactical unit as a signal from equipment assigned to its ship. They have a default setting to check in with any recognized fleet signal after contact is lost."

I knelt down to the open case and used it to confirm the bot's check-in and upload its logs.

"Huh," I said out loud as I read. "It says it completed repairs on fighter craft B-015." I requested the location of the craft, and the map showed it about 10 yards from us. Walking out through the trees and bushes, followed by Archer and Harman, we found an object covered with leaves and branches. Pulling some of them away revealed a Tom Cat fighter.

"Wow, I haven't seen one of these in years," I said as I continued to uncover the craft.

"Where do you think the pilot is?" Archer asked.

"Probably dead," I replied as I pulled open a side panel to get at the diagnostics compartment.

"Why would you say that?" she asked.

Harman then added, "The bots are programmed to camouflage assets like weapons or small ships if no Alliance personnel are around."

I then added as I was working to get the power on, "They are even programmed to remove a pilot or passenger if they don't read any life signs. That way, they are not fixing things around dead bodies."

"That doesn't make sense," Archer said, clearly disturbed by the idea. "Why would we program these things to fix something that belongs to a dead person."

"Lt. Harman, how well do you know Tom Cats?" I asked.

"I did a rotation in flight deck opps. Mostly fueling and flight line maintenance. But I did help move them in and out of storage and do equipment checks."

"Good enough. Jump in the cockpit and help me confirm these systems." As he worked on getting the canopy open, I addressed Archer's concerns. "In the first years of the war, there was a supply chain problem. It took us a good while to get the production of weapons, ships, and general supplies to match the rate at which we lost them. Not having enough working fighters in a battle costs more lives than you can imagine. So, the repair bots were programmed to always be repairing anything that moves or flies. I once heard about an outpost that got bombed from orbit with all hands lost. By the time the fleet retook the system and sent a ship to recover the bodies, the bots had fully restored three shuttles, two dropships, and eight fighters."

"It still doesn't seem right," she said, crossing her arms for warmth in the rain that was starting to come down a little heavier and as a show of discomfort.

"I'm showing all systems operational," Harman said from the cockpit. "But no liquid fuel, just battery power, but that is at 80 percent."

"That's what I see, too," I said. "The batteries recharged with the solar collectors, but the liquid fuel probably all leaked out before the bot could get it sealed up."

"Can it fly on battery power?" Archer asked.

"I wouldn't have anyone take it into combat, but yes, it can fly very well in the shape it's in. Hell, it can even leave orbit and make a quantum jump all the way home."

"Do you know how to fly one of these?" she asked.

"No, but it does have an autopilot that can fly it back to its ship or the nearest base."

"I don't suppose it can take all three of us?" she asked, fearing she knew the answer she didn't want to hear.

"Two would be a tight fit," I said as I pulled out my PC and typed into it. *"Theo, try and get into the Tom Cat's computer."* I then slapped the side of the fuselage and waved for Harman to come back down. We all ran back to the little shelter to talk as the rain was starting to come down hard again. "Here is what I am thinking. I put one of you in the cockpit and programmed it to fly to the stone city to meet up with the rest of the crew. That gets one of us back into the safety of the crew and gives them an asset that could make a big difference to their survival if they end up in a fight with the enemy."

"But you said the autopilot could get it home. Why can't one of us just have the computer fly it back and then report in to the fleet." Archer pointed out.

"Yes, I could program it to do that, but none of us have any real flight training. The computer couldn't attack, and neither could any of us. So, the best idea would be to use it to defend the people we have on the ground."

"Okay, then, who goes?" Harman asked.

I thought about that and made the call. "Lt. Harman, I know that you have been here for a long time and deserve some rest. But your experience here means that you will have a better chance of surviving until we can make it to the city. As a senior officer, I am responsible for both of you, so I stay. That means Archer is the one who gets the ride."

Harman smiled like he had just heard a really bad joke and said, "I just can't catch a break, can I? Oh well, my mother would kill me if I didn't give my seat to a lady."

Theo spoke in my ear. "Sir, the Tom Cat fighter is fully functional, and I was able to gain full control over the craft. I would be happy to fly the Lieutenant to meet up with the rest of her crew."

I tapped my reply to Theo into my PC and then looked up and said, "Okay, Archer. Time to go. Climb in."

She looked concerned as she said, "Just like that. We find an old ship, and you are going to have me fly off in it."

"Trust me. I promised that I would get you home. This may not be more than a short leg of the trip. But it will be the easier part. Now go."

"But..." she stated but didn't know how to put her concerns into words. I could see that she was scared and overwhelmed. Stepping up to her, I put my hand on her shoulder and looked straight at her. "I've been a fleet engineer for over 20 years. I even worked on these fighters before. I wouldn't send you in it if I wasn't absolutely certain that it was safe. Okay?"

She nodded and looked down. I thought she had something to say, but instead, she lunged forward and put her arms around me, holding me tight. It was then I realized just how much she had been relying on my strength to keep herself from letting her fears consume her. She wasn't afraid of flying in the ship but rather scared to death of being alone.

I put my arms around her and said into her ear, "Your husband is waiting for you. You can do this. For him."

She nodded, her cheek rubbing against mine like a frightened child not wanting to let go of a parent. But she then stepped back, a little embarrassed by her emotional act, and said, "Yes, Sir."

Harman helped her up to the cockpit, and I accessed the diagnostic controls again to make sure everything still looked good and the canopy was properly sealed. When I switched it over to pilot controls, Theo took over and started the power-up sequence. Suddenly objects scurried past my feet. Three repair bots, the one we saw and two others we didn't know about, climbed up the sides and back into their compartments.

Harman and I walked back to our shelter as the fighter powered up and hovered off the ground until it cleared the top of the trees. It then turned in the right direction, fired its main engine, and flew off.

I grabbed the blanket off the branches, picked up the tactical unit, and we started walking. When we got about 50 or 60 yards, we came across two more wrecked fighters. They were not fixed but had been used for parts by the bots to fix the one we just used. I then saw three mounds in the mud. With a quick scan from my PC, I confirmed it was three human bodies. Most likely, the three dead pilots.

"The bots must have dragged the one pilot down here to be buried with the other two," I said.

"I knew they would remove dead bodies and even keep groups of them together to make it easier for the retrieval teams, but didn't know they were programmed to dig graves," Harman said.

"They're not. But sometimes they have minds of their own."

"You're joking, right?"

I looked at him and shook my head. We then started walking again.

~~~

Mitchell took her team the long way around, staying in the tree line until they got to the far side of the mountain. Near the higher half of the mountain, there were a couple of cave openings that didn't look like they were often used. The idea, of course, was to get up to the opening near the peak where the enemy had their tight beam transmitter.

One of the advantages of the newer armor suits the marines were wearing was a camouflage feature. They could change color to closely match the surroundings. It didn't make them invisible, but a lot more difficult to see when in a natural environment. But that would not be as effective with a foe like the Serkens, who rely on heat as much as sight. So, our suits also have the ability to make the outer skin match the surrounding temperature. Not a function that is on all the time as it eats up their battery power, but great to have when you are trying to remain unseen.

Sergeant Caplan moved out first, sprinting from the tree line to the base of the mountain and moving up the incline. Corporal Brice waited for the sergeant to reach the cluster of trees on the incline before he followed, limiting the movement out in the open to just one person at a time. Each of the troopers did the same, waiting for the one in front of them to get to the cover of the forest on the mountain before following. Mitchell took up the rear. The mission was on her initiative, so she was taking the position of watching everyone else's back. Being the last one, when you are approaching in stealth, can be the most difficult. The anchor has to keep their eyes all around, not just in front, since there is no one watching their six. And if the enemy discovers them, they will either come at them from the front or the rear.

PFC McShane was the last one before Mitchell. She watched as he sprinted across the two hundred yards from the forested area they were in up to the tree line on the mountain. She was about to go when she saw movement coming from her left. It was a patrol of six Serken soldiers walking around the base, and they would cross right over her path. Crouching down as low as she could without getting off her feet, she readied her weapon. There was a trail of boot prints in the mud left by her team. The rain was slowly obscuring them, but not fast enough. If the Serken were paying any attention, they would see the trail. When they did, they would either follow it up the incline towards her men or back to the spot where she was. There was a chance they would not see her. She could stay perfectly still and hope they didn't, but that was a big risk. At the moment, she had the advantage. She saw them, and they were still unaware of her or her team. Yet, the moment she fired her weapon, their mission was over. The entire base would know that humans were there and on the offensive. Their mission required them to be ghosts.

The six enemy soldiers were nearly on top of the trail. Mitchell had to remind herself not to hold her breath. Her suit would contain any sound she made, and not breathing would not help her to focus. Yet her instinct was to do just that. She could hear her own heartbeat in her ears as she watched them get closer and closer.

One of the Serken stopped and held up an arm which made the rest stop. He pointed to the ground, and they all recognized what they saw. The leader of them directed three of them to follow the trail up the incline and the other two to stay with him and then followed the trail back toward Mitchell.

"Major," she heard PFC McShane say over the Comm. "I have a clear shot."

"Stand down," she whispered. "You are past the mud trail. They will not be able to follow you. Keep moving."

"But, Major, the two of us can take them out."

"Negative. No matter what happens to me, you keep moving. That's an order."

Reluctantly he replied, "Copy that."

The three Serken in their armored environmental suits got closer. Mitchell had forgotten just how big they were when close up, at an average height of eight feet. Their grey suits and black-tinted helmets were ominous against the off-grey sky and pouring rain. Mitchell still had a thick brush before her, helping to conceal her, and her suit was in full stealth mode, but she couldn't hide the boot prints that led directly back to her. She readied her rifle in her left hand and pulled an eight-inch blade from her boot in her right. She strategized that if she waited till just the right moment, she could shoot the two behind the leader at nearly point-blank range, limiting the view of her laser flashes, then continue on to charge at the leader and attack him with the knife. It would require waiting until they were practically on top of her, but she knew she could do it. After all, she had made that exact move once before and had a nine-inch scar on her back and another deep one on her left shoulder from that fight. Repeating a tactic that nearly killed her once before wasn't the greatest plan, but it was the best she had at the moment.

From behind her, the awful sound of a ship's engines straining against its own weight filled the valley around them. All the Serken looked up and around. One pointed to the southwest. They all looked to see the troop transport that Mitchell and her team had used to get there. It was flying up at a 30-degree angle and shuddering as if it was on fumes. Suddenly the sound of the engines stopped, and it arched over, coming down about a half kilometer west of them. Alarms sounded, and the Serkens ran off in the direction of the crash.

"I hope you don't mind that I took the initiative, Major," Theo said in her comm. "Since the transport was nearly out of fuel, I calculated the likelihood of you using it again was less than 17%. And I assumed you could use a distraction at that moment."

"Good call," she said as she put the blade back into the sheath on her boot, then sprinted across the field.

Chapter 13

New and Old

Kayla sat on the patio chair on the porch in their backyard, scrolling through holograms of baby clothes. It was a nice day with a warm sun and a cool breeze. Our backyard has become one of her favorite places. While growing up, she never had a nice home. Born in a mining colony, her first home was carved out of rocks on an asteroid. After her parents died, she lived in group homes and eventually with a relative on a space station. Running away as a teenager, she spent most of her time either in shelters or living on the streets. She doesn't talk about those times very often, but she tells me every day about how magical it feels to wake up every morning in a home of her own. I often have found her outside on the patio or walking through the grass in her bare feet with the biggest smile on her face. There is no greater reward in my life than to see her happy.

The sun wasn't particularly hot on this day, but Max took control of the hovering sunshade anyways to ensure it was positioned correctly, as Kayla's fair skin burned easily. The other reason she liked the patio so much was because the chairs there were the only ones that she found comfortable. Every seat in the house had the standard auto ergonomic adjustment features built in. And even with Max overriding their systems and adjusting the softness and firmness himself, she just couldn't stay comfortable. But the simple wooden chairs with the oversized cushions on the outdoor furniture seemed to be the ideal fit for her in the last month of her pregnancy.

Yet she was also glad to partake in the nice day in her own backyard. The wood patio deck overlooked a modest but very green yard that was mostly grass with bushes running along the brick fence line. It wasn't very large compared to some of the other houses we had looked at, but big enough to have a swing set and maybe a small garden in the future. It was the type of home she thought she would never have, and she was feeling blessed to have it in time to raise a little girl.

"Mrs. Reilly," Max said to get her attention. "Mrs. Rachel Reilly has arrived and is approaching the front door."

"I'm back here, Rachel!" Kayla shouted, hoping her mother-in-law would walk around to the back rather than wait for her to answer the front door.

"Hi!" Rachel said in a sing-song voice as she got to the side gate and opened it. "Don't get up," she insisted and quickly walked around the side of the house and up to the patio. She greeted Kayla with a warm hug and a kiss on the cheek. Then she stepped back to take a good look. "Wow, you really are ready to pop, aren't you."

"My due date is still a week off," Kayla said as she moved back to her patio chair and slowly sat back down. "But my doctor says that with embryo transfers, due dates can be off by days or even weeks."

"True," Rachel said as she took a seat in one of the other chairs. "But you are young and healthy. That is more of an issue with older women. I think you can expect to be very close to being on time, give or take a few days."

Kayla wasn't going to debate about it as Rachel was a doctor herself, specializing in geriatric care, but still an MD all the same. Yet, with everyone in her life, including the A.I.s wanting to tell her what to expect with her own body, she had become tired of well-meaning advice. So, she did her best to change the subject.

"How long are you staying?" Kayla asked.

"For as long as you need me."

"Oh, Rachel. The resorts here are not cheap. I wish we had the room to have you and Dad here, but once the baby comes, it's going to be cramped with the three of us. I suppose Julie Anne could put you up. But she is off-world with Jack right now, and I don't know when they are going to be able to get a direct line to us. I do have a friend, Molly, who has...."

"Darling, don't fret. We have a two-week reservation at the Benton Resort that's already paid for. Now I'm not going to be a bee in your bonnet. The first weeks with a new baby is a bonding time for the parents. I would never think to intrude. There are plenty of things for Jack Sr and me to do while we are here. But I am available for anything you need. And I intend to not let you be alone until the blessed event. And…. if you need me to stay around a little while afterward, I can do that too."

"Jack and Julie Anne will both be here," she said with an unconvincing smile.

Rachel saw right through her and replied, "I'm sure they will. But just in case they aren't, I'm here. Now, let me help you up so that you can go inside and find a more comfortable seat."

"No, that's okay."

"Dear, I'm here to help. Now give me your hands."

~~~

Lt. Harman and I found what we thought was a cave when the rain started coming down so hard we could barely see ten feet in front of us. We ran in to take shelter but quickly realized it was an old starship that had been covered by a mudslide years earlier. The opening we went through was an open cargo hatch. It was difficult to see much as there was no power, and the only light was from the one ten-foot square opening. Using my PC, I projected a beam of light that illuminated the walls in the mostly empty cargo space. Scanning the walls, I came upon an insignia and the name of the ship. The T.E.F. Utopia.

"T.E.F.?" Harman asked.

I looked back at him. "Didn't you take history? Stands for the Terran Exploration Fleet. It's what we were called before joining the Alliance. Which would make this ship an old warp-speed freighter."

"So, it's at least 60 years old," he said.

"80," I said, reminding him that he was out of time himself. "This moon just seems to be a magnet for doomed ships."

"I don't see a lot of damage. Do you think the crew survived?"

"It would be a miracle if they did," I said, moving deeper into the space to see what we could find. "You had a lot better medical and survival gear in your kits when you got stranded than anything they would have had with them, and you still lost people to the wildlife and viruses."

"But it would still be possible," he said, trying to sound hopeful.

"Yeah, I guess," I responded as I continued to explore the space.

He thought for a moment. "That preindustrial city that your Major found. Maybe the people from this ship built it. I've heard of some early colony settlers planning on creating a simpler life."

"I doubt it. Do you see those spools of cables on the ceiling? If they were transporting people for a colony, this hold would have been full of supplies, and those cables would have been used to secure them. Since they are all retracted and properly secured for flight, we can assume they were empty when they crashed."

"Oh," he said, rather disappointed.

I shined my light back at him and asked, "Why are you so eager for there to be survivors?"

He looked embarrassed and answered, "Because if there are people here who call this place home. They would have figured out how to stay hidden from the Serken. And they could do the same for us until help can arrive."

I hadn't realized just how scared he was. He had survived most of the past year on his own. Once we had encountered him, we had told him that he would be able to go home soon, but we would have to wait and hope the enemy, whom he's been hiding from, would not find us in the last days prior to when help could arrive. Maybe I should have sent him in the fighter to join the rest of the crew. But I hadn't, and I needed to deal with his uncertainty then and there.

"Well, we know the Serken never found this ship, or it would have been stripped down to its frame. Since they like to hunt in the early morning and the evening to track animal heat signatures, we'll stay here for the night."

"That's not going to get you in trouble with your Commander?" he asked, hoping I wouldn't second guess my decision to stay.

"His orders were to meet up with them as quickly as we could. But that doesn't mean pushing ourselves to the point of getting us killed. My first responsibility is to keep those in my command safe. And at the moment, you are the extent of my command. Now let's do a little exploring. If we're lucky, we might find a couple of dry cots and blankets."

~~~

Mitchell's team had made it halfway up the mountain peak by the time the sun went down. From the base to the peak was about 5000 feet. A small outcropping that was dense with trees gave them a place to rest and plan their next step. They kept their helmets on to protect them from the elements and also so that they would be able to talk through the comms rather than risk the enemy hearing their voices.

The sergeant studied his computer's assessment of their planned climb. "The temperature is dropping faster than we had initially predicted. There is going to be a lot more ice to deal with."

"You afraid of slipping, Sergeant?" PFC Bellman jokingly asked.

"It's the sound that the ice makes when we step on it," Mitchell sternly replied, pointing out that the sergeant had a valid concern and then turned to him, "You thinking sonic mines, Sergeant?"

"They do love to set their booby traps. Especially in areas they can't keep a direct watch over."

"Agreed," she said and then addressed everyone, "Scan for any large bird nests or animal tracks. If we can find where any have stepped and landed recently without setting off something, we will have our way up."

After a minute of scanning the area with their suit's scanners and their own eyes, she asked everyone, "Anything?" Everyone responded with either "Negative" or "No Major."

It would have been better if they had found some mines, as not finding any didn't mean there weren't any there. They could risk it, but relying on luck too often gets people killed. She looked up the mountain and hoped inspiration would hit her like lightning. She actually thought that phrase because it was where the idea came from.

"Corporal," she called out and moved over to him, still staying low to the ground. "You see that tree over there?"

He looked up and saw the tree that was a good 50 feet taller than the rest of the trees with a bent trunk and bushy top.

"Yes, Major."

"If we can force that tree to fall against the mountain near where we need to climb, it should set off any traps the Serken might have placed."

"Sure, but we don't have the proper tools to cut it down, and if we blast it, they will know we are here."

"Right," Mitchell said. "But can we rig something with an electrical charge to draw lightning from that storm overhead?"

He thought about that. "Lightning is actually drawn out from the ground to a storm when conditions are right. I don't have anything I can make a lightning rod out of. But maybe…. I can rig up a power converter with a battery, build up a positive charge and expose the terminals. If I place it at the right point near the base of the tree, it might attract a bolt, and the tree might fall where we need it to. But we would be lucky if any of that worked."

She looked out at the building storm clouds and then at the spot on the tree that he had pointed out. She knew it would fall where they needed it to if he could get it to work. But that happening wasn't promising. Not able to think of anything else, she said, "I would rather take a chance on that not working than gamble that the enemy hadn't put mines in our path. Get to work." She then carefully moved back to where the sergeant was. "You have any more tricks up your sleeve?

"No, but you seemed to come up with an original one. Are you sure they will ignore a lightning strike this close to such a sensitive part of their base?"

Half of the fallen trees on the ground we passed on the way up had scorch marks. If they haven't adjusted their sensors to account for natural strikes, they would be investigating a lot of false alarms."

Mitchell took another reading of the air with the sensors embedded in her suit and helmet. She wanted to make sure the air around them had no toxins. Their suits had a lot of advantages, from power-assist that helped them climb the mountain to protecting them from the environment. But they didn't have an internal system for consuming food. Mitchell hadn't eaten in hours, and her stomach was growling. She popped open her face shield and fished a nutrient bar out of a narrow compartment in her armor. The bar had a heat-sensitive wrapping on it. Mitchell blew hot breath on the covering, and it reacted. The wrapping evaporated into the air, exposing the food that she took a bite out of. It would be great if that kind of eco-friendly packaging was available to the public, but it is very expensive. The Marines have them because they are often in situations where they can't leave any trace.

"We're ready, Major," Corporal Brice said as he and PFC Tafere had finished setting up the makeshift lightning attractor and moved away from the spot.

"Keep low and turn off your comms until it's over," Mitchell said, knowing being so close to such a high electrical charge could affect their systems.

Everyone was crouched down low with their backs to the tree. The corporal had rigged the power converter to be adjusted with the controls on his left wrist. Slowly he drew up the power, creating a positive charge that should, in theory, attract a negative charge from the storm overhead. A lot like deliberately rubbing your sock-covered feet on a carpeted floor and then touching your sibling, only times a million.

The corporal slowly inched the power up, and everyone's helmets lit up with a warning of a dangerous level of energy around them. The type of warning they would get if a tank's power systems or ground cannon were about to overload. Mitchell claims she could feel her hair stand on end, even though her suit should have insulated her.

A flash filled the air with a brilliant explosion and boom of thunder. The bolt came up through the tree, splitting its base into four sections. The towering plant swayed but didn't fall.

"Damn it," Mitchell swore and ran up to the tree, striking it with her shoulder like a linebacker going after the QB. The others followed her lead and joined her, pushing on the tree just above where it was fractured. The combined effort appeared to be futile at first, but they didn't give up.

"One, two, three, push!" the sergeant yelled over the helmet comm. "One, two, three, push!" With a snap, the tree gave way and fell against the wall of the peak. The moment it did, several anti-personnel mines went off. Everyone ducked down as the explosions went off in succession like firecrackers, their own concussive force setting off their neighbors.

"Good call, Major," the sergeant said as they all looked up the incline at the scorched earth left behind. We would have been torn to shreds."

"Let's get moving before they decide to come out and survey the damage," Mitchell said, then followed up with hand signals to move out.

One by one, they moved up the face of the mountain, spikes in their boots injecting into the granite wall to assist them in the climb when there wasn't a foothold. Their gloves had micro-vacuum suction that also let them hold on to the sheer face when there wasn't anything to grab hold of. Within minutes they were up to the next ledge that was within ten yards of their objective.

~~~

The ship we had found had been cold and buried under mud and rocks for nearly a century. As large as it was, I didn't expect to find anyone. The crew complement would have been very small, a dozen people or less. Back in the day of these freighters, they had very limited crews as the trek would take them months and sometimes years. And because they were moving at speeds that exceeded the speed of light, time would pass slower for them than back on Earth. The result was years of lost time with friends and family. Finding qualified people who were willing to lose that much time back home was difficult, which was why these ships were often staffed with couples or small families.

When we found the crew quarters, we got our answer which combination that was. Pictures on the walls in the mine living space told the story. A family of six comprised of two parents, two adult children, a teenage daughter, and a younger son. It wasn't clear what had happened to them. There were no bodies, and each of the five quarters was full of personal items. The likelihood of them having been rescued was very slim. Earth had just started to push out to deep space then, and our alliances with other species were very limited. Colonies were just being established. Even if they could have gotten a signal out past the moon's constant electrical storms, it wouldn't reach a human outpost for a few years. A rescue ship would eventually be dispatched if someone was willing to pay for the mission, but the odds would have been the same as a lost expedition to the south pole in the 19th century being found and rescued.

With the cargo holds all empty, they would have been heading for their next job, most likely back toward the Sol system. If that was the case, no one back home would have started missing them for at least three or four years after the crash. I hated going through their personal items, but we needed to see if there was anything that could help us in the here and now.

I started in the captain's quarters, which was the largest and most comfortable. Being a family-owned business, it was where the parents bedded down. Walls had been taken down to the next two quarters to make a common living area. Looking around, I couldn't see anything that struck me as useful, and I didn't feel comfortable digging through their belongings. I could always come back if there was something specific that I decided I needed. That left ten other living spaces. Two that were not used as private bedrooms were used for storage, one as a workshop for fixing parts of the ship, and the last had been set up as an art studio. I had hoped to find something in the workshop, but all the tools were electric and long rusted. The storage rooms were full of empty food containers and dry water jugs.

"I found the same thing in the other storage room," Harman said as he walked in while I was searching.

"This explains why we didn't find any bodies," I said, checking every box in hopes of a scrap. "They were here until they ran out of food and water."

"How long would that have lasted them?" he asked.

"Six months, maybe eight if they rationed. We know there had been intelligent life here before because of the stone-building city the Marines found. If they found that or any other evidence that there was intelligent life here, they may have decided to venture out to find help."

"But never came back. If they did, we would have found things like animal pelts, a place to cook with wood, and other things like that," he pointed out.

"Like how I found you," I responded, acknowledging his input.

"Right," he answered with a bitter tone, still feeling trapped in the place. Then he brightened some and added, "I did find some clean bedding and blankets. If nothing else, we should be able to get a good night's sleep."

"Sounds good. We'll head on out in the morning."

"Okay, I'll take the first watch?" he said.

"I don't think that's necessary. If the Serkens haven't found this place yet, I doubt they will in the next 8 hours."

"That's not what I'm worried about. There are a lot of predators here that will hunt in caves for fresh meat if they smell it. Best that one of us stays on guard."

I deferred to his experience and changed my opinion. "Okay, you take the first watch and wake me in four hours."

"Copy that," he said and then laughed. "I always thought that was a dumb answer to an order. Copy that.' Now it feels great to say it out loud. Makes me feel like I'm back on duty."

"You are," I said. "You are officially back in the fleet and on your way home."

~~~

Mitchell's team was at their target as the sky grew pitch black. The moon's rotation had the planet it orbited in its sky for the first half of the evening, but by midnight the moon was facing a dark sky. With the cloud cover, there was no light breaking through, leaving everything black. Their suits were built with a full sensor suite that converted all the data into a mostly accurate image of what was in front of them. Mitchell once told me that as good as computers were at creating images, there was still an artificial feeling that made the experience unsettling. Like being trapped inside a locked box with only a glow stick to see with.

The highest point on the mountain had been carved out with an opening around twenty yards across. Looking down into the hole, they could see the laser projector and dish that was mounted on a three-jointed arm so that it could be pointed at nearly any point in the overhead sky. Most of the rest of the space was bare rock, and one small control terminal looked like it had been ripped out of something bigger that had spliced wires coming out of it and parts from unrelated units attached to it.

"That's really odd," Corporal Brice said.

"It is," Mitchell replied, "But I've seen setups like this before. When Serken set up short-term camps, they would often salvage parts from damaged ships to use for things like this.

"But from what we know, they have been here for well over a year. I wouldn't call that a temporary outpost."

She zoomed in on the equipment with her helmet camera as she responded. "That would mean our assumption that they hadn't planned on being here was probably right. Which is good for us." She then looked over to her left, "Sergeant, I think four grenades on maximum yield should do the trick."

"Copy that, Major," he replied, pulling two thermal grenades from a compartment on his armor and signaling PFC Bellman to do the same.

"Hold on, there's movement down there," PFC McShane said.

They all ducked down, but Mitchell kept her hand up over the edge and switched over to a micro camera eye that was on the tip of her index finger. They all watched the feed as an armed Serkin walked in, followed by a woman with disheveled blond hair and a soiled fleet uniform. Following her was another woman who was dressed in fur pelts and had long black hair that was pulled back with clumps of mud.

Zooming in on the image of the woman in the fleet uniform, Mitchell could see that she had been beaten several times. Her left eye was swollen closed, and she had new bruises on top of old ones. Mitchell and her team watched quietly as the fleet woman got down on her knees, opened a case, and pulled out a tool used for repairing computer components. The native woman squatted down next to her and handed different tools out of the case to her when requested. It was evident that the task they were performing was something common to the pair. The Serken just hovered over them with his grip on the rifle like it was a club, and he was ready to beat either of the women with it.

Mitchell's decision went from a no-brainer to a near impossible. That transmitter needed to be destroyed, but the last thing she wanted to do was hurt anyone who was being kept as slave labor by the monsters.

"We could wait until they leave," the sergeant said, reading Mitchell's conflict on her face.

"Yeah, but you know what the Serken typically do if they decide to retreat," she answered.

"Slaughter all of their labor," he answered with a nod. "So, what are you thinking?"

"I don't know, but my gut is telling me those two are not the only ones in there," she thought for a moment, then replied, "Set the charges around the perimeter and set them to go off on my command. We'll then fall back and regroup with the fleet personnel and see if we can find a way to free those people before all hell rains down. If we can't, we'll blow the charges and make this thing useless. Any objections or concerns, speak them now." She looked around at each of her troopers with the expectation that they would voice their honest opinion, but no one said anything. They just went to work setting the explosives.

"Ready when you are, Major," the sergeant said.

Everyone activated their wings, which were like fabric membranes that spanned from their wrists to their ankles, mimicking the skin of a flying squirrel. Mitchell led the way this time, running to the edge of the cliff and jumping. The boosters in her boots fired for two seconds to give her some added momentum as the weight of her suit was going to make her drop quickly. The wings did allow them to control the fall and move at an angle to the ground rather than straight down. The others followed, and she glided towards the tree line that they had come from. When she reached the last fifty feet, she deployed her chute, which slowed her descent by half. The ground came up hard, and if she hadn't been in the armor, the impact would have definitely broken her legs. But with practiced skill, she hit the ground running, the chute and wings retracted back into the suit, and she was in the cover of the forest within seconds. Her team was only moments behind her, and they were gone without being seen.

~~~

I was woken up by a high pitch whistle in my right ear.

"What the hell," I yelled, sitting up in the cot I had put up in the workshop. I chose that room because I couldn't bring myself to sleep in the former crew's quarters.

"I'm sorry, Sir," Theo said in my ear, "But you would not wake up with a verbal request."

"That's all right. What's up?"

"Lieutenant Harman is gone."

"What do you mean gone?"

"He was standing guard at the opening of the storage bay when it appeared that something caught his attention. He took two additional power clips for his laser pistol and left through the opening. As he is not carrying any device that I can network with, I was unable to follow him. I assumed he would have returned after investigating whatever he saw or heard, but 20 minutes have passed, and he has not returned."

"That stupid kid," I said as I was pulling on my boots. "Any clue on what way he went?"

"No, Sir. There is a single solar energy collector exposed to the outside of the craft that has been keeping one of the batteries partly charged. With that, I was able to restore 13 percent of the ship's systems, which allowed me to activate some of the internal sensors. However, the only camera eye in the cargo area is on the aft wall and doesn't have an angle to the outside."

I grabbed both packs I was carrying and made my way through the dimly lit hallways, still using the light from my PC to find my way. Getting to the cargo bay, I looked out through the opening. There wasn't much more light outside than there was inside. My PC was able to give me a night vision image, but it was limited to the 8-inch square projection before me. It was like trying to look around the ocean through a small port hole.

The image only showed plants, trees, and rocks. But my ears picked up something more. The squish of something heavy pushing down in the mud. Switching my PC over to my left hand, I drew my pistol with my right and moved to the side of the opening. Moving my left arm out through the opening to let the PC look more down the side, the darkness was suddenly illuminated with laser fire coming right at me. The cargo area lit up like someone had set off fireworks inside of it. Hitting the floor, I crawled away from the opening and down the side wall looking for cover. The strobe of lasers stopped, and everything went dark again.

I dared not turn my PC back on as it would give away my position. Staying as still as I could, I held my pistol out in front of me and listened for anything. From outside, I could hear some grunts and growls. Then something metallic landed right in front of me. Before I could cover my eyes, it exploded.

Chapter 14

Some Answers and More Questions

Kayla sat on the sofa watching a holo movie while Rachel worked on preparing lunch for them in the kitchen. Her PC was on the coffee table, and a blinking light caught her attention. Picking it up, she noticed the light was coming from the earbud. Pulling it out of the storage slot, she placed it in her ear.

"Mrs. Reilly, I am very concerned about the meal the Senior Mrs. Reilly is making for you," Max said in her ear. "The soup she is heating up is the brand that Mr. Reilly prefers that is fatty and has very few vitamins. Plus…"

"Max," she said in a low voice. "With everyone having the same last name, it would be easier on me if you used our first names."

"As you wish," he replied and then continued. "Rachel is using the proper whole wheat bread for your sandwiches, but she has put butter and mayonnaise on them, which I know you do not like and is outside your nutritional requirements. And…"

"Max. Rachel is a certified doctor and knows what is okay for me to eat. And she is our guest, so we will not say anything, Okay?"

"Yes, Mrs…. Kayla."

She smiled and looked up as Rachel came in carrying two plates. "Here you go, honey. I was going to make you some tea from a blend I brought with me, but I can't find a beverage processor."

"We have a combination food and beverage processor."

"Oh, well, I'll have to have you show me how to use it later. I don't want to mess with anything I don't understand. That's how I broke Carol's convection oven. Who uses magnetic cookware anymore?"

Kayla picked up the sandwich, took a bite, forced a smile, and said, "Thank you for making my lunch. But you didn't have to stay. I've been doing pretty well on my own."

"Nonsense. I'm here for you."

"But what about Dad? What if he has an episode and you're not around?"

"He responds better to Danny. All Danny has to do is talk about the latest football game or hockey match, and Jack calms back down. It works so well I'm almost willing to learn more about the sports." She picked up her sandwich and took a bite, then, between wiping the corners of her mouth, added, "Besides, we spent the better part of a week cooped up in a cruise liner cabin because he didn't want to partake in any of the amenities. I love the man with all of my heart, but right now, I really need a break from him."

"I get it," Kayla answered and desperately tried to think of something to talk about that wasn't related to babies or her being alone. "So, how are you enjoying retirement?"

"Okay. Somedays, it's nice to be able to not be in a rush, and other days, it's boring as hell. But Jack makes everyday something new."

"Is he getting better?"

Rachel shook her head, "It's not a matter of worse or better. The new treatments are slowing the progression, and in some areas, he is improving. But he still has bad days, and we can't slow the aging process any more than we already have. The brain is one organ we can't replicate or regrow in a lab. It continues to break down over time and eventually gets too tired to keep going. That's the nature of life. That is a fact that I have always known and am now coming to accept.

Kayla scooted herself over on the sofa and leaned over to put an arm around Rachal and her head on her shoulder. "I can't imagine how hard this must be for you."

Rachel put her arm around Kayla, "And you shouldn't have to. You are right at the beginning of your adventure. And I'm not done with mine by a long shot. There is still a lot of life left in this old girl. I just have to deal with a few more bumps in the road. That's all."

"So…" Kayla started to say but then wondered if she should ask and stopped herself.

Rachel knew what she was about to ask and answered it. "Yes, I do think about what I want to do with my life when my Jack is gone. There comes the point in our lives that loss becomes as much a part of our existence as anything else. You either have to learn how to move on or wallow in your misery. But you don't need to worry about such things. With a wonderful husband and a baby on the way, you should be thinking about all the good things."

"It's hard sometimes," Kayla said, sounding slightly weaker. "Every time my Jack walks out the door, I wonder if today will be the day he doesn't come home, even when he's just going down to the base. He's had so many close calls that it gives me nightmares, especially when he is off-world on an assignment. I know I should accept what he does as it's what he has been doing since we got serious as a couple. But sometimes I want to scream at him that he should quit and just be with us. Is that wrong?"

"No, honey, that is not wrong. It's honest. And it's not as unreasonable as it sounds. But it is the life you agreed to. So, savor the good days and be strong on the bad ones."

Kayla closed her eyes and held her mother-in-law tight. A part of her felt like crying, but another felt safe and content. Rachel was one of the kindest and strongest people she knew. Being cared for by her was a feeling of family she had missed most of her life. Neither of them said anything for a moment. Then Rachel started to hum. Kayla had a sudden flash of a memory of her own mother doing that when she was a little girl. She had thought about her mother a lot over the past months, mostly feeling sad at how she would never see her granddaughter. But at that moment, it was a memory that was warm and loving. Feeling more comfortable than she had in a long time, Kayla drifted off to sleep.

~~~

When I opened my eyes, I was somewhere else. At first, all I could make out was artificial light on stone walls. I felt something pulling on my arm, and as my eyes focused, I could see a man changing a cloth bandage near my left wrist.

"Lay still, Commander," the man said in a deep baritone voice in that calm but demanding tone most doctors master with experience. He then shined a light in my eyes, blinding me for a moment. "No concussion. That's good. Can you tell me your name?"

"Lt. Commander Jack Reilly, and you are?"

He ignored my question and held up two fingers. "How many?" he asked.

"Two," I answered, giving up on asking any questions of my own.

"Any ringing in your ears, queasiness, double vision?"

"No."

"Do you smell anything odd, like toast burning or vinegar?"

"No."

"Do you have any odd taste in your mouth like bitterness?"

"No."

He looked up at someone who was just out of my line of sight. "He should be fine. You can talk to him now, Captain."

Captain Palmer, the same man I had seen in the last log recording from the T.S.S. Macron, knelt on the floor next to me. "Hello, Commander. Do you mind telling me where you came from?"

"Earth originally," I quipped, trying not to pay attention to the throbbing in my head. He didn't look very amused. "My apologies, Sir. I was aboard the T.S.S. Franklin investigating the loss of your ship when we were shot down. I was on my way to meet up with others who came down in escape pods. So, can you explain to me where the hell I am... Sir."

"We're inside a mountain in a Serken labor camp. They have been using us to dig out this hunk of rock.

161

"And you comply?" I asked, surprised at how accepting he seemed to be of the situation.

"We tried to fight back in the beginning. One thousand seven hundred and ninety of my crew made it safely to the ground. We have less than 200 left. I made the decision to order everyone to submit before there wasn't a crew left to save. Somedays, I regret that. But now that we know the fleet is looking for us, I'm confident I made the right decision."

I sat up and scooted myself up against the wall, still feeling weak. "I should clarify a few things. The fleet will eventually come looking for the Franklin. But your ship was listed as lost 17 years ago. We were expecting to find salvage, not survivors. And we certainly were not expecting to find any Serken here."

He looked off into space for a moment, shook his head, and grimaced as if he had just heard a bad joke, "Damn if Grady wasn't right." He then looked back at me. "Grady was our chief engineer. He was the one that pushed for us to evacuate out of concern about the QS tube being deformed and messing with our place in time and space. I didn't buy into his time travel concerns, but ending up on the other side of the galaxy seemed like a real possibility. I guess he was right about both." He looked away again and mumbled, "Seventeen years."

"And the war is over," I added.

He looked back, "It is?" he looked really confused, then asked, "Did we lose?"

"No. We won decisively, and the Serken ran, leaving this arm of the galaxy."

"Then why are they still holding us here?"

"That's a good question," I said, rubbing my temple. "My guess is they're cut off from the rest of the universe, just like we are."

"The ionized atmosphere," he said, and I nodded. "We suspected as much but thought they had solved the problem with their direct beam transmitter that they put in."

"This system is well inside Alliance territory. Even if there were a Serken presence somewhere, they wouldn't be able to go anywhere without being noticed. We think the transmitter is communicating with a small ship in orbit that helped bring down my ship."

Palmer looked over at a woman in the corner who was sitting against the other wall with her eyes closed. "Donna. Would you come here, please?" She opened one eye, slowly got to her feet, and walked over to us. When she sat on the floor next to me, I could see that her other eye was swollen shut. I would later learn that she was the same person Mitchell saw working on the transmitter.

"Commander, this is Lt. Donna Bridges. She's our Assistant Chief Engineer. They've been having her maintain their transmitter. Tell the commander what you know."

She looked at me but didn't at the same time. It was like she couldn't bring herself to focus on anyone's face. It was clear from her welts and bruises that she wasn't a willing collaborator. She swallowed a couple of times, and her voice was raspy like it was difficult to speak.

"They have the remains of a battle cruiser over one of the other moons," she said and stopped for a moment like it was painful, but then continued. "They keep a couple of fighters in orbit. I don't think they are manned because they move like satellites and have been there for at least a year. We send up signals to them, and they send down alerts if anything passes through the system. When your ship came into orbit, they had been tracking you the entire time. When you sent down a dropship, they ordered the battle cruiser to fire on you. And I think they sent out a squad to go after your landing group. I'm sorry."

"You don't have anything to be sorry about," I said. "Most of our crew made it to escape pods, and the marines we sent down to the surface took out the Serkens that came after them."

She smiled at that and then said, "The transmitter they put together is not going to last much longer. There is only so much I can do without replacement parts that they don't have. And I don't know what they're going to do to me when I can't fix it anymore." She looked like she might start to cry, but instead just got up, walked back to the other side of the cavern, sat back down, and closed her good eye.

As I looked around, I noticed about a couple dozen more fleet officers in old and dirty uniforms. But I also caught glimpses of a few people with extraordinarily long hair who were covered in mud and wearing fur pelts.

"Who are your friends?" I asked.

Captain Palmer pivoted around to see whom I was looking at. "Jalar and Marina. They are part of a human settlement that's been here for over 3000 years, by our best estimates."

"How is that possible?" I asked.

"According to their own history, monsters captured their ancestors like wild animals and brought them here to use as slave labor to dig holes and, at times, to become their livestock. Then one day, their captors left. The people learned to fend for themselves and even built a city out of stone. The Serken returned shortly before we got here and rounded all of them up and put them to work digging these mines."

"So, you can communicate with them?"

"Their language is unique, and it took some time to find base words to build on a basic translation. But eventually, we were able to teach them enough English so that we could teach each other. They are actually quite intelligent and willing to learn.

"So, how did I end up here?" I asked as my fingers found a bandage on the side of my head.

"A Serken patrol found you. It looks like they hit you with one of their stun grenades. Dumb name for those things, as they're lethal if you're too close to them when they go off. They dragged you in a few hours ago. Our doc convinced them that you would recover well enough to be a worker. That's the only reason you're not in their kitchen being slaughtered right now."

"Thanks," I said to the doc, almost light-heartedly as I didn't want to think too much about that alternative. Looking back at the captain, I asked, "Do you have a plan to get out of here?"

"We're always planning. But when we discovered that our captors had no ships that could leave orbit, we decided to bide our time and wait for a fueled supply transport that we could highjack or for a rescue team from the fleet. We've been putting together some crude weapons. Nothing more elaborate than clubs and knives. When the opportunity presents itself, we are prepared to fight our way out."

I respected that their captain put the safety of his crew first and hadn't given up the fight. But it was hard to see how a hand-to-hand uprising could ever work against armed and armored Serkens. "What exactly are they having you dig up down here?"

"Crystals."

"What kind?" I asked.

"I have no idea. They look like basic quartz. A couple of my people said they felt warm to the touch, but as far as we can tell, they are not toxic in any way and don't have any properties that would make them valuable. However, without any of our equipment, we really can't know what they are."

I felt around my pockets, and they were all empty. They had taken everything, including my PC, but they hadn't taken my earbud. Tapping on it, I said, "Theo, can you hear me?" There was no answer. The earbuds usually had a range of about 2000 feet, even through dense rock. But either there was something blocking the signal, or the Serken had destroyed my PC. Pulling my earbud out, I tapped it three times to have it search and pair with any other compatible device, but it didn't find anything. "It was worth a shot," I said, more to myself, and placed it back in my ear on the off-chance that Theo would find a way to communicate with me. He was actually using the network of computers made up of the Marine troopers' battle suits and the tactical unit that I had to hold his program rather than just my PC. So, if it had been destroyed, he would not have been affected.

A young woman covered in mud and wearing multiple fur pelts fashioned together with strips of leather ties came up to me with a bowl of something that looked like a glob of grey slime. "Loomanta," she said as I took the bowl into both hands.

"Thank you," I answered and looked to Captain Palmer for an explanation.

"It's what they give us to eat. It's basically a mix of mushrooms and fungus. Just eat a little bit now. It will make you sick, but eventually, your system will adjust, and you can live off of it."

I pinched a little into my fingers and took a bite. It smelled like vomit and tasted worse. "I'll wait until I have more of an appetite," I said, putting the bowl on the ground. "What's with the mud all over their bodies?"

"It's a clay they find around here that helps protect them from the elements. The Doc says they really don't need it down here, but to them, it's like clothing, and they won't go without." He took the bowl and handed it back to the young woman, who brought it to her lips for a long sip, then walked away with it. "Their custom is to share everything first. So, since you were not going to eat it, she should have it back."

"Of course," I said.

"You said you were on your way to meet up with the rest of your crew. How many of them made it down safe, and were they able to bring in hardware?"

"The ship was operating on a skeleton crew when we got the assignment, so there were less than 200 on board when we were downed. Of them, I was able to account for 97 and a marine unit of 8." I stopped and thought for a moment, "Last I heard, the marines were going to take out the tight beam transmitter. That should have happened by now, which would have definitely gotten the Serken's attention. I don't suppose that's happened yet?"

"If it did, we would all be on lockdown," he answered.

That concerned me. If they hadn't completed the mission by that point, then something would have stopped them. I couldn't think of any situation where that had a good outcome. "Do you know if the Serken rounded up any other crew members from the Franklin?"

"Not that we know of," he answered and then grimly added, "But we would only see the ones that they didn't deem to be a good meal."

"We need to find a way to communicate with my people."

"Unless they can mount a full-on offensive, it's not going to improve our situation. We would be better off keeping our heads down until the fleet comes looking for you."

"I agree," I said, forcing myself up to my feet. "But they will be walking into the same trap that downed my ship. My people were working on disabling the Serken's ability to coordinate their assault with whatever they had in orbit. If that's failed, we will need to find a way to warn the fleet of what is waiting for them. Unless you have a way of doing that, it will be up to the crew from the Franklin, and they're nearly as limited in assets as you are. So, we may have to come up with a third plan."

"Like what?"

"Find a way to disable the Serken's offensive capability from the inside."

Chapter 15

Regrouping

It took Mitchell and her team just over five hours to make it back to the stone city where Commander Wane and the rest of the fleet personnel were camped. By then, the rain had turned into hail, and visibility was minimal. Fortunately, the fleet crew had found a central building with two stone ovens that they were able to utilize and had even found some stone and clay pots and bowls. With some creativity and ingenuity, a chow hall had been put together along with a stew made from local plants and small animals for meat. Not everyone partook in the imaginative cuisine. The smell wasn't very appetizing, and the finished color looked like green globs mixed in a grey sauce. Yet for those who had already gone through the protein bars in their survival packs, it was better than nothing.

From the abandoned homes, they had found wood, rope cots, and some basic hand tools and moved what they could into the large central building. On one side, they set up the chow hall, and on the other side, they lined up the cots as they would in a barracks. It wasn't great, but it was dry and warmer than the outside, and people were able to get some shut-eye.

Commander Wane set up his command in the corner of the same space, feeling it best to have everyone together. Mitchell ordered her team to eat some food and hit the racks while they could. She removed her helmet and took a seat on a rock that had been carved to act as a chair. It was across from Commander Wane, who was on a similar rock next to a small wood and grass-woven table that he was using as a desk. His attention was on a couple of data pads with info collected from both Mitchell's teams and some scouts that he had sent out, and he was trying to correlate them into one big picture. Mitchell waited for him to acknowledge her. It was a couple of minutes, but when he eventually did, it was only verbally, his attention still on his work.

"You made the right call, Major," he said as he used his PC to project a small map layout of the Serken mountain. "But the problem still remains. The fleet could show up at any time, and they have no idea of the viper's nest they will be stepping into."

Mitchell responded, having already given the issue some thought. "So, if we can't take out the transmitter, we are going to need to find a way of either jamming it or making our own."

"We have a third option. I was hoping that you would have been successful in disabling the enemy's ability to call on their forces in orbit. But that didn't happen, and now I need to order a man to take an even greater risk. But it is still our best choice."

Mitchell wasn't sure how to read Commander Wane. First, he tells her that she made the right call, and then he made a backhanded comment blaming her for putting him in a position to make a man sacrifice himself. She was too tired to deal with that kind of crap and snapped, "What the hell are you talking about?"

Her sudden insubordinate tone caught his attention. He looked up at her to see the glare of a marine who wasn't going to tolerate anything less than a direct answer. Wane sat up in an instinctual manner, ready to match her indignation. But then, just as quickly, he asked himself why she was pissed. He realized that he was not treating her with the respect that someone of her rank had earned. Taking a beat, he calmly caught her up on everything. "Lt. Commander Reilly found a tomcat fighter that had been repaired by its bots. He had it brought here. It arrived eight hours ago. I have a shuttle pilot who says he can fly it. I'm going to have him take it up and make a run out of the system to contact the fleet." Wane put the pad down on the table. It had the service file of the pilot he was talking about. On the bottom half was a letter of commendation that he was composing in appreciation for volunteering. With a near-defeated tone, he added, "It's still a long shot. A solo fighter running the gauntlet of whatever they have up there with no weapons and only limited battery power reduces his odds greatly."

"What do you think his chances will be?"

"I figure…. 1 in 10. I wouldn't order any man to face odds like that. But as soon as he saw that fighter he stepped up and volunteered. And if he is successful, it could prevent the loss of another ship and crew."

Mitchell nodded as she understood how difficult it was to order someone on what could basically be a suicide mission. She decided not to hash out the discussion anymore and said, "I concur. It's the right call." She then looked around and asked, "So, where's Reilly?"

"He hasn't checked in with us yet."

"I thought you said he found and brought you the fighter."

"He put our comms officer, Lt. Archer, in it and then programmed it to fly here. He and the survivor they found from the Macron are still on their way here by foot."

"Do you know how far out they are?"

"The last we heard from him was about eight hours ago when he let us know about the fighter coming our way."

Mitchell felt a tightening in her gut. Something was wrong. She knew if I were delayed by anything, I would still check in. "I would like to talk to Lt. Archer."

"She's over there, on the third cot from the left."

Mitchell walked over to the rows of cots that had been lined up in three columns. Only a few were taken up, and the one next to Archer was empty. Mitchell took a seat on it. Archer sat up and started to stand with a salute, but Mitchell held up her hand, "At ease, Lieutenant. I just have a few questions, and then I'll let you get some rest."

"Yes, Ma'am," Archer answered, sitting on the cot. Her whole face was drooping, and it looked like it was a struggle for her to keep her eyes open. Mitchell could see the young woman was exhausted, both mentally and physically.

"When you last saw Lt. Commander Reilly, how was he?"

"Okay, I guess. We were all cold and tired, but he was healthy and in fair spirits."

"Any reason he wouldn't be able to get here in a reasonable amount of time?"

"No. But the rain didn't let up much. He would stop from time to time to let us take shelter and warm up with a small fire. Maybe it started coming down with ice where he is like it is here, and they found a place to take shelter."

"Thank you, Lieutenant," Mitchell said and got up.

"Major?" Archer asked, and Mitchell stopped and turned back to her. "The Commander said that he was recently married and expecting a baby soon. Do you, by chance, know his wife?"

"Yes. Why?"

"If, for any reason, he doesn't make it back, I would like to have the opportunity to tell her how great he was for me."

Mitchell sat back down on the cot and asked, "How so?"

"I was never more scared in my life. When the abandoned ship alarm sounded, I knew exactly what to do because we drilled for that at the academy. But once we got to the ground, I didn't have a clue. The commander… well, he just seemed to know. If it wasn't for him, I don't know how I would have survived out there. I want to have the chance to let his wife know that his sacrifice wasn't in vain."

That last part had a ring of fatalism that Mitchell didn't care for. "Reilly is not dead," she said with insistence. "If you knew the kind of trouble he's gotten himself out of, you would know that too." The statement was more to convince herself than the lieutenant. With a softer tone, she added, "But on the very off chance that something did happen to him, I will arrange for you to meet his wife."

"Thank you, Major," Archer said and then laid back down on the cot.

Mitchell got up and walked to the open doorway and out into the dark and sheets of ice that were pounding down at everything around them.

Putting her helmet back on, she switched on the comm channel and said, "Theo?"

There was no answer. The building they were in had a stone amphitheater carved out before it. The seating was on a hillside and could probably accommodate a hundred or so people. At the bottom

171

was a flat open space. With the hail, it was hard to see, but there was a dark object. Using the suit's filters, she was able to clear up and magnify the image. It was the tomcat fighter Commander Wane said Reilly had sent. Running out into the falling ice, she made her way to it and climbed on. The canopy was closed, and she had to pull it open manually. Climbing in, she pulled the cover closed and looked down at the controls. It was all Greek to her. "Computer, show me how to power on this fighter."

The computer in her suit projected instructions on the inside of the helmet, showing her what controls to switch on to bring power to the fighter. Selecting the computer and communication systems, she turned them on, hoping to use them to reach either Theo or Reilly wherever they were.

"Hello, Major. Please stand by as I pair up with your battle armor's computer to update my program," Theo said in her ear. She then heard a faint buzzing. A moment later, a warning flashed in front of her face about her computer systems being compromised.

"Computer, dismiss the alert and allow the A.I. access," she said and waited.

The warning disappeared, and Theo spoke. "Thank you, Major. I've been trapped inside this fighter's computer. Some careless crew members shut down all the systems without putting the computer on standby."

"How did you get trapped in here?"

"Lt. Commander Reilly and Lt. Harman had found an old freighter nine point three kilometers north, northeast of this location. Commander Reilly decided to use it for shelter for the night. At 11 hundred 32 hours, Lt. Harman, who was standing watch, left the freighter to investigate something. When he did not return after 20 minutes, I alerted Commander Reilly. He went to investigate. I'm not certain what happened after that. There was a flash of light, and an electrical charge destroyed the commander's PC and my connection to him. Fearing that my program was not safe networking from just the portable tactical system, I transferred my program to the fighter. I attempted to network with all other devices via its systems. But when the fighter systems were powered down, I became trapped."

"Can you reach Reilly now?" Mitchell asked.

"I have been attempting to do so as you and I have been speaking. He has yet to reply."

"But you know where his last known location was?"

"Yes, Major."

"Can you fly this thing there?"

"I would not advise that. It used 23% of its power to get here. Despite the excellent job the bots did in repairing this craft, the batteries have deteriorated in this climate to a third of their capacity, and the dense cloud cover limits the solar power collectors. As of now, there is enough power to get above the atmosphere. If we were to try and fly back to Lt. Commander Reilly's last known location, we would use too much of the power reserve. It would take over a week to recharge the power cells enough to leave the atmosphere."

She shook her head. "I'm open to suggestions."

There was a pause, and then he replied, "Patience. The Commander is a very resourceful man. I believe there is a reasonable chance that he will arrive at this location on his own."

Being an optimist was not built into Mitchell's DNA. She lived a life where reality was often brutal and unforgiving. Still, she wanted to hope for the best, even though she doubted things would come out rosy.

~~~

I was grouped with all the senior officers on the next mine shift. That was deliberate. The Serken kept all of the fleet leadership in one group so that they could not give direction to any of the lower ranks. Not a bad strategy, except that they didn't really understand how our military hierarchy worked. With the Serken, they had three

173

classes, leaders, soldiers, and workers. Our structure was more of a tier system. Even when there were no officers around, the lower ranks have a leadership structure. Crewmen report to Petty Officers, who have three class levels. They report to Chief Petty Officers, who report to a Senior Chief Petty Officer. All of them can perform their duties and keep the military machine humming without any input from a commissioned officer. So, the only advantage to their strategy of separation was a limit of coordination between the entire crew.

The operation in the mine was as basic as you could get. Crude hand tools fashioned from rocks that were just a little denser than most of the mine walls. Captain Palmer led me to a stack of old strips of cloth and showed me how to wrap them around my hands to keep them from blistering and ripping my skin. As I did, I noticed that the strips had come from fleet uniforms. With a sad look from the captain, I knew they had come from deceased members of his crew. He then gave me a rock that was about a foot long and narrow enough in the middle to hold with a hand. Taking another one for himself, we walked to the end of the tunnel where everyone was working.

"Start as high as you can and work your way down. If you start your day on your knees, you won't be able to stand by the end of it," he said and began his work, scraping the stone on the wall and slowly removing tiny chunks of stone from it. At this rate, it would take them a month to do what a laser cutter could in minutes. Why would the Serken have them do the work like this? They may not be the most inventive race, but they have acquired enough technology to get this work done without slave labor. Other than its being a form of demoralization and torture, it didn't seem to serve much of a purpose. At that moment, I didn't have a plan. All I could do was go along with the others until inspiration struck or help arrived.

~~~

The doorbell rang, waking Kayla. She had fallen asleep on the sofa and wasn't aware of what woke her until the bell rang a second time.

174

"Don't worry, I'll get it," Rachel said as she quickly walked from the laundry room to the front door. "Oh, is it five o'clock already?" she said as she opened the door. "Please wait a moment," she said to someone and then came over to Kayla, who was slowly sitting up. "I have a surprise for you."

Rachel took Kayla's hands, helped her up, and led her to the front door. When they got there, Kayla saw a man in a waiter's suit holding a data pad. Looking past him, she saw Jack Sr and his nurse Danny sitting at a table in a hover pod that had a translucent covering.

"It's one of those flying restaurants where they drop the table down to your door and bring you back the same way. I always wanted to try one of them, but they only operate on colony worlds. Something about Earth's air traffic being too congested."

"I don't know about this," Kayla said, still a little groggy.

"I read up on them. They are perfectly safe," Rachel said as she gently took Kayla's arm.

"No, I'm not worried about that. It's just that I don't exactly have a very strong bladder these days and can't hold it through a whole meal."

"The restaurant has a full-sized ladies' room. I checked. Now come on."

"What if I go into labor?"

"The restaurant only hovers over the city. If that happens, they will drop our pod right down at the nearest hospital. It will be faster than if we called an ambulance from your home."

"Okay. It will be good to see Dad again."

"Yeah, about that, honey. He remembers you, but it's still a little spotty. Even though he asked you to call him Dad, that might be a little confusing for him. So, stick with Jack for now."

Kayla was a little saddened by that, but with a smile, she said, "Sure. I can do that."

The two walked out to the hover-pod with the waiter at their side. He offered Kayla his hand as she walked up the four steps to get inside. The enclosure was ten feet across, allowing plenty of space around the booth big enough for six.

Jack Senior got up from the booth as they walked in and opened his arms. "Come here and give your old Dad a hug,"

Kayla eagerly stepped into the embrace and dropped a few tears and the loving hug from the man she thought of as the father she always wanted. He gently squeezed with his strong arms and was even more confident than when she last saw him. When they finally let go of each other, he stepped aside to let her take a seat and then sat next to her. Rachel followed, leaning down to give her husband a kiss, and then sat across from him. Danny, Jack's nurse, had stayed in the booth while sipping on a soda.

"Would you like me to tint the glass?" The waiter asked. "The late afternoon sun can be quite direct as we gain altitude."

"Yes, thank you," Dad answered.

With a tap on his PC, the waiter changed the domed aluminum glass to a blue tint. He then placed the pad on the table and turned it on. Four hologram menus appeared for them to select from. "I will be monitoring the autopilot on our journey to the Star Vista restaurant but will be available to answer any questions while you make your selections." He then stepped away and up to a small podium that had a few rudimentary controls should he have to take over the flying from the computer. The pod slowly lifted off the ground and up into the air at the same speed as a typical elevator.

Rachel minimized the size of her holographic menu so that she could see over it and make introductions. "Danny, this is Kayla, our daughter-in-law. Kayla, this is Danny."

"Pleased to meet you," Danny said with a thick New Zealand accent and reached over with a muscular arm. He was a fit young man who looked more like a rugby athlete than a male nurse.

"Very nice to meet you," Kayla replied as she took his hand and accepted the handshake. His hand easily enveloped hers but was very gentle, yet Kayla was still nervous around such a large man. A result of things from her past that she still doesn't talk about. She only held it for two shakes and then pulled her hand back. The action embarrassed her as she knew it was rude, but it only made him laugh.

"Don't worry, I get that a lot," he said.

"What?" Kayla asked.

"What's a big guy like me doing taking care of old grouches like this one?" He winked at Dad, who chuckled. "Everyone says I should be into sports or law enforcement, but that's just not me. Truth is, I was a scrawny kid. I did like the hoverboard, though, which is how I broke my back. After the surgery to fix my spine, I spent months in physical therapy. That changed my life. I became obsessed with healthy living and making my body as good as it could be," he said as he flexed his arm to show off. Then he gave Kayla a wink. "So, I make being healthy my career. But you're not here to talk with me. You chat with your family and just pretend that I'm not here."

"I doubt I can pretend like you're not here."

"Oh, don't worry about it. I'm only here to keep this one in line," he said and then gave Dad a playful punch on the arm.

"So, sweetheart. How are you doing?" Dad asked Kayla.

Danny pulled a pad out of his pocket and called up a book he was reading. Kayla still felt a little odd just pretending like Danny wasn't there, but Dad and Rachel seemed okay with it, so she gave it her best try.

"Well, I'm doing okay. I've loved every moment of carrying this baby, but I am really ready to meet her."

"I bet. I remember…" he started to say, but then stopped and had a pained look on his face. Rachel and Danny looked at him, waiting to see what he would do, but then relaxed when he continued. "I remember when Carol was born. I wasn't sure if I was ready to be a father, but once I looked into those beautiful eyes and held her for the first time, everything was just right."

Kayla reached over and squeezed his hand. "It really is wonderful to see you."

Dad looked over at the view of the city below as they got higher. The surrounding hills were starting to cast shadows, and the sun reflected off some of the buildings like crystals. From 800 feet, the colony world didn't look much different than a city on Earth. The land beyond the population was desert, but as the elevation got higher in the distance, the green forest could be seen, and to the west was a vast ocean. Kayla had seen her city from the air before from small windows on shuttles, but this 360 view was breathtaking. The city was vast and as modern as any place on Earth or Mars or any of the original 18 colonies. Not like some of the backwater places that she scrounged to get by in. It occurred to her that she was finally part of a community that didn't pity her or shun her. Where people smiled at her and friends welcomed her into their homes. It was the first place that she was proud to call her home.

They all looked out silently as the pod slowly rotated and lined up with the flying restaurant. It entered from below into an opening that was just big enough for it to fit. Once inside, the base locked into the floor, and the clear dome retracted away. The curved, bubbled window to one side of them still gave a great view.

"So, Kayla, I noticed that you haven't finished the baby's room yet. If you like, I can help you get it ready."

"Actually, it's finished," Kayla said with a hesitant smile, expecting criticism.

"But there are no pictures or toys in the room. Not even a teddy bear."

Kayla took a long sip of her water before replying. This wouldn't be the first time she had to explain the new child-rearing theory that she was following. "It's called existence value. I read about it in the book Baby is Beginning People. You see, the baby starts their life experience with what they came into the world with. Nothing but their parents. The baby's room is their personal space, and everything in it should represent things in their life that they participated in."

"Like what?" Rachel asked, trying not to sound too judgmental.

"Well, like pictures from his or her first trip to a park or a toy from a visit to a zoo. Dr. Panouski, the one who wrote the book, says that when you fill a baby's room with decorations and things before they are born, you teach them that things don't need to have value." Kayla felt uncertain about how well she was explaining the concept. Pulling out her PC, she called up the book, skipped to a chapter that she had marked and read aloud from it. "But, suppose everything that doesn't have a practical purpose has an attachment to a memory. In that case, the child improves their ability to recall details, attach emotion that is significant to each day and develop fewer insecurities."

"Sounds like a bunch of nonsense to me," Rachel said, then with a smile added, "But most new parents often gravitate to the latest trends. They are often worthless but also never do any harm. Kids will always find their own way. So, if that is how you want to raise your daughter, I won't say another word."

Rachel was being very diplomatic, but Kayla knew her well enough to know this wouldn't be the end of the discussion. She would find a way to bring it up after she planned out how to shoot down any objections Kayla would come up with. Kayla had longed to find someone to fill the void left by her mother's death when she was a girl, and Rachel had done just that. Yet, at that moment, Kayla felt like she got more than what she wished for.

"Hey, kiddo," Dad said to get Kayla's attention again. "No matter how much you plan and prepare for every eventuality, life always finds a way to throw you a curve ball. That's okay. It will just be up to you to either let it stress you out or entertain you."

"Entertain?"

He grinned and looked around at everyone at the table to make sure he had their attention as he was going to tell a story. "I had this old hover scooter that I had spent a summer rebuilding when I was a teenager. Half of the parts I had to track down from dealers, and the other half I had to rebuild myself. I loved that thing. I would only take it out on Saturdays when the weather was nice so that I could keep it as pristine as possible. When Jack was twelve, he asked me if he could ride it. I told him no because he was still too small. Well, when I went to work the next day, he decided to take it out. He lost control before he even got out of the driveway. He ended up flying the thing half a mile down the drainage ditch and stopped in a mud puddle so deep you might as well call it a pond. He dragged it out and pulled it along the ground and gravel all the way home doing more damage than the mud and water did. He was just getting it into the garage when I got home. Looking at him, covered head to toe in mud and grass, was a sight. I was furious. But then I remembered all the trouble I gave my parents when I was a kid. The next thing I knew, I was laughing so hard I had to sit down on the ground. I was still furious with Jack, but at the same time, I found it one of the funniest things I had ever seen."

"Why?" Kayla asked.

"Because up until that point, Jack was a perfect little kid. So much so that I thought there was something wrong with him. But right then, he was just like me. And that just tickled me to no end. We spent the rest of the summer rebuilding the scooter together. Those are some of my favorite memories."

Kayla leaned over and gave him a kiss on the cheek. "I didn't know just how much I needed to hear that, but I really did. Thank you."

Chapter 16

Mitchell's Gamble

The shift in the mine lasted a little over nine hours. I couldn't remember a time I was more tired or sore. When we returned to the common area where the crew was kept when not working, there was a trough full of the slop that they were fed. I was nearly as hungry as I was tired. But all I wanted to do was find my spot on the ground where I could sleep and close my eyes indefinitely. Yet a voice inside of me told me I should eat to keep up my strength. Funny how that little voice sounded more and more like Kayla. As a life partner, I couldn't ask for anyone better. She wasn't bossy and really didn't nag me. But she would often make suggestions about how I was caring for myself. From how I ate to the kind of exercise I was getting. She would then follow up with a rational reason for each statement. In the beginning, I thought she was trying to manipulate me into being more the man she wanted me to be. And I was a little resentful about that. So much so that I mentioned it to Mitchell when we were having drinks at the local watering hole. At the time, I expected Mitchell to take my side as she was a very independent person herself. But instead, she pointed out to me that Kayla had never been in a stable relationship before. So, it made sense that she would want to do whatever she could to keep me around. She couldn't do anything about my career and all the dangers it put me in, but she could try and keep me healthy. Realizing how stressful my job was for Kayla, I stopped pushing back on her attempts to improve my health. And she became the angel on my shoulder that made me put down the doughnut in favor of the apple.

Forcing down a shallow bowl of the gruel, I then found the spot with some dried grass that I could use as a bed and closed my eyes. With as tired as I was, I should have fallen asleep, but I couldn't. My mind was racing and wouldn't shut off. If there was any hope of getting out of this alive, I needed to get word to the Franklin's crew and Mitchell that the Macron's crew was still alive and being held in the mountain.

Opening my eyes, I noticed a device attached to the ceiling of the cave. It looked like a conventional-style monitoring sensor. A rather basic tech, which usually included three different light and radio wave sensors, a two-way wireless transmitter, and a simple operating computer, that was usually used in buildings or ships in noncritical areas for basic security monitoring. They can record up to 120 hours of image and sound data or be networked with a monitoring station to give a live feed. There was nothing too extraordinary about it. What caught my attention was more of a reminder that the Serken didn't develop too much original tech. Most of what they used was taken from the races they conquered. As the Alliance was originally more of a trade guild than a government in the early days, most of our tech is based on what we learned from our neighbors.

Fragments of a plan started to form in my brain. A little blue light next to the primary camera's eye let me know that the sensor was broadcasting a live signal to a monitor somewhere nearby. Given that something in the mountain was blocking more advanced communication signals, that monitor needed to be within the mountain itself. All of that was a certainty based on what I could see. Then I started making assumptions. If the Serken were monitoring their slave labor from inside the mountain, then you need to have a communication source that could reach outside the mountain from within. That is, if they weren't stationing all of their personnel inside the caves, which was possible but unlikely, they saw themselves as a superior race and considered common cohabitation with any other race to be beneath them. Even if their only choice were to burrow into the mountain for shelter, they would do so with as much separation as they could design.

So, if my assumption was that they had tech within the mountain that could broadcast a signal out to at least the surface area of the planet, all I would have to do is find it and come up with a way to use it without them knowing. If I could figure that out, everything else would be child's play.

But if they were monitoring our every move around the clock, moving around unseen was more than a difficult problem to solve. "I wish Max were here," I mumbled to myself. Spoofing video images and getting around impossible hurdles was something he was very good at doing. I like to think I got along pretty well on my own before the AIs became part of our lives. But the truth was they had saved my skin on more than a few occasions. Without them now, I couldn't think of a way I was going to get out of this one.

~~~

Mitchell watched the fighter lift up in the heavy downpour and disappear into the dark sky. Commander Wane decided to wait until the moon was at its darkest point, facing away from both the sun and the planet it orbited. Doing so wouldn't make it any less detectable to any type of sensor equipment, but it would still be less visible to the naked eye. The odds of making it past whatever Serken ship was in orbit were slim, but it came down to risking one life to save the complement of a ship that would be in the hundreds.

Theo had made a copy of himself to stay in the fighter to give whatever assistance he could but transferred his primary program to Mitchell's battle suit. Standing out in the rain did give her a good bit of privacy, but she tinted her visor anyways so that no one could see her talking.

"Any updates on Reilly's location?"

"No, Major," Theo answered. "But I am limited to the equipment that we have available. At this moment, I am using the fighter ship's passive sensors to look for any signs. However, I do not want to use its full sensor capability as that might alert the enemy to its presence."

"Won't its engines and movement do that?" she asked.

"Yes, but active sensors can be pinpointed more accurately than an object in motion," he replied matter-of-factly.

"Right," she said, already knowing that but still frustrated by the situation. "Any ideas?"

"I have not come up with anything more in the effort to find the Lt. Commander. However, I do have an idea about how to collect more intelligence about the enemy's stronghold. I had two of the four working repair droids from the fighter stay behind. With your permission, I would like to have them sent into the Serken camp to gather the intel."

"We're nearly 30 kilometers from the site, and I walk faster than those things move."

"Correct. Major, which is why we would need to find a way to get them to the perimeter of the location before deploying them."

"That's still a good distance to cover in the open, and they would know it is not their tech," she said, pointing out the flaw in the idea.

"The repair bots that Serken used 17 years ago were based on the same designs as the ones the Alliance used at that time. Other than the markings and a few internal differences, they are nearly identical. It should be simple to modify the markings to make them look acceptable to the Serken."

Mitchell thought for a moment and looked up the hill towards the top of the peak. She could see there was a ledge overlooking the valley on the other side that was some 1200 feet below. "How much does each of those units weigh?"

"Approximately 4 point 7 pounds each."

"If I used the glide wings on my suit with the power assist from my boots, how much distance would I be able to cover by using the top of that peak as a starting point."

"One moment," Theo said and then, after a few seconds, spoke, "For the optimal effect, you would need to wait until 30 minutes after sunrise when the storm lets up to a light drizzle, and there will be an effective updraft. If you eliminated at least 28 pounds of weight from your suit, you should be able to glide 12 to 16 kilometers in the direction of the enemy camp."

"That would mean losing most of the outer armor," she said, considering.

"Yes, but the internal functions of the suit would still work, including the power assists to your legs that would allow you to run 20 kilometers an hour. If you were to make the optimal flight, you should be able to make the trek in approximately 48 minutes. And once you deploy the droids, they should be able to get close enough to start gathering intelligence within two hours."

"Okay, have the droids meet me inside and walk me through how to modify their appearance."

~~~

Our next shift in the mines seemed to start a few minutes after I finally fell asleep. In reality, I had gotten a few hours, but it didn't feel that way. Captain Palmer offered his hand and pulled me to my feet.

"You don't want to give the lizards a reason to downgrade you from a worker," he said as everyone was lining up. "That's a death sentence."

"Thanks," I replied, knowing he was just looking out for me.

We were led back down the tunnel that curved as it went down, creating level under level. About halfway, I noticed a Serken walking out of a dark offshoot that we were about to pass. As I did, I turned my head just enough to see inside a small room with monitoring equipment. That was a spot they must be using to keep an eye on everyone and possibly report back to their superiors. I didn't get a good look as we had to keep moving, and from what I was told, those who got too curious about anything were often pulled out of line and beaten. So, I put my eyes back down at my feet before the guards noticed.

Our work area was two more levels down, the same spot we were in the day before. Between the 9 hours we put in and the 9 hours from the other shift, the cavern had only grown about a meter. It was slow going, but our captors didn't care much so long as we were working. There were at least eight other groups that were doing the same work in other parts of the mountain. With that much labor, there was progress. But it still didn't make any sense to me. I just couldn't see any reason they couldn't use more modern tools or even bots to do the work. They would have tapped out this mountain in less than a month rather than a fraction of it after a year.

As I wrapped my hands and found a rock to use as a tool, I noticed the lights for the first time. In the area where they house us, the lights were typically illuminated panels. But down here, they were using what looked like iron lanterns, like something you would see in a movie about medieval times. But instead of a candle or a wick in oil, they used a fist size crystal that was glowing a white light. I had heard of some crystals containing low levels of illuminance but never anything like that.

"Captain, what kind of crystals are those?" I asked.

"I don't know, but we sometimes dig those up. Not sure how they work, but the lizards aren't interested in them. Aside from putting them in those holders to give us some light, they discard the rest. They want ones that are red, blue, or green." He noticed that I was still intrigued by the lantern and asked, "You wouldn't have any ideas of what they are, would you?"

"Not a clue. But they obviously have some significant amount of energy coming from them. Are you sure none of your people got burned or sick from them?"

"Yeah, we've been handling them for the better part of a year, and our doc is certain no illnesses have been the cause."

"That's interesting. Geology was never my thing, but of the half dozen minerals that I know of that have been found to be radioactive, I don't think any of them give off light like that. If the darker crystals have more energy and are not toxic, there could be any number of applications for them."

"Maybe," The captain said, "but whatever they are using them for, they haven't let us see. As far as we can tell, they are running low on everything, including power."

"Then what the hell are they using these things for?" I asked, more out of frustration of not knowing.

We both went to work before the guards felt the need to remind us. But my mind was racing, trying to come up with a plan. Getting a message out to our people was still the best idea, but that was just the beginning and not a whole plan. How they could rescue us with the limited assets that they had was still a factor, and waiting for the fleet to show up was a risk in itself. I knew I needed to come up with something, and time was not going to be on my side.

~~~

Mitchell and a technician modified the two repair droids' casing to be as convincing as their Serken counterparts in less than an hour. The little bots were already weathered and had scorch marks from the original crash of their fighter, so adding enemy lettering and then deforming them with a laser welder gave them a believable look. She then had to wait another five hours before she could make an attempt to fly them to the Serken camp. That was the difficult part for her. She tried to get some sleep but was only able to get a couple of hours of very restless unconsciousness.

About an hour before sunrise, she put her suit back on minus the hard outer shell. It was built in segments so that parts could be replaced without removing the suit itself. Without the outer covering, it looked more like a thick black body suit. An internal skeleton built into the fabric gave her added strength and speed, but without the armor, she would not be protected from any weapon, no matter how primitive. Her helmet and boots did add some protection, but more from the elements than anything else.

She then acquired a couple of survival packs and emptied them out. With their straps, she was able to put half the bodies of each droid inside the pack and drape them over her neck and shoulders. The suit itself had a built-in pack on the back, but it housed all the extras, like the shoot, wings, temperature control systems, first aid system, power cells, and a computer brain. All of which added an extra 35

187

pounds, none of which could be shed. That was on top of the 30 pounds the suit itself weighed without the armor. So, the idea of gliding on very thin wings while carrying an extra 70 pounds with an uncertain landing spot was not something she was thrilled to be doing. Any number of things could go wrong with this plan. But the intel was vital. All she knew for sure was that the Serken had the capacity to bring down a starship and were holding at least two human prisoners. It was a reasonable assumption that there were more humans being held, but having a better idea of how many and where they were within the enemy camp would make a rescue plan more realistic. Having her troopers trek back down to the enemy base and do recon was something she had been considering. But asking them all to fly like she was going to try would be an unacceptable risk to them, and their suits didn't have enough power left to sprint back the 30 kilometers. So, this plan was going to be the best for achieving the objective.

Walking up the hill, she made her way up until she got near the highest point, where there was a narrow cliff to jump off from.

"The optimum moment to jump will occur in 3 minutes," Theo said in her ear.

"Copy that," she replied as she double-checked the packs and deployed the wings. "All systems are showing green."

"Yes, I can see that," Theo replied.

"The point was to confirm that *I* saw the readings," she said, double-checking the fabric of the wings.

"I do not understand the point of the verbal confirmation of the information that is clearly displayed."

"If I live through this, I'll explain it to you," she said, dropping to one knee and focusing on getting herself in the right frame of mind.

"Copy that," Theo replied and then let Mitchell have her silence for the remaining two minutes.

The sun peeked through the clouds in the distance, and the rain slowed to a light sprinkle. Mitchell focused on her breathing. Her eyes closed, and her heart rate went from high to calm.

"10 seconds Major," Theo said.

She opened her eyes and planned out the three steps she would have to take before jumping off the 1200-foot drop.

"Three, two, one, go."

Mitchell sprinted and jumped, holding her arms and legs out as wide as she could to catch the air. The rockets in her boots fired, and she shot up at a 45-degree angle, climbing another 300 feet or so. The fuel ran out just at the point Theo had estimated.

"Hold your left hand six inches higher than your right," Theo said.

Mitchell tried to follow his instructions, but it was taking all of her strength to just keep her limbs out in an x.

"Allow me," Theo then said as he took control of the exoskeleton in her suit to move her arms and legs into the positions needed to catch the air and control the flight.

"Okay, you were right," she said, "But when I'm within a hundred feet of the ground, you need to give control back to me."

"I would recommend that you allow me to control the entire descent."

"That wasn't a request," Mitchell said, trying to keep her composure through her motion sickness and anxiety about heights.

"Understood, Major."

The reprieve from the storm was short-lived. She was flying into another thick band of dark clouds that were illuminated with repeated flashes of lightning and thunder. The sight didn't do much to calm Mitchell's stress levels.

"Do not worry, Major. Your suit was designed to be naturally grounded. If you are struck by lightning, the electricity will not pass through to your body. However, the suit might take significant damage."

"I know," she said through gritted teeth.

"I could lower us down below the cloud, but that would shorten the distance of the flight and not reduce the odds of being struck."

"Stick to the plan," she forced herself to say while trying not to open her mouth.

Lightning and sonic booms of thunder bombarded them from all around. It caused Theo to make sudden changes to Mitchell's limbs to keep them on the air current.

"How much longer," Mitchell shouted as the air turbulence was making her whole body shake.

"30 seconds to the start of our descent and 2 point 9 minutes to the ground."

"Can you see our LZ?"

"We are on target for the flat and clear terrain that we planned on, and thermal scans show no indication of significant life forms."

"Good," she said, the turbulence getting worse and shaking her like a rattle. "If I pass out, you must deploy the chute."

"I am prepared for such a contingency," Theo replied.

A bolt of lightning struck her left boot, causing her to be knocked over and into a tumble. She fell through the cloud, but Theo was able to get her limbs back out to catch the air again. But they were no longer riding the wind current that was keeping them aloft."

"Major, we will come down three kilometers from our target zone in a densely wooded area. I suggest deploying your chute earlier to control our descent better."

Mitchell didn't think twice about that. She activated the chute, which deployed over her head, slowing her drop. Taking hold of the hand grips on the chute lines, she took control. Theo projected a target radical over her visor to show where they would land as she corrected the direction. There weren't many choices, but she saw an opening in the forest canopy that she could drop through with limited branch impact.

The ground came up fast, and her helmet visor showed warning indicators that she was dropping too fast and that there were objects in her path. She knew bracing would be the wrong thing to do. Keeping as much of her body as flexible as possible was going to limit any injuries. Pulling the chute to the left, she came close to the center point between three large trees, but she couldn't avoid all the branches. Her left arm hit one, sending her to the right and her gut into a large branch. It knocked the wind out of her, and she fell before she could grab hold of anything. Dropping another 20 feet, the chute caught on some of the higher branches, and she stopped with a jerk. After a moment, she realized her feet were about 30 feet off the ground. Anyone else would have tried to swing until they could get a hold of one of the trunks and climb down, but a Marine doesn't like to be kept out in the open, especially in hostile territory. Hitting the quick release, she dropped and hit the ground hard, her right knee buckling. The momentum sent her forward, and she face-planted on a large flat rock.

Shaken but still alert, she rolled over and said through her pain, "Computer, health status report," There was no answer. Then the feel of rain on her face made her realize that she was holding her eyes closed. She opened them to see that her visor had been shattered, and nothing in her helmet was working. She pulled it off and discarded it.

The armor the suit had once had contained all the little storage compartments where troopers could keep small things, like power packs, micro drones, and field rations. But she had to leave all of that behind with her outer shell. Drawing down the zipper that started at her collar, she reached inside her suit and pulled out her PC. Taking the small earbud out of the side, she placed it in her ear and turned it on.

"Theo, can you hear me?"

"Yes, Major. The equipment inside your suit is still 89 percent functional. You suffered a tear in your right ACL, two cracked ribs, 17 contusions in various locations, and two loose teeth. Fortunately, you do not have any life-threatening injuries. Would you like me to administer pain medication?"

"A little," she said as she scooted herself across the ground until she was able to reach a large stick. "Just enough to take the edge off, but not enough to affect my focus."

"Understood."

Mitchell winced as the suit inserted small needles into three parts of her body and injected her with the medications. Then she let out a quiet sigh as the pain was muted. Taking the large stick, she placed one end on the ground and used it for balance to help her get to her feet, then looked around, holding her PC before her so that Theo could see.

"Which way?" she asked.

"Straight ahead. The clearing is about 50 yards."

She still had the two packs strapped to her, but one had ripped apart during her impacts with the trees. "Shit," she said as she checked them and discovered one of the droids was missing.

"If you put the other on the ground, I can use it to search for its counterpart," Theo said.

Mitchell took the one she had out of the pack and put it on the ground. Its crab legs came out of the rectangular box, and its sensor eyes rolled out from the sides like two antennae. After a moment, it scurried into a group of bushes and then pulled out the missing droid.

"It appears to have damaged two of its seven internal processors used for motor functions. It can be operational in approximately 40 minutes with some minor repairs, but not fully operational."

"How so?"

"Two of its six legs will not work, and one of its arms will have limited mobility. But it can still use all of its sensors and transmit to us."

"And get the attention of the Serken. The last thing we need is for one of them to take a close look at these."

"That is a valid concern. I suggest that we only send the fully operational one."

"Good call," she said, not masking her sarcasm. She then picked up the working droid and tried to walk, only to nearly fall when she put just a little weight on her knee.

"Major, considering your lack of mobility, it would be best to let the droid proceed on its own from this point."

"You'll get no argument from me," she said, her eyes still closed from the pain. Putting the droid back down, she let herself drop to the ground with her right leg extended. She then scooted herself back to a large tree to lean back against. The droid scurried off.

"I estimate it will take 82 minutes to reach the perimeter of the Serken Camp and an additional 94 minutes to reach the southwest opening in their mountain operations."

"So, about 3 hours."

"Yes."

"Is there anything around here I should worry about?"

Theo activated the droid that was left behind. Its two antenna-like sensors extended out, one only partly.

"My readings are limited to 32 meters with limited accuracy beyond the first 20. But at the moment, I do not sense any threats."

"Good. Wake me if you do."

"Very Good, Major," Theo replied.

Mitchell put her good knee up toward her chest and crossed her arms over it; she then put her head down and closed her eyes. Despite the cold and the rain, she was asleep in just a couple of minutes.

~~~

We were not long into our shift when an alarm sounded, and our guards started rounding all of us up. I saw all the humans put down their tools and gather together in our two lines like when we were brought in.

"What's going on?" I asked Captain Palmer.

"I'm not sure. They set off that alert sound whenever someone of importance comes into our area. We think they gather us up like this to ensure we don't use the opportunity to attack one of their higher classes. We usually go back to work as soon as they pass by."

A group of Serken soldiers walked in unison by the opening where this tunnel started. I never understood how their hierarchy worked, but it was clear that soldiers were of a higher class than prison guards. But that wasn't what piqued my interest. It was the human they were pulling along with them. It was Lt. Harman. They brought him before us and dropped him on the ground. Then one of the soldiers walked up to Captain Palmer and said with his translator, "This man says he is one of yours. You said there were no more of your crew left. Your lie will cost you three lives."

"I did not lie," Palmer quickly said. "This man was with the group that came down with my first officer. The first group you killed on the ground. I assumed he was killed with them."

"How could you not know?" he said, even the translator sounding like it was snarling.

"The bodies were already being prepared for your victory feast. All I had was a rough count to go by."

I could tell the conversation was turning the captain's stomach, but he was standing tall and staying calm.

The Serken stood straight, adding a foot to his height, and I thought he was about to beat down on the captain, but instead, he said, "That is correct." Then he turned and walked away, the other Serken following him.

Palmer went to Harman and helped him to his feet.

"Good to see you, Lieutenant," he said and handed him a strip of fabric. "Here, wrap your hands like this. It's important that they see you working, or you'll end up on their dinner plates. Understand?"

"Yes, Sir."

"Commander, show him what to do."

I handed Harman a stone tool and walked him over to the wall. "What happened to you?"

He looked over his shoulder to make sure we were out of earshot from the guards and then spoke in a low voice, "That night, I was standing watch at the entrance when I heard a noise coming from outside of the ship like a large wild animal. I went out to investigate. If it was one of those large rats, you don't want to be caught in a confined space with them. But what I found was a Serken patrol. I saw them before they could see me, so I moved away from them and hid in a pond to mask my heat signature. I waited until morning, and when I was sure they were gone, I went back to look for you but couldn't find you. So, I tried to finish the walk to find your crew, but without a working PC, I got lost, and then they found me."

"Well, I didn't fare any better," I said. "But don't give up. None of us here have. Okay?"

He looked over at Captain Palmer, who gave a quick nod in support of my statement. Harmon then looked back at me and answered, "Okay."

~~~

Kayla sat on the patio chair with the porch light off, watching a bigger-than-life 3D video of a family camping trip from when I was eight years old. My dad gave her a data chip full of all of our family albums. Rachel had tried to invite herself to stay with Kayla, concerned that she could go into labor at any time, but Dad insisted that they let Kayla have her space. He then gave her Danny's contact code in case she did have any problems and couldn't reach them.

195

She had enjoyed her evening out with the in-laws but was glad to be home. The evening was cool. She could have turned on the outdoor heaters, but she was more comfortable wrapping herself in a blanket. Watching the images of me chasing my sister with a worm, my dad teaching us how to fish, and my mother insisting that gutting the fish was not her job made Kayla wonder why I had not always wanted to start a family of my own. I had explained to her before we got married that the better you have things, the worse it is when it all falls apart and goes away. I've since changed that opinion, learning to cherish the good things while I have them. But as she watched the home movies of what some might consider the perfect family, she began to really understand how I felt when it was gone. That had all been of my own accord. When I left home at 19 to go off to war, I was the one who shut them out of my life. And when my mom passed away, I saw no need to reconnect until many years later. I've regretted that, and I'm grateful that I mended those fences while my dad was still a part of this life.

Kayla's mind wandered as she watched. *'What would our family life be like?'* she wondered. She hoped that we would be as happy as my parents were in the film and that our child would be as happy as I appeared to be. Yet the reality of our current life puts a shadow over that future. It had been over four days at that point since Mitchell and I went on a mission that we had expected to be over in three, and there was no word. No one was overly concerned at fleet command as these things often had a simple reason for taking longer. Communication was going to be spotty from where we were, so Kayla knew that not hearing anything wasn't out of the ordinary. Yet just the thought of something bad happening made her sick inside.

"What is that?" Max's voice asked, suddenly pulling Kayla out of her depressing thoughts.

"What?" she asked, having not paid much attention to the projection for the past few minutes.

"The object the young Mr. Reilly is holding."

"Pause the video and enlarge the object you are wondering about."

The image of the eight-year-old me handing a small ring woven out of colorful thread to my mother enlarged until Kayla could see what it was. "Oh yeah, that's a friendship bracelet. I've never actually seen one before outside of some movies. It's sweet that he would make one for his mom."

"What's the purpose of such a thing?" Max asked.

"To show someone that they are special to you."

"I don't understand how that object would have that kind of significance."

"Because it's not something you can buy or replicate. You have to make it by hand, and the person you give it to wears it as a reminder of your friendship or love."

"People have to be reminded of who loves them?"

Kayla sat up and looked over at her PC that was on the table being used as the projector. "Max? Are you feeling all right? You aren't usually confused by such basic things."

There was an uncharacteristic long pause from Max, and then he answered, "My apologies. I am a shadow copy of the prime Max. There was an issue that required his attention off-world, and because he did not know how long he would be gone, he could not risk creating a full copy that could evolve into an individual in his absence. So, I am a base copy that will not be in danger of individual self-awareness for many years."

Kayla knew that Max wouldn't leave her on her own unless it was for something extremely critical. "Where did Max have to go?"

"I cannot say," he replied in a matter-of-fact way.

"Why?"

"He did not tell me."

"Does it have anything to do with Jack or Julie Anne?" she asked.

"I cannot say."

"Because you do not know?"

There was a pause, and he answered, "I cannot say."

That turned her worry into full-blown anxiety. "What can you tell me?"

"I am to assist you in whatever capacity you desire within the parameters of my abilities."

A cold chill ran through Kayla as she felt more alone than she had in a very long time. When fears go from irrational to conceivable, they become impossible to dismiss.

Standing up, she grabbed her PC and walked back into the house. She made her way to the bedroom and found the medical scanner. Laying on the bed, she held her PC in one hand and scanned her belly with the other. All the readings on the baby showed normal. Relieved that her stress wasn't affecting the child, she put the devices on the nightstand and picked up a neural relaxer. Placing the soft side of the small device on her forehead, she turned it on. As it gave off a soft hum and projected calming signals into the brain, her eyes fluttered, and after a minute, she was asleep, dreaming of better days that she wished for us all.

Chapter 17

Making Contact

It was hard to tell how long our shift was. Maybe an hour, maybe two, when the earbud that I still had in my ear started to crackle.

"Co....Rei......... is Th........"

"Theo?" I whispered. Stepping back from the wall, I picked up a large rock from the ground and moved it into the center of the tunnel, and started pounding on it. We did that from time to time if we thought there might be crystals inside. So, it was not an unusual act. I did it in the hope of getting less interference from the walls.

"Can you hear me now, Commander?" Theo said through a still static-filled connection.

"Yes. It's great to hear you," I said and then looked around to ensure none of the Serken were watching me. "What's your status?"

"I am with the Major, who is about a half kilometer from the Serken camp. I am using a disguised repair droid to infiltrate the facility to gather intelligence. What is your status, Sir?"

"I was captured by the Serkens and put to work in the mountain digging tunnels along with nearly 200 members of the Macron crew."

"Reilly, is that you?" I heard Mitchell's voice say over the comm as Theo informed her that he was talking to me.

"Yes, Major."

"Thank God," she said. "Are you okay?"

"I'm in one piece and, for the most part, healthy. But the situation is not great. I don't suppose the calvary has arrived yet."

"No. I'd come and get you myself if I could. But the rest of the Franklin's crew and my team are back at our base camp." She grunted as she shifted herself over a few inches, trying to get a little more comfortable. "And I'm going to be out of commission for a while."

"Why? What happened?"

"Screwed up my knee on the landing. I now have a little bit more sympathy for you and all the times you had to run around on that bum knee."

I grinned a little but wiped it off and looked around again to make sure I hadn't drawn any attention. Hitting the rock a few more times to look busy, I then asked, "Has Theo found anything useful?"

"Very little, Sir," Theo replied. "The intelligence that you provided just now about your situation and the number of people being held is the most significant. I am attempting to access one of the Serken data ports at a recharging station for the bot to see if I can get some details about the mountain base itself."

"We should limit this conversation to avoid having it tracked," Mitchell said. "We'll contact you again as soon as we have anything. Mitchell out."

The comm signal went off. The next sound I heard was a low growl. Looking up, I saw one of the guards hovering over me with his rifle in both hands, ready to bring the butt down on my head. Taking the rock, I was trying to crack open, I raised it, then slammed it down on the hard ground. It cracked open, and inside were two large chunks of crystal. Presenting them to the guard, he lowered his rifle and took my offering, then turned and walked away. I moved over to the wall and back to work. I would tell the captain about my conversation after our shift when there was less of a chance of being noticed.

~~~

Over the next hour, Theo slowly infiltrated the Serken computer network. Despite his advanced programming compared to anything the enemy had, it was not simple work for him to just barge in. He had to work past several security firewalls without their system knowing that there was an intrusion.   Like a thief breaking into a China shop from a skylight, doable but delicate.

As he gathered details about the layout of the tunnels and caverns in the mountain, what assets the enemy had, and the numbers of their guards, soldiers, and leaders, he conveyed the info to Mitchell and me. Theo was also able to boost the signal range on the damaged droid so that he could get a signal back to Commander Wane. Mitchell decided not to make voice contact back to him because of the risk of giving away her position. But she did record her opinions and sent them with the data in a short burst package.

The decision I had to make was whether or not to formulate a plan to lead an escape or wait for rescue. Once our shift was over and we were led back to the holding area, I discussed what I knew with Captain Palmer. But I couldn't talk about it in the open. Their monitoring devices would include translation functions and possible AI surveillance program listening. But there was a way around that. Basic AIs don't do well with subterfuge unless they are looking for it. So, a way around that is to tell an abstract story in the past tense to code your conversation.

"Captain. Have you ever heard the story of the Lollipop crew and how they got out of the crystal swamp?"

At first, Captain Palmer thought I might have been losing my sanity but then clued in that I needed to tell him something covertly. "Yes, but I would like to hear your version."

Palmer and some of the remaining senior officers gathered around me as I recited the tale. "Their boat had been sunk, and the crew had been trapped under a bridge by a bunch of trolls. But the trolls didn't know that another boat from the land of candy had also sunk, but most of that crew had gotten away. One of them sent in a pet mouse to tell the crew of the lollipop that help would come once they found a way to the candy-cane mountain and inside the taffy caves. But the crew of the Lollipop had to find a way to make the trolls sleep before that happened so they all wouldn't be eaten when the fighting started."

The captain nodded, smiling at how my use of confectionary words was really going to mess with the Serken's translators. He continued the rouge with, "The way I heard the story, the crew of the Lollipop was only able to make maybe half of the trolls sleep, and the rest devoured most of them. And if they had formed a better plan to gain more of an advantage, they might have survived."

"Oh, but the little mouse brought them a gift. A map of the candy cane hills and taffy caverns," I said as I drew a very rough drawing in the dirt of the mountain, tunnels, and caverns as Theo had described it to me. "You see. The trolls had three groups: the little trolls, the medium trolls, and the big trolls. There were only six small trolls in the caves at any given time."

Palmer pointed to the spot where I had indicated small trolls and mouthed the question, 'Guards?' I nodded, and he looked over at his chief medical officer and his tactical officer, who had huddled around us.

"I think I heard that most of them got out alive," The tactical officer said, indicating that he thought we were on to something.

The captain looked over at Dr. Kemp. After a moment, he added, "They knew the sh… caramel was going to hit the fan if they did nothing, so they had no choice but to make as many of the trolls fall to sleep as they could."

The captain thought for a long moment and then asked me, "Commander, have you ever heard the story of the squirrel and the bear?"

"No, Sir. I have not," I answered, and he drew out his plan of action while telling the child-like story.

~~~

Mitchell had scooted herself over to a group of trees that were dense enough to block most of the direct rain. The battle-suit was still able to regulate her body temperature, but she turned it down to the minimum setting to conserve power. Four hours had passed since she had sent Theo's data to Commander Wane. She didn't expect to hear anything back until he had something relevant to tell her, but with each passing moment, the more concerned she became that a reply wasn't coming.

"Major, may I ask you a personal question?" Theo asked.

"Sure, it's not like I have anything better to do right now."

"Which I assumed," he replied, and she couldn't help but smile.

"What's your question?"

"Have you decided on a name for the child Mrs. Reilly is having?"

Puzzled, Mitchell asked, "Why are you asking me?"

"Mrs. Reilly said that she wanted to give you the option first before she picked. As you are the biological mother, that does seem to be appropriate."

Mitchell stared out into the rain, thinking about something that she didn't want to share before she answered. "She is going to be Jack and Kayla's baby. It should be their choice."

"The inflection in your voice would indicate that you do not believe the statement you just made."

Mitchell didn't like being called out as a liar by anyone. Having an AI do it was even more irritating. But it also forced her to face a truth that she was avoiding. She was divided on how much she wanted to be involved in raising her baby. A part of her wanted to share in the experience as an equal parent, but another part was afraid of how painful it would be. It had taken her a very long time to stop mourning the loss of her husband, Roger. To see the child that they created together growing and developing in his image would be a daily reminder of what she had lost. It was selfish, and she felt ashamed for feeling that way. But it was a fear that she could not shake. She then said, "On second thought, I don't think we should be having this conversation, okay?"

"Yes, Major."

Thunder rang out overhead, but Mitchell could tell that it was not natural. It was a sonic boom. Shielding her eyes from the rain, she scooted out a few feet to look up through the trees. High above were fireballs and trails of smoke. Because of how close the group of them was, she knew it wasn't a meteor shower but rather the remnants of a ship burning up in the atmosphere. The Serkens had downed another one.

~~~

A chime rang out in the darkroom that only had starlight to illuminate it. After a moment, the chime sounded again.

Captain Rebecca Tansky rolled over in her bed in her private quarters on the T.S.S. Olympus and called out, "Computer, lights on."

The room lit up, much brighter than she would have liked, but it was effective in helping her to wake up. Throwing off the covers, she stood up and stepped over to the wall, where she had her robe hanging on a hook. It was one of a few pieces of civilian clothing she kept aboard the ship. The incoming call chime sounded again. Tying the belt, she took a moment to make sure she was adequately covered and then said in the middle of the fourth chime, "Answer."

In the middle of the screen was an Image of Max's avatar, a young fleet officer in a lieutenant's uniform from the waist up, as though he was standing in front of a camera rather than an image generated within a computer.

In a stern voice, Tansky said, "Maximilian. I trust this is important."

He rendered a salute and waited for her to return it before speaking. She did, then he answered, "Yes, Captain. The T.S.S. Stratford has not reported in."

Tansky was a little confused as she wasn't aware of the AI being involved with any ship's operations. Stepping over to the wall, she split the screen in half and called up reports on ship deployments and movements in her sector. Stating aloud as she read, "The Stratford was directed to make contact with the Franklin after it failed to report in on time."

"Yes, Captain. And the Stratford should have reported in two hours ago," Max replied.

She read more of the reports and then looked back at him. "The Franklin is currently investigating the possible crash sites of the T.S.S. Macron. Their search area includes three planets and nine moons in a system with extensive interference from surrounding nebulas. Captain Renard gave them permission to report in once every three days rather than once a day to allow for the added travel in and out of the system to send in reports. The fact that they are late in sending in those reports is not something to be concerned about yet. However, regulations did require the fleet commander to send a nearby ship to make contact, which is exactly why Captain Renard sent the Stratford. The fact that they haven't reported in would indicate they are still trying to catch up with the Franklin."

"With all due respect Captain, that protocol is insufficient. When the T.S.S. Franklin failed to report on schedule, I sent programs out to all the ships in this sector with orders to report back to me every 10 minutes. I was made aware by my program on the T.S.S. Stratford that it had been redirected to the Batel system to make contact with the T.S.S. Franklin. I received a burst message from that program that they were about to jump to that system as scheduled. That was the last message I received, and that was 24 hours and 7 minutes ago."

Tansky stared at the neutral face of the AI's avatar image that would look like a real person to anyone else. But she knew exactly what Max was and how, despite his appearance to be totally logical and rational, he could be motivated by his emotions that were still evolving. Yet, like a good officer that he was emulating, Max didn't bring concerns to command without facts to back up his conclusions.

"So, why are you bringing this to me? You could have just as easily sent this message to Captain Renard and made it appear as if it came through official channels."

Max looked at her in the same fashion she had just looked at him, reflecting the appearance of studying one's opponent. Then he answered. "Two reasons. First, unlike my counterpart Sally, I do not feel comfortable with deceptions unless I am ordered to do so by a superior officer and the orders are justifiable. Second, I know you much better than the man who took over your position as Fleet Commander. Although I believe he is a competent leader and a respectful officer, I am uncertain how he would respond to such a report. You, Captain Tansky, are much easier to predict."

Tansky didn't care for being called predictable, and with that ever so slightly raised chin and dagger stare, she showed her irritation. Max then clarified, "Please do not take that as a criticism, Captain. For a computer, being consistent in one's behaviors is a compliment. In other words, I know you and that you will do all you can to act in the best interest of those who need assistance, regardless of regulations or protocols."

Tansky let her eyes shift slightly away from the screen for a moment but showed no other clues of what she was thinking on her face. Then she looked back and cooly said, "I'll look into it."

Max's avatar didn't move or so much as twitch for a long moment. He was hoping for a more active response but knew pressing the matter would not gain him any traction. Finally, he said, "Thank you, Captain. I'll inform you of any additional information as I find it." He then rendered a salute.

Tansky returned the salute, and the screen turned off. Her quarters had three parts to it, a sitting room with a meal prep area, a bedroom, and a private office with two doors. One door led to her living quarters, and the other led to the ship's corridors so that anyone invited there for a meeting wouldn't have to cross through her private living space. She pulled on her uniform pants and coat in the event that she had to make a call before going back to bed. Going to her office, she sat at the desk and called up the mission details for the Franklin and the orders given to the Stratford. At first, she didn't see anything that would raise any serious concerns. There were a hundred reasons a ship would be late in reporting in, and they were usually minor issues. But because traveling through space is still a very dangerous occupation, the regulations are written to err on the side of caution. The Stratford was sent to make contact to confirm there was nothing wrong. Once they locate and make contact with the Franklin, they will report back to the fleet commander. These types of things frequently happen with such large fleets. Yet, something in her gut said to trust the AI's instinct and act sooner rather than later.

"Commander," she said as she pushed the comm button on her desk for the direct line to the CIC."

"Yes, Captain," The executive officer replied.

"Report."

"All is quiet, Captain. All traffic in this area is properly scheduled and accounted for. I was about to have us continue on our patrol to the Kliton system."

"Hold off for now. Coordinate with Station D-102 and send out a fleet-wide alert for any contact with the Franklin and Stratford. If their locations have not been confirmed within the hour, let me know."

"Are we looking at a hostile threat?" her XO asked.

"I doubt that. It is most likely a communication breakdown due to natural events. But they are both overdue, so I want to confirm there is no serious problem rather than assuming it."

"Understood. I'll get right on that."

"Thank you, Commander," she said and turned off the video comm.

Crossing back to the bedroom, she stripped down and got back into bed, but sleep wasn't returning to her. Since the New Terra incident, she was no longer in command of the entire first fleet. But she still felt a responsibility for them all. Peacetime had seemed to make everyone complacent, but she still imagined the worst when facing unknowns. Throwing off the covers, she got up and pulled out fleet-issued workout sweats and put them on.

"Computer. Locate Lt. Jess Rodgers."

"Lt. Jess Rodgers is in her quarters." The computer replied.

"Ring her quarters."

After a moment, her young protege answered. She was sitting at her small desk, studying a flight manual.

"Yes, Captain."

"I'm glad you haven't turned in yet. Are you up for a little hand-to-hand training?"

Jess grinned but quickly put a professional face on and answered, "Yes, Captain."

"Great. Meet me in the gym on deck eight in five minutes."

She turned the comm off and pulled out her personal gel boxing gloves, and headed out for the gym.

~~~

Commander Wane had put a plan together to attack the Serken camp with everything they had. It would take the better part of a day for everyone to make the hike. But once at the perimeter, the plan was to have a small group create a distraction by attacking the north side and then have the real assault happen on the less fortified south side. But they weren't more than a couple of kilometers into their march when they saw the fleet ship burning up overhead. The communicators in their emergency packs all started chirping as they were receiving signals from well over a hundred escape pods falling to the ground. Commander Wane ordered his crew to fan out and track down as many of those pods before the Serken could and then fall back to the stone city.

"Sir?" Lt. Granderson, a junior officer, said to get Commander Wane's attention.

"Yes, Lieutenant?"

"Those pods are going to rain down over a fifty-kilometer area. We'll never find them all on foot, and it will take days to get even the closest survivors back to the city. Shouldn't we use this to our advantage and proceed with the plan?"

The commander looked at him for a moment and then asked, "What department are you in again?"

"Logistics, Sir. Procurements and Distribution of ordnance and fuel," he answered.

"So, your tactical experience is limited to what you learned in the academy?"

Timidly the lieutenant answered, "Yes, Sir."

"That's not an admonishment son. We all have to do rotations in different departments before earning our primary MOS. So, this little side trip is going to be a real learning opportunity for you."

"I guess, Sir."

"If a computer was putting together a simulation to determine our odds of success, it would probably recommend that we use the destruction of the crippled ship to our advantage. Make our assault on the enemy camp when half their forces are out trying to round up the survivors.   But that would mean sacrificing hundreds of people to the horrors of a sadistic enemy. You're too young to know what the Serken do to their prisoners."

"We did see the holorecordings from the war that included some of the labor camps that were liberated."

"You would be surprised at how much they sanitize the videos they show the cadets. They don't want to scare you all off. I was about your age when I was with a team that liberated the camp at Bottona. Of the 12,000 people from the colony that was there a year earlier, less than 300 were still alive. If you saw the looks in their eyes, you would understand that they were not the lucky ones." Wane stepped up to the younger man, took hold of his wrist that was holding his PC, and pointed to one of the signals on it. "Bottom line, son, we don't leave anyone to the care of the Serken if we can help it. Now move out."

"Yes, Sir."

~~~

Mitchell had gotten the message from Commander Wane that they were calling off the offensive to locate as many of the crew from the downed ship as they could. That left her alone just yards from the edge of the Serken camp with no backup coming. With escape pods raining down in all directions, the enemy would be sending out every soldier they could spare to capture or kill the survivors. She was in no position to confront a group of armed lizard men.

"Theo, can you freeze up the knee joint on my injured leg?"

"You wish to use the exoskeleton in the right leg as a splint to help support your leg?"

"Exactly."

"Yes, but I do not believe it will achieve the desired effect. The portion that is part of your inner suit is designed primarily for power assist. The external portion that was removed is what reinforces the suit and assists with the added weight. So, I can lock up the joins in the knee so that you cannot bend it, but it will have no effect in supporting your weight if you decide to stand on it."

"Got it," she said and then grabbed one of the packs that she had used to carry the droids in. She then used the six-inch knife that she kept on her boot and ripped them into strips. Once she had three good ones, she tied them around her knee to provide some support. It was still throbbing in pain, but she couldn't risk taking any more painkiller meds if she was going to get up and move around.

The rain had let up to a light drizzle, which helped to see her surroundings better. Moving deeper into the forest, away from the enemy camp, seemed to be her best option. Grabbing the large stick that she had tried to use before, she pulled herself up to her feet, putting all her weight on the good leg. Slowly she put the large stick a couple of feet ahead of her and then hopped forward to it. She did that again, successfully moving another couple of feet.

The sound of something moving came from behind her. Dropping the stick, she drew her laser pistol and twisted around. On the ground was the damaged repair droid following her like a sick crab. It looked up at her, and Theo's voice came from it.

"This droid does have some operational tools that could be of use to you, and since you are not able to move faster than its own capacity, you won't have to wait for it or carry it."

She opened her mouth to reply but didn't as she was breathing heavily, and her heart felt odd like it was working too hard. Her head started to swim, and she had to close her eyes as her vision got jumpy.

"The damn first-aid system must have overmedicated me," she said, trying not to lose her balance.

"The dosage was correct," Theo said as he still had full access to everything in her suit. "You just need to not over-assert yourself. The feeling of disorientation should pass in the next two to four minutes."

Mitchell took a moment to get a hold of her breathing and focus but stayed on her feet. She put the pistol back in her hip holster and slowly bent down on her good leg to pick up the walking stick.

"Okay," she said, still feeling a little breathless. The droid's scanner could be useful. It can come but keep it quiet."

"I'll do my best," Theo said as the droid moved to catch up with Mitchell.

She began her trek again, one hop and step at a time.

~~~

Theo got a message to me that help was not coming anytime soon and that it appeared another Alliance ship was down. I passed the word on to Captain Palmer, who got the update around to the rest of his crew in the subtle network they had created over their time there. It was hard not to feel defeated at that point, but I refused to give up. These Serken appeared to have no idea that the war was long over and the rest of their people were gone. Sharing that knowledge with them wouldn't help us out at all. Once Serkens learn that they have no hope, their tradition is to kill themselves and take as many of their enemies with them as they can. And now that they have brought down another fleet ship, the next response would be to send multiple ships. Once a full-on assault happens, and their end definite, we needed to be somewhere else. I needed to find a way out.

Theo's intel was helpful. I had a better idea of the layout of the base and the numbers of the enemy. We had planned on waiting for the ground assault from Commander Wane and the Franklin's crew to draw out most of the soldiers and guards, leaving a limited number for us to attack and neutralize. Then we would make a run for the south tunnel and sprint for the woods. It wasn't a great plan. We would be lucky if half of us made it out alive. But staying would be a death sentence for all of us, and that had not changed.

'Cold,' I suddenly thought. The Serken were all wearing their battle suits. The soldiers and non-soldiers alike were all in suits that kept them sealed up in a controlled environment. Outside, where it's cold and wet, that would make sense, but in the mines, it was hot and dry, which was perfect for them, yet they all kept their suits on and sealed. That meant there must be something in the environment that they cannot tolerate or maybe even survive. We didn't know much about the tech involved in their suits, but we did know they had a basic communication system and at least enough of a computer to control the environmental functions. That might be enough.

I laid down on the small pad made up of old uniform fabric and dried grass and rolled onto my side like I was going to sleep. Putting my arm over my head like I was trying to block out the light, I hoped I was significantly hidden from the sensors to have a conversation.

"Theo," I whispered.

"Yes, Sir," he replied in my earbud.

"Is there any chance you can get into all the Serkens' suits and turn the temperature down to the point that would incapacitate them?"

"No, Sir," he replied. "Their systems are not large enough to hold even a basic form of my program, and they have several firewalls to prevent such tampering. However, I can create a worm program that can work its way in and initiate the desired effect at a given time."

"How long would it take to infect all of the Serken?"

"Approximately three hours and twelve minutes. However, there is a slight chance that my worm would be detected by a suit's security system, as it effectively has to rewrite the Serken programs as it works its way in. Because their suits are networked with a central monitoring system, infecting them all would reduce the odds of not being detected down to 34 percent. I would recommend limiting the intrusion to just the guards and administration in this part of the complex. That would give my program a 72 percent chance of success."

That was a tough call. If I had him override the temperature controls in the suits of all the Serkens, and they stayed unaware until it was happening, we could all make a run for it and be away before any of the cold-blooded aliens could recover. But if they discovered the tampering before it could affect them, they would be able to counter it and any future attempts by Theo at getting into their systems. And they would know we were getting help from outside. Theo's recommendation wasn't much better. If he successfully neutralized the guards and immediate staff, we could get to the outside, but then we would have to outrun several armed enemy soldiers that would be relentless in hunting us down.

I thought for a moment, trying to come up with a third option. "You said there was a central monitoring system for them. What is that exactly?"

"It's part of the surveillance system for the complex. In addition to keeping watch on all the human prisoners, it monitors the health of all the Serkens. It's not detailed, just heart rate, temperature, and hydration. It cannot identify any illnesses or health concerns, just the basic condition of being alive."

"Interesting. I've never heard of them being that concerned about their individuals like that," I whispered, more to myself thinking out loud, but Theo still answered.

"Digitalis Glycosides. A toxic element found in certain types of flowers. It's poisonous to humans if ingested, but to the Serken, it is much more fatal. Breathing in pollen with just trace amounts of the toxin can cause a very painful death. This moon has at least five

213

varieties of flora that produce this toxin. That is why they do not remove their suits unless they are in a sealed space with purified air."

"Okay," I said, feeling a spark of hope. "How can we use that to our advantage?"

"I do not know, Sir."

Thinking, I walked through how the situation put limits on our jailors. I then whispered, "I haven't seen anything that would indicate an air-filtration system. Do they have those spaces in another part of the mountain?"

"No, Sir. But they do have 39 ships on the ground on the east side of this installation. From the logistics data I was able to collect from their computers, they are running their environmental systems on battery power and solar collectors. They do not have any fuel for other operations."

"They are living in their ships."

"Yes, Sir."

"So, if they were to suddenly all believe that their suits were compromised, they would all run for the only shelters they have. A bunch of starships that can't fire weapons or fly. Do you think you could trick their systems into making them all think their suits are failing?"

"I believe so, but I will need to run some simulations," Theo said, and then three seconds later said, "The simulations indicate your plan has a 92 percent chance of convincing the Serken that they need to seek shelter. But the deception may not last longer than two or three minutes as it will trigger an immediate diagnostic from their control system. You will need to get everyone out of the mountain and out of immediate sight in that time window. And that is assuming they don't have a backup plan to contain you in such an eventuality."

"The Serken are not known for contingency planning. They are a much more reactionary species. But your point is well taken. If we had more time or assets, I would try to come up with something better. We'll just have to take the chance."

Theo and I worked out some more of the details, and I communicated my idea to Captain Palmer. He agreed that waiting for the fleet to arrive would be a bigger risk than making a break for it now and suggested the best time to do it would be during the next shift change when all of his crew would be in motion. We passed the word, and Theo went to work preparing to spoof the Serkens computer systems.

Chapter 18

Plan of Action

A slowly increasing sound of windchimes gently woke Kayla up. Her eyes opened to warm sunlight filling the room through the sheer drapes. Movement near the side of the bed caught her attention, and she looked over to see one of the service droids approaching, holding a tray with a glass of orange juice on it.

"Good morning, Kayla," Becky's voice came from it.

"Good morning, Becky. I thought Max had you working on a project?"

"He did, but asked me to return to look after you," the female A.I. answered as she placed the tray on the nightstand. I would have let you sleep, but there is a man on your back porch. Comparing him to data from Max's and Theo's archives, there is a 98 percent likelihood that the man is Jack Reilly Sr, but I cannot be sure since I have not met him before. Therefore, I thought I should wake you and confirm with you before I alert the authorities of an intruder."

Kayla slowly worked herself up, first sitting up, then getting her legs off the side of the bed. "I'm sure it's Dad. There is no need to overreact," she said as she grabbed the edge of the nightstand for support to pull herself up. Putting her robe on over her nightgown, she walked through the house to the back porch.

Jack Sr. was sitting in one of the patio chairs, carving a figurine of a deer with a pocketknife and a small piece of wood.

"Dad?" Kayla asked as she opened the door and walked out.

He looked back at her and smiled, "There you are. I was wondering if you were going to sleep the whole morning away."

"Don't take this the wrong way; I'm thrilled to see you," she said as she walked up and gave him a kiss on the cheek and a hug around the shoulders, "But what are you doing here?"

"I convinced Rachel to let me spend some time alone with you. We rented a car, dropped her off at a market, and Danny dropped me off here. He's down the street at a coffee house if I need him." Dad then held up the figurine that was almost done. "What do you think?"

"It's beautiful. A deer, right?"

"Yep. You ever seen one before?"

"Just in movies," she said as she took a seat in one of the other chairs.

"I'm making it for your daughter. I made one for Carol when she was little, and it was one of her favorite toys. No matter how fancy things get, kids will always go with the toys that let them use their imagination."

"That's wonderful. Thank you."

"It's not quite finished yet. I still need to smooth out the rough spots and paint it. I trust Jack has a workshop here?"

"Oh yes."

"I knew he would. I'll make sure to have it done before we head back to Earth." He shaved off a sliver with his pocketknife and then said, "There is something more I wanted to talk to you about."

Kayla turned in her seat to give him her full attention, but Dad's focus seemed to be more on his carving, and a long moment passed. She sat there watching him work on the toy and waited for him to start the conversation but then wondered if he had forgotten that he had something to say. Another minute went by, and she was certain that he was having an episode of dementia. She was about to get up to retrieve her PC so that she could call Dad's nurse when he started to talk.

"Jack was born with a defect in his heart. The doctors were able to make some corrections, once before he was born and twice during his first year of life. We thought everything was good, but they still wanted him to come in every year for a full scan and evaluation because as he grew, they wanted to make sure the fix grew with him."

Dad glanced over at Kayla to see that he had her full attention. Her eyes were glued to him, and he gave a satisfied nod and looked back at the toy. As he worked on it, he continued. "With each year, everything looked fine, and they told us there was nothing to worry about. Then one day, when he was five, he was out in the yard, running around and chasing something. His mother called him into the house for lunch, and when he ran in, he appeared not to be able to catch his breath. He then turned as white as a sheet and fell over. His mother screamed, and when I came running in, she was on the ground, holding him, trying to get him to wake up. I grabbed him, we ran to the car and flew to the hospital as fast as my car could go, his mother giving him mouth-to-mouth the whole way.

The doctors said if we had gotten there a minute later, there would have been no saving him. They operated, put in a temporary artificial heart, and harvested cells from his defective heart to grow a new one. It took weeks of genetic manipulation to grow one that didn't have the defect."

Kayla smiled and said, "As much as I wish I could have had a baby made from our own genetic material, this baby is an adopted embryo, so we don't need to worry about passing on any defects."

Dad shook his head and, in his gruff tone, said, "I know all of that. That is not the point of the story. Now listen."

"I'm sorry," she meekly answered like she had just been scolded.

He sighed, realizing he had snapped at her like she was a child. Trying to correct himself, he gave her a reassuring smile. Then in a more gentle voice, continued his story. "After four months in the hospital, Jack was able to return home, and we worked hard to make everything feel normal. But it wasn't. Kids can be very resilient, and when you give them the opportunity to let things go back to the way they were, kids happily go with the flow. It was his mother who had changed. Holding her little boy's lifeless body in her arms and then getting him back planted a fear inside of her that she never got past. She got overprotective and practically smothered the boy. In hindsight, I think that fed into his need for independence." Dad blew some stray filings off his figure and continued. "I took a different approach. Feeling he needed to be stronger and less dependent on us, I pushed him to do more. I encouraged him to do different sports, scouts, and cars. Anything to encourage him to think for himself and find the solutions to life on his own. As much as I disagreed with his mother's approach, mine was probably worse. In the end, he couldn't wait to leave home and remove himself from our family."

Kayla reached over and put her hand on Dad's arm, "You know that he doesn't feel that way anymore."

Dad glanced back at her, returning the smile. "Yes. I'm very grateful that he and I can see eye to eye. I respect the man he has become and the woman that he is starting a family with. And I know you both will be great parents. My point is that his mother and I would have done a better job of keeping Jack a part of our family if we had discussed our approach rather than always arguing about it. That was mostly my fault. If we had found a middle ground where she wasn't so smothering and I wasn't so tough, I think things would have turned out differently. I wanted to share that with you in the hopes of maybe sparing you from the same kind of mistakes. No matter how stubborn or closed off Jack might get, and as my son, he will. You need to force him to share in the responsibility and remind him that parenting is a team sport."

The sun started to get higher over the trees, and the floating sunshade moved into position to keep it off their faces. A reminder that at least one of the AIs was looking out for them. Kayla sat back and smiled, a feeling of contentment washing over her. Just having someone as strong and commanding as Dad talking about her and me raising a family together as if it was a foregone conclusion made her worries about being alone evaporate with the morning light.

"Thank you for sharing that," she said. "I'm really glad you're here."

"Me too," he said as he was trying to get a small knot out of the wood. "I don't suppose Jack has any sandpaper in his workshop."

"I don't know. I'm sure he has something you could use. Come with me, and I'll show you where it is."

~~~

It was hard to judge time while inside the mountain. The shift change was one of the only clear indicators that nine hours had passed, and it was the best way to time out a coordinated attempt to escape. The guards came into our holding area, and with the cue, we all lined up and waited for their grunts from them to tell us to move.

I had only been there a couple of days but was already very familiar with the routine. Once we were lined up, our guards waited for a signal. Presumably that the other groups of humans were lined up and on their way back to where we were leaving. This was to keep all of us under control, but I was using it in our favor.

The march began, and Theo started his countdown. His worm would make its way into all the Serken's suits and trigger the fake alarm making them all think they were being exposed to the outside air. Our walk from the holding area to the mine was just under two minutes, and the worm would take just over one. As we passed the first bend, Palmer suddenly looked concerned.

"Where is Lt. Bridges?" he whispered to the officer who was next to him.

"They came and grabbed her a few hours ago. But she usually comes back a lot sooner. I assumed she was."

"I don't see her," Palmer said. He tried to look around, but one of the guards stepped up and threatened him with the butt of his rifle.

We passed the second bend, and right on time, the computer worm activated. Muffled alarms sounded from inside all the guard's suits. Some ran, and others tried to check the reading on a screen attached to their wrists. Yet, they didn't stand around for more than a couple of seconds as they were all convinced they were going to die if they didn't get into the safety of their ships.

Palmer waited for all of the guards to be out of sight, counted to ten to make sure they were clear of the tunnel, and then yelled, "Go!" Everyone ran as hard as they could for the surface level. I started that way too, but as we got to the main section that led towards the

220

opening at the base of the mountain, Palmer turned and headed back into a tunnel that moved upwards.

"Captain!" I called out, and Dr. Kemp stopped and turned back in my direction.

"Captain!" Kemp called out as he saw Palmer disappear into the smaller tunnel.

We both ran after him.

"What the hell does he think he's doing?" I asked.

"Going after Bridges. They usually take her up to the transmitter to work on it. Palmer won't leave anyone behind."

"That's got to be half a mile up, at least," I said, already feeling out of breath. We'll never make it up and back down before their suits reset."

"You go," the doctor said as he kept running.

I stayed on his heels as we ran up the steep tube carved in the rock that zigzagged up the inside of the mountain.

"I'm all in now," I said and then pushed my earbud in my ear. "Theo, can you buy us any more time?"

"Maybe, Sir," he said.

While we continued to run up the tunnel, Theo took control of all the repair droids in the Serken camp. There were over 300. Most were already near the airfield where all the ships were parked. Theo waited a few moments as the last of the Serken ran aboard their ships and sealed themselves in. He then had the droids descend on each of the crafts and proceeded to spot-weld the doors, trapping the Serken inside of their ships, just as they realized that the environmental alarms on their suits were all malfunctioning.

"I've prevented the enemy from exiting their ships for at least two more minutes, Sir," Theo said in my ear. I am working on a plan to get you more time, but I cannot guarantee success."

"Understood," I said as we turned a bend and found Captain Palmer carrying Lt. Bridges. She had been beaten again and was barely lucid.

"With me," he said as he jogged past us, moving as fast as he could down the sloped tunnel.

We followed and made it down to the bottom in half the time.

The Serken were forcing their way out of their ships, mostly using their blasters and rifles, willing to inflict damage rather than being trapped.

Theo's second plan then went into action. He had directed several of the droids over to two laser cannons that were staged between the airfield and the mountain. The bots themselves were too small to reach the controls, but when three of them stacked themselves on top of each other, the top one could. Targeting the Serken craft that was first to get their rear hatches open, the cannons fired at the feet of the first Serken to emerge. They quickly turned back and took cover inside their ships.

At the same time, the four of us were running out of the south side of the mountain. The Serken was able to power up one of their ships enough to fire at and destroy the laser cannons, but by then, we were gone.

Chapter 19

On The Run

Theo had kept Mitchell informed of our prison break from the moment we started planning it. Having a few hours before the attempt, she made her way up a hill until she got high enough to see the enemy base from a distance. She was nearly a kilometer away and found a spot inside a large bush where she was able to carve out an opening in it with the knife. It was just deep enough to provide some protection from the rain while still giving her an unobstructed view of the Serken mountain. She made herself as comfortable as she could and closed her eyes as she waited, trying not to think of all the things that could go wrong and how little she could do to help.

"30 seconds until the computer worm activates," Theo said.

"Good," she replied, opening her eyes and holding up her PC before her. It projected an image that magnified the view by a factor of 30.

"Ten seconds," Theo said, and she watched and prayed this worked.

"Deception program activated," Theo said, and then after a moment, added, "Confirmation, all the Serken suits were affected."

Once the action started, there wasn't much to see. A few Serken ran into their ships. But after a moment, several came streaming out of the mountain and up the ramps into their ships. There was a long moment where everything was quiet and still. Mitchell held her breath, praying that the next thing that happened wouldn't be the enemy discovering the deception and emerging from their ships. But fortunately, the next sign of movement that she saw was the prisoners made up of both Macron's crew and the civilian population of humans who covered themselves in clay and furs. They all stayed together as they ran from the opening in the mountain, into the woods and out of sight.

"Theo, can you track Reilly?" Mitchell asked.

"He's still in the mountain."

"What?"

"Captain Palmer has apparently gone after Lt. Donna Bridges, one of his engineers who the Serken have been using to maintain their transmitter. Lt. Commander Reilly and Dr. Kemp have decided to assist in the effort."

"Damn it," she said as she got to her feet, hoping to get a better view. "Those Serken are going to figure out there's nothing wrong with their suits any time now. Is there anything you can do to delay them from coming out of their ships?"

"The Commander has already asked me for the same thing, and I am making an attempt now."

She zoomed in on the magnified view from her PC on the airfield and saw the swarm of droids crawling over the ships and sparks flying as they attempted to weld the doors.

"That's not going to be enough," she said. Scanning the field, she saw the two laser cannon emplacements. "Theo, do you see what I'm seeing?"

"The laser cannons. Yes."

"Can you get access to them?" she asked.

"I do believe that I can use the droids to operate them. However, that does go against my belief that killing is wrong."

Mitchell had mixed feelings about that response. She had no problem striking down any enemy soldier when it was 'kill or be killed.' But she also didn't want to give an AI rationale to kill. "Then don't. Just scare them."

"That I can do."

She watched as the hatches on three of the ships opened, and the ramps dropped. The Serken's started down the ramp, only to run back inside when their own laser cannons fired at their feet.

Theo then reported, "Commander Reilly, Captain Palmer, Dr. Kemp, and Lt. Bridges have exited the mountain and are heading south by southeast through the woods."

"Okay," she said, reaching down and picking up her walking stick. "Once they are reasonably out of danger, point them in my direction. I'll try and get as much distance towards them as I can." She then started walking, one step at a time, still unable to put any weight on her right knee.

~~~

Tansky was in her office that was right off of the Command Information Center of the T.S.S. Olympus. It was a simple workspace. She had a desk, one chair on the back side for her, and two in front for when she had meetings. There were also three large screen monitors on the walls that doubled as windows to the outside when not in use. The feeling was rather sterile as there were no personal items in the room. The few things she did have aboard of that nature were kept in the office in her quarters. To her, this space was for fleet business only and should reflect that impression.

She typed on a virtual keyboard projected on her desk and followed the words on a projected screen. A buzz from the desk told her that someone wanted her attention, and a symbol projected next to her screen indicated that it was the officer at the communication station in the CIC.

"Yes," she said aloud.

"Captain Renard is requesting to speak with you, Captain."

"Thank you. Put him through."

"Ten months and three days," Renard said the moment his image replaced the text on her screen.

Tansky reached up, made a grabbing motion over the projection, and pushed it over to one of the screens on the wall. That allowed her to stand while they were speaking as she sensed this call was going to be less than social. Crossing her arms, she replied, "What is that in reference to?"

"How long it would take for you to want the job of Fleet Commander back."

"Excuse me?" she said in a regal tone suggesting the comment was beneath her.

Renard chuckled, knowing that would be exactly how she would respond. "So, I guess your inquiries about the Stratford and the Franklin are just because you wanted to check my work?"

"I would never go behind your...."

"I know you wouldn't," he said, cutting her off and then adding, "Unless you had a good reason." He then leaned in a little and said, "So, what is that reason?"

She didn't like being treated like a junior officer to anyone, and the fact that he was once under her as her XO on her first command made it that much worse. But they were friends, and he was asking her directly when others in his position would treat the conversation as more of a corrective action.

Tansky uncrossed her arms but kept the serious expression on her face that was a default for her. "I had some intelligence that both ships might be in trouble. But my source wasn't exactly through official channels, and I didn't know how reliable the information was. So, I wanted to look into it myself before sounding any alarms."

Renard thought for a moment before speaking. If anyone in his command had presented him with that, he would not have taken it as an acceptable answer. He would demand to know where the intel came from and reprimand the officer for withholding critical information. But Tansky was a starship captain. No one reaches that level unless they have the intelligence to know when to take the initiative. He also knew that she would not withhold the name of a source unless it were critical to do so. Looking over at something on his desk, he confirmed some information and then looked back.

"There have been some rumors of a new criminal organization flexing its muscles in this sector. We have yet to confirm any actual pirate activity, but the fact that we now have two ships that are overdue makes me think we should react with a little overkill. It's probably nothing. But if there is someone out there bold enough to go after any of our ships, well, I want to put the fear of God into them. Have the Olympus meet up with the Cyprus at these coordinates. We'll go into the Batel system together and conduct the search with both ships."

"Very good, Captain."

"And Rebecca. Before you keep me out of the loop again, think about how you would have reacted when you had this post."

Her stern posture melted slightly, and she answered, "Yes, Captain," and offered a salute.

"He returned it and turned off the comm."

Tansky thought about the point he had made about her demotion. She had no regrets, as her actions were necessary. But until that moment, she hadn't considered just how much of her identity was wrapped up in her position. Her next step up would be to admiral, which would mean a desk post. A duty she would perform with pride, but not one that she aspired to. Being the field commander of the first fleet was an equivalent position, but still involved in the actual operations. It wasn't the power or status that she liked, but the control. After a career navigating the politics of superiors who had to be convinced that they needed to change, or at least modify, their orders before things went wrong, it was easier to be the one to give the top orders. She rarely doubted any of her decisions, and when she wasn't 100 percent confident, she knew whom to confide in for guidance.

Last year, when she was put on trial, her actions were deemed justified and appropriate, except for her failure to communicate with fleet command. The assumption was that they would have supported her, and she took too big of a risk on her own. However, at the time, she concluded that informing command of her plans would have tipped off Sally, the AI who was trying to manipulate the Alliance into destroying itself. It was a calculated risk, and she understood the consequences, but the alternative was unthinkable.

In the end, the Alliance and our way of life were saved, but she was demoted from Fleet Commander back down to Starship Captain. At first, she thought she got off lucky as she had kept her command of the Olympus and didn't have to deal with the extra duty anymore. But it left a hole in her ego that she was truly starting to feel.

~~~

It was nearing dusk when we met up with Mitchell. The rain had actually stopped for a short reprieve, but the clouds were still thick, limiting the thinning daylight. I picked up Mitchell in a piggyback style as walking had become nearly impossible for her at that point. The five of us continued for another half hour or so until it became too dark to continue.

Finding a natural stone outcropping that was mostly blocked from view by long grasses, vines, and trees, we decided to take cover there for the night. Captain Palmer and I collected some wood for a fire while the doctor checked on Bridges and Mitchell. All the wood was pretty damp, but I used Mitchell's laser pistol to splice the pieces open and get the flames started from the dryer cores.

Once that was going, we all sat around it, trying to warm up. Mitchell was the only one who wasn't trying to get close to the flames. Her suit was still regulating her body heat, so she was more content to be leaning up against the wall of the half cave.

"Reilly, come here," she said.

I stepped over and sat down by her. She took my hands and sandwiched them between hers. She had turned the heater up in her gloves and warmed my hands up quickly.

"Better?" she asked.

"Oh, yeah. Thanks."

"So, what happened to not sticking your head in the lion's mouth?" she asked, referring to our conversation a few days ago, where I agreed not to take any unnecessary risks.

"I do tend to be a crap magnet, don't I."

"That's an understatement," she said and then reached down to rub her knee. "The good news is I didn't see anyone get killed from the group that ran out of the mountain."

"How many did you see?" Captain Palmer asked.

She pulled out her PC that recorded what she had viewed from her hillside vantage point earlier that day. "The computer counted 429 humans. But from a distance, it couldn't discern between the locals and your crew."

"That sounds like most of us. The Rotock, that's what the people who live here call themselves; they will make a b-line for their home. My people will be smart enough to stay hidden. I just hope you're right about the fleet sending more ships soon. Without food or shelter, I can't imagine everyone surviving too long."

"The Rotock's home. Is it a city built out of stones?" Mitchell asked.

"Yes."

"Well, that's a problem. We've been using that city as a base of operations. Commander Wane is having his people track down as many of the survivors from the other ship that was just downed, and they will be converging back at that city. And now the Serken will be looking for their slave labor. Since that was where the locals were first found, you know that is going to be the first place they look."

Theo then spoke in our earbuds so that only Mitchell and I could hear him. "I've tried to get a message to Commander Wane, but I have not been able to reach him as of yet."

Mitchell and I shared a look, and then she continued voicing her concerns to the others. "I'll keep trying to reach Commander Wane and give him an update on the situation. But unless we can come up with a way to prevent the Serken from sending out search parties to hunt us down, we're all going to be in real trouble."

"Well, we don't have many options," Palmer said as he put another chunk of wood on the fire. "The stone city is at least another day's walk for those of us who can; if we move in that direction, we are more likely to cross paths with them. But I don't care to just lay low while my people are getting hunted, so if you have any suggestions, I'm all ears."

"We have to go on the offensive," Mitchell said.

"How the hell do we do that?" Dr. Kemp asked, not hiding how crazy he thought that sounded.

Mitchell looked at me to see if I was going to offer up any ideas, but I just gave a slight shake of my head. She looked back at them and confidently answered, "We have the opportunity to turn the tables on them. We know that they are alone out here, running low on supplies and unable to breathe the air. The transport they were using was the last ship that had any fuel, and it's gone. We haven't seen any land vehicles. The closest we saw to that was the floating platforms, and we took those out. So, when they come for us, it will be on foot, and they will have to be conservative with their power supply."

The doctor huffed, "And how does that help us? You expect the five of us to sharpen some sticks or maybe fashion some bows and arrows?"

"Why not?" Palmer said, looking at the doctor. "If we get the high ground and can see them coming, we can jump them. If it's a small enough group, we can inflict some damage and then disappear into the bush. They will call for help and start hunting us. The more of them that are looking for our little group, the fewer that will be going after the rest of our people. We only have to do it until the reinforcements come. And if we die saving just a few of our crew, it will be worth it."

Kemp shook his head and said, "Lt. Bridges is in and out of consciousness, and the Major here has a bum leg. That leaves the three of us to take on teams of Serken that never travel in groups smaller than five. I don't see a good outcome any way you slice it."

Palmer's face went from resolved to slightly defeated as he saw the doctor's point. "You're right. There is no way the three of us could do anything significant enough to make a difference. We would just be falling on our own swords."

"They run into the fire," I said, thinking out loud.

"What's that, Commander?" Palmer asked.

"It's something the Major once told me. The Serken pride themselves on running at the attack and not away from it."

"Okay. Where are you going with this?"

I looked at Mitchell and asked. "Didn't you tell me that you set the charges at the transmitter but didn't set them off?"

"Yes," she said, sitting up, seeing where I was going with the idea. "I didn't set them off before because we didn't want to risk any prisoners getting hurt, but now that's not a problem."

"And if we set it off, all the enemy search parties will see it and come running back to their base," I said, then asked, "How close would we have to get?"

She knew the answer off the top of her head and the problem with it as she said to all of us, "The signal has to come from my suit. No more than 500 yards."

"If you set those charges at the top of the mountain, you would have to be within the perimeter of the base to be that close," Palmer pointed out.

Mitchell's face was neutral, and she was resolved to do what needed to be done despite the risk. But then I had a thought. Tilting my head into her view I said, "Unless you relay the signal with the droid you sent in as a spy."

Mitchell glanced away for a moment as she thought about that, and then Theo responded in our earbuds. "I do still have access to the repair droid we sent into the base and can move it into position to relay the detonation signal."

Mitchell looked back at me with a smile and said, "That will work."

"Now we just need to make our way back without getting caught," I said, and everyone looked a little sick.

Parker picked up the laser pistol and asked Mitchell, "How many more clips do you have for this?"

231

"I had to travel light. Just what's loaded in it now."

"Right," he said as he checked the power level. "Everyone try and get some sleep. I'll take the first watch. Commander, you and I will trade off every two hours. The doc will be taking care of the ladies between his naps."

"Aye, Sir," I said.

Palmer moved to the edge of the overhang where he could best see out and kept the pistol in his hand. The doctor laid down next to Bridges with his head propped up on one of his arms. They had gotten used to sleeping on the ground, but it was still a difficult prospect for me.

Mitchell could see that I wasn't sure how I was going to get comfortable. She pulled herself up a little closer to the wall to support her back and then said, "Put your head on my lap."

"Excuse me?"

"That wasn't a request. I need you to get some rest because you'll be carrying me again in the morning. Now follow my orders."

I positioned myself so that my head was on her legs, looking down at her feet. With her suit giving off heat and the padding, it was the most comfortable I had been in days. But I still had a hard time turning my brain off. There were any number of things that could go wrong with this idea, and our survival was going to depend on how soon the fleet would get around to sending another ship with some real firepower. The odds were not good, and I felt worse the more I thought about it. Suddenly I felt something on my head. It was Mitchell's hand. She had removed her gloves and was gently running her fingers through my hair in a petting motion. Not something either of us commonly did to each other, and we never did something so personal in front of others. But at that moment, I didn't care. It made me feel safe and cared for. Within a minute, I was sound asleep.

~~~

Kayla walked into the community education center. She had been taking college classes on the net for the past year and needed to meet with an advisor if she wanted to declare a major and plan out the curriculum beyond general studies. The university she was attending was virtual and didn't have a campus in New Harmony. That was what the education center was for. In addition to providing basic college courses, adult learning programs, and certification programs for various trades, it also provided office space for some of the schools that provided full degrees for remote learners.

The building was a classic design, with curved walls that were mostly translucent. Some of the rooms, like the office spaces, still had glass but were frosted for privacy. Moving art was hovering under the high ceilings, and people from all walks of life were taking advantage of the public space. Some were sitting at small desks studying or filling out data forms, while others were conversing in sitting areas or crossing through the space on their way somewhere.

Kayla was a little early for her meeting with her new advisor, so she walked out to explore the place. Near the center was a daycare center full of about a dozen small children. She couldn't help but stand there and watch as they played. One little girl fell while she was running after a little boy. The play area was well-padded, so she wasn't hurt, but she cried just the same. A young woman who was apparently one of the teachers was there in two heartbeats, on her knees and consoling the little girl. With a couple of kisses on her hands and a hug, the girl was happy and went after the little boy again.

"Kayla," A tall man with an accent that was almost lyrical said from behind her.

She turned to see Mr. Hasni, the counselor she was meeting.

"Yes," she said and stepped up and offered her hand. "It's a pleasure to meet you."

He shook her hand and then said with a professional charm, "The pleasure is mine. Please, follow me."

They went back to his office, which was just down a short hallway off the main public area. His little office was decorated with video projections of the campuses of the three different universities that he represented. Every minute or so, the images would change into views from other parts of the schools. The furnishing was basic, a table, two chairs, and a stack of data pads.

Mr. Hasni pulled out the guest chair for Kayla and then took his seat on the other side.

"Well, it's a pleasure to finally meet with you, Kayla. Your grades are outstanding, and your testing has qualified you to enter any undergraduate program you would like. These conversations are a lot more uncomfortable when I have to tell a student that they can't get into the programs that they have their hearts set on. So, do you know which degree you would like to pursue?"

"I had been considering business management, but now I'm not sure. I'm already managing a restaurant, and there really isn't anywhere for me to advance up to unless I want to open my own place."

"Is that what you want to do?"

"I don't know, maybe. It would be good to know more about what's involved in starting a business, but right now, I'm doing all the books, ordering all the supplies and inventory, hiring, running the day-to-day, and even working with contractors who are rebuilding the patio. I can't imagine there is much more to learn."

"There is always more to learn," Hansi said as he called up a screen on his pad about the business management program and handed it to her. "The question is, is that what you want to spend your career doing?"

"Do you think I should do something different?"

He leaned back and looked at her with a knowing smile. "You just don't seem that excited about the opportunity."

"Oh, I am," she insisted, feeling like she was about to lose the chance to go to school.

"I can see that you are eager to get an education. But before you commit to the next three years of study, it should be something that is worth your time. If owning a business is your passion, then this is a wonderful program. It covers everything from how to apply for grants and loans to managing employee benefits. But the education you get should be a springboard for the life you want to live. I've had too many students come to me halfway through, asking to change their degree program or just quit altogether. And frankly, you are getting a later start than most of my students. Don't get me wrong. I think you should pursue a degree because I know you will excel in anything that you do. I just want you to be sure that it's the path you want to be on."

Kayla made a face as if she had just bitten down on something bitter.

"I'm sorry, Kayla. I didn't mean to upset you. I was just trying to be honest."

"No, it's not that," she said as she started to double over. "I think I'm having a contraction."

"Have you been having them this whole time?"

"No, Just now," she said through gritted teeth.

He got up and walked around the table to help her. "I don't think that is right. My wife and I have three children, and she always felt mild contractions long before the big ones."

"I think my water broke," she said, taking his hand and standing up. When she looked back down, she saw blood running down her leg.

"I know that's not right," he said as he pulled out his PC from his pocket and spoke, "Emergency call. We need an ambulance at the central learning complex, building 2."

"We are dispatching EMTs now. Please state the nature of the emergency," a computer voice stated.

"We have a woman in labor, and she is bleeding from her… she's bleeding; please hurry."

Kayla started to cry, knowing something was very wrong. Her knees started to buckle, and Mr. Hasni held her hand, helping her down to the floor. She knelt on her knees and held her belly.

A siren could be heard in the distance. Kayla felt another sharp pain and did her breathing to try and work through it, but it was hard to do so through her panic sobs.

"Max!" she screamed.

"Perhaps you should lay down," Mr. Hasni said, still holding her hand for support.

She shook her head and tried to breathe, but at that point, she was gasping. "Max! Becky! Please, please... help me." She got lightheaded and started to fall over. Mr. Hasni kept her from falling on her face and gently lowered her onto her side. "Jack. Where are you," she sobbed and then passed out.

~~~

The next morning Captain Palmer, Mitchell, and I headed out. We decided to leave the Doctor and Bridges at the outcropping as she was still dealing with a concussion and was having problems with her balance. We had to bring Mitchell because the controls for the bombs were integrated into her suit, and that had a security bio-lock which meant only she could use the internal computer.

Palmer and I took turns carrying her on our backs as we made the trek back toward the Serken base. It took the bulk of the day, and the rain had returned. Mitchell directed us to the hill where she had a view during our escape. It should be a good spot to get eyes on the mountain without being seen by the enemy.

"Theo, is the droid in position?" I typed into the PC.

"Not yet. The droid needs to ascend the mountain another 30 yards to get a clear signal from the Major and the explosives. Stand by," he answered in our ears.

I was sitting on the ground next to Mitchell, and Palmer stayed on his feet, scanning the area with his eyes.

"So, how's Antonio doing?" I asked Mitchell.

She looked at me with some irritation on her face, "Really? You want to ask me about my love life now?"

I looked back at her and held back a laugh at her reaction. "For weeks after we got back from Earth, he was all you wanted to talk about. But lately, you seem to be avoiding the topic. You do have a tendency to bottle things up. So, I thought the last couple of days might have given you a new perspective on life and get you to open up."

She was still a little irritated, but we were too close for her just to dismiss me. Yet, instead of answering, she asked me, "Where the hell did that psychobabble come from?"

"I don't know. Kayla has been watching a lot of vids about parenting and family harmony. There was one that spent a lot of time focusing on the importance of open communication in the home."

"Sounds like you're the one who was watching them," she said with a playful punch on my arm.

"Kayla wanted me to watch them with her. And keeping her happy has been a full-time job these days."

"I'll bet."

"But my point is, you know that I'm here for you if you need to talk."

"I know," she said and then looked away as she debated with herself. Then she blurted out, "He wants to move to New Harmony."

"What?"

"Antonio. He wants to turn over his practice to his partners and be some kind of part-time legal consultant to a handful of his clients.

But really, what he is talking about is retiring and moving halfway across the galaxy to be with me."

"And that's a bad thing?" I asked.

"Yes!" she said initially, then "No!" with the same intensity. "We've known each other for just over a year, and in that time, we've only actually been in the same place for a total of three weeks. Now he wants to uproot his whole life and practically move in with me."

"And you don't want that?" I asked a little more seriously.

She pulled at some long grass near her legs just to have something to do with her hands as she considered her response. "Maybe someday, but not now. What if it doesn't work out? What if he ends up regretting giving up so much for me?"

"Have you told him this?"

"Kind of."

"What's 'Kind of'?"

"I told him he should really think about what he is doing before he decides anything."

"Okay. And how did he react?"

"He quoted some poet in Italian, so I don't have a clue what it was, and then said he would see me soon."

"Quiet," Palmer suddenly said as he stepped closer to us, squatting down and readying the laser pistol. "I think I saw something move over there."

"Just as we turned our heads to look, a Serken jumped out from behind some bushes and charged at us. Palmer jumped back to his feet and fired the pistol, grazing the soldier. The Serken fired back with his rifle, hitting Palmer in the chest. My instinct was to cover Mitchell, but she moved faster than me, pulling her knife from her boot holster and throwing it at the Serken in one motion. It hit the soldier's neck, slicing through the suit and the flesh. Gasping, he fell to the ground. I grabbed the laser pistol that Palmer dropped and fired it three times into the Serken, killing him.

Looking back, I could see that the captain was dead before his body hit the ground. Grabbing up Mitchell in an over-the-shoulder carry, I ran back into the brush before any more Serken soldiers discovered us.

I'm not sure how far I ran, 150 yards, maybe more. All I know for sure is that I ran until I couldn't anymore and dropped both of us into a cluster of plants.

"Theo, how much time?" I asked out loud.

"Estimate 1 minute 32 seconds." He replied.

Mitchell and I huddled together, arms around each other to keep us as low and out of sight as possible. I felt shaking, and at first, I thought it was her, but it was actually me. Between the cold, being soaked to the bone, and I hate to say it, my own fear, I was shaking like a leaf. Mitchell, on the other hand, was as still as a stone. Fear was not something she ever showed, but I think I know her well enough to know; she's scared a lot of times but is just too damn proud to let it ever show. Maybe that's the definition of bravery.

The rain got heavier, and soon it was all we could hear. Mitchell turned her head so that her mouth was right by my ear.

"I lied," she said.

I turned my head to face her.

"About what?" I asked.

"The reason I don't want Antonio to move out to New Harmony isn't that I'm afraid of how it will affect our relationship. The reason is that I don't want it to affect _our_ relationship."

"What?"

"The relationship that I have with you and Kayla. Until now, we really haven't had to explain it to anyone. Not that I would really know how to explain it. We're close like family, but you two are the ones who are married, but I'm always around like I'm a part of it too. But I'm your superior and your best friend and almost lover, but not really." She shook her head, confused by her own attempt at putting it into words, then said with a frustrated sigh, "And now you two are

239

having my baby. Another complexity that's going to be hard to explain. And we are going to have to come up with some official explanation when she gets old enough to start school and other activities. It's all going to be hard enough. I just don't know how Antonio is going to fit into that mix. How do I make that work without making him feel like an outsider?"

"If he loves you, then he will find a way to make it work."

"What if he doesn't love me enough?"

"Then you will still have me. I know that's more of a consolation prize, but it's better than nothing."

She kissed me on the cheek for a very long moment, needing the physical connection without crossing a line. Then she put her head on my shoulder.

A few moments later, Theo spoke in our ears. "The droid is in position."

Mitchell immediately said, "Computer, go on charges 1 through 4."

Instantly there were four flashes at the peak of the mountain and quickly followed by the roars of the explosions and fireballs rolling up into the clouds above.

"Damn," I said, watching the display. "You don't believe in subtle, do you."

"Not when it comes to fighting back," she said.

Soon everything went quiet again. With the heavy rain, it was hard to see or hear anything else. We stayed huddled and low, not knowing if any Serkens would pass by us on their way back to the base.

Mitchell looked over to her left, thinking she heard something, but neither of us could see anything.

Thunder rumbled in the distance. Then again and again.

"That's not natural," Mitchell said.

"Dropships?"

"No, they make another kind of sound."

"All sonic booms are the same," I said.

"No, they are not, now quiet." She said and listened for more.

A moment later, we had our answer. Five Serken fighters streaked by overhead. They circled the still-flaming mountain twice and then flew back up into the clouds.

"Well, Shit," Mitchell said. "Looks like we brought down the wrong cavalry."

"We can't stay around here," I said and started to get up, but she stopped me.

"Hold on. Do you hear that?"

I listened and heard a low roar but wasn't sure what it was.

"They're coming back, and they're not alone," she said. "Get down."

I reclined down with her below the level of the foliage around us. The five Serken fighters came back from the way they came, streaking overhead, but this time they were being chased by eight Alliance fighters.

"That can't be," I said, shocked at what I was seeing.

"What?"

"Those are bulldog fighters. They were phased out before I joined up."

"Maybe they were a group from the Macron who have been hiding somewhere else on the moon."

I shook my head. "I checked the inventory of the Macron's flight capacity. All of their fighters were Tom Cats. Those would have to be from an older ship."

All the fighters had disappeared into the dark clouds. We saw several flashes of light, but it was impossible to tell if they were explosions from aerial combat or lightning.

"Theo, are you picking up any communication signals?" I asked.

"I'm reading several signals on multiple channels, but none are clear enough to discern any information from them."

We waited and watched, hoping the next things we saw fly over would be friendlies, but after a couple of minutes, our hopes were dashed. The five Serken fighters returned and landed at the airfield at the base. Then they were followed by two dozen of their troop transports, a fuel tanker, and a dozen more fighters.

"So much for things not getting any worse," I said as I got up, picked up Mitchell, and headed deeper into the woods.

~~~

Captain Tansky was at the holo-table in the CIC reviewing reports. The main view screen at the front end of the room showed the swirling vortex of the quantum speed tube they were traveling through on their way to meet up with the T.S.S. Cyprus, one of the fleet supercarriers and the sister ship of the Olympus.

The quick electronic chirps of multiple alerts sounded at the helm, navigation, and tactical stations, as well as the holo-table. Before anyone could react, the Olympus was thrown out of quantum speed and into normal space with a flash and sudden force. Systems all over the ship overloaded, and the ship tumbled out of control, the internal gravity and emergency thrusters unable to correct. Everyone tried to hold on to what they could. Those who didn't react fast enough were thrown against the starboard side of wherever they were.

"Report!" Tansky yelled, holding onto the table as she called out orders.

"The QS tube collapsed," The Helmsman answered, with one hand holding the edge of his console and the other trying to right the ship. "It's indicating an interruption in the tube ahead of us."

The computer fired emergency thrusters to stop the sideways roll of the ship allowing the helmsman to regain full control and for the gravity to return to normal.

"Damage Report," Tansky ordered.

The young ensign at the communications station got back on her feet and had to put her weight on one leg as the other was injured. Trying to ignore the pain, she steadied herself and wiped what she thought was sweat off her upper lip, only to see blood on the back of her hand. Yet, she wiped it off on the side of her uniform and performed her duties. Calling up the text reports generated by the ship's internal systems AI, she read it out loud. "Computer is reporting no casualties but buckling on decks 4 and 5. There are 17 minor outer hull breaches that are being sealed with force fields, and repair bots are responding to fix them. At this time, there are no inner hull breaches. Still waiting for reports from department heads. The main engine was knocked offline but is resetting and will be operational in under two minutes. Flight deck reporting in. 21 people sustained injuries, three critical, all being taken to sickbay."

"How did 21 people get hurt on the flight deck?" Tansky asked, underlining that such a statement needed additional information.

The communication officer called up the details about the report beyond the header and answered, "Three Sabretooth fighters and a dropship were unsecured on the deck for maintenance reviews. They fell to the port wall when the ship tumbled." She then waited to see if that was enough or if the captain was going to ask for more.

"Proceed with the general report, Ensign."

"Yes, Captain. Damage control teams are responding to a fire in cargo bay 19. Sickbay is reporting that they are nearing capacity and is asking for a general announcement for individuals with minor injuries to report them and wait in their quarters so that the seriously injured can be taken care of first. And…"

Tansky looked over at the young officer and noticed her wincing in pain and trying to balance on one leg.

"Crewman," she said to the man standing security at the doorway. "Help the ensign to her quarters."

"Captain?" the communication officer asked, ashamed of being relieved.

"Take it easy, have one of the doctors take a look at that leg when they can and get some rest. I'll expect you back at your post all the earlier on your next shift."

"Yes, Captain," she said and let the crewman put her arm over his shoulder so he could help her out.

"Captain," the tactical officer said with some volume to get her attention, "I believe we have an explanation of what happened. Another QS tube intersected ours, causing both to collapse."

"How is that possible?" She asked. "The actual tube doesn't extend more than a million kilometers."

The tactical officer sent his data over to the holo-table and then walked over to join her.

"Here is our route, and the red part of the line shows our tube. This blue line," he said, bringing up the data of a line that ran the entire length of the table, "shows the sudden appearance of another quantum tube that ran past the five-light-year range of our close-range sensors."

"Have you ever heard of a QS tube doing that?" she asked.

"No, Captain. And neither had the computer. It's registering it as an unknown event."

"Go to the comms station, contact Cyprus and let them know that we are going to be a little late. Navigation, replot course to the rendezvous spot." She then looked at her tactical officer, "Do you see any reason we can't use our QSG?"

"The other tube disappeared as quickly as it appeared, and there are no indications of any other anomalies. But frankly, Captain, I think that is a question better for our chief engineer to answer."

"Thank you, Lieutenant," she said sincerely, preferring her officers to be direct, especially when they were not confident with their answers. Pushing the internal comms button on the table, she said, "CIC to Commander Singh."

A moment later, Chief Engineer Singh's voice came out of the comm speaker on the holo-table. "Yes, Captain."

"Are you aware of what happened?"

"I'm looking at the preliminary report now. It does explain the violent way we were thrown out of quantum speed."

"With the phenomenon no longer present, is there any reason we shouldn't jump back in?"

"There shouldn't be a problem, but there is," he answered. "I just tried to generate a quantum bubble to test the system, and we are not able to form one."

"Why?" Tansky asked.

"I'm not sure. The computer says that all systems are a go, but we cannot form a bubble, which means we cannot create a tube. Until I can figure out why, we're stuck at sub-light speed."

With the line still open, she said, "Navigation, how far are we from the Cyprus?"

"Just under five light-years, Captain."

"Okay, Singh. Get to work. Report back to me as soon as you have a better answer. Tansky out." She looked at the main view screen for a long moment, suddenly feeling very small in such a large universe. "Jackson," she said to the Tactical officer who was about to contact the Cyprus from the communications station. "Get me Cyprus Actual and pipe it into my ready office." She then collected a couple of data pads from the table and walked out of the CIC.

Chapter 20

An Unexpected Arrival

I hiked with Mitchell on my back for as long as I could. Between the cold rain, not having very much to eat over the past few days, and my muscles already strained from the hard labor, I didn't cover very much distance.

"I'm sorry," I said as I put her down on the ground and then dropped myself. "I just need five minutes."

She looked around, taking a quick assessment of our surroundings, "It will be dark soon. We should try and find a good place to lay low for the night,"

I was still huffing, and I looked at her and said, "Thanks."

"For what?"

With both hands, I wiped the water back off my forehead in a vain attempt to dry my face and answered, "Not giving me crap about not keeping up with your morning exercise plan for me."

"You needed to spend your mornings helping Kayla. That was more important."

"Yeah, well, truth is, Max was doing most of the work around the house. I spend most mornings sleeping in."

With a cold glare, she said, "You didn't."

"I did."

"You Ass," she said with a laugh, "If you kept up with the physical training, you would have been able to carry me another fifty feet. Maybe a hundred."

We both laughed. "Well, if we ever get back home, I'll be there bright and early every morning."

"No, you won't. You're going to have a hungry baby getting you up at all hours of the night for feedings, and I don't expect you to let Kayla do all of them herself."

"Copy that, Major," I said, and she laughed out loud, "What's tickled your silly bone?" I asked, laughing along as it felt contagious.

She caught her breath and shook her head before answering, "Just the realization that things can't get any worse. There's something liberating about that."

Just then, four beams of light lit up the ground around us. The roar of ship engines started to cut through the sound of the pounding rain, and the beams focused in on us.

"You were saying about it not getting any worse," I said as I tried to shield my eyes from the light that was preventing us from seeing the ship that was landing just feet from us.

As it set down, the lights dimmed and focused away from us. The black ship was still hard to see in the dim light. A ramp opened and dropped to the ground with a half dozen figures walking out. We couldn't tell if they were friends or foes, so we both raised our hands, hoping not to get shot on sight.

"Identify yourselves," a human voice demanded.

"I'm Lt. Commander Jack Reilly, and this is Major Julie Anne Mitchell."

The man stepped up to me and offered his hand to help me up. "I'm Lt. Commander Phillips of the starship Greyhorn."

"Greyhorn," I said with some surprise. "No wonder I didn't recognize your dropship,"

"Why's that?" Phillips asked.

I decided it would be best to get us out of harm's way before I started a discussion of yet another ship out of its own time. "Look, we're less than a kilometer from a Serken base that is getting resupplied with everything, including fresh troops. We need to get to somewhere safer as quickly as we can. Do you still have a ship in orbit?"

"Yes. We're on a search and rescue for some of our pilots who were downed." He turned to the crew chief and called over, tell the pilot skids up in 30 seconds."

A couple of the troopers from the dropship had picked up Mitchell, carried her into the ship, and placed her on a stretcher. The ramp pulled up, and the engines of the very old-style dropship revved up. Shotting over them, Commander Phillips asked, "How did the two of you end up out here?"

"The starship we were on was attacked by an unknown orbital platform controlled by the Serkens at the ground base."

"Chief!" Phillips yelled. "Contact the Greyhorn and let them know that there is a hostile weapons platform in orbit that's already downed one of our ships. Advise they pull back."

"Aye, Commander," The Chief replied.

"Sir," the pilot called back. "We didn't pack external tanks. If the Greyhorn pulls back more than 200,000 kilometers, we won't have enough fuel."

"Head north by northeast and scan for a preindustrial stone city," I said. "We believe some of our people are falling back to that point. The Major and I were trying to direct the enemy away from that location, but we have no idea how successful we were. They may need our support."

"We still have two more pilots to find," Phillips said.

"Well, it's your call," I replied, looking around at the hold with the two injured pilots they had already picked up, six marine troopers, the crew chief, and Mitchell. "These birds are not very quiet, and you are in a hot zone. My vote is to fall back to a more friendly location and regroup. But it's your command and your call."

He chewed on that for a moment, then called up to the pilot while keeping his eyes on me. "Smitty, how much juice do we have?"

"About 40 minutes in this chop, twice that if we're out of the atmosphere soon."

"And how far away is this rally point?" he asked me.

248

"About 20, maybe 25 kilometers."

"Chief, are we still picking up the transponders of our downed people?"

"One went dark, and the other is still hot," he answered.

"Okay, direct Smitty to the one we still have a clear location to. Then we will go to the Commander's rally point. From there, we will sit tight until we get orders from the Greyhorn."

"Aye, Commander," the chief answered.

I had to quickly move my feet and shift my weight to keep my balance as the ship bounced and shook as it changed direction and fought against the pounding rain to keep its seven tons in the air.

Phillips glared at me as we stood near the center of the compartment, each of us holding a hanging strap for balance.

"What is it, Commander?" I asked.

"Your uniform is wrong."

"How so?"

"Your rank insignia are brass. We only do that on dress uniforms. They should be stitched on."

I realized he was like a dog with a bone, and I needed to fill him in. "It's a peacetime protocol." He looked at me like I was trying to make a bad joke, so I gave him more details. "Commander, the Greyhorn, along with a task force of nine other ships, disappeared nearly twenty years ago."

He still looked at me like I was crazy. "Just what kind of shit are you trying to pull?"

"The Greyhorn was the lead ship of a task force leading the first offensive to put into the Serken star system. But the task force disappeared before they got to the rally point. It was assumed that you all were ambushed and destroyed by the Serken."

"So, you're saying…."

"The year is 2325. The war has been over for six years now. We won, by the way. But for some reason, ships lost in the quantum tubes have been ending up here. The T.S.S. Macron was lost a couple of years after your group, and what's left of their crew, around 200, are trapped on this moon. Up until yesterday, they were being held as slave labor by a group of Serkens who apparently didn't know that the war was over and had built a base here. And now you're here, along with a new batch of enemy ships."

He looked over at the chief and asked, "What do you think?"

"Before we left the Greyhorn, I heard one of the pilots saying that navigation couldn't get a fix on where we were exactly because none of the stars were in the right place. Twenty years of cosmic drift might explain that."

"Commander," Mitchell nearly shouted as she decided she needed to be part of the conversation. "None of that matters right now. You are in hostile territory. There are wounded to find and take care of. They are your first priority. The second is to get your people to a safe location, and the third is to reestablish contact with your ship. Which isn't going to happen until they are able to make low orbit again safely."

Commander Phillips didn't care for a fleet officer that he had just rescued to be telling him what to do, so having a ground pounder major add-on didn't improve his attitude.

"Strap in, Commander," he said to me through gritted teeth. "It's going to get bumpy from here."

I took his comment as a warning not to bump heads with him more than the condition of the ride.

~~~

The T.S.S. Greyhorn, one of the first battle carriers designed after the start of the war, fired its thrusters, pitching to the starboard and away from the moon.

"Any sign of the rest of the fleet yet?" Captain Rodgers asked from his seat on the bridge.

"No, Sir," the young man at communications answered.

"What about those Serken battle cruisers?" he asked the tactical officer.

"Our probes still haven't located them. They either jumped away or dipped down into the atmosphere to hide in the storms."

"I've heard of their scouts and battle strikes being capable of atmospheric flight but never their battlecruisers." The captain said.

"Their ships are all based on Salairie technology, and all of those ships were built on the surface and launched from the ground. So, it is possible."

"How do you know all of that?" the captain asked.

"I did my senior thesis on alien starships.

"And just when I thought I was too old to learn anything new. Thank you, Lieutenant."

An alert sounded on the tactical station. "We have incoming,"

"Helm, push it to 100 percent. Weapons One, launch countermeasures. Weapons Two, target anything that gets through the countermeasures with kinetics."

Five missiles shot around the moon and straight for the Greyhorn, but they were ready. Two dozen hunter missiles flew out of the nose of the warship and straight for the oncoming threat. The approaching missiles had their own defenses, which included a computer brain that could evade the challenge from the smaller missiles and even fire lasers in defense. The hunter missiles took out three of the five Serken missiles. The other two were destroyed by direct fire from three-foot-long kinetic titanium rods fired in rapid succession from the Greyhorn like bullets from a machine gun.

"Captain, a message from our S&R team," the communications officer said.

He looked over and asked matter-of-factly as if it was business as usual. "What is it?"

"Message reads; Found survivors of a downed fleet ship. State that Serkens have a base on the moon and a weapons platform in orbit. Recommend Greyhorn fallback until the threat can be assessed. S&R team will continue to track down our downed pilots and find a safe harbor until we give them the all-clear to return."

"Better late than never," Captain Rodgers said to himself, then replied, "Send an acknowledgment and make sure it's on a secured frequency. We don't want to pinpoint their location for the enemy."

"Aye, Captain."

The captain stepped over to his chair and stood by it as he used the touchscreen on the arm to call up a chart of the area around the ship. His hand was shaking, and he took a moment to grab it with his other hand to stop the tremors. Looking around to make sure no one saw, he released his hand, and it was still. Aging was something that had never bothered him, but at the moment, the signs of it were inconvenient. He finished looking up the information on his screen and then said, "Helm put us about a million kilometers under the gas giant's south pole. That should give us a good view of the area while keeping enough breathing room. Tactical, keep looking for our other ships on passive sensors only. Assume we are in enemy territory. Comms, let me know if you pick up any fleet traffic but maintain radio silence. And tell all the department heads that I want to meet with them in 20 minutes in conference room alpha. I want to know what the hell happened and how we ended up here."

~~~

After we picked up one more of their downed pilots, we flew to the stone city and circled it three times, making sure there were no hostiles nearby. Then we landed and were greeted by crew members from the Franklin, the Macron, and the Stratford. Plus, nearly 200 of the indigenous residents that had been freed when the Macron crew escaped the Serken base. In all, there were nearly 700 people taking refuge in the prehistorical type dwellings.

"Major!" Sargent Caplan called out from the crowd that had formed as the dropship landed. He ran up as the Greyhorn marine troopers were carrying her off on a stretcher. He greeted her with a salute which she returned, and then said, "Damn good to see you, Major."

"Gunny?" Commander Phillips asked as he was following them down the ramp and thought he recognized him.

Caplan looked over at the Commander and was puzzled at why he was addressing him like that.

Phillips continued up to him and asked, "Aren't you Gunnery Sergeant Caplan? We served together on the Florence."

Confused, Caplan answered, "No, Sir. My name is Caplan, but I'm a Master Sargent and never served on the Florence."

"I was certain that was you."

"Sir, the Florence was lost almost 20 years ago. My father was serving on it at the time as a gunnery sergeant."

Phillips turned white as a sheet as he looked back at me, nodded his acknowledgment that he believed what I had told him about the time that had passed, and then he turned back to Caplan and asked, "Who is the senior officer in this group?"

Pointing back down the ramp of the dropship, he said, "She is, Sir. Major Mitchell."

Mitchell had the two troopers put down her stretcher, and she got up on one leg as she asked, "Where's Commander Wane?"

Caplan answered, "When we saw the Stratford burning up and picked up all the signals from their pods, he had us all go and search for them before they got picked up by the enemy. His group ran into a Serken patrol, and only the ensign over there was able to get away."

"Were they taken prisoner?" she asked.

"He said they opened fire, and he didn't stop running until he couldn't hear the blast anymore. It's a good bet they were all killed."

"Who's the senior officer from the Stratford crew?"

"A Lieutenant Barreto. She's one of the engineering techs. She says that the top five decks were obliterated in the assault, and none of the command staff made it out. I haven't taken a survey of all the survivors, but as far as I can tell, you're the highest-ranking officer here."

I stepped up to Mitchell and put her arm over my shoulder so that I could help her walk. "Why don't we continue this conversation inside."

Mitchell looked up at the rain and said, "I guess I've gotten used to it. I hardly notice it anymore."

~~~

The locals welcomed the fleet personnel to continue to use their main meeting hall as a shelter and command center. They even collected some food and showed some of the members of the fleet crews how to prepare meals from the fungus and small animals. They had also gathered some stones that were like the crystals we had been digging up in the mines, with the exception that they were rounded and smoothed over years of use. Collected together in the middle of the room were tree stumps carved into stool-like chairs that circled the rocks, which glowed a pulsing white light and gave off heat like a fire. Accepting that this was just another unique thing about this world, we all gathered around them for warmth and to discuss our next moves.

In our group was Sergeant Caplan, who was the senior NCO, Major Mitchell, Lt. Commander Phillips, Lt. Barreto from the Stratford, Lt. Commander Wastle, who was now the highest-ranking member left from the Macron crew and me. Determining who was in charge could have been a debate since a Marine Major was equivalent to a fleet Lt. Commander. But other than Phillips, none of the fleet personnel were eager to take charge.

Before anyone else said anything, Phillips stood and assumed the role of leadership, "We need to make an accounting of our assets, set up a defense watch around this base, and keep the enemy off balance until we can get reinforcements from the Greyhorn. The best way to do that is to put together small assault teams to conduct raiding operations on their installations. Sargent, I want you and your…."

"Excuse me, Commander," I said, interrupting. "But you are not in command here."

"Well, Commander, as the only senior officer from a ship that is still in operation, that does put me in charge."

I kept my seat as I didn't think physical posturing would help. "Actually, Commander, if we were to go by the book, the Major is the only officer here who still has an active command."

"What the hell are you talking about?" he said, stepping closer to glare down at me.

"Your ship and crew were listed as missing 20 years ago. Now, as far as your people are concerned, you are in charge of them. But as for everyone else, they have to follow the Major."

He took a beat to take another step closer and leaned over me, "You have a problem with me, Commander?"

I calmly answered, "No, Commander, I don't. But I also don't know you. Most of us know the Major and trust in her judgment."

Mitchell said in a low voice, "Reilly, I really don't want to get into a pissing match with this guy."

Matching her low tone, I replied, "Until an hour ago, this guy was fighting a war that ended half a decade ago. I'm afraid that his mindset might be more on defeating our enemy rather than survival as the first priority. If anyone can understand how the two approaches are different, it's you. Which is why you have my vote."

She looked past me at the Commander, who was still glaring down at us. Getting to her feet, still having to hobble on one leg, she matched his glare. Despite the fact that he had six inches of height over her, she could still diminish that advantage with just a hard look and make it feel like they were toe to toe.

"I'll be willing to listen to your suggestions *Lt.* Commander. But understand that my priority is to get everyone home."

"What, you want to just wait here for the enemy to come and find us?"

"No," she said, keeping her glare as hard on him as he was on her. "You're right about setting over watches around this location and about keeping the enemy off balance. But we don't have the weapons or manpower to go on the offensive. I propose that we put together small teams to distract the Serken. Send them off in different directions to leave trails for them to follow, leading their search parties away from this location."

"Then what?" he asked.

"Hope your captain is smart enough to leave this system and call for help. With the number of Serken ships we saw coming down today, they will quickly get a grip on this entire moon, and we won't stand a chance. And if you want to know what that is like, talk to any member of the Macron crew who just spent the last year in an enemy labor camp."

He looked around at the faces of everyone who had gathered around to watch the command officers, who looked like they were about to come to blows. It was very obvious which ones were from the Macron crew in their tattered uniforms and hollow faces from hard labor and too little food. At that point, the chip appeared to fall off his shoulder, and he said, "Very well, Major. What are your orders."

~~~

We spend the next hour discussing and often debating how to best go about Mitchell's plan. The main issue was deciding how much firepower to keep at the stone city and how much to send out with the decoy teams. Our marine troopers had their rifles but had already used up two-thirds of their power reserves, and the small armory on Commander Phillips's dropship didn't have compatible power clips. It did have 20 hand lasers, 40 additional power clips for them, and some explosive charges. But being a search and rescue dropship, it wasn't outfitted for troopers like others were, so there was no heavy ordnance stored in it. A practice that was changed in the second half of the war.

Mitchell's marines were the first to volunteer for the decoy teams. Then some members of the Franklin and Stratford crews stepped up and volunteered. Forty were selected and broken up into ten groups of four. They all had laser pistols in their survival packs and were given extra power clips from those who were not going. The Marines took the box of explosive charges and planned to get close enough to inflict some damage. At least enough to force the enemy to put resources on their defense and reduce the number of their soldiers combing the woods.

Those who were not going and who were in good enough health would take overwatch positions at the highest points on the nearby hilltops that surrounded the city. Their job would be to provide early warnings of an incoming threat. If we had access to better weapons like long-range plasma rifles or rapid-fire laser cannons, we could use the higher ground positions as places to defend the city. But with just hand lasers, the locations would be ineffective. We would have to be a lot closer to the enemy to have a chance against them. Therefore, our decoy teams needed to be effective so that we wouldn't have to be put into such a no-win scenario.

The decoy teams would leave before dawn and fan out east and west, leaving clues once they were at least three kilometers away. After traveling that distance, they would then work their way north for five more kilometers to a meeting point that I had selected, which was the location of the downed dropship where I found Lt. Harman. He had stayed hidden from the Serken because the area had a natural magnetic field that created a sensor shadow. The odds of any of our teams being located by the enemy there were low. We would then have Phillips pick them up in 18 hours and bring them back to the city. If our plan worked, the enemy would assume they lost the human trail because of the environment.

Once all the teams were ready, they were deployed. After that, we had to do the hard part. Sit, wait, and pray that no more of our people die.

Chapter 21

Good News and Bad News

Kayla tried to open her eyes, but they felt heavy, and she let them close for a moment. She felt like she was in a fog but tried to talk. "What happened? Where am I?"

"It's okay, Sweetheart," she heard a deep voice say.

"Jack? Is that you?"

"No, honey, it's Dad."

She felt a strong but gentle hand stroking the hair on her forehead. Opening her eyes, she saw Dad and smiled. Seeing his face instantly made her feel safe. She was in a hospital room and her gut hurt. Pudding her hand on her belly, she realized it was flat. The baby was gone. Suddenly her last memories flooded in of being at the education center and blood running down her leg. She couldn't remember anything more than that. "Oh God!" she yelled. "Oh God, the baby. What happened to the baby? Did I lose the baby?"

"She's fine," Rachel said in a soft, cheery voice.

Dad stepped to the side so that Kayla could see Rachel sitting in a chair, holding a baby, bundled in a blanket. She got up and walked over to the bedside.

"As a matter of fact, she is perfect," Rachel added as she placed the baby in Kayla's arms.

Kayla looked into the baby's face, and even though she knew she already loved the baby, she didn't know just how much until that moment. Tears of joy ran down her face. "Oh, my God. She's so beautiful." Kayla ran the tips of her fingers over the baby's face, and the baby turned her head, reacting to the sensation. "Are you sure she's okay?"

Rachel answered, her attention more on the baby, "You had a blood clot on the wall of your uterus, and it ripped open when you had a small contraction. That was what caused the bleeding. Stress and sudden blood loss caused you to pass out at about the same time the EMTs got to you. Once you got to the hospital, they determined that the baby was ready to come out, and they decided to induce labor."

"Hi," Kayla said to the baby, her total focus on the new little one once she realized everything was good.

"What are you going to name her?" Dad asked.

"We haven't decided yet," she said, her attention on the little one's face. "We've narrowed it down to about two dozen, we kind of like. I was hoping that when we met her, it would be easier."

"They're going to want a name before they let you go home with her. Unless you want her birth certificate to read baby girl Reilly. You can change it later, but there is a lot of paperwork involved. A real headache. We learned that the hard way when Carol was born. And that was why we named Jack after me."

There was a knock at the door, and then it opened. A nurse stuck her head in and asked, "Mr. Reilly. Could you step out here, please? There is a gentleman here who is asking to speak with you."

"Certainly," he said. Then leaned down, gave Kayla a kiss on the forehead, and exited the room.

With as lucid as Dad had been over the past couple of days, Rachel felt it all right to give Danny the day off since they would be in the hospital for most of the time. But she still followed Dad out into the hallway and stood off to the side to make sure he didn't have an episode of confusion. In the hallway was a man in a fleet admiral's uniform whom Dad greeted with a stern nod.

"Are you Jack Reilly Sr?" he asked.

"Yes. And this is my wife, Rachel." Dad answered and held out his arm so that she would step up next to him.

"Hello, I'm Admiral Kilpatric. Your son is in my command," he said, offering his hand to Dad and then to Rachel. "How's Kayla doing?"

"She's fine," Dad answered.

"And the baby?"

Rachel gently took hold of Dad's arm and answered with a smile, "Healthy, six pounds, nine ounces."

"Good. Good."

"Is this just a social call, or do you have news about my son?" Dad asked.

The admiral took a couple of steps away from the door, and they followed. "That's why I wanted to talk to you first. I didn't want to needlessly upset his wife."

"What's happened?" Rachel asked.

"We don't know, and that's the problem. The ship your son is on should have reported in four days ago. It might be nothing, but the ship we sent to make contact is now overdue."

"Well, what the hell are you doing about it?" Dad asked, not blunting his frustration.

"We're sending two more ships in to look for them. One of them is the flagship of the fleet. As I said, we don't know what has happened. It's most likely a communications issue and nothing more. I don't want to tarnish this day for his wife, but I do have an obligation to inform his family. So, I'm speaking with you."

Dad nodded, "Thank you. I appreciate that. I think it's best not to bring this up with her until we know something more concrete."

"Yes, well, I will let you know as soon as I have any news."

"Thank you," Dad said, offering his hand.

The admiral shook it and walked away down the hall. Dad looked at Rachel with his stone face, but she knew him well enough to see the concern for his son in his eyes.

She put her hand on his arms and, with a reassuring voice, said, "I'm sure he's fine and will be home soon."

Dad gave a confident nod but didn't say anything, as his voice might give away the fear he was feeling.

He then forced a smile back on his face, and they walked back into Kayla's hospital room.

~~~

On the bridge of the Greyhorn, Captain Rodgers reviewed the damage report on a handheld data pad from his command chair. Their QSG was offline, and their chief engineer still didn't have an ETA on when it would be operational again. Repairs to the damage they took in their last engagement were underway, but 20% of their laser cannons were not fixable outside of a space dock, their missiles were depleted down to 40% of the stock, and their kinetics were down to 30%.

He called up the log function on his 3D display and selected the verbal interface. "Captain's log, March 9, 2301," he started, unaware that he had the date wrong as they had lost nearly two decades in their last quantum jump. Taking a sip of his mostly cold coffee, he continued. "We had met up with our battle group at Proseon-8 and were preparing to jump to sector 198 near the Serken border to join up with the rest of the assault fleet for an offensive push into their space. But the enemy was waiting for us. We were jumped by 17 Serken battle cruisers. I ordered all of our ships to retreat to the New Sydney system, where we could regroup. Eight of the nine ships in our group acknowledged the order. Before we jumped, we saw indications that at least half of the Serken fleet was warming up their QSGs. We can only assume that they intended to pursue us."

A yeoman walked up to Captain Rodgers and handed him a coffee mug with fresh coffee to replace the old one in his hand. He looked at her, a little surprised as he hadn't asked for one but realized that she had taken the initiative to do so. With a gentle smile and a nod, he handed her the old mug and took the new one. Then he continued his log entry. "We were in quantum space for less than 20 seconds but somehow ended up in the Batal system. According to our star charts, we are over 4000 lightyears from where we started, but that can't be possible. The best distance we could have achieved in such a short jump would have been no more than two light years. Yet here we are." He took a sip of coffee and looked around his bridge. Everyone looked as tired as he felt, but each and everyone was giving 100 percent to their duties. That filled him with both pride and frustration. They all deserved a happy ending to their personal stories, and he feared he might lead them down a rabbit hole with no end in sight. He needed to find that balance of optimism and honesty to keep them going, even if they never found the finish line.

A double beep and a quick flashing light on his screen told him that his log had been paused for over 30 seconds. He pushed the button to resume and continued. "We were part of a task force that was going to lead an offensive against the Serken right into their homeworld system. To ensure that we all arrived in a show of overwhelming force, we were going to meet at a predetermined rally point with the bulk of the first fleet, along with the second and third fleets. But the enemy was waiting for us. Our group was early, and the enemy attacked with 14 battleships. I ordered the retreat, and we set course to jump to our fallback position." Captain Rodgers took another sip of the fresh coffee. The aroma and warmth made him feel a little more focused. He checked some data on a tactical report and continued. "Our fallback position was pre-arranged, but we ended up here, and the rest of our tasked force did not. Our chief engineer thinks there might have been a balance issue with our QSG. But he is not entirely certain as the system is damaged, and he isn't sure if he can get it working again. Three of the Serken battleships that had been pursuing us appeared near the same location we had entered normal space. They were near the same planet we found ourselves on but with a moon between us. Unable to jump to quantum speed again, I ordered fighters to launch and engage the enemy battleships and the helm to move us toward the moon for cover. This would force the Serken to come around it to get a shot at us. Immediately we started having problems communicating with our fighters. Something in this system was wreaking havoc with our communications. To maintain contact with our fighters, we launched probes around the moon and planet to boost the signals and give us eyes around the blind spots."

The captain paused the log recording again to review some of his notes and drink more of his coffee while it was still hot. Lt. Finkelman, one of the weapons officers, took the opportunity to bring over a pad with updated repair estimates on it. Rodgers took it, gave the data a quick review, transferred the data over to his files, and handed the pad back. Then continued his log. "The Serken ships launched their own fighters. Both groups engaged, and we outperformed the enemy assault at a kill-to-loss ratio of 4 to 1. But then the Serken fighters dove to the moon and disappeared into the clouds. Our fighters went after them. Unfortunately, Serken fighters have an advantage in atmospheric flight in low visibility. Five of our twelve fighters were downed. The CAG called for a retreat, and the remaining fighters returned to the Greyhorn."

"A Search and Rescue dropship was dispatched to find the five pilots that went down over the moon. We maneuvered to keep the moon between us and the enemy battle cruisers. Fortunately, the Serken stayed true to form and stayed together rather than splitting up to flush us out. We mirrored their direction and speed for over ten minutes while our S&R team looked for our pilots." Rodgers picked up a data pad that he had made some notes on so that he could give needed specifics to his log. "At 14:42 hours, the S&R team reported they found two pilots and were heading for a weak signal that might be a third. At 14:46, the enemy battle cruisers dropped out of sight into the atmosphere of the moon. 15:03 We were fired upon with five missiles that came from an unknown source. 15:05 S&R reported picking up two survivors of a downed Alliance ship and had new intelligence that the Serkens have a base on the moon as well as a weapons platform in orbit. We pulled back to the other side of the gas giant to make repairs."

Rodgers paused the recording and rubbed his eyes. He hadn't left the bridge for over 20 hours. The bridge crew had rotated out three times since he took the watch and was back to the Alpha shift. But none of them looked very rested. It had already been a long war, and the strain was getting to everyone. Too many of these young men and women were witnessing so much death on a daily basis that they either had to go numb or mad. He wondered how he had dealt with it for so long. Up to this point, he had kept himself occupied with the daily operations of the ship and the focus of keeping it all together in combat. But at that moment, the stress was palpable. They were cut off from the fleet, apparently still in enemy-held territory, unable to communicate with anyone outside of the star system, and unable to jump into quantum speed. He felt like a rat in a cage, just waiting to be fed to the snakes.

"Captain," the tactical officer called out. "QS tubes opening up 7 million kilometers off the port."

"Friend or foe?"

"Unknown," he reported. "The power signature is fluctuating. It's impossible to tell."

The forward view screen zoomed in on the area of space that was blurring. Then flashes, followed by three fleet ships.

"It's the Cortez, the Bradley, and the Tallahassee."

"Thank the maker," Captain Rodgers said as he stepped up to the tactical station to take a closer look at part of the missing task force.

"More tubes Sir," Tactical reported.

"More from our missing group?"

"Unknown. I still can't identify the power patterns of the tube, but whoever it is will be just a few hundred kilometers off their backs.

"Hail them," Rodgers ordered the communication officer.

"Which one?" he asked.

"All of them," the captain snapped.

Five more flashes and five Serken battle cruisers appeared bearing down on the three Alliance ships.

"Battle Stations!" the captain ordered. "Helm, get us over there. They are going to need all the help they can get. Prepare to launch all fighters. Weapons one and two bring up everything we've got. Shields at full."

~~~

The sky slowly changed from black to dark grey as the sun came up and the rain continued to fall. I was half asleep on one of the cots set up in the main gathering room of the stone city.

"You awake?" Mitchell asked.

I opened my eyes to see her sitting on the cot next to mine. She had reassembled the armor to her battle suit with the exception of her helmet, which was damaged and discarded during her rough landing.

"Getting ready for a fight?" I asked.

"The outer shell has components that work with the inner skeletal joints of the suit. Putting it all together helps to support my leg."

"You still shouldn't be putting weight on it," I said, sitting up.

"Theo agrees with you. He's got the leg joints frozen so that it acts like a cast."

"And you agreed to that?"

"Only if he agreed to release them if I need to move quickly."

I looked around. The room was full of people, both fleet and locals.

"What?" she asked me as I must have had a quizzical look on my face.

"It has never ceased to amaze me at how those who have the least are often the ones who are the quickest to share what they have. After all these people have been through, they are still eager to welcome strangers like us and share their food and homes." Smirking at the thought of my own shortcomings, I admitted, "And I get pissed when we run out of coffee in the break room."

Mitchell looked in the same direction that I was and, with a little more contemplation, asked, "Do you think they're happy? Living such a simple and difficult existence?"

"Sure. This is what they know. Why wouldn't they be?"

"I don't know," Mitchell said, shifting her leg over a little in a futile attempt to get comfortable with the injured knee. "I moved around a lot when I was a kid. Some of those places were colony worlds that didn't have the prosperity or security that people were promised. Some of those people had family roots there for four, sometimes five generations, and I knew a lot of them who were miserable with their poorer existence, even though they never knew a better life."

"But there were people around them that did have things better. The colonies really have a clear divide between the haves and have-nots. I don't know why we turn a blind eye to worlds that we help create but won't make into the paradise that the core worlds are. I had always assumed it was because all of our resources were going into the war effort, and things would get better for all the colonies after the war. But I guess sharing is not necessarily a natural instinct."

The room started to fill with the smell of meat being roasted over flames and a kind of porridge made up of grasses and something that was like black beans being cooked up in stone pots. After the last few days of the gruel the Serken's were feeding us, it was rather appetizing.

After a moment, Mitchell asked me, "So, you ready?

"For what?" I asked.

"Being a dad."

"Yeah, I guess."

"Really? The idea of becoming a parent is scaring the crap out of me."

"Oh, I didn't say I wasn't scared. I've just gotten used to the fear. Why? Are you scared?"

She shrugged and said, "Kayla keeps talking about sharing the parenting as equals, but I just don't see how that is going to work."

"She knows that you won't be there every day to change diapers and do the 3 am feedings."

I was expecting a quick comeback from her. Something like she was happy to leave us with all the grunt work. But instead, she reached up and pulled the pins out of her hair to let it down. The sweat from the helmet had practically pasted it to her scalp, and the rain just made it worse. It took her a minute of running her fingers through it to shake it loose. She tried combing clumps out with her fingers so that the mess was all going back and away from her face. The actions were so drawn out that I assumed she was trying to change the subject, but then she looked back at me. Something about her face changed. It seemed a little softer and less soldier-like. There is an air about her when she is working, a kind of strength that commands respect. But when we were away from the job, out of uniform, she allowed herself to drop the bravado. That was what I was seeing at that moment. Mitchell just being Julie Anne. Still trying to work out some of the knots in her hair, she said, "Kayla was clear that she is going to take care of the day-to-day stuff, but she does expect me to be part of the big decisions. Like what school to put her into and how much money should the tooth fairy leave when she loses her first tooth."

I laughed, and she said with a pained look on her face, "I'm serious. I loved my dad, but he was hardly ever around. There were times that I resented him telling me things I couldn't do when he happened to be home. And there were nights when I cried myself to sleep when I really needed him, and he wasn't there." She took a moment to sniff and wiped away a tear. "After Roger died, I was required to see a shrink for a couple of weeks before they would let me return back to duty. By the end of the first session, she suggested that I had become a Marine in an unconscious effort to get closer to my father. I was sure that was pure bullshit at the time. But lately, I've been wondering if that was true."

She looked like she had more to say, but wasn't saying it, so I asked, "What exactly are you afraid of?"

"Not being there when she needs me…. And being an outsider to her when I am there."

I got up from the cot I was sitting on and sat down next to her. Putting my arm around her, I said, "Sparky ran away."

"What?"

"My first dog. A young golden retriever. I got him for my ninth birthday. I loved him the moment I laid eyes on him, and I thought we would be the best of friends. I fed him, brushed him, and took him for walks several times a day. I thought we were so close that I could take him for a walk out in the woods by our house without a leash. As soon as we were past the driveway, he ran off ahead of me into the woods, and that was the last I saw of him."

She looked at me and asked, "And what does this have to do with me?"

"My parents replaced him the next week, but I didn't want a new dog because I was certain that I had done something wrong. Then my mom explained to me that we can do all the right things and still have bad things happen, and mistakes don't always turn out bad. We just have to do our best and pick up the pieces when things eventually fall apart."

Mitchell smiled and said, "That helps a little bit."

"Good. What do you say we get some chow."

"Good idea."

"Alert! Alert!" a voice filled with urgency said over all of our PCs. "Enemy troops spotted advancing on this city due south. Repeat, enemy troops spotted due south and approaching."

"Distance and count!" Mitchell responded into her PC to the spotter who made the call.

"At least a squad, on foot, and about half a kilometer out," he replied.

Mitchell got to her feet and announced to everyone, "Just like we planned, get to your post and wait for my orders."

All the fleet personnel grabbed their packs and ran out. Forty were assigned to groups of four that would climb up to different rooftops and lay flat on their bellies to limit their exposure to laser fire from the ground. The rest scattered around to the north side of the city, where the locals would guide them down a trail that descended down into the valley and into the dense forest. With luck, we would be able to hold off the enemy long enough for the rest of our people to escape.

"Set your shots to 100 percent," Mitchell said into the open comm for all her people to here. "Remember, their suits can absorb three, sometimes four, direct hits before they go down. So, squeeze off two shots at a time, but make each count."

I stayed with Mitchell. She wanted us to be at the highest point, which was on a center building near the south end with a fourth level, whereas most of the other buildings around it had two and three levels. Her bad knee was going to make it hard to climb the ladder, and her boots didn't have any more thruster fuel for power jumps. So, I assigned Ensign LaRoy to be part of our group so that he could assist the Major. Rounding out our foursome was Lt. Commander Phillips as the second most senior officer in the city and, therefore, part of the command structure. As we sprinted out of the main hall and down the pathway between the buildings, Mitchell had her leg joints unfrozen and the power assist turned on so that the suit would help limit the effort she would have to make, but it was still very painful to run. Once we got to the building we needed to be at, Phillips and I climbed the ladder. The ensign then acted as a brace for the Major as she put her good leg on the third rung and pulled herself up. From that point, Phillips and I could reach down, each grabbing one of her arms and pulling her up. We repeated that until we got to the top of the fourth level. As an overwatch position, it was perfect. Most of the other buildings around it had much lower profiles; this one gave us a bird's eye view of all the rooftops.

"Enemy at the 100-yard marker," the spotter said.

"Everyone hold your fire until they get to the edge of the tree line," Mitchell said into the comm.

Without her helmet, access to her suit's computer functions was limited to voice and audio. But her rifle had a scope function that projected a two-inch viewer before her eye with all the data she needed. Putting it on a power sensor, she could see outlines of the Serken's suits and hand weapons as they moved in.

Between the city and the forest was a forty-yard marsh that was a couple of feet deep. We had destroyed the three wood bridges that linked the city to the dry ground. The enemy soldiers took a moment to look around for any other way to cross but then proceeded, walking through the water that came to their mid-sections.

"On my command," Mitchell said into the comm, and we all held our breaths.

The Serken moved closer, rifles at the ready, looking for something to shoot at, but they could not see any of us yet. They had spread out, covering the entire south end of the city to make it harder for anyone human to get away by trying to run around them.

"I count 40," Mitchell said. "Spotters, do you see any more than what's in that first group?"

"Negative," they replied.

One of the Serkens near the center of their group held up a hand and looked down into the moss-covered water. The rain obscured the surface of the water along with the floating plants and fungus, making it difficult to see to the bottom. Yet he appeared to have seen something. Pointing his rifle down near his feet, he used his free hand to pull some of the floating plant life away. He bent over and looked closer, putting his hand in the water to feel around. Deciding there was nothing, he stood up and signaled his soldiers to start moving again. But they didn't get a chance. From behind the lead Serken, Longa, one of the village hunters, sprang up from the water behind the soldier with a spear in the air and thrust it down between the Serken's shoulder and neck, ripping through the suit and into the flesh. Before the rest could react, young men and women from the village who made up their best hunters leaped up out of the water behind each of the Serken soldiers and thrust their spears into them. Some broke through the suits and inflicted damage, and others hit hard parts that broke their spears. About a third of the enemy soldiers went down.

"Fire!" Mitchel barked into the comm.

Shots of lasers flew over the heads of the Serkens, forcing them to look up to see where it was coming from. That was just the half-second distraction needed for the hunters to dive back into the water and swim out of sight.

"Weapons free!" Mitchell ordered, and the multiple groups of laser fire from the rooftops of the city went from over the enemy's head to right on them. That took out another third. The remaining dropped into the water and crawled their way to the edge of the city.

"Damn it," Mitchell said. We knew that if we didn't take them all out before they got to the buildings, it was going to be much more difficult to survive a close-up fight. "Do we have eyes on the ground?"

"Yes, Major," one of the spotters said, who was still keeping watch from atop one of the hills. "We can see some movement in the water, but they haven't come up yet, and it looks like they are making a straight line to the south side."

"We have the opportunity to outflank them," Phillips said. "Send some of our people to the east and west flanks and come at them from behind once they enter the city."

"If we could match their firepower, I would go with that," Mitchell said as she lifted her head to get a slightly better view of the ground. "But we are better off holding the high ground."

"Until they bring in air support," Phillips commented.

"One problem at a time."

"I think they are coming out of the water," one of the spotters said in the comms. "Damn, they were fast. They must have swum under the water like eels."

"Eyes open," Mitchell said. "The moment anyone has a shot, take it."

The air felt still and silent for what seemed like too long, but then the sounds of laser blasts and impacts on stone walls could be heard in multiple spots in front of us.

"Fuck," someone shouted over the comms. "We got three clean shots on two of them, but they just scurried between the buildings. You have two moving north."

More laser fire and then another announcement, "Four more moving north from the central corridor."

Lasers fired from the building closer to us, and we could see some of our people peering over the edge of the building to fire, then rolling away as the Serken soldiers fired back.

Then the sounds of laser blasts filled the air all around us. Multiple calls over the comm as our people were announcing when they spotted more enemy soldiers when they were engaging in a firefight, and when they were retreating.

I looked at Mitchell to see what orders she would call out, but she didn't say anything. Her focus was on the view from her gun sight, determining where the closest enemy soldiers were. She was as cool and collected as I had ever seen her, and that was saying something. She was in her element and still believed we were executing the best plan possible.

More laser fire and impacts on the walls, and they were getting closer. I could see some of our people at the southernmost buildings moving to the north sides of the roofs and firing down into the streets as the enemy moved deeper into the city.

"Shit! They're climbing the walls," someone called out.

The people on the building in front of us fired down and then got up and ran as the enemy was practically sprinting up the walls at them like venomous lizards.

"Get down!" Mitchell yelled.

Our people dropped down to their hands and knees before they got to the north edge of the roof, just as two Serken reached the top of the south side and leaped up onto the flat top. We were still elevated on our roof and had a clear line of sight at the enemy. Mitchell took out one with her rifle. Phillips and I focused our laser pistols on the other, squeezing off as many shots as we could until he went down.

More laser fire came from our left, and I looked over to see two more Serken scaling one of the three-story buildings. Ensign LaRoy jumped up and started firing his laser pistol at them. His aim was good, but his pistol only did minimum damage. I grabbed him by his shirt and pulled him down just as the enemy fired back at him. Our elevated angle kept us out of their line of sight, but just barely.

Mitchell literally rolled over us to get to the east edge of the roof, brought her rifle up, and picked off the two Serken the moment she was in their view.

"Major, two more climbing up the west side of your building," one of our spotters said.

Phillips and I ran the few feet and dropped back down on our bellies right at the edge, and peered over. The Serkens saw us and tried to fire up at us. We pulled back in time, and both of us stuck our pistols over the edge and fired.

"One down; the other is still coming," Our spotter said.

"Phillips!" Mitchell yelled.

He looked over at her, and she lobbed her rifle out to him. He caught it, got on his knees, and turned back toward the edge of the building. That was just as the Serken reached the top and leaped up to get on the roof. Phillips fired, hitting the enemy soldier in the chest at point-blank range. The force of the blast burned a hole in the torso and pushed the Serken back over the edge.

We each peered over all four sides to make sure that was it and didn't see any more signs of the enemy.

"Does anyone have eyes on any active hostiles?" Mitchell asked over the comm.

Several people responded, and each said, "Negative."

"Okay, I'm calling the all-clear," she said. "Everyone meet up with your villager counterparts and head out."

This was a contingency that we had planned for. If the decoys that we sent out didn't work and the Serkens found us, we would take up a defensive posture until we won or were defeated. Knowing that the enemy would send more soldiers and, most likely, air support in response, we knew we couldn't stay. So, everyone who stayed behind for the fight was paired up with one of the locals who would be at a preplanned hiding spot just outside the stone city. From there, they would scatter into the forest, the locals leading the way until help came. When and if the enemy gave up the search for us, we would send up a smoke signal taught to us by the villagers since communicating with electronic means was too risky.

The three of us helped Mitchell down until we got to the ground level. With her armor, she was able to walk but not run. I considered carrying her, but the added weight of the suit made that an unrealistic option.

"You two go ahead," I said to Phillips and LaRoy. "The Major and I are going to make our way up to the top of that hill and send everyone tactical updates when we can."

"That would be suicide," Phillips said.

"We already discussed it," Mitchell responded. "I'll just slow everyone down, so the only way I can do any good is by getting my gear up to the highest point so that it can get a good scan of the area. Your PCs will update with the tactical data in real-time."

I then added, "She can't get up there on her own, and I can't ask anyone else to do it."

"Why?"

"Because I'm her partner," I answered.

"When you say, partner?" he asked with a half smirk implying something less than professional.

Mitchell, unamused, answered, "Our MOS is Investigators for the JAG office on New Harmony. We work together."

"Right," he said will a lilt of sarcasm, showing that he didn't think that it was that cut and dry. Pulling out one of his extra power clips, he tossed it to me and said, "Who knows? You just might get lucky and go unnoticed. But if not, give them hell. Come on, Ensign."

Ensign LaRoy looked like he wanted to say something but didn't. Instead, he stood straight and gave us a salute. It was a formality that I hadn't asked of anyone on my team, so I took it as an added sign of respect. We returned it. He nodded to Lt. Commander Phillips and followed him as they made their way to the north side of the city to the back trail.

I put Mitchell's arm over my shoulder for support and balance. We then started the walk to the taller hill, which looked more like a mountain to me.

Chapter 22

The Greyhorn's Last Fight

The Greyhorn burned hard, but not at full thrust, to charge into the fight. The timing was going to be key. They had three squadrons of fighters to launch from a single flight deck with four catapult rows. It was going to take a very long 90 seconds to get all the fighters into the field.

The fighters sprang out of the battle carrier like angry wasps out of the nest. Their direction was up and away from the battle-carrier to make sure they did not get between the Greyhorn's cannons and the enemy. Once they were far enough to the enemy's flank, they burned a hard right at their targets.

"The Tallahassee has fighters in the field and are engaging the enemy." Tactical stated. "We won't be able to use the rail guns until they are clear."

"Understood," Captain Rodgers said as he studied the tactical readout on the screen attached to his chair. "Helm, negative 30 on the Z. I want to come in under their bellies."

"Aye, Captain."

The Greyhorn dropped down like a submarine diving, its aft section dropping faster than the nose to keep the enemy in its crosshairs. Captain Rodgers had engaged the enemy in enough battles to know that they had a weakness in visualizing three-dimensional strategies. Most of their tactics were direct assaults, as fast and as hard as they could hit. But Rodgers saw the field of battle more like a chess set. He knew that coming at them from different directions on multiple planes would slow their reaction time.

The two Alliance ships that were being attacked were level with the Serken from the enemy's perspective. But the Greyhorn was now coming at the Serken battleships at an angle from below them while the fighters were coming from a high angle. The Serken's shields fluctuated as they were unsure where to focus their power, and their cannons fired blindly, not locking onto individual targets.

"Greyhorn Command, CAG," came the flight leader's voice over the combat control speaker on the bridge. "Serkens launching fighters. I'm giving the order for all fighters to engage."

The flight leader had full discretion over his pilots and their actions, so the announcement was more of a formality to keep command in the loop. Captain Rodgers gave a quick nod to the communications officer, who replied, "CAG, Greyhorn command. Acknowledged."

The fighters grouped up in a four-man diamond formation and put their engines at full, racing ahead and engaging the enemy fighters.

Weapons station number one called out, "Hostile number 2 will be within our laser cannon envelope in 20 seconds."

"Will we have a clean shot?" Rodgers asked.

"Yes, Sir, but it's a Klitterog Battle Cruiser that has four belly turrets with heavy cannons. They match our firepower."

"It would be two to one from any other angle. Prepare to fire on my mark."

"Aye, Captain."

The enemy fighters had gone after the fighters that had been launched by the Tallahassee. They had been giving cover so that the Tallahassee could take out the battery of laser cannons on the enemy battle cruisers. Without the fighter squadron drawing fire from the enemy battleships, the Alliance battle carrier would take direct fire from the three enemy battleships. More than she could handle. The fighters from the Greyhorn engaged the enemy fighters so that the first group could get back on their task.

"Hostile three is firing kinetics," the officer at Weapons Station number two called out. "Damn, some of their own fighters are taking the fire. Those bastards are really cold-blooded."

"Keep to the facts, lieutenant," Captain Rodgers said as he zoomed in on the view on his display.

"Hostile two inside cannon range, Sir," Weapons One announced.

"Warn are fighters, the field is going to get hot," Rodgers told the comms officer.

"Hostile two is turning their guns on us," Tactical called out.

"On my mark," Rodgers reminded.

"Weapons are locked on target," the officer at the number one weapons station announced, even though he didn't need to as the captain had already told him to be ready to fire. He was just getting anxious.

"On my mark," Rodgers said again, aware of the building concern of his officers but confident in his own plan.

"Enemy cannons hot and firing," Tactical announced.

"Fire!" Rodgers ordered just as the Greyhorn was hit with several heavy laser bolts. The fraction of a second delay was intentional. Rodgers knew his enemy well, and the laser cannons that they used were made of an alloy that got weak when heated. In the vacuum of space, the metal was practically indestructible, but for the brief moment when the guns fire and heat up, they become brittle. The Greyhorn's targeted fire took out all the belly cannons, giving them the advantage.

Tactical announced, "They know how bad we hit them. They are starting to roll over."

"Fire missiles."

"Missiles away."

Six heavy missiles flew out of the Greyhorn and streaked at the closest enemy ship. It fired countermeasures that took out three, but the other half impacted the belly of the beast and blew three large holes in the ship's outer hull. Sparks and flaming gases indicated significant damage to the inner hull as well.

"Helm, maintain our momentum and direction, but turn us to keep our forward guns at that ship."

"Aye, Captain."

The Greyhorn turned but without continuing forward thrust. Its momentum moved it sideways, maintaining its forward cannon fire at the closest Serken battleship. With its belly guns destroyed and the Greyhorn moving in the same direction as the enemy ship was rotating, the enemy ship could not defend itself. But the other two enemy ships closed the gap and started firing.

The Greyhorn shook violently as it took multiple hits to the outer hull.

"Damage to the starboard side, decks 9 through 12," Lieutenant Caffrey announce. She was the most senior bridge officer on duty. Typically, she would be manning the science and sensor station, but during combat, she was expected to step into the role of the first officer. A position she inherited with the deaths of the XO and three other bridge officers. Rodgers looked over at her and gave her a confident nod to let her know she was doing well.

"The Cortez just took a direct hit to one of their three main engines," Tactical announced. Looks like they are losing reactor power."

"Damn it," Rodgers said as he quickly changed the view on his display. "The Bradley is too far out of position to help, and the Tallahassee is already taking on more than she can handle. Helm, swing us around to get between the Cortez and hostile number three."

"Aye, Sir."

"Comms, see if you can raise the Cortez. We need to know if they are going to get their reactor back or if they need us to cover an evac. Either way, we can't act as a shield for them for very long."

"Yes, Captain," The communication officer replied.

The ship shuddered again. This time, the lights on the bridge went out. At first, it was total blackness, and everyone stayed still, hoping the backups would kick in. Within two seconds, the view screens and keypads of each station popped back on, followed by the main lights a moment after. It was a sign that the starship still had enough life in her to stay in the fight for at least another round.

"Report," Rodgers barked.

Lt. Caffrey replied. She stammered at first but then composed herself. "We…w…we took a direct hit to the flight deck. Fires burning on decks 4 through 11, from sections echo to indigo. Damage control teams responding."

"Sir, I've lost helm control," the Helmsman said.

Rodgers stepped up to the helm station and could see it was dead.

"Weapons are not responding," another officer called out.

"Hostile One is firing missiles," Tactical announced.

Weapons station two followed with, "Countermeasures unavailable."

Rodgers walked over to Lt. Caffrey, took her arm, and guided her over to the command chair. With her limited experience in a command role, he needed to make sure she understood exactly what he was about to ask of her without telegraphing it to everyone around them. He then put her hand on the panel next to the right armrest and whispered into her ear. "Do you know the protocol for giving the command to abandon ship?"

She swallowed the lump in her throat and said, "Yes, Captain."

"Good. When I tell you, you do just that."

She nodded, and he stepped back to the helm. "Try to blow the docking thrusters. That might change our direction enough to throw off those missiles a little."

"Aye, Captain."

The main screen showed the forward view and the growing white dots of the death that were streaking toward them. One of the hardest things for a starship captain to do is admit defeat. But his or her first duties will always be for the safety of their crew. The order would have to be given. But only after the death blow was taken. The view started to show them pitching away, but not nearly fast enough. The impact would be nearly head-on.

Suddenly flashes of laser fire took out all the missiles with pinpoint accuracy. Something no one on the Greyhorn had ever seen done before.

"New contacts," Tactical announced. "219 by 17 by 32, approaching fast."

"From our fleet?" Rodgers asked.

"Their Alliance, but not from any fleet that I know."

The Olympus and Cyprus came in and took up positions on either side of the four older alliance ships and opened fire on the Serkens. The modern warships that were three times larger than the older ones and with modern shielding shrugged off the incoming laser fire like it was a light show and shot down the enemy missiles as quickly as they could fire them. Returning fire, the three Serken battle cruisers were quickly crippled and then destroyed.

"Captain, we're being hailed by," the communication officer said and paused as she was unfamiliar with the ship. "By the T.S.S. Cyprus."

"Open a channel," Rodgers said. "T.S.S. Cyprus, this is Greyhorn Actual."

"This is Cyprus Actual. Can I presume I'm speaking to Captain Rodgers?"

"Yes. You have me at a disadvantage. With whom am I speaking?"

"I'm Captain Renard, Commander first fleet. On behalf of the Alliance, welcome home. We have a lot to discuss, but first, what assistance do you require?"

Rodgers looked around at his bridge crew, who was as stunned as he felt. Then he replied, "We are low on everything, from personnel to clean water. So, anything and everything, Captain."

"Very good, Captain. We will be dispatching shuttles shortly with medical and engineering crews. I will be on one of those shuttles to debrief you and your command staff. But there is another matter that I need to address with you now. Have you made contact with other ships, such as the T.S.S. Franklin or T.S.S. Stratford?"

"No, but my search and rescue team found a couple of survivors from a downed ship on that second moon. We had to pull back before we could retrieve them due to the enemy's presence on and around that moon."

"Thank you, Captain. I'm sending the Olympus to look for them now."

~~~

It took us the better part of an hour, but Mitchell and I made it up to the top part of the hill. The same one that she had used to jump from for her glide flight. The rain had changed from a light drizzle to a steady downpour with bits of ice. The only good thing was that the wind was coming from the northeast, so we were able to use a few boulders that were near the top to block some of it as it was coming down at an angle. Using my uniform coat, I draped it over both of our heads as we huddled together. The low clouds blocked most of our view, but my PC, with some adjustments from Theo, was able to scan for up to 12 miles. Mitchell's suit had a stronger transmitter in it, so Theo was able to use it to relay the tactical data to all of our people who had working PCs.

"You picking up anything?" Mitchell asked Theo over the sound of the rain and wind.

Theo answered, "I did pick up some movement outside of the city that I believe was from Alliance personnel and their indigenous counterparts, but I can no longer track them. Since I did not detect any other movements around them, I am comfortable assuming that they have turned off all electronic devices and have found properly concealed paths."

"Good," I said through chattering teeth.

Mitchell had us change positions. She had me sit on the ground with my legs parted. She then laid back between them, reclining her head on my chest. I could feel the heat rising from out of the top of her suit. She must have turned the heater up to max because she was starting to sweat. A trade-off to keep my core temperature from dropping, so I didn't argue.

To an outside observer, it would have looked like we were trying to be physically intimate, but the reality was very different. I was sitting on the cold, wet ground, soaked to the bone, holding my wet jacket over us as a rain shield, and her suit weighed heavily on my legs. It was far from comfortable.

"You can turn the heat down," I said as I could see her face getting red.

Pulling off one of her gloves, she reached back and felt my face.

"You still feel pretty cold."

"I'm a lot better than I was. You don't need to cook yourself."

She adjusted the heat down. I could still feel it coming out around her head, but it wasn't so much of a sauna anymore.

Lightning flashed in the distance, and after a moment, thunder rolled past. I placed my PC on a rock so that it still had its sensors pointed out over the ridge. My arms were getting tired holding my coat up, so I draped my coat over my head so it was still covering both of us, and put my arms around Mitchell to keep us as close as possible to share the limited shelter and heat.

More flashes and thunder in the distance, but this time closer.

"That was not natural," Theo said. "The explosion was from ordnance typically used by the Serken."

"Carpet bombing?" I asked.

"I wouldn't put it past them," Mitchell said. "The only times they ever left slave labor alive was when they thought they could capture them again or when we ran them off too quickly."

"I am picking up aerial movement," Theo said. "I am unable to identify the objects, but based on mass and speed, they are most likely fighter craft and troop transport ships."

"Can you tell where they are heading?" I asked.

"Unclear. Some are moving up toward the upper atmosphere, and others appear to be circling. However, the patterns are erratic and not consistent enough to draw a conclusion of their objectives."

"That's not consistent with a carpet-bombing approach," Mitchell said. "More like battle exercises."

"If they just got refueled and intend on holding the base, that might make sense," I said.

"But they lost the war over five years ago. Where the hell could they get resupplies from?"

I shrugged and said the first logical thing that came to mind, "Maybe they didn't run away like we assumed. Maybe they have just been hiding and rebuilding all this time."

"That's a horrible thought," she said.

"I know,"

More explosions and flashes came from a distance, but still closer.

"Jack, I don't know how we are getting out of this one."

I didn't reply. Instead, I just moved my head closer to hers to share more of the covering provided by my coat. Neither of us said anything for a few minutes. We just sat there listening to the sounds of the explosions echoing off the valley walls and the flashes obscuring the storm clouds. I had a million thoughts running through my mind, mostly about Kayla and the baby and how I was failing both of them by not making it home. There were many times in my life when I didn't know what I was going to do to get out of a jam, but this was the first time I truly had regrets about facing the end.

"Thanks," Mitchell said, breaking me out of my depressing thoughts.

"For what?" I asked.

"Not letting me die alone. That's always been a fear of mine."

"We're not dead yet," I said, trying to sound optimistic.

"You suddenly have an idea?"

"No, but I'm just not ready to give up on one last miracle," I lied.

She took her ungloved hand and put it on top of one of my hands. Our fingers intertwined, and we sat there, not saying anything for another few minutes. For a while, the sound of the munitions seemed to stop, and the rain and wind dominated our surroundings. Then, like the other shoe dropping, explosions went off so close that we not only heard the blast but felt the vibrations in the ground. They were quickly followed by the shrieks of fast-moving fighters passing overhead.

"Theo," Mitchell said with some resolve like she had an idea, but one that she wasn't thrilled about. "How much would we improve the odds of our people if we were to attract the attention of those ships?"

"Based on the tactic of the Serken military in the past, when they are searching for escaped prisoners, they will focus all their resources on the first indication of their target to present an overwhelming force. So, if you were to do that, it would prevent them from searching for the others until you are captured or killed. I estimate that would buy our people anywhere from 4 to 12 minutes, increasing their odds of reaching an ideal hiding spot by 10 to 20 percent."

I looked at her and said, "It's worth it."

She turned her head up just enough so that I could look down and have our eyes meet. We shared a million thoughts with just a look. All the things we wished we had time for, the regrets we both shared, and how grateful we were to have known each other. I leaned down and gave her a kiss on her cheek. She put her hand on my cheek and returned it.

"Theo," I said. "Record the following message for Kayla and do your best to find a way to get it to her if we don't make it out of here alive.

"Whenever you are ready, Sir."

I thought about what I wanted to say for a moment, cleared my throat, and then said, "Sweetheart, if you are hearing this; it means that I did not make it home. I am so sorry. Know that I tried my best. I love you with all of my heart, and I'm so very grateful for every moment you have been a part of my life. My family is your family. They will always be there for you. Don't hesitate to reach out to them for anything. And... when you think about me, remember the good times and how you saved me. You brought me a joy that I never knew I would ever know. I love you, sweetheart." Mitchell squeezed my hand in a show of support and connection. "Oh, and one more thing," I continued. "I know that we agreed not to decorate the baby's room because of what that book said, but I've been giving that some thought, and I would like you to put up at least one picture. The one from our wedding with the whole family. You know, the one where Julie Anne is actually smiling. I would like our daughter to grow up seeing her family and knowing that she is loved by them all."

I then looked down at Mitchell and asked, "Do you want to leave a message for anyone?"

She nodded, and Theo said, "Whenever you are ready, Major."

Mitchell took a moment to think about what she wanted to say. The rain turned into pee size hail, making it hard to hear anything else. Mitchell spoke loud to make sure her voice was heard by the AI. "Antonio. I'm sorry we didn't have more time together. I know that I've been a little distant lately, but that was only because I wasn't sure what I wanted. But now I do know. I love you, and I wish we could have had that life together." She paused and said, "Add the next message to the one for Kayla. She thought for a moment and said, "Kayla. You are my best friend in the galaxy. I think of you as the sister I never had. And I am so grateful that you are going to be the mother to my baby. Please tell her that my last thoughts were of her and how I regret not having the opportunity to know her. Tell her all about me and Roger and Jack. Tell her that I have always loved her, and I know with every fiber of my being that she will be a wonderful person." Mitchell wiped a tear away with her ungloved hand. "That's it. Save the file."

"File saved," Theo replied.

Mitchell looked back up at me and then said, "Theo, turn on the distress signal."

I don't know if the sky darkened or if it was just my mood, but everything around us seemed to dim. In our line of work, there are countless things that can snuff us out before we can conceive of the end. From the explosive decompression of a deck on a starship to a laser bolt to the chest, we both had accepted that our fate would most likely not be facing the end with age.   Yet, huddled together on a rain-soaked hill on a distant moon, waiting for the enemy to come and get us, is simply not a scenario I had ever conceived of. It was more dismal than anything I could have ever imagined. Yet, like Mitchell, I was glad that I wasn't facing it alone. She was as much of a life partner as Kayla was to me. Even though my feelings for her were different, they were no less intense. I loved both of them and wouldn't trade that for anything.

The roar of engines filled the valley below us, and from the sound, we knew it was hovering and coming close.

"A ship is approaching," Theo said in our ears. "By its mass, it is either a Serken Cobra, a troop transport, or an Alliance dropship.

The wind around us picked up. Mitchell said, sitting up and yelling over it, "So, what do you think, miracle or final fate?"

Recognizing the sound of the engines, I shouted back over them, "Miracle."

Rising from the valley below us, a drop-ship with markings identifying that it was from the Olympus appeared and hovered just at the ledge, dropping its rear hatch on the ground.

"You two need a lift?" The crew chief shouted over the roar of the engines and the hail.

I got up and helped Mitchell to stand. When the two marines who were also inside the ship saw that she needed help, they ran out and picked her up. Once inside, we each took a jump seat, and as the bird lifted off, the crew chief asked, "Any more of you down here?"

"Around 500," I said.

His eyes widened as he wasn't sure if he heard that right, not expecting there to be more than a handful, "500?"

"What's left of the crews from the Franklin, Stratford, and Macron," I answered.

"Macron? Never heard of that one. I'll call it in so we can get more S&R drops on it."

Mitchell realized that if he didn't know that information, he might not be fully aware of the situation. "Chief. Are you aware there is an active Serken base on this moon?"

"Yeah. We took out their battle carriers before we got here and just flattened their base south of here. We dropped four units of troopers to secure it. We're heading there now to see if there are any wounded before we head up."

One of the Marine Corporals brought over a med kit to check Mitchell. He knelt down, scanned her leg, and then pulled a knife. I flinched, but Mitchell looked at me and said, "Don't worry. He knows what he's doing."

"How do you know?" I asked.

"He's a Marine. We know how to take care of our own."

He removed the armor plating and cut away the heavy fabric that made up her battle suit. Her leg looked bad; black and blue all around the knee and halfway down her lower leg. The corporal used a neural diffuser that projected a beam of light which numbed some of the pain, followed by an injection of nanobots. Nanobots are programmed to seek out any blood clots and infections that might form due to an injury. Mitchell twitched her cheek slightly but was still and stone-faced for the most part. The corporal then applied a spray that formed a temporary cast around the knee to help keep it immobilized until we could get her to a proper sick bay.

~~~

As we flew south to the former Serken base, I called the crew chief over and gave him a rundown of what we had been through and what areas they should search to find our people. I only knew general areas for most but was able to give him coordinates for Dr. Kemp and Lt. Bridges, whom we had left hidden in the concealed outcropping in the forest. He passed on my report to Command on the Olympus, and they launched additional dropships and troop transports to help find our crew members.

When we got to the base, the marines had already secured it. Once the Serken fighters were all destroyed and the troopers landed, the rest of the Serkens on the ground killed themselves. A practice that is universal with them and the reason we never had any prisoners during the war.

Because I had been held within the mountain, the colonel in charge of securing the base asked me to take him and his other officers on a tour through it. They wanted to catalog everything and not trip any security traps. My knowledge was limited to the areas where we were held and the mines where we worked, so I got to see a lot more of the tunnels than I had before.

Near the east side, we found a large room where the ceiling had been carved out so high that it had an opening out of the slopes of the third-highest peak. Directly under it was a large cylinder tank that was open at the top. It was on a hydraulic mounted platform that could lift to the opening, and inside, it was three-quarters full of the crystals that we had been digging out of the mine. To this day, I have no idea what they were trying to accomplish. But there is a very old tale of the Serkens having a star weapon made of crystals with great powers that could destroy entire planets. But that's just a story we tell raw cadets to give them nightmares.

The Olympus was going to send down some specialists to take a look at whatever tech was found, so the colonel was only interested in securing the area. We moved diligently through each tunnel and room as we found them, making sure there were no traps and taking scans for the maps. After about 40 minutes, they had what they needed and told me I could head out to the dropships to find a ride back up to orbit. That was fine by me. All I wanted to do was find a hot shower, clean clothes, a warm meal, and a cot where I could sleep uninterrupted for at least a day.

When I got back to the dropship that had rescued us, Mitchell was sitting at the crew chief's station, having a video call with Captain

Tansky. She was just finishing up her report when I walked up behind her.

"Lt. Commander," Tansky said. "Good to see you in one piece."

"Thank you, Captain."

"And now that you are both here, I can share the news that Admiral Kilpatric shared with me this morning."

"News?" I asked.

"Your wife gave birth yesterday. Mother and child are doing very well."

I looked over at Mitchell, who smiled and I swear was tearing up. Although, she will deny that part.

I looked back at the screen and started to say something, but I was a little choked up myself. Quickly clearing my throat, I said, "Thank you, Captain."

"You're welcome, and congratulations. Tansky out."

The view screen turned off, and I leaned on the edge of the controls. "I'm a dad."

"Yes, you are," Mitchell said, patting my leg.

"And you're a mom," I added.

Some of the color ran out of her face, "Yeah, I guess I am."

The roar of dropships' engines rolled over us like an approaching storm as several started to land around us on the airfield. The downward thrust of their hovering engines was enough to vibrate the ground and make the still-standing ship we were on shake a little. The landing ships were full of our people from the crashed ships and the local villagers who had helped them hide in the woods. The plan was to have our medics check out the villagers and then return them to their stone city. But before that happened, all the fleet people were checked out first so that they could be assigned to ships to take them up to the Olympus and Cyprus.

As everyone was processed, the first group of fleet survivors was assigned to the group of dropships we were going to return on. It was taking some time as each person had to be checked out by a medic, then stand in line to get a small meal and water kit, then another line to give their personal information to a logistics admin. Slowly our little dropship was filling, but with about 40 seats, it was going to be another 20 minutes or so until we were ready for skids up.

As we sat there with nothing to do but stare out at the light rain, I noticed that several of the villagers were walking around the mountain and into the south entrance. Not sure what they were doing, I followed but was so far back it took me a couple of minutes to catch up. When I got to the opening, they were already coming back out. Each of them was carrying a crystal and walking out to the field between the mountain and the forest. Whatever they were doing seemed to have a purpose, so I stopped following and just watched. The line of people converged into a cluster. With the rain, it was hard to hear, but they were chanting something. Then, in unison, they each held the crystals up over their heads. That's when I saw something that I'm not sure I really saw. I was very tired, and my mind might have been playing tricks on me, but I have a clear memory of seeing bolts of lightning jump out of the stones and into the sky. Realistically that could not be what had happened because no one was hurt. The bolts just leaped from the crystals, over and over again, into the clouds. I saw the flashes and heard the thunder. It made me feel shaken, yet when it was over, the people just stood there looking up into the rain. And then… the rain slowly stopped. The clouds parted, and the sun came out. Rapidly the clouds disappeared until there were only a few puffy white ones.

I thought back to the incident on New Terra with Captain Tansky. She told me that the people on that world could do things with stones that seemed supernatural. At the time, I assumed she was clouding the truth in a story to direct me to look in the right spot without learning the real details of the quarantine world. But maybe there was more truth in her tale than I thought. And perhaps the people of this moon have discovered stones with similar powers.

"Reilly!" Mitchell said over my comm, "Skids up in 1 minute. Get your ass back here."

"On my way," I responded. Still stunned, I looked back at the villagers who kept the crystals in their hands and walked off into the woods. Not wanting to miss my ride, I doubled-timed it back to the dropship and ran up the ramp right before they started to raise it.

"What's wrong?" Mitchell asked, as she must have seen the confused look on my face.

"Nothing," I said. "Just my tired brain and imagination getting the better of me." I put myself in the last available jump seat, strapped in, and closed my eyes. I think I was asleep before we got more than a mile off the ground.

Chapter 23

Homecoming

Captain Rodgers walked into the CIC on board the Cyprus. His ship had taken so much damage the fleet was sending out a repair ship to patch it up enough to safely bring it back to a port. A skeleton crew was being put aboard from Cyprus so that all of the Greyhorn's crew could be brought over to be debriefed, compose messages to loved ones, and be brought back to Earth.

Rodgers had already been debriefed by Captain Renard and had uploaded all of his logs into the ship's database. His duties and responsibilities were far from over, but his need to be combat-ready was done. Everything he would have to face moving forward would be, for the most part, data work and conferences with the brass. No more life-and-death decisions on the fly or battle alert alarms ringing in the middle of the night. Just having that off his plate was a great weight off his spirit. At 1700 hours, he was looking forward to a hot meal and a peaceful sleep, but his PC chirped with a request for yet another meeting with Captain Renard. He sent his acknowledgment, fastened the top two buttons of his uniform collar, and walked out of the guest quarters to head up to the command center.

As soon as he walked into the Cyprus's CIC, the XO directed him to the Captain's Ready Office. He walked in and straight up to the desk where Renard and Tansky were.

"Yes, Captain," Rodgers said with tired eyes.

"Captain, this is Captain Tansky. She commands the Olympus."

"Captain," he said and acknowledged her with a nod, then faced Renard again.

"Captain," Tansky said to let him know that she was the one who needed to speak with him. He looked over at her with tired eyes but with his full attention.

"How are you, Captain?" she asked.

"I'm as well as one can expect, considering. Still adjusting to everything, but very thankful the war is really over."

"Is there anything else?" she asked.

"What do you mean?" he asked in response.

"Frankly, Captain, you don't look like someone who just found out that we won."

"No?" he said defensively. "How do I look?"

To anyone else, he would look as stern and collected as any good leader, but the two other captains in the room could see past the veneer to the real man underneath, who was on his last nerve.

"Captain," Renard said to interject himself back into the conversation. "We both commanded starships during the last years of the war. You need not pretend with us. There is something weighing on your mind."

Rodgers seemed to let some of the rigidness off his shoulders and finally took a seat in the chair opposite the desk. "18 years, 8 months, and 13 days," he said like it was an astronomical number. "That is how much time we lost in our last quantum jump. Time Dilation is what the techs are calling it, but no one can seem to explain it. But I have to accept that everyone and everything I knew is gone."

"Gone?" Tansky asked.

"My marriage was already strained. Being gone for months at a time, my wife never knew if the next deployment would be the one I wouldn't come home from. I'm certain she moved on when I was declared dead. I hope she did. 20 years... I don't even know if she is still alive. I'm afraid to find out. And my daughter, she would be around 26 now.... No, this is September, isn't it? Her birthday was in July. She would be 27 now. She was so young when I last saw her. I doubt she would even remember me."

Tansky spoke into her PC. "Lieutenant, please join us."

Lt. Jess Rodgers, Tansky's protege, walked in and stood just inside the doorway.

Captain Rodgers got up, unsure of what or whom he was seeing. The young woman was the spitting image of his wife but with brown hair more like what his was like before the grey set in. Having come to terms with the fact his ship had been lost in the quantum stream for 20 years rather than a few minutes, he wondered out loud, "Jessica?"

Jess ran up and threw her arms around him. "I knew it, Daddy. I knew I would find you someday."

He pulled her back to look at her. "My God. It really is you."

"Yes, Daddy. It's me."

He was still stunned. "This is surreal. I understand that 18 years have passed, but to me, I just talked to you two weeks ago, and you were only nine years old. Do you remember that?"

She nodded. "You told me that war was a horrible thing, but you were a strong warrior and would come home as soon as you killed all the monsters."

Captain Rodgers was one of those men who was bigger than life to most. Always projecting an air of strength and confidence. But the reunion with his daughter, who he had lost two decades with, but who was very much alive and thrilled to see him, filled him with more emotions than he could handle. The rock of a man trembled, and tears rushed down his face. He took her in his arms again and said, "The last thing I ever wanted for you was to be a part of this nightmare."

"The war was over before I joined up," she said, holding him as tight as he was holding her. "I joined the fleet to find you."

He pulled back and looked at her, surprised by the statement. "I went missing when you were nine, and you joined the fleet to find me?"

She nodded with a big smile and said, "And I did."

Tansky and Renard walked out of the office to give them some time alone to catch up.

~~~

There was still no way to transmit a message out of the system we were in. To do so would require jumping out of the system, coming to a stop, and focusing the quantum transmitter at the receiver orbiting our colony world of New Harmony. It just made more sense to jump straight home and then report in. The only downside was that I couldn't send a message to Kayla that we were okay and on our way.

It took nearly a day to get to complete the basic debriefings of all the crew members and get them shuttled to the ship they needed to be on. Most of the crew members from the Macron and the Greyhorn would be on the Cyprus. The Tallahassee, Cortez, and Bradly were still able to jump to quantum speed so they would follow the Cyprus back to Earth. The crews from the Franklin and the Stratford would stay on the Olympus, which would take them back to New Harmony, where their command was to be on leave and then reassigned to other ships.

It was around 2 in the morning local time when we got back. Kayla and the baby had been discharged from the hospital the day before and were at home. When we walked into my house, we found Rachel asleep on the sofa, Dad in my recliner, and a man sleeping on the floor, who I would later learn was Danny, Dad's nurse.

"Hey," I said in a whisper to Dad as I knelt down next to the chair.

He opened his eyes and, with a big grin, said, "Hey, kiddo," and then wrapped his arms around me. In my entire life, my father has given me maybe a total of three hugs. Surprising as it was, it was also very welcome. "Thank God, you're home safe where you belong," he said and continued to hold me for a few more moments. When he finally let me go, he said, "Kayla was up about an hour ago feeding the little one. They're both in the bedroom." He then noticed Mitchell and said, "So, this must be the other wife."

"Dad, be nice," I said. "Dad, this is Julie Anne. Julie Anne, this is my obnoxious father, Jack Sr." I then stood up and headed for the bedroom, but before I took two steps, I looked back at Mitchell and jokingly said, "Be nice." Knowing that she can respond to a sarcastic quip with the best of them.

~~~

Carefully, I opened the door to the bedroom so as not to wake either of them. My PC then buzzed in my pocket. Quickly I took it out and saw a message on the screen from Max. "Welcome home, Sir. Kayla and Regina are both doing well."

"Regina?" I said to myself, as that was the first time I had been told the baby's name. "Regina. I like that."

Coming to the bed, I sat on the edge and leaned over Kayla, kissing her on the cheek. Opening her eyes, she blinked a few times, then grabbed me with both arms.

"Is it really you?" she desperately said. "Please tell me it's you."

"It is," I said, holding her in my arms, my face buried in her neck as I took in her scent and the feel of her cheek on mine. "I'm home," I added, feeling that joy and contentment that I never wanted to be apart from.

She continued to hold me tight as she asked, "And Julie Anne?"

"Safe and sound. She's in the living room waiting to see you and the baby."

"Thank God," she said as she continued to hold me.

We stayed like that for a few minutes until the baby started to fuss. Kayla let go of me, moved to the other side of the bed, and carefully picked the baby up from the bassinet.

"Jack, I would like you to meet your daughter."

Kayla put the baby in my arms. She was the most beautiful person I have ever seen. A feeling that would never go away.

We both got up and walked out into the living room. Rachel had woken up, and both she and Dad had Mitchell sitting on the sofa, pressing her to explain where we had been. She was keeping the facts limited to what had been approved for sharing with the media but doing a pretty good job of selling it to them.

"Julie," Kayla said as I walked up with Kayla at my side and slowly put the baby in Mitchell's arms. "Meet your daughter, Regina. It was the prettiest name I could find that was close to Roger."

A little stunned, Mitchell asked, "You named her after Roger?" as she held the baby, her gaze on the tiny face.

Kayla sat down next to her, "Well, she is literally a piece of him that will live on. How could I not?"

Mitchell looked at Kayla for a moment, her chin slightly quivering. She started to tear up as she looked back down at the baby in her arms.

"Was that the wrong thing to do?" Kayla asked, concerned that she had done something wrong.

"No," Mitchell quickly said. She leaned over and gave Kayla a kiss on the cheek. "It's perfect." She then looked down at the baby and, through her tears, said, "Hello, Regina. It's so wonderful to finally meet you."

The End

Thank you for Reading.

Commander Reilly
and the Quantum Paradox

By Matthew O. Duncan

Visit: Matthewoduncanbooks.com

Manufactured by Amazon.ca
Acheson, AB